To my fr[...]
I hope y[...]
the story with all the
bad editing. At least it'll
be worth something in
seven years.

A Werewolf's Redemption

Cheers.

Darcy John Ebenal

PUBLISH AMERICA

PublishAmerica
Baltimore

First printing

ISBN: 1-4241-3674-1
PUBLISHED BY PUBLISHAMERICA, LLLP
www.publishamerica.com
Baltimore

Printed in the United States of America

To Jennifer Little

The roses still bloom, though with a different colour.

Acknowledgments

Trevor Strand, who's always been an inspiration through the dark times.

To Mark, Val, Kevin, Mandy, Nan, Ron and all the others in my family for their ongoing support and encouragement.

To Doug and Marg Teise, for the kick in the pants and the hospitality when I needed them both the most.

Rob Van Doorn and Reverend Raymond Guimond for putting up with the neurotic writer while he lived in their midst.

To James Graham, who still knows the value of loyalty and trust.

And Luise Chokan for the education in books and book publishing.

Author's Note

Like the dragon, the werewolf appears in nearly every culture's mythology across the globe. The Norse have their Fernir, the Egyptians their Anubis, the Aztecs their Chantico. The Celts have their Arawn's dogs. Even remote South American tribes speak of half jackals, half men, while the Windego terrorized settlers as late as western times.

In writing *A Werewolf's Redemption*, I hoped to seamlessly blend some of the stories of old with the modern myths of the vampire and the werewolf: two elements I am sure have as much appeal today as the legends did in their day.

It was not my intention to write an offensive novel, but rather I wrote to expand the vampire/werewolf genre with a look at both the new and the ancient, to use vampires, and in particular werewolves to show how they must have been thought of in past civilizations and how their presence may be included within interpretive fiction of today.

But ultimately, my greatest goal was just to write a good story.

I hope you enjoy the efforts.

Sincerely,
Darcy Ebenal

Book One
Priest of Osiris

Chapter One

Like a great serpent thrown to the sands, the River Nile slithered across the endless deserts. Yet, though the endless seas of sand were lifeless and hostile, the river was rich with fertile soil. Kement, known as the Black Land after the dark earth, would one day separate what would be known as Egypt from the rest of the world by a blanket of wealth and prosperity. There would be a ruling class of dark intentions and human sacrifice to appease the gods. Kement was a civilization that worshiped the dead. They practised a cacophony of black magic in the pitch of the night. This was what would become Egypt, the spawn of the mighty river Nile. Along its banks, the Nile had built for herself a land rich with wealth and power, of statues and pillars and monolithic architecture that would challenge the genius minds of every culture to follow. We would come up wanting. For she was a merciless serpent, the Nile, thrashing recklessly in her bed of wealth to mark all of eternity passing before her.

The lush vines of the fertile valley grew tall against the glistening sunlight, yet did little to obscure the shadows of manmade mountains cast down upon the earth, now made irregular in hideous discontent. The riverbanks overflowed often. The fields were always green with new harvests, busy with the hands of slaves that toiled endlessly through the years to bring in greater and greater crops. The Nile teemed with merchant ships and fishing vessels; every waterfront market was a place of chaos and wealth.

It was a time of blood in those days, when storms and death were common, where the death of a slave meant nothing worth a blink of an eye to a child, yet the children younger still laughed and cheered the slaughter on.

The gods were pleased. As children fell and blackened mists dwelt over the land, a great horde of demon vampires rose out of the temples and catacombs at night to dine with the mortals in their beds of dynasty. The mortal rulers were ever-present guardians of the dead ruling class. Known as Nomarchs, this elite ruling class of provincial governors vied for power with each other through a deadly and bloody battle that pitted thousands of slaves against each other in an inexhaustible hunger for death.

And the vampires, priests of Osiris, caretakers of the tombs, came out of the sands at sundown to feed on the reckless carnage left in the wake of every bloody battle, despite who the victor was. It was the Nomarchs who won the favour of the vampires through promise of greater wealth, more servants, more blood and bigger tombs. The ancient relics that symbolized the humans' devotion were a small price to pay for the luxury of having a vampire drink blood within such places.

* * * * *

Iminuetep was born to the city Deir El Medina, in the Valley of the Kings. This valley was the great place where all Kings wallowed in the afterlife from their preserved thrones of immortality. And this was where the mighty craftsmanship that went into the making of those tombs took place. Iminuetep was born a free man, an artisan working under the tutelage of his father since birth. Though he was still but an infant, the Nomarch of the land took an interest in Iminuetep's family after he raided the catacombs of Karmack, the thriving city across the Nile.

Iminuetep played in the corner of his family's workroom, a mound of wet clay in front of him. The room was not large, though it was not cramped either. His entire family worked from this one place. They lived in adjoining rooms off to the side and back, and built the larger statues outside. Knowing their work, Iminuetep's father and mother, as well as his father's brother and his wife, went about their tasks in relative silence, dedicating their attention to the mastery of their craft.

When the door opened and the royal Nomarch strode into the room, work froze. The Nomarch ignored the adults as he walked past them, carrying his own child, a male babe that slept trustingly in his arms. They were followed by a woman of surpassing beauty. She flowed through the meager shop, glistening in wealth brought to her for her devotion toward the Nile. The women stared at her in awe while the men flinched under the gaze of their mighty ruler and looked at the floor or the corners of the room nervously.

The Nomarch placed his heir next to the little one playing with the wet clay. Iminuetep laughed and clapped his hands, celebrating the occasion of meeting a new friend so soon in life. He regarded the younger one for a moment, and then looked up at the towering man in front of him in awe. He jumped, made a piping sound, and clapped his hands joyously as he bounced up and down in his spot. Water sloshed over the edges of his bowl and wet clay smacked across his face, causing the child to laugh even more.

The governor stared back at the two children, and then motioned for the woman to come forward and watch over them in his absence.

She stood between the children and the others in the room, mute and watchful of their safety. No one would risk harming the children now that she was present. At the door to the workshop, the Nomarch turned back to the family staring at him in mute devotion. The governor announced, "Montuotep is destined for greatness. In death he shall be revered."

His family looked over at their child playing next to the heir to the throne of Thebes.

It was here that the sleeping prince was brought because it was here the mighty one would be buried. His father had chosen Iminuetep as the one to join the prince in the afterlife as his protector, that his tomb should forever be a place of greatness. Iminuetep had been chosen to craft the tomb, to design its mighty walls and heliographs that would etch the cavernous chamber from floor to ceiling. He would be the one to command the slaves that would lift the tomb's pillars into place, and it would be he that would close the door forever from the outside world, then set the traps that would bring death to any who broke his seal. And then, finally, after satisfied the governor had been properly mummified, he would lie down and take his place in death next to his master.

Yet with such thoughts, the baby would cheer, knowing full well that the vampires would be the only ones left alive after their catastrophe of blood was finished being spilled. It was to be a day of reckoning, and all of Egypt would quake under its wrath. Yet the immortals would sleep soundly in their tombs, far out of reach of punishment.

Chapter Two

Ra's merciless presence beat down upon Iminuetep's sculpted muscles as he laboured under the sun-god's ever watchful eye. Yet he ignored the heat and discomfort as he studied the immense standing stone in front of him. The stone had been brought to him only that morning, before Ra's full wrath had fallen upon the land. The slaves had carefully lugged the stone in from the desert under the guiding eyes of their masters, and Iminuetep was eagerly studying the rock that stood easily twice as high as he did. He ran his hands over the stone, feeling its texture more than seeing its surface, imagining the statue waiting from within. It had a rounded, curving face to it that Iminuetep decided he would cultivate, while the rougher backside of the stone could be chiseled down into a smoother surface. He would use the stone as part of a pillar, and though the task was a simple one of skill, the labour would be daunting. Montuotep would be pleased.

It had taken him all of the morning to come to this decision, and as the sweat now flowed freely on his brow, he could not help but look toward the Nile and long to bathe in its cool waters. But quickly enough, his eyes darted nervously toward the great statues and the architecture that loomed all around him. The priests of the dead were asleep at this time of the day, but their ever watchful agents saw and heard everything. Iminuetep could not allow a bad report to reach his nomarch's ears, not when there was still so much work left to do.

He took a careful drink of water and wiped his brow. This was all the respite he dared to take and it would have to do. Then, with the humble hands of a master craftsman, the young man took up his chisel and hammer and made his first notch in the great stone. One blow followed another until he was lost in the rhythm of the rise and fall of his hammer. Chips flew away from the stone with each blow. He worked through the heat of the afternoon, labouring through the worst of the Egyptian sun until shadows began to cast their wavering lengths over Deir el Medina.

Shocked to find so much time had passed, Iminuetep looked up to admire the work that he had done in the setting sun. "Bring the scaffold!" he shouted as he ran his hand over the smooth surface of the pillar's face. "Scaffold, now!" He was too consumed with his work to waste patience on sleeping slaves.

Four of them rushed forward, carrying the apparatus that would allow Iminuetep to work on the higher surfaces of his piece. He stepped back out of their way as they reached the stone and his eyes swept up to the untouched upper surface. He would work from the place he had started, chiselling out a line of the finished surface and using it as a guide for the rest of the pillar.

Impatiently he looked at the slaves still struggling to rise the scaffolding around the stone. "Hurry up with you!" he bellowed. He was not a cruel master, by anyone's standards. But he did not have the time to waste on the negligence of his slaves. They jumped at their task with renewed vigour, yet struggling to assemble the scaffold properly. "I cannot wait!" Iminuetep cried angrily, feeling the inspiration that had carried him throughout the day slipping from his grasp. "It is just a scaffold!" he barked. "Here, do it like this!" He put his hands to work with the slaves. They used the last of the sunlight to construct the platform, and Iminuetep was satisfied only after torches had been lit in a circle around his project.

"Now be gone, all of you," he said in a quieter voice. "I have work to do." The slaves bowed and backed away from him before they turned and scurried from his presence. He did not watch them go, but rather kept his eyes on the pillar, trying to envision the work he had started. Finally, he sighed and climbed onto the scaffolding, carrying his hammer and chisel with him.

Carefully choosing the place for his chisel to strike first, Iminuetep brought his hammer back to swing, and suddenly the platform under his feet swayed. With little warning, Iminuetep threw his tools into the sand, afraid for their safety before his own. The scaffold pitched and threw him onto his back before the supports gave way and he came crashing down to the earth on top of a heap of lumber that was supposed to have supported him with firm footing. The breathe was knocked from him and the stars spun in the sky as he stared up at the standing stone over him. He was dazed and only a little aware that other artisans had dropped what they were doing and were running to his aide. The stone pillar began to pitch, and Iminuetep groaned in despair as the piece fell into the sand, dangerously close to crushing his life.

In moments, other artisans had reached him and were pulling him out of the rubble and helping him to his feet. Yet, his eyes were fixed only on the fallen stone before him. He was silent and bitter tears stung his expression with an outrage to match the loss before him.

Then he felt the presence of a dark one and looked up to see a priest watching the commotion from the shadows. Dressed all in black, as was the custom of the vampires, he stood motionless, assessing the damage, assessing Iminuetep. Iminuetep glared back at him, not trying to hide the anger in his eyes, or the grieving loss he was suffering. He was not afraid of retribution, only of failing.

Having made up his mind, the vampire glided forward. The other artisans grew silent as they noticed his approach and stepped back respectfully to give Iminuetep and the priest room. They lowered their heads and looked at their feet, though Iminuetep watched the vampire approach him fearlessly. Once the creature stood before him, Iminuetep also lowered his head respectfully. But he looked back into the vampire's eyes quickly enough as he said, "The pillar is ruined."

"The damage can be repaired," the vampire declared. "The stone is not lost."

A collective sigh of relief went up through the artisans, though none felt more relieved than Iminuetep.

"Bring the slaves responsible to me," the priest announced.

Artisans jumped to do his bidding and Iminuetep watched dispassionately as the four of them were led before them.

The vampire held out a small, ornamental dagger to Iminuetep. The artisan gasped when he saw the weapon, a ceremonial blade used only for human sacrifice. It was a great honour to be given such a tool, and Iminuetep, unsure of the priest's intentions, took the blade carefully. He looked at the weapon in his hands for a moment, and then at the vampire, who only nodded his head toward the slaves responsible for the scaffold's collapse.

"Have them stand on the stone," Iminuetep announced to his companions. The other artisans took the slaves forcibly by the arms, ignoring the panicked cries that began to rise from their doomed throats.

Iminuetep grasped the knife and leapt onto the stone. Then, one by one, he slit the slaves' necks dispassionately. The vampire priest took each slave as the life slipped from him and feasted off of his blood as his life drained away.

When they were done, Iminuetep leapt from the pillar and looked up at the priest.

He stood swaying over the bodies of the slain men. His eyes were glazed and he stared off into space as he relished the sensations, the memories, and the experiences of the dead men as though they were now his own. In a few moments, his vision cleared and he too leapt from the fallen pillar to stand at Iminuetep's side.

"It is best not to erect the scaffold in failing light," the vampire said flatly.

"Yes sir," Iminuetep said as he dropped his eyes and knelt before the great priest. He held the blade up for the vampire. "My life is forfeit," he said fearlessly. "I will gladly die to compensate."

"You will gladly die," the priest repeated. "But not today." He motioned for Iminuetep to keep the blade. "Finish your work, artisan. There is still much to be done." With that, the vampire strode into the darkness, leaving the stunned free men of Deir el Medina to stare at his back as he left. Iminuetep was more shocked than any other as he gripped the dagger the vampire had given him.

* * * * *

Montuotep came for him when he turned sixteen.

The young prince's father was on a bloody campaign defending his temple from an invading Nomarch, and Montuotep, in high spirits, strode into Deil el Medina with an entourage of servants and slaves in his wake. He was on foot, despite the oppressive heat of the black land, dressed lightly in a white robe plaited with gold thread worked into the seams. He wore an immense gold necklace, befitting his station, and looked neither right nor left as he strode toward the pillars Iminuetep was working on.

Iminuetep had completed three more of them since the catastrophe that awarded the artist his ceremonial dagger, and he kept them close at hand, adding hieroglyphs every now and then to depict the wondrous things his master Montuotep had achieved. He knew his space was limited, so he chose his words carefully, running them through his mind again and again as he worked on more pillars that would grace the young prince's tomb.

As Montuotep walked through the city of artisans, the other artists pointedly ignored the prince and stayed focussed on their own work. But when Iminuetep saw the prince he stopped his work and smiled as he dusted the sand off of his hands. Then he took a water skin from his workbench and went out to meet his future Nomarch.

He went down on one knee before his master. Montuotep lifted him to his feet and pulled him into an exuberant embrace.

Breathless from the force of Montuotep's fierce affections, he returned his master's hug and said, "You seem excited today, master. The battle fares well with your father then?"

"The battle hasn't even started yet," Montuotep declared as he held Iminuetep at arms' length. He was grinning from ear to ear.

"Then what, may I ask, has delighted you so?"

"You may ask," Montuotep declared. He took Iminuetep by the arm and guided him away from his work, back in the direction the prince had come from.

He waved his free hand in the air and his small army of slaves jumped forward and rushed past the two wordlessly.

Iminuetep looked over his shoulder and saw they were dismantling his work and carefully taking his pillars down. But Montuotep was pulling him forward and began to speak, so Iminuetep had no choice but to follow and remain silent.

"The battle will be held at sunset," Montuotep said. He leaned into Iminuetep's ear. "You will be there to witness it."

"Thank you, master," Iminuetep said, unsure of what else to say. "But there is much work to be done in preparation for your death. You will have the greatest resting place in Kement, I swear it."

Montuotep smiled again. "Oh, I have no doubt of that." He lowered his voice so only Iminuetep could hear what he was about to say. "My father dies tonight. It has been arranged."

Iminuetep was careful not to let any emotions show on his face. "By whom?" he asked instead.

"By whom! The man asks by whom. By the vampires, of course!" Montuotep laughed. "Who else?"

Iminuetep was silent. The Nomarch of Thebes was going to die, leaving Montuotep with the daunting task of stepping into his father's shoes as the provincial governor. It would be a great day for Montuotep, if he was ready to assume leadership in these troubled times. And though Iminuetep had no doubt about his master's capability, he could not help but wonder how much

Montuotep was responsible for the priests' decisions.

"So what is to happen to me?" he asked. "And your tomb, where will I continue working on your tomb?"

Montuotep grinned. "Tonight we watch my father fall in battle and we watch the vampires feast on the dying. Tonight we celebrate!" He looked at Iminuetep mischievously. "With women!" he added.

Iminuetep rolled his eyes and shook his head, though he returned his master's grin. Though he and Montuotep had been raised to be the closest of friends, Iminuetep could never understand his master's lust. Iminuetep had his art, his work, his responsibility to immortalize Montuotep's legacy, and while he channeled his energies into exploring new ways to express what needed to be expressed, Montuotep was exploring women.

"Your legacy, as great as it is, may not be able to afford to take a night off," Iminuetep admitted. "I am not as great an artist as I could be, nor as fast with the chisel as I should be."

Now it was Montuotep who shook his head. He laughed and put his arm around Iminuetep's shoulder. "Do you still have that ceremonial dagger?"

"Always," Iminuetep answered as he patted the blade where he kept it sheathed at his side. As they walked through Dier el Medina, Iminuetep had to force himself to ignore the envious stares of the other freemen as they headed toward the Nile. Barges were waiting for them on the shores of this side, and in the distance, the temples of Thebes could be seen on the other side, rising above the palaces and rugged wilderness of Kement. "Why?"

Montuotep only smiled secretly to himself. "You can take the night off," he assured Iminuetep. "Everything changes after tonight."

"Why, master? What changes?" Iminuetep was not usually this inquisitive with Montuotep, but his life's work was at stake, and he knew Montuotep would not be angry when his diligence was not in question, nor his loyalty.

"In time," Montuotep would only say. "In time."

* * * * *

The barges carried Iminuetep and his few statues memorializing his young master carefully across the Nile with a host of Montuotep's personal slaves to oversee the transportation. But although Montuotep was in high spirits and insisted the young artist join him in celebration, Iminuetep kept one eye on the barge with his precious pillars, massive stone sculptures that were each over twenty feet tall. "If they so much as make a scratch on any of those,"

Iminuetep muttered as he watched the slaves and his pillars on a different barge. He pulled the dagger from his belt and placed it on the table between him and his master. "With my own hand, I swear it," he muttered angrily.

Montuotep snorted his approval and kept his eyes on Thebes as they approached. This year had brought a good flood season, enriching all of Kement's fertile soil with new silt from Ethiopia. The fields were now rich with emmer wheat and barley; the slaves were now into their second harvest. The temple of Osiris rose in the backdrop behind his father's fields, soon to be his fields. "We will usher in a new era," he said, more to himself than to Iminuetep. "We will conquer the other Nomarchs and bring them under one rule, under one temple, and Osiris and his servants will be pleased."

"You will, more than I, master," Iminuetep admitted, tearing his eyes off of his precious works and looking at Montuotep. "I am simply here to record the events."

Montuotep shook himself out of his dream and looked at Iminuetep. "What was that you said?" he asked. "Oh yes, of course." He was silent for a moment. "I trust you have enough papyrus for the story."

Iminuetep waved at the stone pillars floating across the Nile at his side. "Your youth has been recorded on something more resilient than the fibres of a reed."

Montuotep glanced over at the pillars quickly. "All of it?" he asked, surprised. "Already?"

"Yes, master," Iminuetep declared proudly. "All of it."

Montuotep picked up his servant's knife and flipped it expertly in his hand. He held the blade out to Iminuetep, hilt first. "Kill as many of them as you wish," he declared.

"Thank you, master," Iminuetep answered as he took the blade and replaced it back into his sheathe. "Hopefully, I won't have to kill any of them." Then he too looked toward Thebes and the wealth that awaited them there.

Montuotep looked at him, surprised.

"Slaves can be replaced," Iminuetep continued, still looking at the dominating presence of the temple of Osiris. "What they destroy can't, even though I have the words memorized."

Appreciative, Montuotep nodded and looked toward Thebes once again.

When they reached her shores, Montuotep ordered the pillars to be sent to the temple of Osiris. Iminuetep, not questioning the will of his master, watched carefully as they were unloaded, and with the rest of his work, carried away.

Montuotep watched for as long as his restlessness would allow and then guided Iminuetep away from the procession, toward an awaiting caravan. "We will see them again, old friend," he announced. "No need to fear." They mounted up on fine desert stallions and Iminuetep followed his master's lead as they kicked their horses into a gallop. "But tonight!" Montuotep cried, "Tonight we celebrate!"

They galloped ahead of the rest of the caravan, racing toward the temple of Osiris as the slaves laboured behind them with Iminuetep's life's work in their care.

At the base of the great temple, far enough removed from the desert looming in the background as to be out of the way of danger, a table was set up under a protective canvas against Ra's heat. Servants were already there awaiting Montuotep's arrival. When he and Iminuetep galloped up and pulled the reins of their horses to a stop, the slaves rushed forward to help them from their saddles and to take the horses from their care.

"Come, Iminuetep!" Montuotep laughed, motioning for his friend to follow him. "Tonight we get to witness my rise to greatness!"

Silently, Iminuetep was guided under the shadow of the tent. Food was brought forward, along with chilled wines. Iminuetep kept his eyes on the horizon of the desert and on the setting sun, promising himself he would not miss a thing. Montuotep stared at the slave girl that served them, leering at her appreciatively as she bent over the table in front of him. "Patience, Iminuetep," he said. "Patience."

Iminuetep only ignored him and kept his gaze steady on the setting sun. Then, as if the mighty eye of Ra was the signal, when it touched the vast deserts behind Deir el Medina, his home left behind, the first of the invading army made itself known on the opposite horizon in front of them. Iminuetep swivelled in his seat, already caught up in the drama of it. Even Montuotep quieted as he watched the army appear out of the shimmering heat waves.

His father's army approached from the city beside them, answering an unspoken challenge and marching out in steady columns to meet the oncoming soldiers. Montuotep pointed to where his father rode out in a chariot, surrounded by men on horses, all carrying heavy bows and swords they would use to guard their nomarch's life with their own. The two armies stopped in front of each other, with no signal Iminuetep could see passing through their ranks. Montuotep's father rode out to meet the other Nomarch, also in a chariot. Each governor brought with him a select few of his trusted advisors and bodyguards. They met, exchanged a few words Iminuetep could not hear, and then rode back to their men. Montuotep's father looked over at their tent, as if waiting for a signal to attack. Iminuetep glanced around them nervously and jumped with fright when he realized they were surrounded by the silent presence of three priests of Osiris, vampires.

The night was still young, the sunrise not quite over; yet these stoic overseers of the dead bore the sun in grimacing silence. One of them, with clenched teeth, nodded his head toward the Nomarch, giving him the signal to attack.

Iminuetep heard the governor yell at his horses and whip his reins, urging them into a gallop. And then the rest of his army was thundering over the desert with him, charging into an oncoming wave of soldiers, seeking to shed blood for the glory of Kement, the Black Land.

The armies clashed with a thundering roar that echoed up and down the desert horizons. Not much made sense to Iminuetep as he watched, but it appeared as though the battle fared in favour of Montuotep's father. It was bloody, and gory, something out of his worst nightmares, yet Iminuetep could not look away as he watched in macabre fascination. Death was sweeping across the land before him. Then, as it looked like the battle was just over, when the enemy was divided and separated into small pockets of resistance in an ocean of his father's warriors, a cry of anguish went up from the conquering army, and Montuotep leaned forward in his seat with excitement. From where they sat, they could not see what transpired, but Montuotep quickly looked over at one of priests of Osiris.

The vampire nodded sagely and said, "It has been done."

Montuotep, abandoning all pretence of grief, jumped to his feet, and hollered his victory. Iminuetep was grateful his father's army could not hear him over the sounds of battle, lest they turn on him as well. But instead, they cut into what was left of the opposing forces, grief stricken and blinded by rage.

The vampires, seeing the battle ended, glided out into the desert night, eager to dine on the blood spilling into the sand.

* * * * *

They came for him early that morning. Iminuetep lay in a heap in the middle of the largest, most comfortable bed he had ever imagined. His blood was still rich with alcohol and exotic drugs, his mind was groggy and his perceptions were unclear. His head throbbed, though he lay motionless and asleep with exhaustion. On either side of him slept a woman Montuotep had chosen for him the night before. They were beautiful women, models of pre-Egyptian finery and splendour. The night had been unlike any Iminuetep had imagined.

Yet, as cruel, cold hands tore him from sleep with mean efficiency, he would soon wish he had died that night.

Priests, with eyes that shifted toward the coming dawn, yanked him naked from the company of the women.

"What is the meaning of this?" Iminuetep cried. His head throbbed so badly he could make no sense of the cruelty he was being handled with.

The priests forced him to his knees at the foot of the bed. The women, wakened by his outrage, remained silent and fearful, with eyes wide in the morning gloom. Another priest entered the room. The vampire was tall and lanky, and the rest of the priests gave him a wide berth with eyes downcast in respect. Iminuetep tried to look up into the vampire's face to determine who this man was, but one of the lesser priests struck him hard with his fist, sending Iminuetep crashing to the floor for his disrespect.

He was dragged back to his knees. Blood gushed from a cut above his eye. His vision swarmed and blurred through the terrible pain, the tears and the blood.

Then, suddenly, he felt something rip into the back of his neck. The blood flooded from his wound and he crashed into unconsciousness again, not knowing if he would ever wake.

Chapter Three

He awoke chained to a mud brick wall surrounded by the light of a thousand torches, each burning into his eyes like the light of an undead Ra. He realized where he was and shuddered. For this was the temple of Osiris. This was the resting place of the undead. This was where the immortals raised mortals up to the status of gods. Iminuetep's head spun with the ramifications of where he was more than it did the agonizing pain his body was in.

The cavern was immense. In front of him slaves embalmed the dead with wraps of linen. The perfume and incense in the air was thick enough to coat everything with a thin layer of oily sweat that glistened like liquid lighting under the torchlight. The dead were laid out on slabs of rock. They were kept in endless wooden sarcophaguses lining the walls and stacked in piles while clay jars preserved their internal and critical organs. The cavernous tomb stretched its yawning maw over the masses of the dead and swallowed them with frightening efficiency.

Scattered along the outside wall of the room, prisoners like Iminuetep stood wearily on their feet while they gazed out over the proceedings. They were chained to the walls, their hands spread wide and above their heads. All male, slim, strong, and with the hands of free men and artisans, they watched everything in front of them with rapt awe. Iminuetep noticed with growing approval that all of them looked to have been beaten and stood barely conscious or hanging limp in their shackles.

One prisoner was kept on a larger chain, held not by his wrists up and over his head, but by a collar shackled around his neck. He lay curled on the floor, half buried under a small mountain of moulding hay. All about him was a wide berth, as though the entombers of the dead knew full well the extent that chain could reach. The creature looked pitiful, shriveled to sticks, his bones protruded through his muscles at strange angles, as though the man was more a skeleton than flesh and blood. He was covered over with scars that crisscrossed across his back, accentuated with bruises the size of both Iminuetep's fists clenched and held together in front of him. Iminuetep pitied him for a moment, and then looked away, confused by the mix of emotions that played in his mind.

There was no way to tell the time, shut away from Ra as they were, but Iminuetep thought perhaps it was still the same day. The last night he remembered he had celebrated Montuotep's ascension to power with a roomful of vampires that sampled the blood of slaves while he dined on delicacies imported from the farthest riches of the known world.

There were no vampires here. And even should they wish to disguise themselves among the slaves before him, he could not imagine they would be able to hide their greatness for long.

Throughout the day work continued undisturbed and in total silence. Bodies and mummies were brought in and out of the underground vault. Never a stitch of sunlight struck his face, and as the hours dragged on in unending silence, he wondered if he had been cast into eternal dark, shut away forever by the sun's piercing rays. It made his heart sick to think that way, longing to be with the sculptures he was preparing for Montuotep.

Then, at one moment, the slaves shifted their attention on what they were doing. Bodies removed were not replaced. Wraps were being rewound and placed into awaiting piles. Oils were being carefully dumped into larger jars and seals were being replaced with dripping wax. The sarcophaguses were shut. The old torches were replaced with new ones and were relit. Slaves that left did not return.

The last slaves to leave refilled the incense burners and placed a bowl on an empty slab of rock before the pitiful creature Iminuetep had been ignoring. There were two of them, working in continual silence, though they moved with practised efficiency as they worked together, as though they had done this countless times before. One slave handed a small knife to the other one, and then, taking up the wooden bowl himself, he moved forward behind his companion. The two of them crept up on the pitiful motionless creature and took the sleeping prisoner's chain about his neck.

Then, with a shocking explosion of violence, they heaved the moaning prisoner to his feet and slammed his head against the brick wall behind him. One priest held him there as he sought consciousness, even as his body tried to faint from the blow. His eyes rolled in his head with a vicious effort. "No," he mumbled. "Don't let it…not again…have pity on me…" The priest with the knife cut the man's arm and held the wrist over the other slave's outstretched bowl. Blood swelled from the wound and dripped from his fingertips. He tried to speak again, but the words were nothing more than weak moans.

Yet as the blood drained from him, strength returned to his muscles. His moans grew louder and angry, audibly growing in power. The slaves ignored this phenomenon, although Iminuetep stared on in growing fascination. Then, satisfied they had collected enough, they jumped away from the slave to let him collapse at the base of the wall.

But, he remained on his feet where Iminuetep expected him to crumble. He leaned against the wall for support, yet he was now growling in inhuman outrage. The slaves did not turn back to him as they placed the bowl on the table before him. Instead, they shuffled out of the room as the man started to roar and flex his pitiful muscles under the torchlight. Muscles bulged on his neck and his face contorted in inhuman expressions of rage. He thrashed at the wall behind him and beat upon his chest with his fists, tore at his hair and clawed at his face in ever increasing rivulets of blood that only infuriated him more. Iminuetep watched in maddening horror as his body grew larger before the captive's very eyes; his legs and his arms grew strength beyond human grasp. He threw his head back and howled his beastly furry. Fur was growing on his shoulders and face. His eyes seemed to be glowing red with hate under the torches.

Then, all at once he stopped his ranting as the sound of an iron door crashing shut echoed across the vault. They were sealed in for the night, buried under immeasurable weights of stone and sand. The world of the living was cast away from them and life inside the tombs had begun.

Unexpectedly, the demon noticed the bowl of blood on the table before him. His nose quivered and he roared as he pulled against the chain at his neck. Yet the blood remained out of his reach before him.

As if awakened by the madman's torments, mummies from the wooden sarcophaguses lining the walls came to life with startling, united abruptness. Among the bodies piled in the corners and laid out on the slabs of rock, many of them shuddered as they all drew breathe and became animated at once. Iminuetep jumped with surprise when he felt a powerful presence of dying life come from the jars along the walls. Among the richer, gold-plated sarcophaguses that lay on the floor, the lid from one of them slowly pushed upward amongst the roars of the creature that seemed half human half dog, though of what kind of dog Iminuetep could not imagine. Then, with resolute authority, the lid crashed against the coffin, silencing the beast as a vampire rose from his sleep.

Dressed in black silk, his skin was pale, his hair was a bleached blonde and stringy, hanging about his shoulders in thinning clumps. On his finger was a gold ring with the largest red ruby set into it Iminuetep had ever imagined. It was the size of a child's fist and reflected the torchlight as though it was the eye of a god under a fiery sun from the underworld. Straight away, he moved toward the bowl of blood waiting for him before the beast. He ignored the dog's howls of fury as he lifted the bowl to his lips and drank down the blood of the man/demon before him. The creature, now with the head of a wolf, pulled against the chain about his neck as he paced in an arc, straining the chain to its full length between him and the wall behind him. The chain did not touch the floor as it stretched taunt and creaked under his efforts.

The vampire took his time with his drink and even glanced at the demon a few times, though with no interest. Then, when he was finished, he dropped the bowl onto the table and strode from the room by the same way the slaves had left. He left the demon to howl now in outrageous grief rather than fury. By then, other vampires had unwrapped themselves from their death shrouds and were unceremoniously dumping the discarded linen into jars kept between the torches next to the prisoners. They too were dressed in black silk that clung to their bodies with the same tenacity the linen had. Then, all at once, Iminuetep realized that the vampires were dressed in black strips of silk, were wrapped in the same manner of the dead even while awake. Iminuetep stared at them in open awe, catching the interest of a few of them as they neared him.

Self-consciously he realized he still had his ceremonial dagger, hung by a loop around his neck, as though someone had placed it there after he had been rendered unconscious. He looked around the room at the other acolytes and realized that not every captive hanging from chains wore a knife around his neck. Three or four others did, though. And they were also capturing the notice of some of the vampires.

Then, wordlessly, one of them came forward and unfastened his chains with a golden key kept tucked away in his hand. "Acolyte, you have earned trust among the priests of Osiris," the vampire said callously. "Your chains may be removed." Then, with little ceremony, he let Iminuetep crumble into the sands. The other acolytes carrying the knives were similarly removed from their shackles and cast to the floor.

One of the priests bent over Iminuetep and nodded toward the beast still howling with unending passion. "Anubis," the vampire confided to Iminuetep. "He is Osiris' son, though the bastard child of his brother's wife." Iminuetep and the vampire stared at the demon in silent loathing while he raged against his constraints. "He would devour anyone in here, as he would the body of his own father," the vampire added.

Several of the other vampires glared at their companion angrily. But none of them raised a finger to stop the vampire from speaking. He spoke the truth, and as they filed past Anubis, they kept well away from him, though held fast by his restraint. Then the vampire that had spoken joined the other priests filing from the room in silence, keeping a wide berth around Anubis.

Exhausted and weak from the day and night before, he collapsed onto a pile of the linen wraps and passed into a grateful, dreamless sleep.

Chapter Four

He was woken by the infuriated outrage of slaves coming in to perform their daily tasks upon the dead. They grabbed him and slammed him against the wall, blabbering on at him about something Iminuetep could not seem to grasp. He was weak and disoriented, and though he was sure the slaves spoke the same language he did, the meaning to their words escaped him, and he stared at them with dazed, unblinking eyes. Angered but not surprised by his incoherence, they gave up trying to reason with him and left him hanging on the wall by his shackles.

Another day passed, and Iminuetep's tongue felt like it was swelling from lack of water. Desperate and tormented, he looked at the other acolytes. Some of them were awake, and as the day began to progress, many of them moaned and begged for water or food. They were ignored completely by the workers going about their daily routines. But the body of the man possessed by Anubis lay motionless, as though dead. He was ignored, along with the rest of the acolytes, but he remained so still and lifeless that Iminuetep feared he had died by the manifestation of the night before.

Then, in an immeasurable stretch of time, the slaves began to pack up for the day. The body of Anubis' sleeping form was dragged to its feet, and blood was drained from its arm by the same two slaves from the night before. Anubis awoke with howling ferocity, the vampires awoke from his outbursts, and that great high priest of Osiris rose from his gold plated tomb to drink the jackal's blood. Iminuetep was once again released from his chains, though the vampire that unleashed him shook his head in utter contempt that he was there at all. This time he would not dishonour himself and he kept his feet in respect as they filed from the room.

When the acolytes of Osiris were alone with Anubis once again, Iminuetep looked around the mummification chamber, dying for want of water or food. He was one of the few that not only were free, but still had enough strength to stand on his own feet. The entire time, Anubis roared against his chains. Yet, eventually he gave up on the bowl that had contained his blood. He quieted for a moment, and Iminuetep, still rooted to where he stood, stared at him from across the chamber. He was sniffing the air, searching for something with his powerful sense of smell. Iminuetep's skin crawled at imagining what he could be searching for.

All at once, Anubis began raging again. But this time, his attention was focussed on one of the clay jars kept not far from where he was chained. Iminuetep watched him silently for a while, still too weak to risk venturing from where he swayed on his feet. Then, all at once, he realized what was kept in that jar and shuddered, understanding what it was Anubis longed for.

Iminuetep collected all the strength he could muster. Then, on shaky feet, he took one hesitant step away from the wall experimentally. He expected to fall. The strange narcotics in his system were still affecting his equilibrium. But he kept his balance, and eventually he was able to take another step toward the clay jar on the other side of the room.

In time, using the rock tables as support and rest, Iminuetep made his way over to the jar.

Anubis saw what he was doing and went into a lather, ferocious with envy as the chain creaked against Anubis' efforts to break it.

Iminuetep looked from him to the jar and looked over the brim of it. Then he wretched and crumpled into a ball at the base of the clay jar. Human hearts, pulled from the dead bodies of newly brought in corpses were inside it. They were kept in some kind of liquid that prevented the blood from congealing and the flesh from drying up. Iminuetep gasped and choked on his own bile, realizing these hearts had been preserved fresh, and it was the flesh of them that Anubis was craving.

He remained as motionless as he could until the spasms passed. Then he struggled to his feet in determination and reached into the gory mess with both hands. He pulled a bloody heart out of the jar with each hand and held the meat up to the torchlight while Anubis went hysterical. He looked at the demigod frightfully, honestly believing that his leash would break at any moment, and that Iminuetep would be destroyed in the jackal's mad lust for blood.

He tossed the dog one of the hearts and immediately Anubis pounced on it, devouring it within a few moments. When he was done, he looked up at Iminuetep longingly. Although he was now quiet, his hunger still radiated over him. He was pleading with Iminuetep with his eyes, and a whine escaped from his throat. Iminuetep tossed him the other heart and watched horror stricken as Anubis devoured this one as well. Three more times he reached into the jar, each time pulling out two human hearts, and each time feeding them both to Anubis, who devoured them with ever growing complacency. The last time, Anubis kept the heart in his mouth, not chewing it or swallowing it. He carried it to the corner of the vault and deposited the organ into the sand. Then he lay down beside the heart and passed into a restful sleep.

Iminuetep watched all this, fascinated and shocked into silence. Then he reached into the clay jar and pulled out one more human heart. He forced himself to eat it slowly, lest he gag on it and be caught in the morning in the middle of the chamber. He made his way back to his own chains as he ate, pausing as often as he dared to catch his breathe and swallow a few more mouthfuls of meat.

By the time he made it back to the wall, most of the heart had been eaten. He was amazed at how much his strength had returned. He still felt confused, traumatized. But he knew he would not die in his chains as many of the other acolytes would. He sat with his back resting against the wall while he finished the heart and then risked nodding off to sleep.

But this time, with the strength of his macabre meal in his stomach, he awoke when the priests began to return. They left him and the rest of the acolytes alone as they took their places upon the empty stone slabs. Anubis was still quiet, content—though awake—to stare out at the silent proceedings from his place on the wall. He still guarded his prize fearlessly against them. They in turn looked not at all surprised or concerned with what he held in a paw that was half human. They only lay down and went to sleep. Stillness settled over them quickly enough, and hideously, Iminuetep realized they had died.

The high priest was the last to enter the chamber. A few of the other vampires were still awake, though already motionless as they stared at the ceiling. He was followed into the chamber with an entourage of slaves ready to begin their daily routines. The vampire stopped in front of the jackal, and noting the demigod's contentment, he nodded to himself and smiled. Then, he went straight away to his own coffin and pulled the lid down over himself.

Iminuetep stood when the slaves took notice of him and waited for them to chain him to the wall once again. Instead, they regarded him with disinterest and left him there to watch as the day began anew.

Anubis growled, and then began to morph into a human. The change was painful, accompanied by many howls of rage and pain. He would scream and then all of a sudden the muscles off his back would melt away. Then, painfully, he would scream again and the jaws of a terrible dog would retract to leave human lips and teeth in its place. There seemed no set order to Anubis' gruelling changes, and eventually his screaming ceased as he lay exhausted on his back, breathing hard. All traces of the dog were gone, and the skinny acolyte dressed in sackcloth pants lay panting but awake in the sand.

Eventually, he came to enough to sit up. He realized he still gripped a human heart in his hand and was relieved to tears when he saw it. Throughout the day, he would eat the heart as he watched the slaves work. Iminuetep, realizing his own hunger was reawakening, began to wish he kept another heart for himself.

* * * * *

Eventually Iminuetep could detect patterns to what the slaves were doing. After carefully rewrapping the dead bodies of the vampires and disposing them randomly, though carefully around the vault, new bodies were carried in and placed on the stone slabs. These were operated on; their organs were removed, and each organ was placed inside one of the jars along the wall. Then, the bodies were wrapped in linen, and carefully laid aside with the bodies of the vampires. Many cadavers were taken out of the room, though Iminuetep could not understand what reason lay behind carrying one body away and leaving another behind.

As the day came to a close, no more bodies were brought into the tomb. All the jars that contained human body parts were removed except for the one that held the hearts. The slaves finished their work, approached Anubis, and cut the acolyte again. This time, he raged all the more ferocious, with strength he had not possessed before.

Still, the slaves collected his blood and placed it on the table in front of him. They left, and the High Priest of Osiris rose from his sleep. This time he looked at Anubis with a renewed interest that was not there before and drank the jackal's blood, savouring it more than he had the night before. When he was finished, he left, and the other priests followed him wordlessly from the chamber.

Iminuetep looked around the abandoned room and realized that many of the acolytes had died in their chains while a few of them had gone utterly insane, babbling incoherently to themselves or staring motionlessly into space.

Eventually Anubis realized that the bowl of blood in front of him was empty and he calmed. He sniffed the air again, found the jar of hearts once again, and then, with determined strength he did not have the night before, he broke his chain and roared his celebration in his newfound freedom.

Iminuetep's eyes grew round with fear. Paralysed, he watched as Anubis overturned the stone slab in front of him. The bowl flew against a wall and shattered into pieces, but already Anubis had moved on. He tore into the lifeless corpse of the acolyte chained next to him and ripped his heart out of his chest. Hungrily he ate it in only a few bites and moved on to the next acolyte. This one was alive, though barely. And Anubis howled his anticipation as he ripped out the still beating heart with one powerful grip of his claws. He savoured the warm flesh, licking the fresh blood from his hand and then moved on.

He roamed the vault at will that night, overturning sarcophaguses and scattering linen. Iminuetep remained where he was and was ignored in turn, although Anubis showed no mercy as he killed every other acolyte one at a time throughout the night. He feasted on their beating hearts, and when he was finished he returned to his corner with a heart in one of his hands. He hunched down with his treasure and went to sleep.

Iminuetep, daring at last to venture from his place against the wall, made his way over to the clay jar and looked at Anubis quickly. The jackal was awake, looking at him with fierce animal eyes that glittered in the torchlight. But he had not moved, and in another moment he closed his eyes. Iminuetep sighed and took two hearts from the jar. He carried them back to his place and forced himself to eat one. The other he would save for during the day.

* * * * *

He awoke well into the day. He had missed the high priest's reactions to Anubis' escape, or the slaves that had to restore the room after the destruction

33

done to it. What was left of the acolytes Anubis had killed had been removed from their chains, and now it was only Iminuetep and the man Anubis possessed that stared out at the wordless proceedings in front of them.

Iminuetep still had his knife.

He ate the heart early in the day and took a daring step into the room, away from his previous chained captivity. None of the slaves made a move to stop him. He avoided their work, staying completely out of their way, and he realized he could walk around the room at will, as long as he did nothing to prevent them from their dissection of the dead.

Carefully he made his way between the working slaves and came before the man Anubis possessed. The man was awake, though chained to the wall once again. And as he looked into Iminuetep's eyes, the artisan realized that not one shred of sanity or reason remained with this man. Iminuetep pulled the knife from around his neck, looked at it, looked at Anubis again.

Then, realizing it might cost him his life, Iminuetep plunged the dagger into the demigod's own chest, piercing his own inhuman heart. Iminuetep could not rest knowing the vampires of Osiris were in danger.

Chapter Five

No one tried to stop him when he stabbed the frightened man a second time. The body of Anubis, though mad beyond reason, knew what fear was, Iminuetep could tell that much. And though he was in too much pain to make a sound, Iminuetep knew he was terrified when Iminuetep plunged his knife into his stomach. He twisted the dagger before he pulled it out, issuing a font of blood from the demigod's gut.

Satisfied that no mortal could survive the wounds Iminuetep had given him, the young artisan stepped away from the dying corpse to look at his handiwork. Whatever punishment Iminuetep would receive, he would know there would be a priest to oversee Montuotep's mummification. And at whatever costs, he would see this end was guaranteed.

Still, the body of Anubis would not die. Instead, the man lay paling on his side as the blood flowed from him. His eyes remained open and he remained very much awake. He was not dying.

Horrified, Iminuetep looked at the creature with a mixture of pity and dread. If he could not kill him in his weak, mortal form, Anubis would avenge himself upon Iminuetep in ways he could not imagine and perhaps on the vampires as well. He cared nothing about the slaves. Slaves could be replaced. Iminuetep knew even he could be replaced. But the vampires could not be, and now, with Anubis' wrath awakened, there would be no telling what the canine would do once he escaped from his chain once again.

There was nothing to do for it, but to finish what he started. Setting his teeth to the gruesome work ahead, Iminuetep readjusted the grip on his dagger and went to work skinning the pathetic creature alive.

Iminuetep lost track of time, as he usually did when he had a task set out before him. He ignored the slaves who worked silently on the bodies of the dead behind him; and they ignored him, too preoccupied with what they were doing to take notice of the desecration taking place in their presence. Then, suddenly, Iminuetep came to, realizing that the creature was still alive, though he had been nearly completely flayed. The human pelt was all but peeled off of the creature. Iminuetep had been careful to keep the pelt in one piece and the work had been hard, demanding his full attention. The slaves had all but departed for the day; the two slaves that usually drew the bowl of blood from the creature's flesh were standing above him, looking on with faces that remained passive and calm. Iminuetep reached his hand out for the bowl and they complied. Then they left him to finish his work.

Anubis was awakening, though he could not tell by anything but the eyes. The creature lay panting, too weak to so much as move a muscle, in too much pain to even try. But his eyes stared at Iminuetep hatefully, and Iminuetep was shocked by the intensity he saw there. With deft, quick movements, he cut away the rest of the pelt and hung it to dry over one of the empty stone slabs.

Then, knowing that the vampires would awake soon, Iminuetep cut his own arm and let the blood collect in the bowl the slaves had given him.

He did not have long to wait before the High Priest of Osiris rose from his final resting place once again.

The vampire looked surprised, but any trace of emotion was swiftly removed from his countenance as he came to stand before Iminuetep.

With perfect sincerity, Iminuetep lowered his eyes and knelt before the great lord of the underworld. He held the bowl above his head as an offering and waited for the hand of the High Priest to strike him dead.

There was a long pause instead. Eventually the vampire took the bowl and raised the blood slowly to his lips. Anubis moaned as he watched the priest begin to drink, but right on the edge of death, the beast was too weak to suffer the vampire his usual ranting. The High Priest seemed to ascend into ecstasy as he savoured the blood; his eyes rolled back in his head and he licked his lips before drinking the rest of the bowl slowly, carefully remembering the taste of every drop.

Iminuetep kept his head lowered as he heard the bowl placed on the table behind the vampire. There was silence through the chamber and Iminuetep realized that the other vampires had awakened and were watching him.

"The beast has died," one of the vampires finally managed to whisper.

Iminuetep looked over at the body reflexively. He was grateful beyond words and had forgotten all etiquette in hearing the joyous news that the vampires were safe. He could not tell if it was the still form of Anubis or of his mortal host that Iminuetep looked at, but when he dared to look at the pelt still dripping from the table behind the High Priest, he was surprised to see that what he looked at was the fresh hide of a wolf, though he was sure the hide had been of a man when he had taken it.

"We have other beasts that can take his place," the High Priest said over his shoulder. "Besides, I grow tired of the blood of dogs." To Iminuetep, he said, "Come with me." Then he led the stunned artisan from the chamber of death and into the bowels of the Temple of Osiris.

Chapter Six

Anubis stared up at Iminuetep from the bottom of a stone pit. He was still a puppy, half human child, half dog, looking up at Iminuetep with an obscure and hideous innocence of infancy that left Iminuetep's skin cold and clammy. The baby was naked, yet filled with the passions of a playful beast, not uncomfortable in the harsh stone pit. He was not alone either. His mother, a ghastly beast morphed more fully into a wolf than Iminuetep had yet seen, lay on her side panting. Her entire body was covered with hair, yet it was unmistakable under that coat of wolf fur that a beautiful human body was captured. Three more puppies, all female, played fiercely with each other, making a game out of pinning each other down. They growled and yipped at each other as they rolled and pounced around their mother. They took no notice of their brother or of the human watching them from the mouth of their pit.

"Chose one from this litter," the High Priest said over his shoulder.

Iminuetep turned and regarded the icy eyes of the undead for a moment, then looked back at the Anubises before them. "Will they always remain this docile?" he asked, relieved that the danger of the other dog had still been extinguished.

"No," the vampire admitted. "If you don't feed them, they get angry, like the other one. Yet, if you feed them too much, they get too strong and escape their chains."

Iminuetep's quick mind jumped to somewhere he did not want to go. "All that in the place of embalming," he began to ask. "That was a test?"

"Chose one," the vampire said again.

Iminuetep picked the male Anubis quickly. "That one, then."

Slaves came forward to do their bidding while the priest turned and strode from the chamber. Hesitant, Iminuetep followed, and had to hurry to keep stride with the tall vampire.

"I am known as Hamenemmon," the High Priest said as he strode through the temple with Iminuetep on his heels. "This is my temple. These are my priests."

"Do all vampires sleep in the same room?" Iminuetep asked.

"No. During the initiation ceremony, those that wish to see the acolytes brought to us may do so. We sleep there during the ritual, letting the slaves care for our bodies while we are dead."

"That was just an initiation?" Iminuetep asked, remembering the hideous nightmare the place of embalming had been.

The priest was silent and kept walking through the temple.

Iminuetep kept pace and tried a different approach. "Those others in chains, who were they?" he asked instead.

Hamenemmon stopped before a wide wooden door and looked at Iminuetep with his hand on the door handle. Iminuetep was silent as he waited for the vampire to speak. "They were artisans," he said, "just like yourself."

Before Iminuetep could respond, Hamenemmon pushed the door open and they stepped outside, onto a wide paved courtyard built high up in a pyramid overlooking the Nile. Montuotep, his master, stood with a small group of vampires on the other side of the courtyard. When he saw Iminuetep and the High Priest emerge, Montuotep stopped talking and ran toward them. He looked surprised to see Iminuetep, but he masked his emotions quickly, replacing them with feinted joy. "I knew it would be you!" Montuotep cried as he embraced Iminuetep like a brother.

Stiffly, Iminuetep embraced his master in return and then pulled apart before Montuotep could sense that something was wrong. "I am happy to serve you, master," he responded with a bow and eyes downcast in respect.

Montuotep took the knife that hung around Iminuetep's neck and held it in his hand, still looped about the artist's neck. "Every vampire has one, you know?" Montuotep asked.

"I can only hope to aspire to that high a station," Iminuetep responded carefully. "To guard the greatest tomb in all of Kement."

Montuotep smiled and let go of the knife. He walked away from Hamenemmon and motioned for Iminuetep to follow him. Iminuetep glanced over at the immortal to make sure he was permitted. When the vampire nodded, Iminuetep caught up with his master at the edge of the courtyard. Montuotep was silent for a long moment while he took in the Nile under the silver light of a half moon. "I have done it," he said at last.

"Done what, Master?" Iminuetep asked.

"United the nomes under one rule," he said as he turned and faced Iminuetep. He held his fist between them and shook it passionately as he said, "Kement, all of Kement, is mine."

* * * * *

Hamenemmon did not waste time. The greatness of a fledgling empire was in his hands, and to memorize the occasion of Kement's unification, he could think of nothing better than to immortalize the man who would watch over the first emperor of Kement as soon as possible. Iminuetep had been filled with strange, intoxicating narcotics that barely left him able to stand. His head was shaved and he was wrapped in black linen by a group of slaves that treated him as if he had already died. Iminuetep found the icy treatment frightening and he had to suppress a shudder as goose bumps rose over his arms.

Then he was brought before the High Priest of Osiris and a legion of silent vampires stood rock still around the vast chamber. Their expressions were unreadable and frightening. Even the High Priest Hamenemmon looked foreboding as he sat in his stone throne, looking down at Iminuetep and studying him dispassionately.

Montuotep stood to the side of Hamenemmon, looking at Iminuetep as if he was something other than human. All traces of Iminuetep's lifelong friend were gone. Tonight, Iminuetep would die, and it looked as if Montuotep had already moved on. Iminuetep swallowed his fear and looked into the dead eyes of the high priest.

All at once the priest disappeared. Iminuetep jumped, but before he could look around the room, Hamenemmon's powerful hands had him by the neck. Mercilessly, he tore into Iminuetep's throat as he strangled the artisan. Iminuetep would have screamed in pain had he been permitted his voice, but in a moment, in the midst of the pain, he felt a swooning come over him, the sleep of death reaching up to swallow him for itself.

Hamenemmon broke away just as Iminuetep was about to faint. Holding the artisan with one hand by the throat, the priest prevented Iminuetep from falling. With his other hand, he held his wrist out before Iminuetep's face. "Bite into it," he said. "And drink the Alexis of immortality."

Horrified, yet somewhat calloused since his initiation with Anubis, Iminuetep did what he was told. Blood flooded through him once again. An ocean of memories and experiences that were not his flowed through him, a tempest sea of emotions that even immortals could not express. Part of him shuddered and tried to scream, yet Hamenemmon was careful not to let him do anything but drink as he held him still by the throat.

He was dying in agony. The blood in him felt polluted and sought to kill him as it streamed through his arteries. He imagined himself turning to stone. His soul, that part of him that could experience and grow old, had fled. Now he could sense the other vampires standing around the room, could even hear their thoughts. Yet, still he drank, and he closed his eyes as he felt himself merge with the consciousness of the High Priest. Time seemed to stop, and Iminuetep could not tell if he stood drinking from the undead for a few moments or a few hours. But at last Hamenemmon pushed him away.

"You have had enough," the priest said victoriously. "Welcome to the order of Osiris." He handed Iminuetep the skin of Anubis, the pelt the artisan had taken from the beast in the place of embalming.

Iminuetep looked at it as though it was an alien thing, then shook the carefully folded pelt in his hands. The pelt had been made into a rough tunic, tied together at the waist by a leather belt. A slit had been made for Iminuetep's head and he donned the skin, slipping it over his head reverently. When he raised his icy eyes to Montuotep once again, the human flinched and Iminuetep raised his head proudly. He was immortal; he wore the skin of an immortal demigod about his shoulders, and all of Kement was at his disposal through Montuotep.

Now he knew Montuotep's sarcophagus would be nothing more than a centrepiece in Iminuetep's immortal mansion, that Montuotep was nothing more than a pawn, though history may record him as one of the most powerful mortals ever to walk the earth.

Iminuetep smiled to himself as he looked deep into his mortal master's eyes. The man would make Kement great, Iminuetep would see to it.

Montuotep swallowed his fear and ever so slightly nodded his respect. Iminuetep nodded back. They understood each other.

Chapter Seven

Though the stone vaults echoed an eternity of merciless death, and though the desert sands blew oblivion across the known world, the children within his care scampered and jumped to see Iminuetep, too young and innocent to see or understand the death that lingered behind his eyes.

"Uncle Iminuetep!" they cried as he flowed into their chamber. "Uncle Iminuetep!"

"Children!" he cried back with open arms, kneeling before them with care not entirely feinted.

Just young enough to speak, they laughed, the four of them, as he caught them all up in a rough embrace that lifted them off of their feet.

He was hurting them, but only a little, and these children were well accustomed to harsher treatment than this, though mercifully they could not remember the incidents.

He put them down quickly enough, and played with them as the sun went down, wearing them into exhaustion as quickly as he could.

Then, gradually, they began to change, to morph into dull witted monstrosities known singularly as Anubis.

Confused, they became disoriented and edgy, yet Iminuetep was there to comfort them through their transition, until trusting and docile werewolves lay cuddled about him as he sat with his back against one of the stone walls.

Though wide awake, the usually aggressive Anubis was content to rest in their master's caring arms.

One of his human slaves found them as such, and fearfully, timidly, edged into the chamber.

At his approach, the Anubis, all four of them, looked up from their docile state and growled menacingly in warning. Their razor sharp baby teeth were no less deadly for their infancy.

"They can smell fear," Iminuetep said without looking up, himself sensing the slave's hesitancy.

The slave did his best to mask his reserves and Anubis quickly lost interest. Iminuetep smiled.

"Master," the slave whispered, afraid despite his best efforts. "The nomarch Montuotep is here to see you."

Iminuetep wordlessly disentangled himself from the puppies, comforting them as they whined for his affections. He stood and strode wordlessly past the slave.

The slave backed out of the chamber, taking the light with him, and closed the door behind the Anubis, locking them inside a stone vault.

"Leave the torch," Iminuetep commanded over his shoulder. "They like the light."

"But master," the slave began. "Without you there—"

"Leave the light."

The slave swallowed his fear, though beads of perspiration were forming on his face. He nodded to Iminuetep's diminishing back and took another torch from a scone on the wall.

As he opened the door, Iminuetep closed another behind him and locked it.

Quickly enough, the slave's screams could be heard through the stone walls until they were abruptly silenced.

Iminuetep smiled as he went out to meet the emerging pharaoh of Egypt.

"Master," Iminuetep hissed as his eyes glinted with the humour of it all.

Montuotep, startled every time he saw the vampire, jumped with fright when he appeared like a shadow at his side. "Don't do that!" Montuotep cried, frustrated at the priest's ability to dance nightmares under his eyes.

Iminuetep only smiled, showing his teeth for what they were.

"The trade routes now extend throughout the known world," Montuotep said boldly, restraining his fear once more.

"I need blood," the vampire said.

Montuotep fidgeted and stepped hesitantly away from the priest of Osiris.

"Not your blood," Iminuetep hissed, showing his fangs once again. Then he recovered and said in a more human tone, "I need more sacrifices."

"Of course," Montuotep said quickly. "I'll have another army destroyed."

"No," Iminuetep said, raising a hand to restrain the first pharaoh of Egypt. "I need them alive and I need them sent here."

"Here?" Montuotep was shocked. "What for?

"That is my business, Master. Not yours."

Montuotep looked at the vampire carefully. "You forget yourself, slave."

Iminuetep laughed outright. "Of course I do!" he cried. "You are mortal." He lifted a handful of sand into his hand and held it out for Montuotep. The pharaoh watched as the sand slipped through his fingers and was gone. The pharaoh looked at the priest of Osiris for a moment and Iminuetep's eyes shone with ambition. "Make your time count, little man," Iminuetep declared. Then he was gone, vanished as smoke right before the pharaoh's eyes.

Montuotep, sweating from fear, looked about nervously and then fled the temple of Osiris.

He was shouting orders to his awaiting slaves before he was completely out of the temple.

Iminuetep watched from the top of his temple, crouched in the shadows under the moon.

Anubis was growing in numbers daily. The children were more intelligent than he could have ever hoped; genius minds were tormented by beastly desires. Yet eventually, that same canine insanity would consume them and leave them empty husks dumber than the cattle that grazed along the Nile, yet a whole lot less docile. If he could find a way to preserve the intelligence of the man, Iminuetep was convinced he could come a long way to controlling the demigod that slept under the surface. Many of the werewolves had to be destroyed lest their numbers get out of control. And Iminuetep spent much of his time trying to understand how he could bolster his number of immortals without all of Egypt becoming aware of it.

Chapter Eight

Egypt continued to grow and solidify under the leadership of Montuotep. The priests of Osiris, weighted down under a tradition of blood baths and terror, were kept busy with their own nomarchs and their priestly duties while Iminuetep's secret army of Anubis held his own nomarch within an iron fisted gauntlet. Totally loyal to the vampire priest, the Anubis were uncontrollable at night, yet idolized their "uncle" during the day. The problems behind housing and feeding a secret society of werewolves was carefully being worked out with surprising ease.

He kept them housed in Montuotep's crypt, a two day trek across the deserts for mortals, yet Anubis could cover the distance within a few hours if he set his mind to it. Iminuetep, who had spent his entire life preparing the pharaoh's final resting place, visited the grave site as often as he could, and trusted the young nomarch to run his own dynasty. Yet, with the strength of the Anubis behind him, Montuotep relied on the vampire like no mortal nomarch before them. It was obvious to both of them who the master was and who was the slave, yet it was an unspoken arrangement. Iminuetep often wondered how many other vampires had the same relationship with their nomarchs, and though it was never talked about, it was not hard to see that the priests of Osiris were the true masters of the known world.

The Nile, rich with life, was also a place rich with death. The crocodiles within the Nile were many. Revered as gods by the people of Egypt, the

Anubis found them as playthings and even in human form the Anubis' hosts admitted a diet of mostly crocodile meat was not that bad. Harvesting their food source gave the creatures a worthy pastime that kept them out of the cities and away from the prying eyes of other vampires. Iminuetep was well pleased to have been able to find a pastime for the army of killers growing larger by the day. Though the war between the Anubis and the Nile was fierce enough to draw attention from the older, wiser vampires within Egypt's ranks of immortals, it allowed the Anubis' numbers to grow undisturbed. His ambiguity was a sacrifice he was willing to make. He was sure no other vampire could stop him now, even if they did understand what he was doing, which he doubted.

And still Egypt continued to rise out of the sands. Montuotep's caravans stretched their reach across the known world, and Iminuetep's army of Anubis scoured the sands, continuing their exploration of the horizon. Montuotep was quick to make use of any find that was useful, growing rich in spices and incenses, as well as in furs and all manner of rare treasures the deserts gave up in the wake of the Anubis' prying eyes.

The other nomarchs, astonished by Montuotep's resourcefulness, continued to bow to his wishes and Egypt continued to solidify under his rule. Taking the opportunity, Montuotep forced his supply lines farther and farther into the womb of Egypt's wealth, forcing the nomarchs under his rule to grudgingly give up more and more of their own wealth before his superiority. It was almost as though this young man that now ruled them was touched by the hand of a god, as though perhaps he was a god.

"He is more a Pharaoh than a nomarch," one of his servants said to another, while watching him cast judgement between two nomarchs kneeling before his throne. The other servant nodded and the title stuck. And still, the other nomarchs grudgingly continued to kneel before his superior leadership.

The other vampires, jealous and contentious at the best of times, thought often of Montuotep and Iminuetep's success, discussing the new vampire's audacity openly when he wasn't around. And yet in front of Iminuetep they were all smiles and congratulations, careful to hide their true intentions to the otherwise oblivious youngster.

He put on his power like a well fitting glove as the Anubis dove into the Delta before him, extending his power out into the Mediterranean and along its coasts. Some of the older werewolves had lived such a tormented existence that they almost smiled when death finally claimed them as they struggled with the magnificent leviathans within the Mediterranean. Iminuetep did not refuse them their play.

Yet, all the other vampires seemed lazy, anxious to linger in the dying desert. Their caravans forged through the rugged hills and endless deserts of nothingness along familiar old-trade routes. Death tolls were still lingering in an ongoing drama within the desert. Other vampires gorged themselves on slave meat, weakening the strength of their own mortal numbers in the name of amusement.

The Anubis played with Iminuetep as puppies and served him blindly, with unquestioning, unwavering loyalty as adults. Iminuetep admitted he rather enjoyed 'the blood of dogs' when offered freely. As Hamenemmon savoured the sensations of a loyal slave, so Iminuetep cherished the blood of his own people, more intelligent than regular humans, and far more passionate. Yet the blood he drank also contained Anubis, and Iminuetep had to admit he lacked nothing from his diet, sampling the best a vampire could possibly have to drink. And supplemented from a diet of crocodile meat, the blood was unlike any another other vampire had ever experienced before. It did not take Iminuetep long before he distanced himself from the other vampires and their tiring life of religious traditions and ceremony. He had things to do, and his empire grew because of his initiative. Every day his temple and Montuotep's tomb grew in magnitude and splendour.

Breeding cells for Anubis had been set up and placed along the halls of his temple. Temple prostitutes came forward diligently to dispose of their wrathful young ones, born of fathers that morphed under the lustful touch of their mothers before the prostitutes fled from the chambers to seal the Anubis in safety against his own uncontrollable passions.

The breeding program had managed to stretch the Anubis' maw. His fangs were increasing in diameter. Those puppies not born with the improved traits were used to supplement the Anubis' diet of crocodile meat.

Every day Montuotep would bring him another statue. Every day another hallway was cleared from the rock walls of the mountains. The sand taken from the mountain was turned to bricks and disposed into pyramids, a place where Iminuetep kept up Montuotep's network of information and control.

He had emerged. They both had, and the spawning children of the damned grew to be the fiercest race of demigods on the face of the planet. Iminuetep once looked around at the exquisite furnishings surrounding him, admitting he was still surprised he had been so naive in life. He continually increased the demands for more blood. As ornaments, artisans from the city of Deil el Medina hung on his walls, artisans just like he had been. He even fancied that he recognized one of them as he watched the man die from malnutrition and the lack of initiative to free himself.

47

* * * * *

Between them was a huge holding tank that held a young werewolf, no older than perhaps five or six years old, yet fully manifested in the form of the Anubis. The child wolf was outraged as it growled and barked at its opponent, a crocodile of equal size. The crocodile showed a very human intelligence, planted there by the young immortal mind of the now scholarly practitioner of the dark arts. Other vampires knelt before Iminuetep out of respect for his achievements and he often drank their blood from ceremonial chalices. He could feast on whatever he wanted, and not another priest of Osiris seemed upset about it. Very few of the others questioned his control, yet he respected Hamenemmon's position as the High Priest of Osiris and kept his ambitions hidden from them all. He sipped from one such chalice now, wondering why blood from his secret army was so much more fulfilling than the blood of a secret enemy.

Another priest, a vampire named Selim, languished in the recliner next to him, bored as he watched the infant child and the crocodile thrash against each other. The Anubis had the crocodile by the neck in a powerful bear hug that lifted the reptile clean off of its hind legs. The werewolf roared as it squeezed the crocodile, showing the vampires its deadly little fangs. The crocodile, sensing itself in a death grip, thrashed its tail wildly and the two went sprawling to the bottom of the tank once again.

The other priest looked at Iminuetep, bored with the fight. "Wager?" he asked. "Just to liven it up a little?"

"What did you have in mind?" Iminuetep asked shrewdly as he sipped his rival's blood.

"A thousand slaves to the winner," Selim said mischievously.

"What am I going to do with another thousand slaves?" Iminuetep responded.

"What do you suggest, then?" the vampire asked, sensing that perhaps Iminuetep could not afford the wager.

"How many Anubises do you have at your temple?" Iminuetep asked.

"Three," the other answered honestly. "And one more I keep in the embalming chamber."

Iminuetep nodded, remembering the terrible conditions of his initiation. He ran his fingers over his pelt as he thought back to the poor beast he had killed to win his own immortality. "How many are you willing to part with?" Iminuetep asked casually.

The other shrugged. "I see no good use for the Anubis anyway," he said. "Why would you want them?"

Now it was Iminuetep's turn to shrug. "Why not?"

"The beasts are stupid and unruly. They are totally uncontrollable, good for nothing more than to feed the myths of the human religion and," he waved at Iminuetep's pelt, "for amusement and clothing."

"Then, perhaps you'll let me take all four of them," Iminuetep said as he leaned forward in his seat, ignoring the battle that raged in front of them. "For one hundred slaves."

The other vampire straightened in his seat as he looked at Iminuetep carefully, trying to sense his thoughts. Iminuetep kept his motives carefully hidden and smiled politely despite his rejecting the other from his mind. His guest returned the smile coldly. "I'll let you have the three," he said. "But I'm keeping the dog in the place of embalming. Every temple should have at least one Anubis, just for show."

"Of course," Iminuetep said. Convinced that the Anubis' strength was one of the most underestimated sources of power within Egypt, he wanted the Anubis entirely for himself and would not feel secure until then. He kept his thoughts well guarded, however, as he averted his eyes back to the fight. The little one was underneath the crocodile, fighting for his own life now as the crocodile sought to sink its teeth into Anubis' flesh. Yet, the Anubis had the crocodile's maw in both his hands, holding the reptile from snapping its mouth shut, and although the crocodile shook its head, thrashing its entire body back and forth, still the child held on, growling with the effort to dislodge the crocodile from his body.

"The other three wolves for a hundred slaves," his guest said, watching the Anubis and the crocodile kill each other.

Iminuetep looked at the vampire through the corner of his eyes. "Which do you expect to win, then?" Iminuetep asked.

"Why, the crocodile, of course," the vampire said quickly.

Iminuetep hid his smile behind the chalice he drank from and nodded slowly, feinting disappointment instead. "As you wish," he said. "It matters not to me. If the Anubis wins, I win."

Selim looked at him sincerely. "I pity you then, Iminuetep, for you have just lost a hundred slaves."

"Enjoy the fight, brother." Iminuetep kept his eyes on the little Anubis in front of them.

"I will," the other priest said as he leaned back in his seat.

The Anubis was still fighting a losing battle, unable to dislodge the weight of the crocodile from atop him. Yet the little creature still held onto the crocodile's mouth with both hands and was now scrambling desperately with its feet, trying to push the reptile away from him.

He gained purchase and rolled the crocodile off of him and then rolled on top of it, still holding onto the reptile's mouth. He continued to roll across the crocodile's body and gained his feet in one fluid motion. Still holding onto the now confused crocodile, he tore it from its back and whipped it off of the ground and around his body. In midair, he changed directions, tossing the crocodile as if it was a rag doll. There was a loud crack as Anubis broke the creature's neck and then slammed the crocodile against the side of the holding cell for good measure. He tossed the crocodile onto the floor in front of it and growled viciously as he waited for the creature to move again. He barked at it a few times and then sat down hard. He cocked his head to one side as he watched the creature's still form and then looked up at Iminuetep and whined, holding his arms out to his master, his "uncle."

Iminuetep smiled despite himself and reached into the tank.

"It seems you are now three Anubises richer," the Selim said. "For all the good it'll do you."

Iminuetep was still smiling as he tore the still heart from the crocodile and handed it to the Anubis as a reward for killing the beast. In a very human voice, the beast giggled and clapped its hands. Then it took the reptile's heart from Iminuetep and allowed itself to be scooped up into his uncle's arms. To the horror and surprise of the other priest of Osiris, Iminuetep kept the beast on his lap while the little wolf devoured the raw heart.

"I will see the creatures are delivered during the day," he said, rising nervously to his feet as he continued to stare at Iminuetep and Anubis. "But I must return now if I am to make it before sunrise."

"Much appreciated, brother," Iminuetep said with a slight nod of his head.

Then the other vampire returned the nod and vanished, leaving Iminuetep and Anubis alone with the dead body of the crocodile. He waited a moment, sensing the other priest's presence still within his walls. Once he was sure the vampire was gone and out of earshot, he placed the little Anubis on the floor and rose to his feet.

In an adjoining chamber, a full grown Anubis stood docile, watching Iminuetep with loyal eyes. Iminuetep strode toward it fearlessly while the little Anubis followed in his footsteps. He stroked the creature between the eyes, then withdrew his hand in a flash when the creature saw the pup. The Anubis barked and lunged at the puppy, who danced back with a whine of submission and rolled onto his back to expose his neck to the larger Anubis. The Anubis sat down in front of the puppy and clamped down on the creature's neck, not too hard to bite through his skin and hurt the little one, but enough to immobilize the creature. The puppy remained completely motionless until the Anubis rose to his feet once again.

Iminuetep stroked the creature's mane as he looked deep into his eyes. "I have a job for you," he said.

Always eager to please his master, the Anubis remained passive under his touch.

"But you will need your mind to do it," he said. "Your brilliant, killer's mind." He smiled as he thought about his departed guest's last Anubis, the one he refused to part with. If Iminuetep could not have it, then no one would.

As the sun began to rise, one soldier departed from the Temple of Osiris with a unit of men for support. Though he looked no different than the others with him, his concentration was unwavering as he jogged through Thebes. Only one thought was running through his mind. *Kill the Anubis and return before sunset.*

* * * * *

In the distance, a train of armed soldiers hustled through the crowds as the sun was setting over their heads. They looked neither right nor left as they pushed through the throng, ignoring the people who dove out of their way. Those unfortunate enough to not move fast enough were trampled underfoot. At the forefront one lone man pushed forward, inspiring, challenging the others with his untiring gait and his unwavering determination.

He mounted the steps to the temple of Osiris three at a time while his men collapsed into the sand behind him. Their mission was finished and he dismissed them with a wave of his hand, yet he looked only toward the main doors of the ancient temple. He came before two guards, who acknowledged his determination but attempted to bar the way, with spears none the less. "I must see the priest of Osiris," he said in a rasping, parched throat. "Let me pass."

In the distance, the sun was fading through the heat waves.

"The priest of Osiris is not to be disturbed," one of the guards said, eyeing the soldier hatefully.

The Anubis growled deep in the soldier's throat. His eyes glittered with the hatred of the guardian of the underworld. "Let me pass!" the soldier shouted in a deep guttural voice that was changing even as he spoke. He grabbed the guard who had spoken by the arm and tossed him down the steps. Weapons and armour clashed against stone as the guard rolled toward the sands of Egypt. "I am out of time!" he shouted as he turned to the remaining guard, this one now standing fully between him and the entrance to the temple.

The sun was still setting, and the soldier was now fighting the transformation, desperate to have his message relayed before the mind of the beast made it impossible.

Another guard from within heard the noise and came at a run. He took one look at the soldier and then another at the guard that lay motionless on the steps behind him. "Brother!" he cried as he pushed the mortal out of their way and embraced the werewolf by the forearm.

"I must speak with the master!" the soldier declared, barely audible. Yet the desperation in his voice could still be heard.

"You are out of time," the other said in a very similar voice. He glanced at the sun, now disappearing before him against the horizon of the desert. "No worries, though," he growled. In a moment he had a flask and a knife in his hand. Without hesitating and without the other flinching, he drew the knife across the soldier's forearm, a deep cut that had the blood spilling over the mouth of the flask.

The soldier who had been cut gave himself over to the pain and Anubis began ripping through his skin with a howl of outrage. Still, his brother held him firm in a powerful grasp that only the Anubis possessed. "Take this," he said to the remaining guard.

The guard, too terrified, stared at them both with eyes swollen in terror.

"Take it!" the other guard roared as Anubis began to rip through his skin as well. "Take it before we kill you!" he shouted, pushing the startled guard away from them with the flask held before him. "See that Iminuetep receives it as soon as he wakes."

The guard, terrified, fled with the blood into the recesses of the temple of Osiris while the Anubis, brothers since birth, released their fury and attacked each other.

Their snarls and roars echoed throughout the temple as Iminuetep rose from his sarcophagus. The guard was running toward him and he looked at the man dispassionately, halting his terrified flight with his icy undead eyes.

"Soldiers have arrived," Iminuetep said to no one in particular.

The guard swallowed his fear and held the blood out to Iminuetep in a fist that shook with terror.

Iminuetep took the flask and tasted it, savouring it. Then he pulled the flask away from him and smiled. The human guard fainted, collapsed at his feet. And Iminuetep, taking another drink, stepped over the unconscious slave as he took another pull from the flask of blood.

Anubis waited at his door, and though he was well accustomed to the werewolves' bad manners, the noise they were making would carry throughout the city of Thebes. He could not have rumours of Anubis walking free filtering back to the other vampires of Osiris. Their deadly play would have to be taken indoors and sealed behind the walls of stone that Iminuetep and the Anubis called their home.

The wolves fought viciously in half human form under the rising moon, yet when Iminuetep stepped from the shadows of the temple, they stopped and as one, turned and looked at him.

"Come," he said, motioning them toward him with his hand. "Come to me!" he said passionately.

The wolves crouched and then pounced, and Iminuetep vanished as he fled back into the temple. The wolves, given over to the chase, rushed through the entrance of the temple, following the scent he left behind for them. The doors were sealed quickly behind and the secret of their existence was kept safe from the outside world.

Chapter Nine

It was time to expand. Egypt was starting to form a bad taste in his mouth. Though Iminuetep appreciated the darker ambitions that drove the priests of Osiris to such a lifestyle, he nonetheless knew the quality of restraint, learning well from the army of the Anubis that served him.

Eternity stretched out in front of him while mankind was spreading like a plague in other parts of the world. Egyptian blood, though infested with the race of immortals, began to spread out as great minds desperately clung together and sought refuge from the ignorant ways of the Egyptian religion. China, Tibet, India, Peru, and hundreds others: a vast network of language was spreading out away from the birthing place of mankind. Iminuetep walked through it all, admiring their expansion as Egypt's comparative power dwindled.

Deep down within the waters of the Mediterranean, embedded partially under a layer of silt, the Anubises of the wild had found themselves a treat. This soul never died. It feasted rarely, perhaps once a month, and day after day those of the Anubis who managed to survive the shadowy depths of the Mediterranean waters brought with them memories of her experiences through the blood they gave him. They were drawn to her with a magnitude of splendour, sensing the powers of the vampire as something familiar, something to feed on. Yet she, in isolation, drew on the strengths of the waters around her. The Mediterranean was never ending to her.

Iminuetep kept himself busy with ruling the increasingly frustrating

Egyptian nation, yet Aphrodite called from the icy waters of her grave, and it did not take an undead priest of Osiris to know Egypt was about to change.

Crocodiles. She drank crocodiles, or so said the wonderful memories tracing back to him through faithful Anubis.

There had never been a female vampire that the priests of Osiris knew about. Aphrodite was the first. He thought often of her, and even went as far as to begin sending Anubis out to her deliberately, that they may correspond with each other through the Anubis' blood. He would one day resurrect her from the Mediterranean, and bring her back to Egypt, that they may perhaps rule openly before mankind as immortal gods for the world to revere.

Then, one day, Iminuetep was sleeping in his sarcophagus when the wails of the Anubis did not wake him. Someone had slaughtered his pets and he awakened slowly because of it. He would have a memory to bring back to her.

Then, the rough hands of a renegade Anubis dragged his still groggy corpse from his coffin and tossed him against the wall. They were there, holding him fast, before he could even crash to the floor. He exhaled as he woke up to stare at the snarling maw of one of the finer beasts with the extended snout. Another vampire must have stolen Anubis from him as a puppy and kept him feasting in secret. Iminuetep wondered how many vampires this beast had consumed before Iminuetep.

Iminuetep was taken by surprise, not knowing if he had awakened fully or not. Lights flared and strange noises came from all around him. For once Iminuetep found he was completely disoriented. But then he remembered where he was and he ripped the beating heart from the Anubis' protruding rib cage. For all of the incredible monster's strength, he wondered why none of them were intelligent enough to remember how easy it was to take each other's heart. He wished one of them could be raised to realize its dominance over its brothers, but though the beasts were uncommonly matched in fury and strength, and though battle could last indefinitely if the creatures were left to sleep where they fell during the day, Iminuetep could not recall the last time a battle had not ended when one of them had accidentally taken a heart from the other. He sucked the juices from the dying corpse as the Anubis fell lifeless to the floor.

The torches flared to life by his silent command and his three highest advisors stood in front of him nervously. The other vampires, caught in their conspiracy against him, looked about the room, wondering if they should flee or fight.

Chained artisans from Dier el Medina hung about them as ornaments.

"What are you doing?" he asked. The vampires glanced around at the vast chamber nervously.

Suddenly, Anubis roared his need for vengeance from a thousand rock caverns and the ground beneath their feet shook with the strength of the demigod's anger. The others heard the personal guard of Osiris rushing toward them in undying allegiance. These soldiers, Anubis one and all, wore chain mail and carried weapons. No vampire could compete with that, yet only Iminuetep stood secure as death rushed upon them. He stood calm and stoic as he watched his most faithful of Anubis devour the traitors completely.

To hell with Egypt.

Darkness fell over much of Egypt that night, and many vampires hid away from Anubis' fierce wrath. Alerted to the conspiracy, Anubis all across the known world turned his vicious head and roared his protest in unending loyal rage. Many more vampires fell that day as Iminuetep unleashed the fearless Anubis upon the streets of Montuotep's dynasty.

The temple gates were sealed, and everything was cast into oblivion when Iminuetep commanded the winds to cover his temple with sand. He had things to do, and the rest of Egypt could not know of his disappearance. Caravans had been arriving daily and were now equipped with kennels. And carriages carrying sarcophaguses were accompanied by sadistic human slavers hungry to see mankind scream.

As he prepared to depart down the Nile by ship, he commanded Montuotep to his tomb, a journey of two days into the desert. Montuotep would receive the message in the morning, just before dawn.

Feinting panic and fear, Iminuetep sent out a silent message, a cry for help to Hamenemmon, the High Priest of Osiris who had made Iminuetep into the vampire he was. "Hamenemmon!" he cried desperately. "The Anubis are out of control! My life is forfeit, yet Egypt is in great danger. We are in great danger!"

Hamenemmon arrived a few hours later.

Still acting, the apparently panic stricken Iminuetep was pacing back and forth in the darkness, distraught beyond control. "What is happening?" he cried when he saw the high priest glide into the chamber. "The Anubis is out there!" he shouted. "And he is devouring us!"

Hamenemmon looked out into the sands and saw legions of Anubis storming through the desert, hunting, prowling, and fighting each other in an ocean of uncontrollable chaos. Yet, remembering his place, he kept his calm and looked at the distraught Iminuetep. "How did I get past them?" he asked quietly, not expecting an answer.

"No!" Iminuetep shouted, startling Hamenemmon. "The question you should ask is, how am I still alive!" Iminuetep pounded on his chest furiously, continuing to storm back and forth in front of the High Priest.

"I don't understand," Hamenemmon said. "Why would you not be still alive?"

All at once Iminuetep dropped his act and became calm, controlled. He looked at the other vampire for a moment and smiled, his fangs glittering in the darkness. Waves of howls stretched across the desert outside them as countless werewolves continued to rage. "It seems the prophecies are right," Iminuetep said. "Anubis will consume his father." Then he glided past the high priest and into the desert to stand before his army.

Hamenemmon, shocked at what he was witnessing, stared at the other vampire as though he had lost his mind. And stunned, he followed Iminuetep out of the crypt to share in their expected fate. Yet the Anubis did not attack and devour the priests as he was expected to. As one, the army of werewolves turned to face Iminuetep and calmed their ranting. They watched him, passive and docile, as he watched them. They stood like this for a time, vampire and werewolf, regarding each other silently, curiously. Then Iminuetep raised a fist into the air and the Anubis roared his approval, every one of them.

Hamenemmon paled as he realized the extent of power that Iminuetep had over the demigod.

Iminuetep turned on the other vampire, and with the strength of the Anubis given to him through the blood of his loyal servants, he grabbed the High Priest and tossed him back into the crypt. The Anubis continued to roar, but the werewolves remained where they were, trusting instinctively that Iminuetep would exact revenge for them all.

"How did you do this?" Hamenemmon asked as he rose to his feet before the now confident and powerful Iminuetep.

"Beasts can be trained," Iminuetep declared as he threw the high priest across the entrance chamber. Hamenemmon crashed against the stone wall, yet rose to shaky feet to face the outraged Iminuetep once again. "But they can also be tamed," Iminuetep spat.

Hamenemmon glanced over Iminuetep's shoulder fearfully, and Iminuetep turned to see three werewolves entering the chamber. Iminuetep smiled at them warmly. "You will feed soon enough," he said to them. "But this one you must not touch. This one is not your father. Osiris is your father. And Egypt is the body Osiris wears in this world. Montuotep is coming in strength." He looked from Anubis to Hamenemmon. "Feed on his armies, on his caravans. But do not touch the pharaoh. He is not worthy of you."

Hamenemmon, horrified at what he was witnessing, looked from Anubis to Iminuetep and then back at Anubis as the werewolves retreated from the crypt to leave them alone. "How can they understand you?" he asked.

"They can't," Iminuetep admitted. "They can only sense the emotion behind my words. And that is enough."

Then, faster than Hamenemmon could see, Iminuetep disappeared and reappeared with his hands around the vampire's neck. He forced the high priest to his knees as Hamenemmon clutched at Iminuetep's wrists. "Remember this?" Iminuetep asked as he leaned over the other vampire. With strength that made Hamenemmon look mortal, Iminuetep held the High Priest in his grip while the struggling vampire fought in vain to free himself.

When Hamenemmon finally weakened and stopped resisting Iminuetep, he looked at the other priest through the corner of his eye and asked, "How do you have this strength?"

"My blood is different than yours," Iminuetep admitted. "The Anubis gives more than what you take. You feed on mortal slaves that eat the meat of cows. I feed on immortal servants that devour the leviathan from the waters of the Nile."

"Selim," Hamenemmon said weakly.

Iminuetep nodded. "He told you, did he?"

Sensing his fate was sealed, Hamenemmon looked up at Iminuetep hatefully. "I should have had the Anubis kill you sooner."

"You should have," Iminuetep admitted. "But you didn't." Then he bit into the high priest's neck and drained the vampire.

When he was done, he tossed the dried, undead corpse into the sand at his feet.

Hamenemmon was shrivelled and in pain. He looked up at Iminuetep, too weak to do anything but draw breathe.

"Don't worry," Iminuetep said as he leaned over the high priest of Osiris. "Montuotep will be here shortly. You can feed on him."

Chapter Ten

Legions of Anubis were gathering in the sands outside, growing angry yet strong as they devoured the caravans that reached the temple's front doors.

Montuotep was not happy as he neared the tomb, seeing the destruction of his wealth spread out like a red carpet along routes he thought he controlled. The Anubis were feasting well, and did not try to hide it. Yet his own caravan had no immortal armies of its own to defend itself, nothing that could compete with this. It was going to take two days to reach his tomb. He would have two days to contemplate what was happening around him as he watched his fate stretch across the horizon in an unbroken line of destruction.

When he reached the doors of his own crypt, it was in broad daylight, and two guards stood off to each side. They stared into the space before them, refusing to acknowledge their pharaoh.

"Your pharaoh stands before you!" Montuotep shouted angrily.

They continued to ignore him.

"Show the respect that is due!"

Neither guard moved. Both continued to stare vacantly into the space in front of them. Then, one of them glanced over at him as if regarding a flea, and pushed open the crypt doors. Darkness stretched its empty mouth in front of him, and Montuotep grew afraid as he stared into the black abyss before him.

"The master waits within," the other guard said.

Montuotep and Montuotep alone walked forward while what was left of his caravan stood nervously in the sands in front of his crypt. He carried nothing but a torch into the infinite blackness. The vast stone doors slammed shut behind him.

Eventually, Iminuetep came to him. He had urinated within his fine silk robes and his torch had long ago gone out.

"What have you done?" Montuotep whispered as he felt the blood begin to flow out of him from a thousand pores in his body.

"Only what is rightfully mine to do." Another torch flared to life in a sconce on the wall, and Montuotep jumped with fright at the unexpected disturbance.

"How did you do that?" he asked, wide eyed with terror.

"Memphis," Iminuetep said.

"The city of magicians?"

"A very interesting place." The vampire smiled and motioned for Montuotep to follow him deeper into the crypt. "I have something to show you," he said proudly.

Montuotep had no choice but to follow.

Hamenemmon was still alive, now maddened with the thirst. When he saw Montuotep, he groaned in longing and struggled on his stomach to inch his way toward the pharaoh and the life blood pulsing through his veins. Calmly, Iminuetep walked over to the High Priest and stepped on the vampire's hand. He looked over to Montuotep to ensure the Pharaoh was watching, and then bent down and retrieved the ring from the shriveled vampire. The ruby shone under the torchlight as Iminuetep slid it onto his own hand and then strode away from the vampire.

Montuotep was horrified and dropped the torch. Instantly, all light was extinguished and Iminuetep's voice was close to Montuotep's ear. "Enjoy your final resting place, master," he said mockingly. Then he was gone, leaving Montuotep and Hamenemmon together in eternal darkness.

* * * * *

The following night, he walked from the vaults of Montuotep's tomb. He was weak and exhausted from the need to feed, but he had won, and the first Anubis came forward with a human sacrifice, a temple prostitute. He ripped the heart from her and sucked her dry. Pleased by the Anubis' choice, he spared the dog his life and moved on to the next in line. The Anubis stretched to the horizon. All of them had brought with them a gift to give to their master, and he savoured the delicacies set aside for him as his own caravan set out from the temple.

Many of Montuotep's slaves and members of his entourage had not been touched. Iminuetep raised his hands to the sky and summoned a storm to wash over Montuotep's crypt. As the sands of the desert began to rise up in the ever increasing winds, Iminuetep had to smile. The humans from Montuotep's entourage cursed and cried out in mercy as the sandstorm washed over them. The desert sand ripped apart what remained of Montuotep's slaves with such a force that nothing remained of them the following morning but wind bleached bones.

Still, the Anubis and Iminuetep strode toward the Nile. Anubis would sleep in the deserts or in the Nile, amongst the raging sand and devouring crocodiles while trusted human slaves watched over the puppies Iminuetep would play with when he arose the following night.

Another nomarch would emerge to become the next pharaoh, or perhaps one of Montuotep's sons would succeed him to the throne. It mattered not to Iminuetep, and he left the great dynasty behind him as he set his mind on the sleeping vampire within the depths of the Mediterranean Sea.

He travelled down the Nile with a selected few trusted puppies stored up in holding pens and chained to his barges during the day. But though Anubis had spread out across the face of Egypt, the finest of the young ones were too difficult to control, and eventually Iminuetep feasted on them, leaving them behind when he realized that the passions of the Anubis were too unruly aboard the confines of a ship. Yet the loyal hounds continued to swim untiring in the waters beside his fleet of barges.

Once they reached the Mediterranean, the tired hosts of the Anubis began to sink into the open waters during the day, where Aphrodite found them, deep within the confines of her watery cage. She drained their lives, and he felt her surface a little bit more with her newfound strength every time Iminuetep opened the lid of his sarcophagus. He was leaving his legion of dogs behind him and his control over her grew with each Anubis that fell to its death. Iminuetep's faithful howled in fury when they realized they could not follow him anymore and he commanded them back to the borders of their land.

The beasts would devour themselves, in time. They would become isolated and confused. Their human hosts would run from mankind in fear, living in weakness and unending squalor amongst the other outcasts of society.

Thankfully though, she was rising, and Iminuetep knew by that hunch, and that hunch alone, which direction to set sail when the black sails of his cargo ship left the view of Egypt behind.

Book Two
Tears for Anderita

Chapter One

The rain was all but invisible in the darkness. It fell heavily upon the sleeping streets, blanketing everything with added layers of darkness and silence underneath its crashing onslaught. It came down in waves, bouncing to knee height off of the cobbled streets. The buildings, in retaliation, seemed to withdraw into themselves, cowering quietly with shudders closed and lights shaded. Children hid under blankets or clung to their parents in sleepless dread. Adults muttered empty assurances to their children, going so far as to lie about the terrors that roared around them and shook the city. Lovers laughed quietly between themselves to dispel their fears, hiding together under their blankets and telling each other how silly they were. The storm was a carrier of death, of horrors, and all the comforts that silence and darkness could bring were dispelled. The storm was master over this night, regardless of what anybody thought.

Outside, one sole woman was struggling through the cold numbing rain with her child. Torn and bleeding, she struggled to put the ocean and the nightmare haunting them behind her. Her once attractive body was now thin from malnutrition and there was a haunted, wild look in her eyes that would drive prospectors away, friends and strangers alike. No one found it comfortable to look into those pools of madness for long. Yet he who now sought her had been the one to cause that madness.

She had been pretty once, though the cruel streets had been unkind and had taken her beauty away, exchanging it for grime and bruises, her finery for torn and dirty rags. Her feet were covered only with loosely bound strips of cloth. Yet her dress, though ripped and ragged, still bore some resemblance to the noble formal wear it once was. The hair pins that once carried her carefully kept hair in royal finery now fell loose as she fled through the empty streets of Eastern Britain. Yet, unhealthy and limp, she had long ago stopped caring what her hair must look like, though she kept the pins and made herself believe she was beautiful still.

The baby in her arms was silent and burned with a fever from the unkind exposure to the rain. She worried over her infant child, the worry gnawing through her as she strained every fibre of her very soul to run yet one more step, to escape the nightmare that was chasing them through the night.

The city hid them well; she knew these darkened streets and hidden alleys. But he who stalked her lived in the night as if all that existed to him was night. The weather was nothing to him. The rain was nothing. The city would betray her this night, and she knew it. No door would open for her, no knock would be answered. She did not waste her time in trying.

A harsh, haunting breathing like the panting of a hunting dog echoed through her ears and the ears of the infant, captivating him with its hypnotic perseverance. It terrified her with the promise of pursuit.

In the distance, far off and unreachable in the night, she heard a horse whiney. Her stomach lurched into her throat with hope. Perhaps, just perhaps, someone was out in this storm who could offer her refuge from her terror. Then she heard the clopping of its hooves and the wheels of its carriage wading through the rain. Her heart soared, though she dared not stop. Perhaps salvation would find her and her little one this night; perhaps she would see another sunrise. But then a snarl tore off the crowded buildings as an echo through the storm. The horse screamed and she cried out in fear as she slipped and lost her footing on the wet stones under her feet.

Aching and weeping with the futility of her flight, she staggered to her feet once again. Her knees were bleeding, but when she looked down at her child, he looked out at the world with very calm, very alert intelligent eyes of a child. They shifted back and forth as if listening to the storm.

She forced herself to remain perfectly still as she strained her ears into the storm. The persistence of her worst nightmare had found them once again.

She stifled another cry with her bleeding hand. The beast was pursuing again.

She moaned in despair and fled onwards, now sobbing helplessly at the sine she had committed. The devil chased her, looking only for what she knew was rightfully his.

She gave up as she realized she had brought this fate onto herself. A calm revelation descended over her with a clarity she had not grasped since the opium pipe had found her. She would die this night.

But the baby—what of the child? Let not the sins of the parents claim the life of the child as well, she silently screamed. She threw herself heedlessly down another dark alley.

The breathing of the beast pursued her as the nightmare was birthed from her mind and her senses betrayed her to insanity. She laughed. If Judas had betrayed Jesus with a kiss, then truly her mind had betrayed her with a kiss as well, a kiss and many nights that followed that simple kiss. As surely as the Christ had been crucified, she was insane. But what hunted her was as real as the infant in her arms.

She ran through exhaustion as every fibre in her cried to stop. There was a great emptiness in her chest, as though she had already died by the beast, yet the infant she clung to was very much alive, and her love for him still burned fiercely in her mother's heart. She ran on for him, dodging down a narrow and darkened alley, mechanically hoping her change in direction would confuse the beast. She knew nothing she could do would free them of him, but she went through the motions anyway and was surprised when she left the alley behind for a large, open space. The darkness was not so thick here, where the buildings did not crowd out the sky.

A flash of lightning ripped across the sky in a jagged three pronged fork lacing through the night. The tall imposing silhouette of a church bell tower loomed over her, partially eclipsing the lightning. She looked haggard and pale and very, very afraid. Her eyes dilated with the lightning strike, illuminating an open courtyard, the city square. The thunder rolled around her and her child. The baby finally started to cry.

She never had much to do with churches. Before she fell from her place in society, she had attended mass dutifully, as part of her responsibilities as a lady. But when she was no longer obliged, she had abandoned the mundane routine, considering it a blessing to be done with it—at the time.

She thought differently now.

Far away, on a rooftop behind her, the sniffing stopped and the beast watched the church just as she did. He crouched like a sprinter before a race. All instinct and sinewy animal strength, he poised motionless for that split moment as the lightning illuminated the night, as though he was afraid of the exposure like a paralysed rabbit under the jaws of a rabid dog.

The lightning faded and thunder rolled. He was the dog once again. The rabbit, sensing somehow the beast had her scent, fled for the church knowing that this was the last of it.

There was no time for doubt, no time for regret or second guessing. The beast was pursuing her, and the life of her child was in her hands. She did not break stride, but rather gave her footsteps purpose. She set her hopes and doubts behind her and ran into the open courtyard with her baby clutched in her arms.

The breathing pursued her as though it was right on her bleeding heels.

Then she saw the candle. The light wavered at first, and she had to blink the water out of her eyes and force them to focus. But though the dim light jumped erratically with each step she took, it remained—the one constant in this night of shifting shadows. It drew her to itself, and she ran for it, keeping her path straight and no longer staggering with fear and exhaustion.

She heard a snarl from behind and above her. Then the beast plunged into the alley she was just in. It had been hunting her from the rooftops and now it had found her scent once again.

"Sanctuary!" she screamed as the rain pelt down upon her. "Sanctuary!"

She reached the steps of the church, broad, rock steps that led up into a stone platform in front of two wooden doors. The candle burned in a window beside them. "Sanctuary!" she screamed for a third time.

She looked over her shoulder.

The dark, muscular shoulders of a disproportionate man glistened under a coat of thick black fur. The large, dripping canine fangs gleamed in a silent smile. Beady, brown, strangely human, haunted eyes stared out at her from above the cruel snout of a dog. Its black nose sniffed the air, continuing in the unbroken rhythm of its panting.

"Sanctuary!" she screamed as she fell against the steps. She turned away from the aberration and crawled up the stairs, shouting, "Sanctuary!" over and over again.

The beast lifted its face to the night and howled hauntingly. Then it lunged into the town square. Dogs all over the city took up its lead and howled a ghostly, inhuman chorus into the stormy night sky.

The woman gained her feet at the top of the stairs and threw herself at the wooden doors. "Please!" she cried.

One of the doors opened inward and the face of a priest appeared in front of her, impassionate and unafraid.

She sobbed her relief as she thrust her baby into the good father's arms. "Take my child!" she cried victoriously as she thrust the bundle into the priest's hands.

Then the beast had her and tore her from her feet and the safety that was so close to being hers.

Her head cracked against the stone as she fell, and her vision swarmed with red dots as it blackened around the edges of her sight. "Sanctuary," she tried to say, though no sound escaped from her lips.

The beast calmly stepped to her side, looking down at her through the rain, relishing its kill. She looked up at it and smiled as consciousness began to fade. She had beaten him. She had won.

The beast fell on her and tore the life from her already dying body.

The priest, helpless and paralysed with the horror, stared out at the murder in shock, the baby with that unbroken curiosity in its eyes. Neither fully comprehended what they saw.

In a moment, the beast rose to its feet. Its maw was glistening black with blood. Its bloodlust had been sated this night, its hunger for death met.

"You will not enter here," the priest said at last, barely louder than a choked whisper.

The beast turned and regarded the priest apathetically.

"This is a house of God!" the priest said, his voice gaining strength.

The beast ignored the man and turned away.

The woman's blood mixed with the rainwater and flowed from the steps of the church in rivers that darkened the stone before the waters washed the streets clean once again.

The candle remained unwavering in the window throughout the night.

Chapter Two

Kerisa walked along the side of her mother's horse, smiling as she listened to her little brother prattling on from his mother's lap about an owl. His hands did most of the talking, describing the size of its eyes to the way it flapped its wings.

Her mother giggled as the story progressed, laughing outright in parts, where her son's antics grew outrageous. But as for Kerisa, she had other things on her mind. Her brother stopped his story in mid sentence and glared at her. "Are you listening, Kerisa?" he asked suspiciously.

"Hmmm?" she asked as she looked up at him again.

"Mama!" Darrel cried. "Kerisa was thinking about James again!"

"Oh hush," their mama chided gently. "Leave her be."

Kerisa laughed as she looked over her shoulder at her papa. He was walking alongside their wagon, smiling at the banter going on.

"Is that so bad, Papa?" she asked, still grinning.

"Terrible," her father said sarcastically.

"I told you so!" the child exclaimed victoriously.

This time, the laughter spread to her father and older brothers in the wagon as well; the two on the bench and the two lounging in the back.

"What's so funny?" the child asked, squirming in his mother's lap to look at his brothers.

"We'll tell you when you're older," one of them piped from the back of the wagon.

"That's what you always say!" the child cried indignantly.

"I don't think it's wrong for Kerisa to be thinking about her future husband," her mother defended her gently.

"But why?" Darrel pressed.

"Well," his mama began. "There's a lot Kerisa has to think about."

"I bet," one of her brothers teased.

Her father held up a hand in warning, and the teenager grew suddenly silent. His closest brother punched him in the leg for his disrespect.

"Have you seen your cabin yet, Kerisa?" her oldest brother asked from the driver's seat on the wagon. He had spent the better part of the summer building it with James and was eager to hear what she thought.

"You know I haven't," Kerisa said defensively.

"Not until you're married, dear," her mother said as she patted the top of her daughter's head. "I wasn't allowed to see our cabin until your father and I were married, so you can wait too."

Kerisa looked up at her mother. "Do you think I'll like it, mama?"

"I know you will. You'll see."

"You'll love it!" her older brother piped up again.

"I want to see it now!" Kerisa declared.

"Now you sound like Darrel," her oldest brother remarked. "You'll see James when we get to the fair. Content yourself with that."

Impatient, she tried to take his advice and found it remarkably easy to fill her mind with images of her gentle giant. She and James had been promised to be wed since the Yule Tide celebration. Traditionally, they could have been married today, at the fair. But Kerisa had wanted to stay with her family to see the harvest in, and James, respecting her wish, had spent the spring and summer clearing enough land to grow crops for their own young family. The cabin and field was supposedly somewhere near her parents' own cabin. But where was entirely a mystery to her. One or more of her family members would sneak off for entire days at a time while the other members of her family kept her busy so she would not know in which direction they went.

It frustrated her to no end, but she contented herself with the extra chores left behind and with the surprise visits from James.

She had been kept a prisoner, always with an escort to ensure she didn't escape and try to find her new home on her own. But such was her fate, and she endured it lightheartedly as the suspense grew day by day.

But James, his sister, and their parents would all be at the fair, and it would be good to have her whole family together in one place.

The afternoon wore on in hazy summer brilliance. The men and Kerisa's mother bantered happily with each other while Kerisa kept to herself and filled her mind with thoughts of her up-and-coming wedding.

Eventually, they crested a rise in the sloping hills and the village came into view. Nestled in the corner of two rivers that met before flowing into the ocean, their young village had long ago cleared the surrounding hillsides of forest. Now the golden stalks of grain rustled gently in the wind as the last lingering days of summer goaded them on to their fullness.

Harvest time would be soon, but for now, a quiet respite of a few days would give the farmers enough of a rest to gather the strength they would need to bring in their crops.

Kerisa could think of no better place to be than in the arms of her fiancée, and she knew he felt the same about her. As they neared the village, a chestnut roan galloped from the little cluster of buildings, kicking up dust as it went. Without a word, she ran ahead of her family, letting the breeze to her hair, her skirts whipping about her ankles as she ran.

James was a barrel of a man, with some of the thickest, strongest arms in the village and a broad set of shoulders with the chest of a blacksmith. Yet the gentle farmer was perpetually soft spoken and would not compete in the annual competitions to match skill or strength against any other man. He never did, and Kerisa knew there was not one man among the contenders who was not grateful for his gentle spirit.

He was laughing as he galloped toward her, the reins of his horse held loosely in his hand and his shaggy brown hair billowing out in every which way.

Hardly slowing, he bent low in his saddle and scooped Kerisa up off of her feet. She laughed as he lifted her up behind him, and with no words spoken, settled into the ride back to her family with her arms around his big barrelled chest and her head resting against his back. One of his hands was entwined through hers, clasping her hands tight to his beating heart. No words were needed. They were together again, and she could not have been happier.

Chapter Three

Deep inside the shadows of the sleeping church, a tiny, sleeping form lay curled upon a deep satin cushion. Space was limited in these troubled times. Fear kept the city populace cringing from the cowardice and arrogance of the Viking invaders. For a little one such as this, no one had time to spend. So the mother had perished, giving the wondrous creature to the church while the dangerous legend Fernir had haunted and stalked her to her death. By whose hand had this child been struck down? How could she have tantalized a deed dark enough to bring about this level of retribution? To whose evil had she catered to deserve the attentions of a creature such as this? The priest could not imagine as he stared over the sleeping form.

"Christopher," he said to the baby, though the infant remained asleep and undisturbed in honest trust. "Your name is Christopher." The wondrous baby had stayed calm and kind through the last few days, and the priest wondered at the manifest goodness in the creature. He shook his head in awe at the special baby and then quietly slunk away from the sleeping form, leaving the candles burning a petition on the angel's behalf.

In the evening of the following day the bishop arrived. His Grace was on a circuit of his diocese, visiting each parish on a tour of his jurisdiction, giving council to his charges, the priests and the holy houses of God they ran in his name. "I am glad you are here, your grace," the priest said eagerly once the common greetings had been exchanged. "I have something to show you that I think will be of a great interest."

"What is it?" the bishop asked eagerly. His trip had been so far a boring one, and any diversion would be of interest.

The priest looked around anxiously, making sure no one would be able to hear his next words. They were alone. "A few nights ago we were visited by a demon, the Viking god Fernir." The bishop's eyes widened with surprise, but the priest hushed the man before he could speak. "He was stalking a harlot, a prostitute of the city waterfronts." He was leading the bishop quickly through the monastery to the small rectory in the back of the church. "Before she died, she was able to deliver a child into my hands. The beast tore her body on our doorstep, but was unable to approach us once I faced him." The bishop was obviously proud of the priest's declaration, beaming with the superior greatness of the story.

The baby was awake, tucked away in a wooden basket that had been used to hold the firewood only a few days ago. But now the makeshift crib was lined with pillows and comfortable linen. The infant stared up at the two men as they came into his view, kicking his feet in amusement and then settling down to mimic the faces of interest that stared down at him.

"He never seems to become upset," the priest said after a moment. "Remarkable, as this child manifests no evil nature."

"All men are evil," the bishop stated. "It is our human nature to be evil."

The priest was silent as he kept his gaze down upon the baby. Finally, he looked up at the bishop.

Wordlessly, the bishop pulled a small travel knife from a scabbard at his belt. Carefully, he took the blade and nicked the baby's arm, drawing the smallest amount of blood.

Shocked, it took the baby a moment to gather the strength to scream, and then scream he did with an aggressive anger that took the bishop by surprise.

The priest was just as shocked, and horrified at what the bishop had done. He reached for the baby and took the squalling child in his arms. Horrified, he looked back at the bishop, who stared dispassionately at the child in his companion's arms. Finally, he nodded at the infant, and the priest looked down at the baby, who now screamed with all the strength he could muster. His eyes were squinted shut with the effort to voice his violent rage and his mouth had changed shape slightly. The baby's expression was so alien to the priest, that the man could not even recognize him as the passive child he'd found.

"I know what I seem to do looks cruel," the bishop said quickly. "But who is this child? And how much of the sins of the mother have been passed on? To have brought on such a cruel fate, surely the stains of the prostitute have been pushed onto the son that nursed at her filthy breast."

The priest was still considering the strength of the baby's anger, the inexhaustible fuel the little one seemed to keep locked somewhere deep inside his chest.

"Who is this child?" the bishop repeated over the baby's screams. "Perhaps even a spawn pup of Fernir himself, though God curses the pagans for believing such a thing."

The priest nodded. "You'll be taking the child with you, then?" he asked.

"In the morning," the bishop instructed. "I must make haste with this creature before whatever befalls its mother takes this place as well."

That night, the priest had left the baby in the crib to continue its outraged screaming throughout the night, unhindered. The full moon crested over the forested horizon and glinted off of the rhythmic waves of the ocean as they lapsed against the Northeast Coast of Britain. The baby was pointedly ignored, though the priest instinctively knew that with a little counselling and soothing, the child would be cooled of its outrages. By the early morning light, he crept back to the kitchen and offered the tiny child a cloth that had been dipped into a bucket of goat's milk. The child quieted immediately, given over to his hunger as he sucked the cloth dry and gummed at the Father's fingers through the fabric.

"Do not worry, little one," the priest mumbled his comforts. "We will travel this dangerous road together."

The child seemed oblivious, so taken was he with his hunger.

The full moon set early as the sun rose over the ocean and the parish church. The priest watched the rising sun quietly while the baby, finally calmed of his inner rage, slept soundly in the Father's gentle embrace.

He would travel with his superior, refusing to give up custody of the child until he could trust the bishop with his well being. Once he knew Christopher was asleep, he gently laid the baby in its crib and carried him back to his place near the hearth in the kitchen. Keeping his footsteps light, lest he awake the house and its sleeping occupants, Jason crept into his room and carefully opened the latch to a large, wooden trunk he kept at the side of his bed.

He knelt beside the bed, keeping his back to the door. Should anyone accidentally open the door to his room, they would find a lowly priest in humble, silent prayer. Yet his eyes were opened, and though his lips chanted the words of the rosary, his mind was far from prayer as he looked down at what lay in his hands. A ring, a hideously large red ruby the size of the child's fist was set in a wide band of gold covered with cryptic heliographs from Egypt's era of legend. The ruby served to keep as a reminder to protect the child despite whatever hideous forces moved within his veins. Even if the child was the spawn of some demon, Jason knew of forces that could free the soul from the demon locked within. Quickly, he placed the ring back in its pouch and slipped the drawstring over his neck, concealing the pouch and its priceless contents next to his skin. Then, ever so quietly, he began to gather their few things for the journey that would take them to Anderita.

By the time the bishop stirred from his night's sleep, Father Jason and the child were ready for the journey ahead of them. The child was bundled warmly within the brown pelt of a wolf.

Patiently, the priest bided his time as he and the bishop sat down together for a light breakfast of toast and silence. The child, having been fed, remained at the priest's side, quietly watching the bishop as he ate.

"You are not staying behind?" the bishop asked the priest.

"No," Jason said, ending all arguments. He looked up from his meal and stared into the bishop's eyes. "I am not."

The bishop swallowed a mouthful of food before looking away from Jason's steely gaze. "I will have another priest sent up from Anderita, then," he conceded.

Jason said nothing as he finished his breakfast and began cleaning up after the two of them.

* * * * *

The city of Pevensey was only a day's journey away. Nestled next to the ocean, it was a bustling port city that never seemed to sleep. Yet it was dwarfed by the enshrouding presence of forests that kept it locked tightly to its dependence of the ocean. Pevensey had once been a popular port city in Roman times, but the Romans were gone now, leaving only an empty shell of their great legacy in the form of a great Roman fort called Anderita. Over the years, it was Anderita's presence that had kept the city alive, a weak promise of safety against the constant Norman invasions. Pevensey was nothing without Anderita, and though abandoned by the Romans when they withdrew from Britain's shores, Anderita was what kept Pevensey flourishing once more, and the docks never slept.

Yet, shadowing all was the constant threat of Norman invasion. The Vikings plagued the troubled towns along the coast of Britain with continuous raiding and pillaging. Anderita, defenceless against the onslaught, had created a militia military that had so far managed to hold back the Normans, securing the trade routes and keeping them undisturbed against their constant invasions. But the time might come when the small army of Anderita would lose, though greatly outnumbering the single longboats that often ground to shore on her beaches.

Plagued by fear, Anderita's citizens clung to any respite they could find, from gambling to drinking to fighting. And on this early Sunday morning, weary merchants and their angry, tight lipped wives crowded into the pews of the local church next to hung over sailors and waterfront harlots who smiled and put on a good show of pious devotion.

Near the front of the church, Jason sat with Christopher in his arms. He was not needed for this mass. The local priest and the bishop would be the ones to carry out the homily. Jason was grateful. He did not want to stray far from the child and kept a close watch on the baby through his waking hours. There was something peculiar about him Jason had come to notice. And attuned to the child's needs as any devoted mother, he wondered how far from the truth the bishop had been about him. But he loved Christopher none the less, and would protect him from the ill-informed, over opinionated bishop and the other, curious priests and monks, despite their best interests. Jason knew a few things about the monster that had killed Christopher's mother, and he did not need to wonder very hard about the outcome of an unfair beginning to the child's life.

If the bishop was right about Christopher, Jason needed to protect the child from the church as much as he needed to protect the church from the child. "But, we'll see," Jason reminded himself.

Mass was starting, so he quieted his thoughts and prepared to receive the homily.

A procession entered from the side door at the front of the church and the bishop and the local priest regally walked to the back of the church in part of a convoy of altar boys and nuns carrying staffs with crucifixes and gold plated incense burners. Then, once at the back, they turned and proceeded down the centre isle, making sure everyone had a chance to see the superior authority of the great Mother Church. The bishop and the priest took their seats in two padded chairs that overlooked the crowded room while one of the altar boys stood behind a wooden pulpit with a golden crucifix emblazed into the front of it. He opened a rarely read book and mass began in earnest.

Jason kept his attention on the child in his arms, making sure the young one did not disturb the religious meeting. He stood when told to stand, and sat when told to sit. But his attention was far from what was happening. Yet, at one point he could not ignore the bishop's words, though he wished dearly that he could.

"In these troubled times," the bishop was saying, "with the threat of Viking hostility so close to our doors, would it not be good to know that the church had the means to protect her children when called upon to do so? It is God who has planted his church here on this earth, to see us through these dark and terrible times of fear. Yet how can she do that if her children neglect her?

"The time will come, I tell you, when you will call upon the church in an hour of need and she will not be able to help. For in *her* hour of need, where were you to invest in her earthly care? Not only are you neglecting your Heavenly inheritance by not giving, you are crippling the one place and the one place alone where you will find the protection, you so readily seek from you fears.

"Give!" the bishop said passionately. "Give as much as you can, and be released from your fears with the certainty of knowing you have a place to go when your hour of need arises." Offerings were being held out in front of the parishioners, little bags attached to long poles, held by the hands of attentive ushers who watched everyone with a disapproving scowl.

One of the plates was held before Jason despite the way he was dressed, which told everyone he was a priest of the Mother Church. He looked up at the usher distastefully and then down at the plate in front of him. He shook his head, still holding fast to sleeping Christopher, and was scowled at as the plate whisked away from him. Jason only shook his head sadly and continued to listen to the bishop.

"Without your help," the bishop was still ranting, "she cannot help you."

At that, Jason had enough and stopped listening altogether.

* * * * *

He left Christopher alone for one minute. The child was placed into a similar makeshift crib as the one Jason had used in his own parish, and then Jason stepped out to find a latrine. Before he returned to the child's side, he could hear him screaming through the walls.

Jason sighed and closed his eyes as he shook his head and offered up a silent prayer on the child's behalf. When he returned, he found the bishop and half a dozen priests and monks standing around the child, dispassionately watching him scream. The child's arm had been nicked again. A tiny trickle of blood was running down his clenched and shaking fist. He had an inhuman expression of demonic rage on his face.

Without hesitating, Jason reached for the screaming child and took him into his arms. Sensing the danger had passed, Christopher began to quiet.

"The child has the blood of a beast," the bishop told Jason. "It would be better to leave him to our care and not burden yourself with him."

Jason glared at the bishop angrily and pushed through the crowd of silent priests.

"You are only wasting your time on him," the bishop called after him. "And it'll only end badly for you in the long run."

"You know nothing about what you speak of," Jason called back, openly defying the bishop in front of the others. He ignored their gasps as he left the room and went to gather his and Christopher's things.

He left within the hour.

He was unsure where they would go when he left, but he refused to turn back. Yet, before the church was out of sight, two monks and a priest caught up to him on the road.

Jason let them approach without saying a word, eyeing the mountains around them and the clouds that threatened them with rain.

"We appreciate what you are doing," one of the monks said when they caught him.

He said nothing and lengthened his stride.

"We'd like to come with you," another monk said. After a moment of silence, he added, "Where are you going?"

"I'm not sure yet," Jason said without slowing down. "I need to hide the child."

"Then hide the child, we'll do together," the monk said happily.

Jason was silent, thinking carefully. This many priests and one child were sure to draw attention to themselves and they'd be easy to find should the bishop decide to send someone after them. He looked at the men around him, not trusting any of them. "You endanger the child's life by coming with us," he said.

The priest, quiet until now, shrugged his shoulders and stepped toward Jason. "Jason," he said. "We have nowhere else to go. The bishop has denied us the right to return. Besides, if we wanted to take the child, we could do so, here and now, and save the bother of betraying you later on."

"I doubt that," Jason threatened darkly. But he saw the other priest's point. Three against one were more than enough odds for most men. The bishop probably saw that no more men were needed.

"We're not going to try," the priest said again.

Jason nodded. "I appreciate that." He turned back to the road and headed away from the city once more.

"Where are we going?" one of the monks asked.

"We have to get off the road," he answered. "We'll be seen if we don't."

"In the forests!" the monk cried. "We'll perish for sure!"

"No we won't," Jason said with a smile. "I know the woods and how to survive inside them. We'll be fine, though it won't be easy."

"Life never is," the other monk said, resigning himself to his own fate.

Jason smiled again and led them off the road into the dark shadows of the uncharted forests.

* * * * *

Thinking to get as good a vantage point as he could, Jason took up the child one morning and announced he would return to camp by nightfall. The others, still too unsure of themselves to be left without Jason's expert guidance, jumped to their feet.

"Where are we going?" one of the monks, a man named Gregor asked. They'd been wandering through the woods for days, and Jason had thought it good taste to learn their names. Despite his earlier reservations, he was glad for the company, and the chore of learning about his companions was becoming easier as the days passed.

"I'm going to climb this mountain," he announced. "I want to see if I can see Anderita from there."

"Why?" Joshua asked. He was the other priest, and Jason had quickly realized the man never did anything unless he had a reason.

"Cold air gets trapped in lower ground. If we find a spring of water nearby, we'll be better off higher up," he answered. "We might move the camp up there. Besides, the farther away from Anderita, the better off we'll be."

Joshua nodded, satisfied with the answer. "Then let's go," he said enthusiastically, being the first out of the clearing.

Jason smiled and lifted his pack onto his back. The others followed suit and they caught up with Joshua quickly enough.

The mountain proved treacherous, yet they found what once must have been a road cut into the cliffs that appeared out of nowhere. Overgrown with disuse, the road was all but invisible, broken by trees as high as the men and grown over with underbrush. Though the going was slow, Jason much preferred the secure footing over climbing the loose shale around them. It took them all throughout the day to reach the top, but when they did, tired and sweating from their excursion, Jason laughed and flopped onto the ground in relief with the child held safely in his arms.

The others, caught in wonder at what they found, ran forward toward the ruins of a huge, abandoned Roman fort. The trees grew right up to its sides, ensuring that no one knew of its existence. Though it had been left neglected for years uncountable, the legendary Roman ingenuity had created an indestructible legacy that still remained mostly intact.

Jason, still laughing with relief, and blessing the Virgin Mother for the bounty her son had given them, rolled to his knees and held the child in front of his face, shaking Christopher gently and drawing a happy laugh from the baby. "Welcome home, little one!" he cried. Then he too jumped to his feet and ran into the building to explore their new home.

Chapter Four

Kerisa stared at the beautiful sky overhead. The sun was just setting and her many brothers, with her father and mother, played and danced together by the cottage back against the woods. She sat down by the beach, separated from them by a broad, sweeping meadow that faded into a long curve of sand that cupped the never ending expanse of the ocean before her. Nothing really separated her from her family, nothing at all. Though she was a goodly distance from them, they could see her easily enough and were in calling range. She did not feel shut off from the revelry. Rather, she felt exuberant knowing she was included, and allowed to express her own joy in life in her own way.

The ocean breeze rustled against her long, flowing hair, filling her nostrils with the salty crispness of life, and her lungs with fresh air that seemed to purify her mind and body. She smiled as she sat and watched the horizon, the way the sky and the ocean met and came together as one: inseparable, one for the other.

She would be married soon, taken from her family to live with her new husband in a little cottage by the ocean so she too might start her own family. She wondered what it would be like to be with her husband the way the sky and the ocean were with each other, the way her parents were together, day and night, always by each other's sides, to be thought of in the minds of other people not as two, but as one, working alongside each other, eating and sleeping next to each other, growing old together, having children and then grandchildren. She revelled in the dream, the soon to be reality of it. And as she sat upon a large piece of driftwood with her knees pulled up to her chin and her arms about her knees, she could not help but glory in her life, in each breathe she took. She relished it, every bit of it.

Though the setting sun was to her back, the ocean still captured the majesty of the sunset as the clouds in the sky gradually flared to a brilliant orange.

"Kerisa!" her mother called. "It's time to come in now!"

She hadn't realized it, but her family had ceased their fun and was clearing their picnic table before the cottage of the remains of their late meal.

"After the sunset?" she asked over her shoulder, not taking her eyes away from the ocean.

Her mother smiled and turned to her father, and reached for his hand. He was watching her too. A tear was in his eyes. He turned to his wife when he felt her hand in his and looked into her eyes.

"Our baby is a grown woman now," she said, giving voice to what she saw in his eyes.

He nodded and swallowed the lump in his throat. "Let's give her her privacy," he said. "She'll have little of it in the months to come," he admitted reluctantly. He took his wife into his arms and guided her into the cottage, leaving his daughter to her sunset and her private thoughts.

Kerisa had no fear of the dark, never had any reason for it, and so never developed one. As the sun set, she simply watched the majesty of the approaching gloom in the clouds as they continued to flare into different colours that reflected the vast stillness of the ocean calm. She did not feel the heat from the sun's embrace leave until it was well gone; and suddenly, a chill swept over her heart.

Startled, she looked around to see the night had crept up on her, but as she started to move, to go home, a powerful set of arms swept around her, holding her in place.

She giggled, thinking it was her to-be-husband, come to call upon her and her family, and she leaned back against the powerful chest trustingly.

It only took her a moment to realize this was not her love. Her eyes widened in fear and a hand clamped over her mouth, as strong as iron. She could not move, she could not shout, and she feared even if she was free to speak, she would not be able to.

She was unable to bring the breath into her lungs, so afraid she was, and her breathing came in shallow, empty gasps.

"Such life," a scornful voice whispered near her ear. She was too afraid to know if it was a woman's voice or a man's. "Such innocence, such passions, always protected by the walls of your log cabin. You were always surrounded by your dull brothers, sleeping soundly behind closed doors and protected by that cross!" The words were spat with such venomous hate, their meaning escaped her completely.

"Well, not tonight," the voice mocked. "Tonight, I had to rise early. Tonight, I had to be pained by the sun. But it is worth it. This will be mine. This will all be mine."

Kerisa would have screamed then, if she were able. Two sharp needles penetrated deep into her neck with a painful tearing that left her on the verge of passing out. She felt the blood flow from her in a powerful flood and her eyes flickered as a wave of darkness washed over and through her.

A wave of hideous evil, of memories and sensations of every kind of unimaginable act penetrated her very soul, covering her with filthy desires she'd never once dreamed of.

Her mind's eye opened with sudden and pain staking clarity and she saw fires of damnation rise up and consume these beastly thoughts and feelings. In her mind it seemed these flames contained her, who she was, who she knew she was, screaming and rallying against the evil that was pulsing through her veins.

Her true self rushed in on the filth, tormenting and striking against it with a righteous anger she could no longer deny than she could the sunset. She felt each blow, each punishment upon her physical body and knew she was dying. Yet even this thought was eclipsed of all fear by the hideous realization that she could no longer recognize where she ended and where the evil began.

"Yes!" the voice at her ear hissed in ecstasy. As it did, Kerisa felt the pain in her neck subside and the evil wash away from her. In that moment, she knew who she was, and that what had taken her was truly not of her.

But as quickly as it came, the moment passed as what had her punctured another two holes in her neck. The blood flowed from her in a rush; her eyes flickered; and she screamed as she fainted in the arms of darkness.

"No!"

Kerisa's eyes flickered again as the scream penetrated the deep layer of unconsciousness that washed over her like the drowning ocean. She was dropped to the beach like rag doll and screamed in pain again, in longing.

She heard the sounds of quiet conflict in the sand behind her and she knew she must stand, must find the strength to stand. She felt violated and torn, as though a piece of her had been betrayed to darkness so hideous and evil, it left her skin cold under the rising moon.

She was slick with blood. She knew it was blood. She knew it was her own blood, knew she had only moments before the spinning world would spin out of control and she would slip and fall to the moist ground once more.

James was there, hugging someone in a monster death grip of his powerful arms. She could not see who it was, but the creature that attacked her was clawing at his fists behind its back. It was thin and winded, and James handled it like a rag doll. His teeth were set in determination as he held it above the ground while it clawed, leaving great rents in his flesh where it dug in with its nails.

"Die!" James mumbled through gritted teeth as he squeezed all the harder. "Die. Die. Die."

The creature, a woman with short black hair, grew still, grew calm. "Oh, but I have, James," it hissed, unable to breathe. "I have." Triumphantly, it opened its mouth to reveal a deep set of fangs, and fell onto his neck, ripping and tearing as it did.

Kerisa took a step toward them, and then fell, knocking into the struggling combatants and bringing them with her to the ground.

The woman, awash with blood, was breaking from James' weakening hold on her when Kerisa did the only thing she could think to save her lover, even as the world began to grow dark.

She bit her.

Fire lanced through her body and the body of the creature. It burned them both as she tasted blood on her lips.

The lady who had attacked them screamed in outrage and Kerisa gave herself over to this new rage, this new sensation. It pulsed through her even as the fire did: some part of Kerisa screamed against all the evil that was taking place, yet that part, hideously outmatched by the darkness enflaming within, faded quickly into nothing.

Kerisa had bitten the creature's leg, and now drank compulsively as the lifeblood flowed out of the weakened monster.

The sensation was like being born, as wave after wave washed over her. She was a presence that had always been, but now the dark presence of vampirism abandoned the body of the first huntress and washed into the body of the dying child to make her into what the first had been.

The other one, who had so mistakenly attacked Kerisa released her hold on Kerisa's fiancée and weakly touched Kerisa's hair. "Oh," she mumbled in dark ecstasy, as their two consciousnesses flooded together, as their memories tumbled together and the one drank of the other, of her power, of her life and her death. They could not tell where one of them ended and the other began. Yet they both knew what had happened, what was happening. The vampire that had attacked Kerisa was dying, and Kerisa drank every last drop of her, taking her into herself. The vampire fainted, and Kerisa knew then she was immortal. Yet she hungered for more, for blood not contaminated by this creature's dark intentions.

"Kerisa," James whispered as she finally pulled herself from the dried corpse. She looked into his eyes under the pale moonlight and it occurred to her some time had passed.

She smiled. "James," she said calmly, and the chill in her voice chilled them both. She was greatly pleased by that.

He reached out a hand to her. He trembled weakly as he did, and she pulled herself over the husk of the vampire corpse to be close to him. He took her in his arm, his strong, gentle arm, and pulled her tightly to the wound on his neck as he began to faint.

She smiled in the darkness as she smelled the blood. "My name," she hissed, "is Aphrodite." Then she drank and drank.

She gorged herself, and when she was done, two empty corpses lay on the beach beneath her.

She rose to her feet on unsteady legs. New blood coursed through her veins and her ears were pounding, keeping rhythm with the ocean waves.

The cabin stood in the distance. Lamplight shone through the windows to cast patches of yellow glows across the shadowy fields. She smiled. There was more, so much more that had been kept from her predecessor that she knew she could have. She knew it. The feelings overwhelmed her with the anticipation of life she would experience this night.

She ran to the cabin and let out a great wail of anguish in a remarkable human voice. Kerisa had been a much loved person, for the door flew open and her father stepped into the night. She could have taken him then, but there was more she wanted, so she kept her façade and sobbed, staying just out of reach of the lamplight. Her mother watched from the doorway with a worried look on her face. Her father glanced around at the darkness fearfully.

"What has happened?" he asked angrily. "What has been done to you?"

"I'm so scared" she cried in a pathetically human, frail voice.

"Hush, Darren," Kerisa's mother chastised her husband. "You'll only frighten the child more."

Sob after sob shook the vampire's frame. Yet she hung back, waiting for the invitation that would set her free.

"Come in, child," her mother finally said. "It is all right. You are safe now. Come in and tell us what has happened." Her arms reached out to Aphrodite across the threshold of her home, inviting her to cross it.

Good enough. The vampire had been set free, and she glided into the lamplight, smiling in anticipation with what was to be.

There were only four rooms to the little cabin; through Kerisa's memories the vampire remembered them all very well. Most of her brothers had stayed in their beds, sleeping through the noise she had made to gain access to the place. She started with Kerisa's parents, silencing them in unconsciousness so she could drink undisturbed.

Then she drank her fill; she drank past her fill. She went from room to room, sampling one and then another, knocking them out cold to make sure no alarm could be sounded to warn the others.

The youngest child, Darrel, slept with Kerisa in her room, and when she opened the door she found the child, no older than six years old, kneeling in the centre of the bed with the blankets up over his head in a protective turtle shell against the terror of the night: her.

She smiled at that, at the innocence of the child.

There was candlelight creeping along through the blankets, further protection against evil, no doubt. She smiled again with all the loving memories Kerisa and her family shared with this child. He was a delight, truly; and Aphrodite could no longer restrain herself with the anticipation of knowing him as thoroughly as she did Kerisa and the rest of her family.

She threw the blankets back and was thrown against the wall. A blinding light lanced through the room, cascading over the furniture and walls like liquid lightning. She shrieked in pain as the light burned her exposed flesh with a fever that set it on fire.

She looked through the painful light. The effort was disheartening, to say the least.

The child was indeed on his knees. A candle was placed carefully between them in a little glass jar. His head was bowed; his eyes were closed; his little lips moved with terrified speed. In his clasped hands he held something she could not see through the blinding, supernatural light. He seemed unaffected by the light; as though he could not tell it was there.

But it was burning her fiercely enough. Her skin was boiling. Her blood, the blood she had stolen from Kerisa and her family, was coming alive with fire, and she screamed with pain.

The child, startled out of his prayers by the sound, fell back on the bed in fright as he stared at the apparition that had once been his sister. In his hands he held a little wooden cross, the source of all this light and all this pain. It seemed to be made of liquid white light, and for the brief moment she looked at it, vertigo seized hold and tossed the vampire onto the floor in front of it. It had a bottomless depth to it and a presence, a life of its own. It not only wanted to burn Aphrodite to ash, but consume her as well, tear her from existence to a place far beyond the reach of imagination, where the horrors of what she was would not be able to touch the conceptualization within the intellect of mankind. It wanted to banish her from creation, to punish her for eternity, and torment the evil that she was, stretching her across existence, across eternity, until she was so diluted in the presence of that burning light, that she would simply cease to exist.

She shrieked again as she fled that cross, that little child and his cabin. She fled into the night and the flickering shadows of the sliver of the moon. But even this small light reminded her of the terror pursuing her from that cabin: that cross.

She plunged into the ocean, seeking only to hide in the inky blackness of those unfathomably depths, where she hoped the light from that cross would not reach.

In the morning, the husk of the other vampire burst into flame. Weakened by loss of blood, she could only try to scream as the flames incinerated her.

Chapter Five

Childhood passed by in a blur. There were many monks and many priests at the monastery he grew up in. It was a large place, far removed and kept secret by the vast tracks of uninhabited forests that lay thick upon the hill the little sanctuary rested upon. The place was called Signa Aquainnus, and if the hill upon which it rested was barren of its forests, the vantage point would allow a view of the ocean and the Roman port city. At one time the monastery had been a Roman fort used to help defend the eastern coastline, yet it had fallen into decay when Rome began to withdraw its armies from Britain during the fifth century. Some time after they left, a handful of monks discovered what the soldiers had abandoned, and Signa Aquainnus was born, named after the founding father, Jason Aquainnus, who led the monks in their discovery.

Christopher loved it there, though there were few other children, other infants left to the care of the Church in other Parishes scattered over Britain. But he was never lonely. With his chores and his schooling, he was given little time to ponder such things as his own fate or the outcome of the universe. He was given over to study and devotion to the Blessed Mother and her most Holy Son, the Christ. And when he was not in mass or school, the monks and the handful of other children crowded his spare time. He was a busy child.

But then puberty came upon him and all of his life turned upside down, into a terrible nightmare that he would never forget.

It began with night terrors. Christopher would awaken in a cold sweat, confused and tangled in his bed clothes, far from his room and the safety he took within its walls. When such a thing would occur, he would go back to his room and lie down to stare at the ceiling in terror until dawn finally found him. What if he fell asleep one day and cast himself off of a cliff, or into a fire? He could not imagine that such an end would be an escape from the terror of what was to come, and so he was consumed with the thought of how he might harm himself while he was unaware of what he did.

Then the nightmares began, and sightings of a wolf prowling through the halls and the nearby forests. He never saw such a creature, though he stayed up many nights dreading the encounter. And perhaps that was why Christopher's dreams began to be plagued by the awful night beast. Night after night, the same recurring dream, the wolf, stalking him and overwhelming him, would leave him wide awake and exhausted. Terrified of sleep, he would take solitude where he could.

He became detached from his extended family of monks and priests, preferring instead the solitude of the forests and the safety of obscurity that aloneness offered. The others began to resent him for his aloofness, and it was not uncommon that one or two of them would chastise him with cruel words when they thought they would get away with their malice.

Christopher never reported the verbal attacks, realizing that all the proof they left him was his word against theirs, and he was the outsider, after all. By his own hand, Christopher had alienated himself from these people that loved him. And though he loved them still, the haunting terror of his continual nightmares left him flinching away from anybody that tried to offer respite from his tormented life.

He did not blame them for their resentment. Instead, he kept to himself and tried to hide the truth of the terror that came from within him.

Still, the terror grew, nearly on a daily basis. The nightmares grew more and more vivid as Christopher dreamt of being devoured and tormented by a demon-wolf with blood red eyes and a passion for destruction unlike any he could reinvent. He continued to awake in strange places, grateful for the few times he awoke in his own bed. He told no one of his sleep walking. He dreaded the priests would try to leach the demon from his body, and Christopher knew instinctively the blood that flowed through his veins did not hold the terror that was destroying him. It was his soul, and no amount of leaches would cure him of his terrible disease, not unless they managed to suck the life out of him before the good brothers and fathers could pull the leaches from his body.

The strange hauntings continued and grew intense. Though he never saw this mysterious wolf, he soon realized that this was the creature that haunted him from within. And he realized that whatever this creature was, it was not something Christopher wanted to meet. Inside his head was bad enough. Outside, the terror of such an encounter was unthinkable.

And then, Christopher realized that he was wolf: that he was the demon, and all along, he was the cause of this horror that now plagued the monastery as much as it plagued him.

* * * * *

One day, when the sun was well up, and sleep was the last thing on Christopher's mind, he crept from the garden where he worked, ignoring the stares and quiet curses coming from his companions. He slipped into the kitchen through the back way and to his relief, he found the place empty. He took a cutting knife, the largest he could find, and tested the edge with his thumb. To his satisfaction, he found the thing sharp enough to cut through his skin before the icy pain of the cut even registered through his exhausted mind.

Christopher smiled at this small mercy and quickly slit his wrists. He did not know if he had cut them deep enough to bleed to death, but the pain was blinding, and his hands shook as the wounds opened. He dropped the knife to the stone floor, where it clanged and bounced loudly in the silence of the kitchen.

A monk came in then. Christopher's back was turned to him and his bleeding hands were out of his sight, so he did not see what the teenager had done. "Christopher?" he asked, with more curiosity than anger. Christopher was touched by the man's care, but it made small difference to him now, after what he had done.

"Get away!" he said quickly. His whole body began to shake, and still he did not turn to face the man.

The monk sensed something was terribly wrong and came around to face the youth. "What have you done!" he shouted. The anger was there now, where Christopher expected it to be, and he had to smile bitterly at his prediction. Somehow, the child always managed to make these people angry at him, no matter what he did.

"Get away!" he shouted back.

The monk looked shocked by the venom in his voice. Christopher could hear the sounds of other monks as they ran toward them through the monastery, and he could see others looking up at him through the windows in the kitchen. The monk grabbed Christopher's arms and clamped down on them, squeezing them below the wounds with a strength all men seem to possess over younger children. Christopher screamed and cried for him to let go, but try as he might, plead as he might, he could not break his grip, and he held the child raging and thrashing in his arms while the others stormed into the kitchen and surrounded them.

"Don't you understand?" Christopher screamed. "I am the wolf! I am the nightmare! I am the demon you all so hate!" They looked shocked and disbelieving. "Let me die!" he screamed with the last vestige of his strength. Still, the monk did not let go of his grip and Christopher collapsed to the floor in self pity.

"Let me die," he moaned, held up in a sitting position by the monk's stubborn refusal to let go of his wrists.

The monks stared at him in horror, at what he had done to himself, and finally, the one who held him looked up at his brothers. "Someone help him," he said. "His cuts need to be bandaged."

As though a bell had been rung, the monks were uprooted from their spots on the kitchen floor and sprang to help clean and bandage Christopher's arms. The bleeding was stopped, and he was ushered back to his room, where a monk sat with him to make sure he did not try anything foolish again. He was too weak from exhaustion and loss of blood to do anything but stare at the ceiling while the room swayed dangerously.

The monk sat next to him in a chair, watching over him as he passed into sleep. "Let me die," he mumbled. And as the darkness began to take over, Christopher grabbed the monk's robe. It was growing dark outside as well. "If it comes," he mumbled as he looked up with pleading eyes at the concerned brother. "Kill me," he muttered anxiously.

"Kill it," he begged with the last of his strength. Then the darkness came once more.

* * * * *

A hill gradually climbed away from Christopher. Sloping up and away from him in a straight line was a broad path he could see up of for miles and miles, until his vision finally faded away from him in a tiny speck of obscurity. It was a clear day, bright and sunny. Tall trees and fields of hay grew against the sides of the road in their turn, swaying gently in the fair wind that blew the summer heat into a pleasurable memory he would cherish against the harsh spray of the ocean storms.

Christopher stared up the road curiously, wondering where it led, and when the obscurity of the distance would ever end. He felt that this road represented his life, and the secrets of what was in store for him was held down this path, could be discovered if he simply walked down this path and found them out.

Yet in the distance, an impossibly large black wolf galloped toward him. The size of the creature awed Christopher even from this distance, and his feet rooted to the ground as he watched the wolf approach. The creature's tongue lolled out of its mouth as its feet ate at the ground, and the forests and fields flew past it as it galloped straight toward Christopher, all the while its eyes fixed upon his with a keen, piercing interest that spread fear over Christopher's entire body and soul.

He trembled as the wolf came on, yet he was unable to stop the creature, unable to even turn and get out of its path. And so he watched: paralysed with fear like a rabbit before the wolf's terrible jaws.

As the wolf approached, it leapt into the air, sailing straight at Christopher's head with its maw open full to devoir him.

Christopher screamed and woke up to find he was alone in his room deep within the halls of the monastery. His wrists still throbbed from where he had cut them; the bandages were bloody and needed to be changed. He wondered why he had been left alone in his room and silently cursed the monk for not killing him when he had the chance. Shaking, he drew himself from his bed and wiped his eyes with a fist as he stood before the window looking into the courtyard below.

Christopher's guard lay on his back within a pool of blood. Another monk stooped over the body, anxious to see what was wrong. Christopher watched dumbstruck and terrified, still by his nightmare, and now by this.

The priest looked up at Christopher and looked deep into his eyes. Christopher flinched at what he saw there, cringing away from the terrible truth that said somehow he was responsible for a man's death. He could see the priest staring straight into Christopher's soul with an intensity that demanded retribution, and Christopher cowered away from the awful truth he saw written in the man's face.

He pulled away from the window as a sob escaped him, and the young man cowered in the corner of his room as he heard the telltale signs of approaching feet. They were coming for him.

In a moment, the room was full of wary monks, banishing torches that cast an eerie light over the room and hurt the boy's eyes.

"He is still in human form," one monk said. Relief was evident even to the child.

"The demon sleeps," another monk said with a sigh. "Still, be wary. The moon is out and the boy could turn at any moment."

Father Jason burst through the crowd, eyeing up their determination before he turned to the young man still cowering and crying with fright. He knelt before him and reached out a tender hand toward the boy. "It is all right, Christopher," he said, going far to dispel the fear and hatred within the room. "You have to come with us, though," he added.

Nodding and still unable to speak through his tears and his sobs, he reached for the priest's hand and was guided from the room. "What have I done?" he managed to moan as the priest led him down the long hallways of their monastery.

"Not you, but what hides inside you," the priest responded stoically.

Christopher shuddered as he remembered the wolf that plagued his dreams and kept silent as he was led to a small room deep within the monastery's catacombs. There was an iron grate in front of the room, and when he saw it Christopher began to panic. Already darkness swarmed around him; his hold on consciousness was slipping.

"No!" he cried in terror. "Not the wolf again! Please, not that!"

The priest gathered the fainting boy in his arms while the monks steeled themselves against the horror of what was coming.

"Leave him!" one of the monks cried. "Kill him, quick!" another screamed.

"There is still time!" the priest shouted back as he rushed the boy into the room. "Get the chains on him, and be quick!"

After that, Christopher slipped into the terrible reality of unconsciousness and the bitter dreams of torment that followed.

Chapter Six

Off the coast of Crete, a slight breeze blew the grain growing on the gentle hillsides with a continual swaying motion that made the tall stalks sway violently in the golden sunlight. Near Venice, in a sparsely populated village community, no one witnessed the wooden coffin ground ashore. No one still would remember the strange vessel that set out across the Mediterranean from the mouth of the Nile in Syria, destroyed during its voyage by an invading pirate ship. Those who were on the ship had taken this box, this coffin, as treasure when they had attacked. Yet a strange sickness had come over the crew of that lost pirate ship, and they were never heard of again, though legends abound of what happened to them. But before that ship and its crew disappeared entirely, this coffin and its cursed contents had been thrown back into the sea by the superstitious crew, to ground to shore here. Its journey had ultimately been a success.

Night came slowly upon the box, and still it remained undisturbed, like forgotten driftwood to cast shadows over the never ending stretch of beach it had marooned upon. But once deepest night had set in, with not even torch flame within sight to offer any hint of human life, with only the wind now howling unceasingly through the grains of wheat, the moon climbed slowly into the cloud pocked sky with only a sliver of its full glory to taunt the surface below with unreliable light.

Something within the coffin shifted, and then there was the breaking of wood as the door was torn off and cast aside. A pale wanderer of the night sat up upon the banks of his new home. He was dressed entirely in fine black silk, with a ruby ring upon his right index finger. His long, bony hands curled over the sides of his coffin as he inhaled the salty ocean air. Then he was up and onto the beach, walking quickly to the cover of the tall grass, continuously on guard for other predators that might give him chase, though he could think of none that would be stronger than him.

Still, it was wise to be cautious. He sat down with a view that would afford him a clear sight of the ocean, and with the infinite patience of the dead, called out a silent invitation toward the waters and their infinite depths. "Come," he called. "Come to me." He waited, knowing that summons had been heard and would not be ignored. Such things as time meant little to him, and he buried his coffin in the sand before the sun came up, still patiently waiting for the fledgling to come from her premature watery grave.

Again, as the sun set and darkness awoke, the wanderer's instincts awoke him as well, and he crawled from his shelter with the expertise gained through uncountable years of practice. His thirst gnawed at him, yet he knew it must be infinitely worse for the fledgling, so he bore the patient longing stoically and retreated to his vantage point of the ocean. "Come to me," he silently commanded. "Come to me." Then he waited.

The third night he arose from his grave on the beach and was rewarded for his patience.

A pale figure surfaced from the depths. Its long, flowing hair was rotting and had been bleached white by the salty depths. Its body was partly rotted and chewed away by the monsters that rested on the bottom of the Mediterranean. It wore only rags that draped in strings around its thighs and over its shoulders. It was the body of a young female, though rotting with the ancient presence of death. She climbed out of the waters slowly, carried by the agelessness of the summons that had called her. And as she shed the ancient remains of her clothing as she stepped fully onto the beach, she smiled as the moonlight revealed to her the nakedness of her body. The night was hers, and her dark passions would once again be released, would be sated. Yet one thing above all else haunted her that night, and that was the need for blood, the aching longing to taste what had for so long been denied her at the bottom of the Mediterranean. There had been other fierce monsters down in those darks, but none of them had proven as fierce as her, and now, as she strode toward the place of her summons, she had earned the right to taste the warm blood of humans once again.

Her fangs contracted with anticipation as the other vampire rose from where he waited for her. They would feed this very night, together. And he would begin schooling her in the luxurious art of survival. Her need drove her forward with an unspoken longing that he did not bother to reply to with human words. Instead, she followed him wordlessly to a small hamlet, where they feasted until daylight and then took shelter for the day amongst the dead of their making.

* * * * *

"Who are you?" Aphrodite asked. She had awoken with a start from the bottom of a root cellar, nothing more than a pit they had found in the barn out back. He had been there. She vaguely remembered the night before, and the uncountable years she had spent half alive, half dead at the bottom of sea, how he had summoned her with his will alone, penetrating deep into her groggy mind and cold body with the sheer strength of his insistence to rise once more. She had surfaced, and had fed, and now, in the preternatural darkness surrounding them, felt as much alive as she had since that fire had driven her into the depths. Her wounds had healed, and her heart once again pumped with the blood of the living. Now, only a weary need to feed again drove her to wakening. And this hole they were in was as much a good place to ask the question as any.

He was already up and studying her silently when she came to, and yet, he took his time to answer her. "I am known by many names," he said at last. "But I was a servant in the temple of the dead," he added. "I became a priest, and this," he added by holding out his hands before her. Even in the darkness, they seemed to shine with an inhuman paleness that would only be found in the dead.

His words made very little sense. "I am who I chose to be," he added, sensing her unease.

She remembered the way she had clung to her new identity when Kerisa had died, the way that human had suffered and been tormented as her blood was drained and then the vampire blood was replaced. She nodded. She understood what this one meant. She smiled as she thought about how readily she had tossed Kerisa's identity aside, how the victims of her thirst were as much a part of her as Kerisa was. And she felt no remorse, only the driving desire to do it again.

"I was dead," she said quietly. "You summoned me back."

97

"Vampires don't die," he said quietly. "They only fall asleep."

She looked around at their hole in the ground and found a cadaver lying near by. It had been human once, but now, drained of blood and life it was as pale as either of them, and just as cold. She reached out to it and idly tried to bite into it, to taste the flesh once more.

The other grabbed her and threw her out of the cellar with such speed and force that the wind was knocked from her lungs. She landed flat on her face in the barn above the cellar and struggled to regain her breathe. She found her way to her knees just as he floated out of the pit and alighted before her.

"Never feed from the dead," he commanded. There was no emotion in his voice, no concern, no remorse.

She struggled to nod that she understood.

"You asked me who I am," he said as he stared down at her. She grew aware that she was still naked by the look in his eyes. "For now, you may call me master."

* * * * *

They travelled together along the coast of Northern Greece, finding refuge where they took their victims, usually on a nightly basis. Death followed behind. When they could not find a hamlet or a farm to visit, they would take shelter in the thick underbrush of the denser uninhabited forests. Pushing the rotting leaves and moss up over their bodies until they were buried alive with the fresh scent of decay, they would spend their days in a dreamless sleep Aphrodite could only imagine was so much like the death she brought her victims.

"Master," she asked one night, as they pulled themselves from the forest floor under a patch of moonlight. "Why is it that we hide ourselves from the sun?"

He looked at her and shook his head. "Why don't you try to reveal yourself to it, and find out?" he asked. Then he turned away and strode from the forest. He was hungry this night, and a little more restless than usual.

She wondered what was on his mind, but his thoughts and his feelings remained ever guarded from her, revealed to her only at his will, and usually taking the form of an unspoken command. Wordlessly, she followed, and it was soon they came across the largest, sprawling metropolis Aphrodite had ever imagined, or had any of her victims, for that matter.

Spanning to the horizon, Venice stretched out before them as a never-ending promise of human flesh. The stench from the cesspools rose to fill her nostrils, and the sounds of the markets met her ears even from this great distance. Every fibre within her quivered with desire, and Venice tantalized her with the promise of meeting every one of her dark desires.

"Try not to kill," her master said in the face of her great emotion with stone cold complacency. "They will track us and try to kill us if they suspect what we are."

"How will we hide it?" she asked, shocked that they could.

"Remarkably well," he said cryptically. "Easily. You will see." With that, he started toward the city again, allowing her to keep pace as he did.

She bounded up beside him, feeling giddy and very much the way Kerisa had toward her fiancée.

"A small bite brings disease," he explained. "The more blood you pull from them, the sicker they become, and with different diseases. If you need to feast, feast from many." But by then, the gates of Venice, now shut up for the night, were looming in front of them. He moved faster than she could see, until he was up on the wall. Then he paused to look down at her and threw himself over the other side. She waited long enough to realize that he was not waiting for her, and then almost as fast, she followed him over the wall.

Humanity was all that she had expected it to be. They were stupid creatures, half asleep in the best of times, timid, excitable animals with passions not unlike hers, yet satiable, where hers drove her on continuously throughout the night. The master was right. They were easy to deceive. Instead of seeing what was obvious and before their eyes, the creatures chose, again and again, to see what they wished to see. And Aphrodite, able to discern what that was, was growing proficient in slipping into any role that would hide her true identity until they were close enough to bite.

She saw her master only rarely, not able to hide herself from him, and he always able to shield his presence from her. But there were times when he let her know he was watching her. He was aloof at the best of times, so she gave him little thought, and gorged on the flesh of Venice.

Bath houses on the edge of poor districts knew her as a public whore. Senators and those of the state knew her as an upstanding lady of incredible resourcefulness. All knew her, though she had the identity of many different people. Most had felt her kiss upon their neck, even if they did not remember it.

Fever ran rampart in the streets. And she gloried in the combined memories and sensations of her victims as they coursed and mixed together with their blood that spilled from her lips. Blood thick with wine left her giddy and drunk, while blood coursing with the drugs from the orient gave her the same sensations they would of any human, except perhaps they had no lasting affect on her.

She discovered she could not take any substance other than blood. All else left her weak with exhaustion after the vomiting had crippled her with stomach pains that left her panting on her knees. But she could enjoy whatever her victims did, and she made sure she did just that, drinking and drinking and drinking, as each night bled endlessly into the next, punctuated only by her instincts that drove her to ground before sunrise and the need to awaken after dark.

Yet in these places of true dark, she remembered nothing. She dreamt of nothing. She was as though dead. Her gorging, to her, felt as though it was truly undisturbed.

* * * * *

She had taken to sheltering in an ancient crypt of the richest citizens of Venice. It was a building above ground, far up into the heart of Venice, and away from the gates and the noise of the city commons. Yet it was not far from her modest estate and she had found the tomb walled in from the inside, so even if someone had come during the day to bury or visit the dead, she would be left alone in peace as she slept. Her cell could only be gained access from the roof, and a large stone had been cut into a rectangular cover and placed over the hole to her den. No human could move that stone and she felt safe in the cover of darkness under its weight.

Daily, she had bedded down on the stone floor and had gone into her sleep of the dead long before the sun began to brighten the horizon. Whatever instinct that drove her to hole before the sun could find her had so naturally led her to seek refuge, that she no longer questioned why she did it. She simply did, and not seeing the sun was a small matter to her in the face of her ever present need to meet her dark lusts.

Yet this day, something stirred on the other side of the wall she lay against, and she came painfully awake as her resting place was threatened.

Her eyes shot open and the sweltering presence of the sun overhead overwhelmed her with fear. Sweat beaded over her face as she stretched her senses across the stone wall that separated her from whatever threatened her.

There was a score of men on the other side, angry men with torches. They were searching the crypt. A few of them had stopped and were talking in angry tones to each other, mere feet from where Aphrodite lay in the dark.

"There is nothing here, I tell you!" one man cursed. "This whole idea of yours is insane! There is no living dead amongst the populace of Venice, no creatures of the night!"

"Steward," another man hissed. "Death has come to Venice! Open your eyes! Plague and sickness haunt us, and now people fear to leave their homes at night."

Aphrodite had missed that. She had had no compunction to enter someone's home, just as she had had no compunction to see the sun, though even now, it terrorized her through her stone crypt. She vaguely wondered what else she had had no compunction to not do.

"Death is here, I tell you. And I will no longer stand by and do nothing while he terrorizes our people." His voice was passionate, and Aphrodite wondered if she had ever tasted of this one's passions. The list of her victims was nearly limitless, yet as she recalled them to mind, she could not seem to recall ever feeding off of passions like this. There was silence on the other side of the wall.

"What is behind this wall?" the passionate man asked suddenly.

"Another crypt," the steward remarked idly.

Something slammed against the wall, echoing the inside of the crypt and bringing down dust from the walls and ceilings. Aphrodite froze on the threshhold of panic. If they discovered her here, now, there was no telling what they could do to her, with the sunlight over head. Another boom echoed through the room.

"Stop it! Damn it!" the steward shrieked. "Stop it!"

"Why?" the passionate man asked calmly. Another resounding crash filtered through the room.

"This man was a criminal," the steward cried. "He was sentenced to death and his tomb sealed, that he might remain separated from mankind even in death. There is no way in."

Aphrodite was thankful he didn't seem to know about the trap door to the vault.

"How long has this place been this way?" the passionate one asked.

"Years. Decades. I don't know. Before my time. Before the plague. There is nothing behind that wall except the dead. And you deface their resting place as it is, just by being here."

"I have to do something," the man spat.

"Go back to the palace," the steward pleaded, "and leave the dead to themselves. Death stalks the living, not the dead."

There was silence as the man seemed to think about what he had been told. Finally, he cursed and left. The soldiers he was with followed their leader.

When silence returned to the crypt, she could hear the steward sigh and sink to the floor on the other side of the wall. Aphrodite placed a hand against the wall to silently thank the man for saving her.

* * * * *

The stone grated above her head, and she awoke again, this time panicked and cornered like a caged animal. There would be no way out, no mysterious saviour of a steward of the dead. Aphrodite braced herself as the stone inched clear of the hole above her head. She fled to the farthest corner of the room and cowered in fear as she waited for what was to come. The stone slid a finger's width and a shaft of light violated her haven, piercing through the dusty air to pool on the floor of the crypt. She hissed at the burning patch of sunlight and pressed herself against the back corner of the crypt, trying desperately to get free from its presence. The walls of the crypt seemed to press in on her, and she felt like they were growing smaller, forcing her toward that burning patch of light.

The stone grated again, and the light spread, growing painfully close to ripping a scream from her. She felt like her skin was going to combust, as though she was going to explode into flames. Though the sensation was unlike that first time in Kerisa's cabin, this light was symbolic of that greater, purer light, and the horror of it was enough to make her skin crawl, even as she knew that if she stepped into that light, she would erupt into flames just like that first time. That experience had been enough to drive her to the bottom of the Mediterranean. This experience was close to as bad.

Eventually, the stone had shifted enough for whatever diabolical purpose the steward had in mind, because it was his voice that filtered down through the light. "Go on," he was saying. "Deliver the master's message. There is nothing to fear if you stay inside the light."

"But why do I have to go down there?" another man asked. He was afraid. "As he should be," Alexis told herself. The punishments she would inflict for having her sleep disturbed by such a nightmare as this sunlight would forever be remembered as legend in this city of Venice.

Eventually, a rope was lowered, and a man crawled down the rope to stand uncertainly in the pool of light in the centre of the crypt.

Aphrodite glared at him hatefully from the shadows, and was surprised that he could not see her yet.

"I have a message from the master," he said shakily. He was urinating himself. "" Death's mistress must feed," he quoted. "You must sate your thirst with death, or death will come to us all." Aphrodite could tell from the expression on his face, the messenger had no idea what that meant. For her, the words were plain enough. She was death's mistress. She had not brought death to this city, as she had been commanded, and now, because her thirst had not been sated, had been denied the satisfaction of knowing someone into death's embrace, the entire city was suffering, and the humans began to suspect that she and her master were here.

Suddenly, the rope was cast down. Now terrified, the messenger stared up at the patch of sunlight. "What are you doing?" he bellowed.

"A gift, mistress," the steward called down through the opening. "From the master." He laughed as the messenger began bellowing in fear. "Learn to control your thirst, fledgling, or we will all die."

"No!" the messenger cried despairingly as he reached toward the vault of the sky above him.

Slowly, the stone began to inch its way closed. "Hurry now," the steward said above the cries of his messenger. "Otherwise he will give us all away."

The stone began to move with renewed effort, and the light slowly dissipated. Aphrodite stared at the man in front of her with hateful eyes of hunger. He continued to cry as the stone closed over head. But the moment the light was sealed from them, his cries turned to screams of horror as Aphrodite pounced and had him for herself.

Chapter Seven

The cage of ravens flew open as it crashed to the floor, scattering the carrier birds into the air in a flutter of noisy chaos that gave the beast more empty space to manoeuvre between him and his attackers.

He burned with a passionate anger no man ever had. He was covered in coarse fur from head to foot; and wild, black, unintelligent eyes stared out from behind the growling jaws of a wolf. Yet he stood upright like a man, panting hard from either exertion or anger, no one was ever sure.

A goodly number of monks advanced on the monster with whips and staves, blunt objects that would leave little in the way of wounds, yet effective enough to drive the demon into a corner and then beat it senseless. At the time little was known about werewolves and the good brothers wanted to make sure they didn't hurt the captive soul inside the beast.

With a bitter anger, the monster roared out his thirst for violence and lunged.

Three whips cracked in unison and he howled in pain and rage as he was forced back. He was bleeding from a deep cut on his face, another on his upper chest, and from a third on his left arm. All three cuts rendered the flesh to the bone.

Maddened, he roared again and threw the now empty cage at the wall of monks. It crashed into one, splintering on impact and dropping one monk like a stone. He tangled up the two closest to him and all three tumbled into a heap of hooded robes and oak staves.

Seeing his chance, the young beast lunged for the opening and the battle began in earnest. Again.

Now the monks were roaring out their own battle calls, shouting, "In the name of our Lord and Saviour," mostly. But they were men of action as well as faith, for faith without works is dead. And so would they be if they relied entirely on one without the other.

Screaming in fury as the oak staves beat down upon his head and shoulders; the demon grabbed one of the staves in his fists and clamped down on it with his teeth, snapping it to splinters with a jagged end in both hands. The monk whose weapon the creature took lost his balance and stumbled backwards.

The other monks, knowing the werewolf's battle techniques by now, whipped him again before he could lunge and rip out the man's throat.

One whip coiled around his right fist and the weapon he carried, holding his fist shut. The other whip coiled around the elbow of his left arm, cutting the circulation and pinching the nerves to the lower extremity. His hand was paralysed and went numb as the staff fell from his unfeeling fingers. The third whip cut another gash in his face, across his forehead. The blood poured into his eyes and mouth, not only blinding him, but confusing his sense of smell as well.

The monks that held his arms hung on, dragging his arms down and allowing the other monks the moment to attack.

In every conflict there is a moment when the enemy is exposed, weak, vulnerable. Once such a moment happens, one must take advantage of that opportunity and chase his enemy into his defeat, his absolute and utter defeat. The good brothers of the distant, remote monastery of Signa Aquainnus understood this and closed in with renewed intent, aiming their blows at the werewolf's vital organs and soft spots, his knees, his temples, his groin, everywhere they knew would take the beast down for good. They rained down on him, only infuriating him a little more as each blow weakened his body, if not his resolve.

He dropped to one knee before he managed to wrap his left hand around the whip at his elbow and pull it from the monk's grasp. But then someone landed a blow between his eyes and the world went dark.

Father Jason watched the entire battle from the security of distance. It was not his choice to stand aside and watch the beast be subdued, but he had quickly realized there was no time to argue. The wolf had broken through his chains, manifesting early enough to escape his cell before the door was closed.

Now, once the beast had been subdued, the monks, with practiced efficiency, dragged the creature back to its cell and chained him to the wall once again. This time, the chains were new, and Jason knew from experience that the demon would not be able to break out of them, not after the beating it had received.

Once the creature was safely restrained again, Jason looked at the weary monks around him. "Leave us," he commanded.

"But—"

"No," Jason cut the protests off angrily. "I am tired of this. Something must be done."

The monks nodded and left.

Deep down inside the unconscious monster, a calm centre stayed eternally separated from the raging storm of emotion that ripped through the beast's body. Deep within, the soul languished in peace and joy; yet the maniacal darkness raged as it began to howl out at the world from the depths of the monastery's catacombs. It was beginning to awaken.

Christopher knew little of what was going on, yet more than the good brothers wished him to know. He took to sleeping during the day and fighting the passions of the night with a commitment to die before he let the wolf come forth. But as the transformations began to rip though his body, he would scream in pain, and the beast would rise up and glory in it; welcome it.

He would pass out and conscious thought as well as conscious control would flee from the presence of the beast. That was when the priests took to chaining him to the walls before the transformations took place.

Now, the creature raged at the need to shed blood as it strained against the chains that held him to the wall.

Christopher was asleep, in the perfect bliss of oblivion until Father Jason spoke up through the darkness. He did not catch the priest's words above the howls hidden behind darkness and silence.

The beast grew silent as he strained to hear the priest's voice once again.

"Why are you angry?" Jason asked.

Christopher could not find a reason.

The beast lowered its head in thought.

Christopher woke up a little more and the werewolf grew intense in his silence.

Father Jason stepped back, startled by the look of intelligence he saw there.

"I don't remember," Christopher lied. The sound translated through the beast as a low, menacing growl.

The werewolf howled passionately at his failed attempts to escape from his wall chains. Yet Christopher tried again, this time with the truth. "I do not know."

This time, the priest nodded. He had understood. Now, he stood by silently, offering the weight of his presence in the room to give encouragement where Christopher needed it most.

Christopher noticed Father Jason carried a coiled whip with him and a walking staff. Christopher wondered if that would help at all. Probably not.

Jason waited while the werewolf thought. There was no reason for the beast's anger, if such things reduced Christopher to this, to the very incarnation of anger.

Christopher realized this, and the revelation let the chains slacken against Christopher's wrists. Though they cut, they did so not as deeply.

Christopher grew very still as he looked out across the darkened cell to the priest that stood on this side of the bars.

In time, he approached and placed a key in the shackles at his wrists, one at a time. As the chains fell from his arms they dropped from exhaustion to his sides.

The priest stepped back to look at him, at his handiwork in unleashing Christopher, though he was still half wolf.

"This is dangerous business," Christopher warned him.

Jason only shrugged. "The outer doors are locked. They've been tested against your strength before. You cannot escape."

Christopher did not doubt his words, nor admit he did not remember the incident. "The chains do not always hold?" he guessed.

The priest only nodded. "The chains do not always hold," he admitted.

"Yet here you stand," Christopher said as he stepped away from the wall and its chains.

Instead, Jason turned away quickly and pointed at a table and chairs next to the wall. Christopher had not noticed them earlier. "I brought something to help pass the night hours," he said. On the table were a chessboard, two wine glasses and a bottle of fine red.

Christopher smiled. The body he was in translated his appreciation and growled quietly with affection for the stuff.

The priest smiled too. "I thought you'd like that," he said, straightening away from the table.

"I would like to sleep," the werewolf growled rudely, not wanting to see himself as the monster he was.

"If that is as you'd like it," the priest said. He was all accommodating this night. "There is a pallet of straw over there, in that corner," he said as he nodded to yet another detail Christopher did not notice earlier. "While you take your rest, I'll be over there." He pointed through the shadows to a scriptorium. "I trust the light of a lamp will not disturb you too much?"

Christopher only grinned wolfishly as he shook his distorted maw from side to side. "Perhaps I may watch?"

"Of course," the priest beamed.

As he lit the lamp, Christopher pulled a wooden stool closer, so he might afford a view while he studied the calligraphy as it was copied from one page to another.

"The style is uniform throughout," Jason instructed without looking up from his work. "The pen stays uniform with the speed of its strokes, neither rushing nor lagging," as he said this, he changed the speed of his strokes, illustrating on an empty leaf of the precious paper. The slower the pen moved the wider, the thicker, the darker the trail of ink. The faster it moved, the thinner the marks on the page. "Even strokes," he said as he returned back to the main body of his work.

Christopher remained captivated and as time slipped by in silence, he sat transfixed to his spot.

Morning found them when two hesitant monks came to check on Christopher and release him from his chains. They were seated across the chessboard and roaring with laughter. The angry manifestations of the werewolf had receded to just below the surface. When Jason saw the monks, he slammed the table with the flat of his hand and raised a glass of wine in salute.

"To the avenging angel!" he cheered.

"To immortality!" Christopher agreed as he held up his own glass of that fine vintage.

Their glasses clinked together. They tipped them back, and had a good dose all at once before they broke out into laughter once again.

Hesitating, the monks fearfully opened the door to the cell. "Father?" one of them asked as they eyed the bottle between them.

"Congratulations, Father," Christopher said in another salute. "You have survived another night in this wretched place." That last part came out more as an angry growl than as a compliment.

Fearful, the monks stumbled back away from the cell.

"And to you," the priest declared, pouring them both another drink. "For accomplishing the same thing!"

They downed their drinks together.

Christopher tuned to the monks standing in the doorway. "I think they think we're drunk!" he confided loudly before he burst into laughter.

The priest roared right along beside him. "I don't care!" he managed between fits of laughter.

That morning, they watched the sunrise together, and the morning rays of light never felt as good on Christopher's face as they did right then.

Chapter Eight

Thirst sated for the day, Aphrodite left the body of her messenger in her crypt and set out once the terrible sun had set once again. She couldn't imagine what it would have been like once the sun had actually touched her skin, but she had no compunction as to her immediate destruction, had such a thing happened. She felt like going after the steward and punishing him for what he had taught her, but she feared her master's wrath, and knew the man to be connected to him somehow. Still, someone had to pay for what had been done, so she turned her focus toward that man who had nearly torn down her sanctuary. She had heard the steward mention that he had been at the palace, and so she headed there, gliding silently from shadow to shadow with a supernatural ability to see into the darkness. No one saw her passage, nor heard her as she swept past them in the dark. She ignored them as well. Let them have a break from death's mistress, this night. Soon enough, they would feel her bite once again.

The palace was surprisingly a place where she did not visit as often as she probably could have. But this night, she did not care. This night she was about getting rid of the threat that had threatened her, about teaching whoever had come after her to fear her, to teach that man about respect and his proper place in life. She was death's mistress. Her master had said so. What was but one mere mortal man to stand in her way?

In the centre of Venice, the palace was enclosed in its own wall. Gates faced toward roads that approached from every direction. The gates were open and well guarded by torchlight and armed guards. But she had very little difficulty passing over the walls without being noticed. She had learned a long time ago that humans were blinded by their own torch light. The very thing they used to give them light actually shielded them from the night and its realities.

Perched atop the wall, she looked down into the palace gardens and the imposing structure itself. What she would find that night was entirely a mystery to her, and she was eager to get on with it. She hoped she would have the chance to feed before the sunlight drove her back into her hole once again.

Noiselessly, she passed back into the gardens and in between the sentinels that walked amongst them. Laughter filtered through the night, along with soft muted sounds of merry making and enjoyment. She ignored all of this, even though her ability to blend into what humans wanted had given her the ability to approach any such noises with confidence and soon win the trust of the people making that noise. Parties and celebrations of every kind were her feeding ground, and in such places as this garden, she would have typically spent the entire night sampling the blood of one person after another. But not tonight. Tonight she had restitution to claim.

The palace denied her entrance. Try as she might, she could not get past an invisible wall that seemed to encircle the entire place, guarding all of its windows and doors from her. It wasn't so much as a physical barrier as it was an emotional one. Yet she could not conquer her sudden urge to be invited into the place before she invaded it with her destruction. Emotions that she could not understand raged through her, and she felt violently sick with the thought of going into this place. Unexpectedly, she did throw up, and the blood of her last victim spattered onto the stones at her feet.

She wiped her mouth with the back of her hand as she stared at the palace in frustration, and then set herself to gaining the rooftop. Suddenly, the barrier was dropped, and she scaled a wall that offered the most darkness. The shadows kept her well hidden from human eyes, and in a few moments, she pulled herself onto the flat ledge that served as a balcony surrounding the roof.

A garden stretched out across the roof. Not unlike the ones down below, this garden was disturbed by small pools full of coloured fish and stone benches. Tall shrubs grew all around her, and torches stood atop tall pillars that cast the entire garden into golden light.

She was pleased she had penetrated the palace this far.

Immediately, she sensed the presence of humans scattered throughout the garden. Couples lounged around the edge of the garden seeking the shelter of privacy amongst the trees and flowers, and one person sat idly feeding fish near the centre of the garden. This person, Aphrodite would confront. She hung back in the shadows as she crept up on her next victim. It was a woman, a little older than Kerisa had been when she had died, a little older than the body Aphrodite now possessed.

She was beautiful, with long, flowing brown hair and dressed in a silk gown that flowed over her lithe form under the torchlight. She seemed totally unaware of Aphrodite's presence, until, without looking up, she said, "You are death's mistress."

Aphrodite was caught off guard by the admonition, as much as she was by the fearlessness in this lady. Abandoning her hiding place, Aphrodite stepped into the torchlight and approached her.

"That is what I've been called, this day," Aphrodite admitted.

The lady threw the last of her food into the water before her and shook her hands. She was utterly fearless when she looked up at Aphrodite, so much so that Aphrodite checked her approach and tried instead to charm her into trusting her. Nothing seemed to work.

"I am Princess Carina," the lady said. "This is my home. You are not welcome here. "

Aphrodite stepped back under the weight of the command and then laughed. "I was able to get here," she responded. "So here I am."

The princess nodded. She stepped toward Aphrodite, who, taken aback, had to force herself to remain where she was. She would feed off of the impudence of this princess before she left, she would make sure of it.

"Why do you torment the people of Venice?" the princess asked, now face to face with Aphrodite.

"I have a thirst," Aphrodite said honestly. "It demands blood."

"Yet you are destroying us."

Aphrodite shrugged and held her hands out in front of her. "I am sorry," she lied. Her voice was full of sarcasm. "What do you want me to do about it?"

"Go away," the princess implored. "Go away and never come back."

"And where will I go, where I will not be turned out again? Where will I go where the blood will be different, and my thirst will be sated for good? Are you so special, you and the people of Venice, that you would push your problems onto the other people of this region, of this world? Are you so privileged, as to command me to discriminate between you and another person, another city?

Should I say to myself in the midst of the blood lust, 'Oh, this person is from Venice, her blood is off limits, but this one, this one isn't from Venice, and so I may take her as food?' And all because you, a mortal woman, asked me too?"

"I am not asking," the princess said, still fearlessly. "I am commanding."

"Oh, you are commanding!" Aphrodite laughed. She grabbed the princess by the arm in a motion that was too fast for a human eye to follow.

The princess did not try to break her grasp, though it was evident that Aphrodite's grip was painful to her.

"You are commanding," Aphrodite repeated, more to herself than to the princess. Then she went to bite the princess' neck.

Light, blinding, searing, hateful light washed over them both, and Aphrodite spat out the princess's flesh disgustingly. She released her and stepped back, pained by the experience and disoriented by the light that still blinded her. Though the flash of light had subsided, there was still a searing pain in her eyes, and she could not see. Her skin seemed to boil and though she was in pain, her anger pushed the pain away from her instead.

She could vaguely hear the sound of boots on the pavement underfoot, pounding toward her as though she or the princess had sent out an alarm.

The princess was holding her neck and looking at Aphrodite. She took her hand from her neck to inspect the blood there, and Aphrodite was surprised to find she had only scratched her, barely puncturing the flesh at all.

"What happened?" Aphrodite asked quietly. She would not try to hurt the princess once more.

"I love the people of Venice," the princess admitted. "You will go now, and harm us no more."

Aphrodite shook her head to try to disarm the strength of the princess's command.

"That is what happened," the princess said, still calmly. "I would give my life to protect them from you. Now go."

Aphrodite fled while she still had the time, escaping the oncoming rush of soldiers that seemed to flood toward them from all directions. As she faded back into the shadows around them, she overheard the soldiers reach the princess. One of them cried out, "Princess, you are hurt!"

"Just a scratch," the princess admitted calmly. "Just a scratch." Even that seemed to cause the princess grief.

Defeated by something Aphrodite could never grasp, she plunged into the night and fled the palace.

* * * * *

"Master," Aphrodite said suddenly, breathing out her wish into the salty air by the ocean. Right on the verge of plummeting back into its depths, she looked across the moon-covered waters bitterly and refused to look at the walls of Venice behind her. Something powerful moved behind those walls. Though the people of slumber dwelt with plague and slept with death's mistress, they had found a source to repulse her, to turn from her embrace and to force her to spit out her kiss to them.

Now, she needed help before she gave up her home in horror and despair and plummet back into the icy depths she knew would have her. Legends of Jonah circulated through these parts, and she knew that the destitute prophet had nothing on her. God had rejected the damned to what they were, and the Mediterranean would never give up her embrace if she asked for it now.

Instead, she looked out across the never ending expanse and called, "Master," this time out loud to the night that would have her.

Nothing happened, though she knew from the urgency in her voice and from past experiences that he would come and that he would be able to offer her some guidance once again.

It only took her moments before she searched the closed gates behind her for the presence of his ageless reassurance. Nothing was coming out of the dark and the terrified barred doors of this great populace to save her from their rejection. The princess's kiss terrified her as much as any she had found from her victims. Once caught in her embrace, once they knew what she was, once they understood that she wanted their terror, that she wanted their experiences, their lives for her own, the fear she shared with her victims in those moments paled to the horror she had experienced in that princess's love for her people.

She turned fully to the city as she regained her feet and paced back and forth down the beach under the pale moonlight. The city was in full view under the ghostly light of the full moon, yet Aphrodite could sense that all eyes were looking elsewhere in fear. No one wanted to see death's mistress this night. For it was rumoured that to see her was to taste her kiss. The terror of that kept people shut away from the dark in cages of fear that would not let her come close.

"Master!" she cried one last time, giving voice to her desperation with a supersonic inhuman cry, with only her dread propelling through the air waves. The wind stirred around her from the effort of her mental call, the waves

114

behind her rippled, and the grain stirred on its stalks upon the hills.

Then she began to dig her grave. She wanted it deep, well below the waterline, so that the citizens of Venice would not be able to find her in the morning. It took her most of the night and well close to sunrise to dig the pit. Yet as the consuming presence of that fiery ball of light and heat began to creep near to her, she shuddered and sank into the miry waters of the Mediterranean. She smiled as a sand crab bit into her arm and closed her eyes as the water covered her face. Then, with a few mighty, deft swifts, she reached through the sand and pushed the mounds of earth back into the pit in which she lay. No one would be able to dig this deep, not during the harvest season. And Venice, she found, always had at least one thing going that kept them busy. Harvest season or not, no one had time to search the beach for the mistress of the night.

By the morning, the ocean's waves had erased any signs of her slumber place. She had vanished from Venice. They were safe from her, and she was safe from them. That was all that mattered. "Master," she called out just before sunrise with as much desperation as she could muster. A few weary flutters of her eyes and she was as asleep as she had ever been, and unsure if she would ever awake.

Time passed.

Then the sand was being removed and a heavy tarp was thrown over her body. Groggily, she began to resist, but the voice of the steward that had brought her that human sacrifice filtered through her sleepy mind. "Rest, mistress," he said boldly, though the sound of his voice told her he knew his life would be forfeit at any moment. She froze at that sound. "The sun is still just under the horizon," he explained quickly. "The master grows angry when his slaves are damaged." To a group of other slaves, the man barked, "Quickly now, get her into the wagon!"

She was wrapped in the tarp like a shawl and lifted clean out of the beach by the powerful arms of a giant of a man. By his scent she knew she had never tasted his blood. "A slave from the south, mistress," the steward said quickly. "One that has never been tormented by your bite, yet guarded in the halls of Venice all this time. The master has resources."

She was placed into the back of a wagon and a door was closed behind her. Curtains were drawn and sealed from the outside as well as the inside. Eventually, the coach began to move, and the sounds of the Mediterranean began to recede behind her to be replaced by nothing more than the blowing wind amongst the grain.

"You may come out now," said a male voice. "It is black as any night out here, and time has passed. The sun will not burn as brightly as before."

"We are passing over water," Aphrodite said as she ripped free of her makeshift death shroud. She could feel the wagon passing over a great empty expanse, and knew that such feelings could only come with being washed away into the depths of eternity and oblivion.

"Most people find such sensations uncomfortable," the voice of her master said through the darkness. The master was not alone and sensed her surprise. "This is your servant now," he confided. "His name is Basheem. If you must drink from someone on this journey, drink from him."

Through the darkness, she felt the slave obediently lift his wrist to her. She looked at her master for an explanation.

"Do not kill him," the master explained. "He has been promised the taste of immortality. But first he must be drained of his humanity."

Aphrodite looked up at the slave from somewhere in the south and then took his wrist and bit into him, drawing the blood out of him in a powerful gout. The sensations of moving and of being carried over water slowly faded in the face of her euphoria and the emotions her slave had given her.

Venice was being left behind.

Chapter Nine

All about him was shrouded in mist and darkness was taking hold. Exhausted, Christopher wanted nothing more than to lie down and pass into a restful sleep, but he knew that would never happen. In the distance, a waterfall played through the forests quietly, lulling him into a false sense of peace. Somewhere above him the monastery perched on the edge of the cliff, looking into the valley he hid in. He hoped that the cliffs and the darkness would be able to confuse the beast when he came awake, but Christopher was realistic as well. He was down here, in the darkness, hoping beyond hope that the creature, the demon, would get sidetracked by an animal and roam the forests instead of return to the monastery. Only time would tell what would happen, and Christopher dreaded waking up in a strange place only to find out he had done someone harm while he was asleep.

He lay down on the ground, too exhausted to take another step, and shivered from the cold. Yet he knew the demon would be oblivious to the weather, and that Christopher would not fall sick from exposure. Another mercy denied him.

He began to fall asleep, knowing it was useless to resist any longer.

In the time between sleep and awake, on the verge of unconsciousness, the wolf roared angrily and pounced at him in his mind's eye. Christopher knew the outcome of this battle, had suffered it every night for as long as he could remember. So he stood his ground and watched the demon lunge into the air with hate filled eyes.

At the last second, Christopher stepped out of the way and the beast sailed past him and roared with frustration as it lost its prey. The trees in the valley shook with the ferocity of the manifestation that came from Christopher's morphing lips.

The demon turned and faced Christopher, who was too numbed by the ongoing torment to fear the thing any longer. "Do your worst," he said to it, though he knew the creature could not understand him. "I won't try to stop you any longer."

The wolf blinked.

"I won't try to hurt you."

The wolf seemed puzzled and cocked its head to the side. It was a huge beast, larger than any natural wolf ever was. Its coat was of black and grey patches that rippled when the powerful creature flexed its supernatural muscles, preparing to pounce again.

"You have me," Christopher said, too tired to fight any longer. "There is no need to fight about it."

Then, the creature lunged, and Christopher did not bother to get out of its way.

Yet, despite the monster's open maw and dripping fangs, Christopher was not touched. Instead, the beast disappeared into Christopher's chest.

Startled from his dream, he opened his eyes to find himself in the body of a terrible monstrosity. Exhausted, he lifted his hands to his face and saw they were more claws than fingers.

The werewolf howled Christopher's unleashed grief into the valley and the trees shook.

Going down on all fours, the creature sprinted toward the waterfall, and Christopher barely clung on to consciousness as he watched the night blur by through the demon's eyes. The creature had taken control, like it always did. Yet from some place deep down inside, Christopher managed to stay conscious this time. He was powerless, and he felt each grotesque sensation from the demon course through him, even as the beast did. But too tired to do anything but remain paralysed somewhere behind the creature's eyes, it was the demon that roamed the night, not Christopher.

The werewolf stopped and smelled the air. The scent of game filled their nostrils, Christopher sensing the deer's presence just as the beast did.

"Go after it," Christopher said quietly, tired.

The wolf, needing no encouragement, agreed. Again, the night blurred past with frightful speed, and with the supernatural hearing of the creature,

Christopher heard the deer give flight somewhere in front of them. He smiled through the werewolf's maw as they broke from the trees onto a rocky ledge that led out of the valley, away from Signa Aquainnus and deeper into the uninhabited regions of the wild.

The deer was disappearing into the forest above them, perhaps two-hundred yards away. And the wolf, seeing its prey for the first time, gave chase with wild, untiring abandonment as its tongue lolled out of its head. The chase continued, though Christopher had no idea of how long. Then, inescapably, the werewolf overtook the deer and pulled it to the ground. Its powerful jaws ripped the terrified creature's throat out before it had time to suffer very much. And then the werewolf set in to devour its prize.

Exhausted beyond reason, Christopher finally dropped into sleep, knowing that Signa Aquainnus, or worse, Anderita, was safe for the night.

In his confused dreams, he thought he remembered the demon wolf approach and lay a bloody haunch of meat at his feet.

Christopher smiled sadly and said, "You go ahead. I can eat when we get back home."

Then, the wolf devoured even that.

Back at the monastery, Father Jason looked out over the expanding regions of wilderness and listened to the beast's howls. He sighed as he thought of his son, locked deep inside the monster's skull, and prayed that Christopher could find a way to stay sane for just one more night.

Yet sane he remained. In the morning, he awoke from the first good night's sleep he had in only God knew how long. He reached the monastery by noon and sought out Father Jason as quickly as he could. He was smiling when he found the man. "Father!" he said happily, embracing him. Then he held the priest at arm's length and looked triumphantly into his eyes. "The wolf can be tamed," he swore. "I'm sure of it."

That night, confident the battles would get easier; Christopher had the monks chain him to his cell well before the manifestations would begin.

"Are you sure about this?" one of them asked.

Christopher nodded. "Just make sure the door is locked, in case the chains break."

The monk's face paled. But he left with his companions and did what he was told.

Christopher was confident as he began to drift into sleep.

The wolf was there, waiting for him. It appeared right in front of his face and grinned wickedly. Then it pounced, and Christopher tried to reason with it, only to find the creature came at him with a single minded determination to do only one thing: make Christopher suffer. To the other inhabitants of Signa Aquainnus, it sounded like Christopher's spirit was devoured alive amongst a chorus of very real human screams of torment and demonic snarls and howls of rage.

The night never seemed to end.

In the morning, they came for him once the noise stopped. He was hanging limp in his chains. His wrists were bloody by the weight of cutting into the shackles, yet other than that, not a mark was on him. He fell into the arms of one of the monks and was lifted into his compassionate arms. The monks took him to a room with a couch in it and he collapsed, exhausted from his tortures, into the soft down cushions. Father Jason sat at a table in front of him.

It was an oak table, finely polished to a black glistening sheen, and a humble breakfast was laid out for Christopher, who looked at it longingly, though he was still too exhausted to join Jason at the table.

"How are you?" Jason asked.

"Tired," Christopher growled.

Jason flinched at the anger in the boy's voice.

"But very much human," he continued with a weak smile. "I realized something," he added.

Jason sat waiting for him to continue in patient silence.

"Only I can win this war. No one can do it for me. It's either me or the wolf, and the wolf feeds off of my emotions."

"Today is the day I ignore all the rules and learn to be free. I've been wondering about my life for some time now and I've come to the conclusion that all the self punishing acts of contrition that people, Godly people I'm sure, have suggested I do will never be enough to put to death the evil that I am. But there is goodness in me as well. There must be. Despite all the terror, from within and from without, the very fact that I am telling you this by the morning light, with the Holy Eucharist inside the sanctuary within these same halls surely proves that I am not all demon, as some have given to suggest."

Jason nodded. "I agree."

"So there must be at least a place where the Holy Spirit can burn inside my chest," Christopher continued. "There must be a place, no matter how small, inside my mind where I can escape to when I feel the onslaught of the beast from within, his awakening.

"Let this body decay. Madness will rule this planet whether the wolf hunts it or not. Sin has been here long before I ever set foot under a full moon.

"The Holy Spirit gives light. The beast is afraid of that light. My mind contains two people, and I am just sort of a substance that floats in between them, mixing them into some kind of half breed: half human, half wolf.

"So be it. There's nothing I can do about that. Still, there must be a greater light than the one I currently live in. There must be, if not a way to tame the beast, then a way to escape it entirely.

Jason looked at him, full of sorrow, yet amazed Christopher could endure for so long. "Is there anything we can do to help?"

Christopher shook his head wearily. "No. I know the answers already. But walking the path and knowing the path are two completely different things. I know that when the cravings of the beast awake, the presence of goodness goes away. I know that when the beast tires from his exploits he dies like a fire after there is nothing left to burn. Then, when all is vacant, the beast lies down and dies. And the Spirit of God reawakens me once again. I am rejuvenated and as my mind is rebuilt once again, the beast reawakens, feeding off of the goodness of my heart, the goodness placed there by the outside, by the source of all light.

"It is I who chose to fall away from this light. I might be driven by the madness within. I might be shaken and tormented by the dark desires of the beast. But ultimately, it is my choice to give in and take my attention off of God. Then everything goes dark and the cycle continues," Christopher admitted.

"Yet now, as I feel the cravings taking hold, I simply desire to die, to them and to everything else. I may not be able to stop them, but perhaps the demon will have nothing to take hold of. Perhaps they will simply pass me by, though they take my life with it. I am but a mortal man, after all. It is the war of the immortal world that rages within my bones, playing me like a tempest organ with two conductors fighting through the music that is my mind.

"There are two wolves fighting in each of us; a black wolf and a white one. It is the wolf I feed that wins, for this wolf has the strength I give it, while the other wolf has the weakness of neglect on its side."

Jason was speechless for a very long time as he looked at his weary son. Finally, he gathered his courage and spoke. "Don't you think you take too much credit?"

Christopher shook his head sadly. "Someone has to. If it's not me, then who?"

"Christ."

"What!" Christopher laughed bitterly. "What does he have to do with it?"

"He died so that you didn't have to."

"I've heard the stories," Christopher growled. "For all the good they do."

Jason looked around the room and made sure they were alone. The others, who had brought Christopher here, slipped out of the room discreetly and shut the door behind them.

Christopher watched them go, wondering what his father had in mind.

"Have you ever seen me eat?" he asked.

"What kind of a stupid question is that? Of course I've seen you eat!"

"Think carefully, Christopher," Jason said as he stood to his feet.

Christopher grew quiet as he thought back through the past. His eyes widened with surprise by what he found. "Just bread," he answered. "And only—"

" Very small amounts of it," Jason finished for him. "Yes."

"The Eucharist," Christopher said, eyes wide with disbelief.

"You're not the only one in this room who stalks the night," Jason admitted. "But you are the only one that is tormented by the creatures that hide in it."

"What are you saying?" Christopher asked. "That you can defeat a werewolf?"

Jason looked out the windows of their hidden sanctuary, at the vast wilderness stretching away from them as far as the eye could see. "No," he said. "I'm saying that I don't have to." Then he turned back to Christopher. "Let me show you something."

When Christopher nodded, Jason suddenly turned to a stone statue. The transformation happened so fast, that Christopher screamed in horror and jumped to his feet as he pressed himself tight against the wall.

The door opened, and in the time it took for Christopher to look from the monks rushing into the room and then back at Jason, the priest had already turned back to human flesh. "It's all right," he said to the monks. "The child just had a reminder of last night."

The monks, uncertain, looked at Christopher, still cowering on top of the couch next to them. He nodded and relaxed, and they left again.

When the door closed, Jason continued. "My body cannot die," he said. "I am possessed by a demon that won't ever let me die and burns me from the inside out with a hunger you will never be conscious enough to realize. Never."

"Are you so sure of that?" Christopher asked as he sank back into the couch.

"Yes. But when I turn to stone, the demon dies, for the time being. My thirst goes away, and I am restored." Jason looked into Christopher's eyes. "When I turn to stone, I die, and I am taken to Heaven, where there is no more pain, no more suffering, no more hunger."

"What is it you hunger for?" Christopher asked.

Jason shuddered. "I pray you'll never know."

"Then why don't you just remain as stone? Just know peace."

"Because of you," Jason answered. "I stay here because of you. Keep fighting Christopher. If I found a way, then I know you can too."

* * * * *

The air, held crisp with the burning lighting strikes that pierced the darkness with their sporadic flashes, was empty of noise and scent alike. Instinctively the beast knew to stay its paws from invading any buildings. So it roamed the streets, hunting them with its empty, enslaving passions. With a mindless hunger that would not be sated, it had been haunting these empty streets for many years, though the streets had long ago learned to be empty at night. The people cowered –though they denied it. They shuttered their windows and burned their lanterns brightly, though they laughed at such childish notions of fear to fill the emptiness they ran from. Boisterous noises made their way to the streets, revelry to bury the fear, smiles to hide the pain.

Many people had died in the night in this city. Many more had gone mad with fright. But the screams of terror had been reduced to whispers when they learned to watch the setting sun and note how much time was left before darkness descended upon them. The whispers of warning were exchanged with guarded knowing looks of fear and jars of ale were raised in denial of what stalked them.

Now, all that remained of the legacies of fear were children's' tales said with fascination to frighten each other, and always said in secrecy. Such tales were forbidden by adults, and certainly by priests.

Yet they knew. They all knew. Enough people had screamed; enough people had died. Some still did, as fortune would allow; they were the ones that found themselves out after dark and overwhelmed by the creature that lurked about the city.

It howled as the cravings flooded through it, giving their fear voice in the darkness, physical presence with no physical form. Hungry for more, yet empty from the addictions that drove the soul from the beast, it roamed ceaselessly, aimlessly, now trotting slowly, now sprinting with the speed of a wolf, now gliding from one shadow to the next with virtual invisibility, now and again howling suddenly with unexpected emotion, inhuman with its longing, its sorrow.

The moon waxed overhead, disappearing now and again as wisps of cloud drifted in front of it. But for the most part, it shed enough light to taunt the city with a false sense of daylight and with more than enough light for the beast to see by. The beast needed no light, and this was but a rare luxury.

The streets were empty. The beast knew that, yet it roamed, chasing the silence and emptiness as if these were a reflection of what was in its soul and longed to fill.

It stretched its senses in desperation or anger; it never knew which and was incapable of considering it. The darkness only grew more intense; the emptiness only became more severe, like a lantern that had only been turned up to cast its hideous light with brighter intensity.

Then, with random unexpectency, it stumbled to the front of a cross, a stone statue some artisan had carved and left in the streets. It stood upright and embedded into a stone block that could have served as a carving for a tomb. The artist had chiselled a flowering vice over the cross, entwining it as it wrapped its way around and around the stone statue until the statue was covered with leaves of stone and blossoms and the immortal cord of a stone vine, as though the plant took its nourishment from the cross, as though its roots were embedded and hidden deeply under the foliage.

The beast stopped and watched with curiosity as it sensed some kind of presence from the stone, as though the cross or the vine was alive.

A fire ignited from nowhere, burning dully and giving off a yellow and orange light that flickered the shadows of the night until the entire rock statue, cross, vine, and platform, were on fire and awash with an unwavering light.

The beast watched the strange fire fearlessly, with an interest kindled by the alien sight of what it witnessed. Then, slowly, the fire seemed to ignite upon the stone of its own dead intellect. Though the beast's coat of fur remained untouched by any physical fire, it felt the unearthly heat radiating from its chest, and slowly, it sank to its knees with the strange burning pain as it stared at the cross and the strange manifestation upon it.

As the heat spread throughout its body, it felt a gentle and subtle awakening of its consciousness, as though some part of it, some piece of its soul, once cast out, now returned and forced itself into the beast, merging with it and fighting with it, though the empty soul of the maddened monster put up little enough of a fight.

The wolf simply seemed to vanish, like a candle flame with no more wick and no more wax to burn. In its place, in the body of a beast, where once an empty host of addictions once raged, now a holy fire burned, and the intellect of a man slowly surfaced in the mind, taking up residence in the empty places where only darkness had been before.

Christopher looked down at the coarse fur of the beast upon his arms and bare chest. He knew this beastly form was his and he belonged to it, as his rightful place in creation.

He seemed to remember, though he was only admitting to himself, all the ghastly gruesome acts this body had performed, and he fell before the cross, weeping uncontrollably at his own shame, at the unrighteousness and the evil that was his soul.

Words of regret, of apology, of sorrow and repentance fell deformed into the emptiness between him and the cross, sounding more like the growling whines of a dog than the utterances of an intelligible human being.

Peace descended with her gentle, invisible wings of light and the tears he did not know were there ceased to dampen the face of a wolf as he stared at the heavenly light in wonder, in awe.

Silently, he smiled. He did not know how long he remained there, how long he stared at the stone cross and its strange light. But when he came to he saw with a quick glance to the sky that dawn was fast approaching. The moon had set and the night was pitched in darkness.

All the better, Christopher said to himself. He did not want to be seen this night, nor did he want his passage marked for fear of blame being placed where blame was not deserved.

When he looked back, the cross was once again only a stone statue. The strange unearthly flame had gone out.

* * * * *

Wary of the approaching dawn, Christopher made his way back to the monastery.

A monk appeared near the front gates, out of the shadows. He seemed frightened and confused and wanted only to hide from the monster Christopher now knew he was. He looked at Christopher silently for a long time. With predator sharp instincts, Christopher assumed he was desperately trying to understand what was different about the monster.

"What is it, brother?" Christopher asked in his beastly form. "Cat got your tongue?" He laughed at his own joke, though it came out as a growl that erupted into a howl he bitterly cut short.

The monk was wide eyed with fear.

"I usually come over the wall in the back, I know," Christopher said.

The brother only nodded. His eyes were as wide as saucers and his mouth was open.

"Do not fear, brother," Christopher said quietly. He was noticing if he talked quietly, his voice sounded more human. He stood there, waiting for the monk to react. When he didn't, Christopher gestured toward the gate. "Well. Open it, will you?"

The monk nodded and jumped to do his bidding, fumbling with a great set of keys and looking over his shoulder at Christopher, afraid to expose his back.

"I am tired of climbing over walls," Christopher admitted.

The doors were unlocked and the monk pushed them open. As he did, the first ray of the sun struck the horizon.

"I'm tired of doing a lot of things," Christopher said in a much more human tone. His transformation was already taking place.

Startled, the monk turned back to see the very human, very weary and sorrowful Christopher Aquainnus standing before him in naught but a pair of leggings.

"I am tired of a lot of things," he repeated as he trudged through the gates and into the courtyard beyond.

The monk only stared in silence.

"Waken Father Jason, would you?" Christopher asked. "Tell him I will meet him in confession."

"Of course," the monk stammered with a nod. "Right away." He set out at a run, leaving the gate and its keys in Christopher's care.

He shook his head and sighed, closed the gate, and pocketed the keys. He would give them to Father Jason the first chance he got.

Chapter Ten

Deep into the wilderness and the unnamed hamlets of the Carolingian empire, Aphrodite travelled with the priest vampire from Egypt known only as the master. They had spent at least two-hundred years plaguing Venice and the Mediterranean Sea, though they had spent very little time together, choosing instead to live in solitude with their own devices as vampires.

For all that time spent, Aphrodite had nothing to show for it except a plethora of lost experiences from a dying population. The master sustained her on their trip with a caravan of servants and chariots, wagons and horsemen, with tents packed on the backs of stubborn camels, and donkeys carrying the weight of a household of servants and slaves, jewels and trade goods from the Mediterranean. They were travelling north, and their riches would only increase as they passed through the scarcely populated regions between the Mediterranean and the Atlantic Ocean.

When they reached the Danube, they began to pick their way west, rather than risk a crossing. And it was between the Rhine and the Danube that the master's other slaves found the statue. It was a lifelike statue of a frozen human pointing with an outstretched arm toward the east, heralding an unknown region and the mouth of the Danube. The caravan had come across it during the day, and overtaken by the lifelike details of the statue, had decided to risk the master's wrath and wait until the night that he may see the statue and what it might portent.

Slow to punishing his servants before understanding what had taken place, the master had been taken to the place early, before Aphrodite had risen. When she found out through her slave what was happening, she had left the safety of her carriage and had found the master shortly after, staring into the face of a man, not taller than himself. The two seemed locked in a conversation only they could hear, and not wanting to break the master's concentration, she crept up silently behind him to peer into the statue's unblinking stare as it pointing back toward the Mediterranean.

The statue was utterly dead, made only of rock, though with a human countenance that only the greatest of sculptors would be able to capture.

Aphrodite looked at the back of the master, dressed still in black silk with his shining ruby ring, then back at the statue. There was something eerily similar to the two of them, the way they stood frozen in front of each other. Then she had it. This statue was not of a human, but of a vampire, and her skin began to crawl as she realized that this thing was alive, though untouchable by her young senses. She waited patiently through most of the night.

The dawn was touching the horizon with a painful brilliance, and still she stood with the master before the monstrosity of the creature before her. What end had this thing met that could so take her over as well? What unknown danger of the night had overtaken this god of death and how long had he stood here under the sun's full brilliance, impartial in his stone sleep? She prayed desperately to the dark that she may never know, and was pulled out of her own shallow trance when the master suddenly stirred in front of her. The sun had almost touched the horizon.

"Back to the carriage," he said quickly as he glided past her.

She followed and asked, "What was that?"

"A vampire," he answered.

"What could have killed it like that?" she asked.

"Vampires don't die, fledgling," he said as she pushed the door to their carriage open. Without looking at her, he climbed into its sealed darkness and prepared himself for the day's travel. She followed and when she had settled next to her slave on the other side of the carriage, he said. "They only fall asleep."

"Where was he pointing to?" she asked, shuddering at the thought of standing under the sun like that, in frozen slumber.

"Romania," he answered distantly. "He was pointing the way to Romania."

Then the carriage began to move, and the master would speak no more. Aphrodite held her tongue and closed her eyes to the oncoming sunlight.

* * * * *

They boarded passage on a ship travelling north along the Rhine, and Aphrodite could not help but feel the master was choosing to hasten their distance between them and the infamous living statue behind them. He seemed distant, uneasy, and spent much of the night alone lost in thought. He would not be disturbed, as if he could not hear what went on around him, and Aphrodite began to suspect the statue had told him much that was not revealed to her. She left him to his melancholy and feasted on the hamlets they passed through as they traveled closer toward the Atlantic Ocean.

One small farming community sat huddled against a tall brick building in the centre of their village. While the huts that surrounded it were made of wood and straw held together with mud, this place sported a polished oak door and glass windows. Intrigued by the paradox, she was drawn to the building curiously, wondering what could be worth so much to simple people.

The ship and all of the master's wealth was kept out in the centre of the river, away from both banks and any chance of being at risk of invasion. Though Aphrodite could think of nothing that would warrant any such caution, she nonetheless left the master to his paranoia and crept up onto the bank of the hamlet soundlessly. While the water sluiced off of her body, she giddily reminded herself she was naked, and that she should not draw attention to herself this night, lest she invoke the master's wrath.

"Gold," Aphrodite muttered to herself as she crept from the bank. There was only one reason in her mind that could justify why these poor creatures would live in mud while in their midst, almost built right into the sides of most of their homes, was a mansion of unspeakable wealth for those parts. And she would have it. It had shamed her how she had been driven from Venice by a princess with wealth that could outmatch the master's. Further, it shamed her that when they went into Venice together, he was as poor as she. Now, it was he that controlled the riches in the hull of his ship. And it was she who had barely escaped Venice with nothing more than the clothes on her back. And those had been soiled by the bank of the Mediterranean.

This seemed as good a place as any to begin massing her own wealth. And after two-hundred years of indulging herself with no thought to her future, she realized she could have any future she wished.

The night was still. There was enough light gleaming off the banks of the river from the moon above that even a mortal could see by it. But the clouds were out as well, and there was a wind high above. Shadows flickered over the sleeping hamlet and its mysterious building, and she easily traversed through these, too fast for human reason to follow. In seconds, she stood before two huge, double doors of planked oak held together with iron bracings. She braced herself and pushed, and the doors slammed open under her supernatural strength.

A large room, as large as any she'd ever seen, stretched out before her. The vaulted ceiling loomed up into shadowed darkness, and benches lined a centre isle she stood before. Directly before her, on the wall opposite, was an immense cross with the figure of a man nailed to it. She flinched at the sight, remembering the cross in the child's hands that had burned her so brilliantly. Yet, this statue had no supernatural light to it, nor did its cross, and the room remained in darkness. Below this figure was a smaller golden cross. "Yes," Aphrodite hissed when she saw it. Such a treasure would make a good start to her fortunes, a very good start. She strode into the building fearlessly, confident and anxious to take the treasure for herself.

"Who goes there?" someone asked as candle light emerged from a side passage. She looked at the man in the simple wool robe and smiled again. He wore a wooden cross around his neck, but this cross was also dead of any power to burn her. He didn't see her right away, and she guessed it was because of the candle in his hands. He was shut away into a cocoon of candlelight, but his soul was surrounded by a wall of darkness thicker than the natural shadows she hid in.

She did not slow her pace and met him at the front of the room. His eyes widened when he saw her, and then they widened some more when he took a good look at her.

Aphrodite followed his gaze and looked down at her body. She was still naked. And she was dripping wet from the river she had crawled out of.

"You're naked," he muttered, surprised beyond being able to mutter more.

She did not slow her pace and reached under his robe, moving too quickly for him to put up a startled resistance. In a moment, her hand found what it was looking for and his eye lids began to twitch. When he moaned in ecstasy, she took him by the shoulder with her other hand and pushed him to the floor. He did not resist, and in a moment, she was on top of him, thrusting her hips over his to an unending chorus of surprised and ecstatic groans.

Aphrodite snorted with contempt at how easy it had been, and now that he was within her clutches, she could truly have him at any time, and he would not even know what had happened.

Unable to restrain herself any longer, she sank down upon him and pushed his chin away from her. He did not try to stop her. She could feel his jugular pulsing under his skin. She closed her eyes and prepared for the glorious sensations that were about to take place and sank her teeth gently, ever so gently, into his neck. Immediately, he was paralysed, and like a fly caught in a spider's web, he was hers to suck dry. She would take her time with this one, drawing out her drinking as she held him tight in her swaying, rhythmic embrace. She began to moan as well, ignoring the fact that his mutterings had turned to something begging for mercy, rather than a longing for more.

Yet what he asked for now was the same as what he asked for not too long ago, and she would not be cheated her reward for his eager cooperation. It wasn't her fault the crosses did not burn her, and in the face of these ancient symbols of power and superiority to her life in the darkness, she could not help but relish her victory, nor would she deny herself the chance to take as much of that victory as she could. She tried not to shudder as she remembered that first cross and drank deeply of her victim's life.

"What is going on in here?" another man roared.

Instantaneously, fire fell from above and sheathed her in searing heat. The crosses at the front of the room, mere feet away, flared to life with such a searing light, Aphrodite screamed as she tore her fangs from her victim's neck. She was blinded as the light filled the entire building, and she screamed again when she began to feel the fire consuming her flesh.

She stumbled to her feet, the victim between her legs and between her teeth forgotten. Then she ran blindly from the room. Though she could not see, and the pain was not allowing her to think straight, she still remembered where the doors were, and was able to back track through the blinding pain. She stumbled against one of the benches and spun onto her back. But she was on her feet again within the moment, and continued to scream in an undisturbed cry of anguish as she fled the building and threw herself into the dark waters of the Rhine.

The master sat on a reclining chair placed on the deck of his ship. The ruby on his finger shone in the moonlight as he held his hand in his chin in thoughtful, deep contemplation of what he had witnessed. He knew she would survive, though she had been utterly beaten. Yet despite what he kept trying to tell her, vampires could die, and now he knew what could do it. He remained where he was, motionless, staring out across the waters to the church and its inner power, a power he could now see, now that he knew what to look for.

A few hours later, Aphrodite pulled herself from the Rhine onto the deck of his ship. He was tired of existence and the endless passage of time. He was tired of the predictable sense of loss that came with the unravelling of any finite lie worn away and exposed by the merciless wrath of the days' never ending. Iminuetep looked at Aphrodite as, charred and burned and full of anger, she crawled out of the river. Her skin was parched black, yet her womanly figure was undamaged. Once she slept, she would be restored, and she was hungry now, ravenous for an experience that would help her forget what had happened that night.

Nothing would help her forget.

She stared back at him, as if unaware that his attention was on her at all.

The master did not acknowledge her as she made a few tenuous steps toward him. His gaze was locked upon that building. She stopped when she realized her advances were being utterly ignored. And chastised, she turned and headed below deck. At the hatch leading below, she turned and looked back at her master. He had not moved, not one tiny bit.

"You look like that sun gazer," she scolded. She stared at him for a moment longer before she realized he was not going to answer her. Then she stormed below deck, pain fuelling her anger.

Pointedly, he forgot her and looked back across the waters to the church that stood sheathed in mystery and the night. Her words had struck a chord of life in him. It was from this building that she had come screaming out of. She was not invincible, she was not indestructible. And though inexperienced and naive as she was, the powerful Aphrodite, locked under the Mediterranean for time uncountable, was one of the most powerful creatures Iminuetep had ever known. If this vampire could be defeated, then surely any vampire could.

There was a higher power than Iminuetep, still. And bored to death with eternity, Iminuetep had nothing left to do but discover who or what this higher power was. He remained motionless throughout the night, contemplating such things as his gaze kept fast upon the sleeping hamlet and its mysterious church. Then, just before sunrise, Iminuetep stirred from his contemplations and went below deck. He had not fed that night, yet he had no interest in feeding his passions any longer. He climbed into the empty coffin next to hers and closed the lid over himself.

The ship set sail not long after, and began its slow and steady trek down river, toward the Atlantic Ocean.

Chapter Eleven

The sun was setting.

Christopher watched it from the solitude of a quiet glen of trees tucked away from the monastery. He was perched on a cliff, and his feet dangled over the edge of a steep valley whose floor was hidden from view by the dense foliage of leviathan evergreens. Yet it was the sun that caught his attention. Two monks sat nearby, discreetly giving him room, yet close enough to beat back the demon that could lurch from him uncontrollably at any moment. And the sun was setting.

He waited until the very last moment and then sprang from his perch and sprinted out of the trees. The monks followed, though without protest. Yet Christopher outran them both. And while the werewolf began to tear through his skin, he fed it his desire to run, to run and run. And run. The wolf listened as it took control and they sprinted into the underbrush and a path that led toward the sun, to the west and out of harm's way.

The monks, now labouring dutifully to keep up, gave up the chase in relief and panted desperately as they watched the creature and Christopher disappear into the oncoming night.

Jason watched Christopher and the wolf from the tall windows of his study. He could just see them disappear and then reappear as the trees hid his view. For weeks, he'd been watching Christopher carefully, wondering when this day would come. Far off in distance, deep in the night when Christopher was usually fast asleep under the howling madness of what haunted him, a similar cry would pierce the wilderness while the wolf ranted in the catacombs far underneath Signa Aquainnus. Knowing what that sound meant to the inhabitants of the uncharted wilderness behind their monastery, Jason had suggested Christopher take this night into the wilds. His son had hastily agreed, knowing there was less of a chance to do harm away from people than there was in the monastery. Jason had stoically kept his peace. Only time would tell what would happen, and he had to let his son go sooner or later.

They ran for hours, undisturbed and in peaceful bliss. Patches of moonlight filtered through the trees, altering the terrain from pitch black to a silvery surreal blur that seemed like the water of a silver stream they swam through with powerful, untiring strokes. Christopher had wanted to run west when he began to tire of fighting the beast back, so when the beast came forth, he ran west, never veering from his path, never stopping to stalk a kill.

Eventually, the terrain began to change. They entered into new territory, places within the uncharted wilderness Christopher had never been before. He doubted anyone had been, and began to wonder how they would get back to the monastery without endangering anyone. Then he laughed, and the beast stopped to howl into the night. It didn't matter anyway. Christopher was ready to sacrifice his life to prevent the creature from hurting someone else.

Heaven knew he had died enough times before.

As the werewolf's howls died into the night, the creature froze, instinctively testing the air for a response. Christopher could never understand why the creature did this, but then another howl echoed through the trees and the hackles on the werewolf's neck rose. The creature was terrified. And Christopher, able to feel and be tormented by everything that the werewolf experienced, was just as terrified, and filled with a loathing of what was to come.

When the strange howl dimmed away, the werewolf answered it. And the other answered that.

They did this for a while, and then grew bored of the game, seemingly at the same time. Then both grew angry that the game ended.

The trees melded together in a blur as the werewolf went to all fours. He tore at the ground with each powerful paw that pushed him forward. Wind filled their ears in a deafening rush, yet Christopher had no compunction about the werewolf's limitations. He could hear through this racket, even as he tore through underbrush and branches both.

The other wolf was doing the same.

They crashed into each other with a chorus of furious snarls and barred teeth. Their eyes glinted in the darkness, shining with inhuman rage, and they ripped mindlessly into each other with a savage hatred that sent Christopher reeling on the brink of unconsciousness. Knowing he was about to lose control, he fell into a dream and watched the wolf snarl in its full fury. Christopher sank to his knees and looked past the wolf. "I cannot hold this creature any more," he prayed. "Into your hands, I commit him." Then he went reeling into unconsciousness as the wolf jumped forward.

He awoke in a horse stall. He was curled on his side on a pile of hay. His shoulders were aching from the wounds the wolf had earned during the night, yet his body had not a bruise or cut on it. The injuries would have faded as the wolf relinquished control. Sunlight filtered through the dusty air and the quiet nicker of a horse came from another stall not far off.

Christopher was too confused to move. He did not recognize where he was, and he couldn't imagine what had taken the wolf here and left the horses unafraid and undisturbed in their stalls. Whatever had happened left him as terrified as he was of the wolf.

Eventually, he heard footsteps approaching from outside. Still too disorientated to understand completely what was happening, he remained where he was and waited for the person, whoever it might be, to find him.

The doors of the barn opened, though Christopher could not see them from where he lay in his stall. Only an ocean of dusty sunlight opened up onto the barn, announcing for good that morning had come and the wolf was safely locked back in its cage. Christopher exhaled as he relaxed a little, and listened as the footsteps shuffled closer to his stall.

All at once, the head and shoulders of a young woman appeared over the stall, and she cried out when she saw Christopher, then gasped as her eyes widened when she saw that he was naked. She paled, and then blushed, and then screamed.

"Wait!" Christopher cried, jumping to his feet. "It's all right."

He saw all at once that she was a nun by the dark robes she wore.

The wolf had probably recognized this sheltered convent and thought to come here to heal from its wounds.

The nun screamed again and ran from the barn.

Exasperated, Christopher rolled his eyes and then chased after her.

The nun had gained a good distance on him, and he was surprised at how fast she could run. Still, he was gaining on her when she disappeared into a side door of the convent and slammed it shut behind her. Christopher crashed through the door a moment later, hardly slowing from the impact.

He slid to a stop as he came face to face with an angry, elderly sister who wore the weight of authority as plainly seen as she did the robes of a Mother Superior. He was in her study. Sunlight shone through open windows onto a broad, oaken desk. White drapes flared as the light summer breeze blew through the room. Beside him was a statue of the Blessed Mother, and on the other side of her was another door Christopher guessed would open onto the rest of the sanctuary. There was a bookshelf lining one wall, and a couch of brown cloth sat in front of it. The Mother Superior's desk sat facing the couch. She stood behind that desk, while the lady Christopher had been chasing was standing next to her in front of it. While the Mother Superior scowled with open hostility, the other nun was as pale as ever with her wide eyes staring unblinkingly at Christopher. Her mouth was covered with one of her hands, as though she had to forcefully stop herself from screaming again. Her other hand held her wrist tightly, adding its strength to the first.

Christopher looked down to see that he stood naked in front of the women.

"I'm not a demon!" he cried reflexively as he brought his hands up in front of him, preparing to ward off any attack that might come.

The younger woman began to faint, and Christopher rushed to her side and held her up in time to stop her from crashing to the floor.

"Get your filthy hands off her!" the Mother Superior roared.

He ignored her and helped the fainting woman to the couch.

The Mother Superior roared in outrage and flew at Christopher, flailing against him, screaming in rage and beating against his chest and shoulders. Each blow was surprisingly strong, yet after what Christopher had endured, he only stepped back and tolerated the Mother Superior's angry flailing calmly, stoically. Quickly enough, she realized he was not threatening her or the other lady. She calmed, and then stopped to glare at him in silence.

"Where is the wolf?" the young lady who had found him asked once the Mother Superior had stopped pummelling Christopher.

He ignored her. "Mother Superior," he said. "I need clothes. And a fast horse. I need to get back to Signa Aquainnus as fast as possible."

"And who are you?" the Mother Superior asked through her brooding.

"I am Christopher Aquainnus," he answered honestly enough. "Father Jason is my adopted father."

"He will hear of this," she swore.

Christopher tried to suppress his smile. "Yes," he said. "He certainly will."

"Sister," the Mother Superior barked. "Get him some clothes. And you!" she spat as she pointed a shaking finger into Christopher's face. "Cover yourself! Use a cushion or something!"

He nodded and sat down on the couch as far away from the nun as he could. Then he ripped a cushion off of the couch and did what he was told. He sat motionless, staring out into the space in front of him and doing his best to ignore both the women.

"Where is the wolf?" the sister asked again.

Christopher glanced at her experimentally to see that she was still staring at him with those wide eyes of hers. He looked away again, back to his focus point on the far wall. "I am the wolf," he admitted.

The sister gasped.

"Go!" the Mother Superior screamed. "Go now! And tell no one of this!"

The sister fled the room in terror.

"And be quick!" the Mother Superior shouted after her.

"Margarette is a little shy," the Mother Superior said angrily. Christopher sighed as she sat down at her desk, discreetly covering his naked form from her view. All she could see was the child of Father Jason Aquainnus; she was no longer distracted. She gave him a moment to feel safe. "Why are you here?"

Christopher swallowed his fear. "I have been charged with caging a beast," he said at last. "Sometimes the beast gets out, and I then become responsible for making sure it doesn't hurt anything."

The Mother Superior said nothing, sensing he was not finished.

"So far, he has done well," he said. "He is learning to love. Yet last night he found one of its kind. The fact that we made it here tells me he won." Now Christopher watched the Mother Superior carefully. "You won't have any more wolf problems for a long, long time."

A single tear of gratitude rolled down the kind lady's cheek. "Stay in the hallway!" she yelled as she pointed at the closed door." When Christopher jumped, she smiled and said, "Margarette is also the most curious of us all, though as tight lipped as they come."

Christopher sighed in relief.

"Our three fastest horses," she said with finality. "And two of our best riders to accompany you. They will know the trails between here and there better than you."

The sister, Margarette, finally came boldly through the door and threw a pile of clothes at him as she passed by on her way to the door she had fled through, the one that still lay off its hinges. "They might be a little tight," she

137

said. "They're made for riding." With that, she was gone, leaving Christopher to blink in shock at the Mother Superior. Sister Margarette was already striding across the lawns between the stable and the convent.

"We leave immediately," the Mother Superior said as she rose to her feet.

"Doesn't it take time to saddle the horses," Christopher said as he came to his feet as well, holding the clothes in front of him.

The Mother Superior laughed. "Get dressed," she commanded fiercely as she followed the nun out.

Christopher stood motionless, in shock.

"We don't want to have to wait for you!" she called across the lawns.

They galloped into Signa Aquainnus before midday and made it into the stables without being seen. "Very few of us know about the wolf," Christopher confided as he closed the stable doors behind them.

Margarette dismounted and looked around the stable disapprovingly. "Men," she said, shaking her head at the way the stables were kept. Then she looked around at the horses and their stalls a second time. "Where does the wolf sleep?" she asked.

"There are catacombs underneath the monastery," Christopher said. "This place was a Roman Fort before we found it. Father Jason has converted one of the catacombs to a holding cell for the wolf." He looked from one nun to another. "I sleep chained to one of the walls."

Even the Mother Superior paled as Margarette gasped and held her hand in front of her mouth.

"Stay here," Christopher said. "Let me get my father." Then he slipped from the stable and went to fetch a robe that would hide him amidst the other monks living there.

* * * * *

The lowly scribe passed into the halls of the great monastery. Timid from the majesty there, he kept his head down and headed for the doors at the end of the grand hall. Other monks, head bowed, hands clasped before them in prayer, went about their chores in the grander scheme of things. They were invisible to the one lone monk, and he too them.

The doors, though tall and made out of solid oak panels, swung away from the monk's push and crashed against the rock walls on either side. Christopher couldn't help but take satisfaction in how close they came to shattering.

Father Jason looked up from his maps spread across a table at the front of the colonnade. He smiled when he saw Christopher's purposeful gait. "Ah, the triumphing hero has returned!"

"If I remember correctly, that was fine wine," Christopher said bluntly. He strode across the space between him and his father with those same meaningful imposing strides, not the measured gait of a scribe. "Ah," Christopher said loudly, draining the wine and then admiring the glass in his hand. If it once held wine, it was a great glass worthy of appreciation.

"You make a mistake," Christopher said with eyes full of mock surprise. With no warning, Christopher tossed the glass at the priest's head. He caught the priceless glass. He too cherished the vintage of victory. "The closest thing I've had to human food in days," Christopher accused as he strode past the priest.

They both knew what he meant by that, as did everyone else in the room. It did not affect a thing.

"Did you manage to track the other wolf?" the priest asked.

"No," Christopher said, surprised his father knew about that. He looked around the room for more wine. He found the wine bottle easy enough, not needing to read the label to know its value. He unstoppered the bottle and looked at the priest and nodded toward the glass in his hand.

The priest levelled him a commanding stare as he asked, "Then what happened?"

Giving up, Christopher reached for the matching glass that stood always at the ready. This one was clean. He hesitated for only a moment before he looked over at the father. He tossed the wine bottle from one hand to another. "May I?" Christopher asked respectfully.

Jason smiled. "Of course. Just make sure it's clean and put back in its place before you leave." He looked down at the maps and charts scattered across the table at his side.

Christopher poured the glass full as he watched the maps as well. "That mountain range is barren in the spring," Christopher said.

"So?"

"So the creature came into the cover of the lowlands, where it plagued a convent. After I fell asleep, the wolf within me won and made it to that convent before I woke up."

Father Jason looked up, worried. But Christopher's attention was locked on the map as his finger stayed pressing it to the table. He remained silent as he drank the wine in his hand. In time, he looked at the father again.

"I'm sorry. The Mother Superior and another sister are waiting for us in the stables."

He didn't ask why, only blinked and nodded his acceptance of the facts. Finally, the priest nodded. He was silent for a long time while he contemplated their next move. "So be it," he said, finally looking up from the map. He tossed his own wine glass at Christopher, who caught it menacingly.

"Come with me," he said. "It's time you introduced me to our two guests." The Father waved at the doors while two priests standing nearby jumped to move the massive hinges.

Christopher followed with a wine glass in either hand. He placed them in the care of another monk. Surprised, the man looked up and met his gaze. Christopher only growled until he saw fear in his eyes.

The monk nodded and turned away as Christopher hurried after the priest.

Both wine glasses were carefully washed and put back in their proper place next to the bottle of red wine.

Chapter Twelve

Orleans. A sprawling metropolis not much different than Venice, Aphrodite nonetheless found the rolling hillsides and the encroaching forests soothing, even if she found the cramped city of human meat a little unsettling. She had become a huntress since that night on the River Rhine. Not wanting to be caught by flames from a Hell she could not imagine, she stalked her prey silently, often for more than one night, looking for any clue of that divine power that might light her up like a torch.

There was no outward sign that could discern who was safe prey and who was bait for a trap. The crosses were becoming popular, and as more and more people wore them, other amulets were added to the religious fervour that surrounded them. Yet there was always prey to be had. Though many of her would be victims seemed wrapped in unapproachable light if she looked at them a certain way, others, no matter how they appeared outwardly, were filled with the kind of darkness Aphrodite relished, and these people she stalked confidently, waiting only for a chance to not be disturbed before she sent them to their own hells and fed her with their experiences and their memories, the very essence of who they were.

She struck continuously, yet sparingly. Fear of another Venice kept her wary of revealing too much about herself, yet the streets of Orleans still flowed with the blood of her victims. She did not bother with disease. She struck and killed on a nightly basis, sometimes twice in one night. The old, the young, the lost, the drunk, the destitute, the rich, the healthy; it did not matter. If they embraced darkness within their lives, they gave a telltale sign of not being associated with that mysterious light of those religious amulets. By rights, these belonged to her.

The master remained close at first. They settled into a manor on the outskirts of the city, using much of his wealth to buy the property and ensure they had enough privacy to remain undiscovered for a long, long time. But as the years wore on in perpetual continuity, she saw less and less of him; in part because she returned less and less to his manor, and in part because if he was around, he chose to mask his presence from her, and it mattered little to her either way. His demands were only that she help sate his dark desires, which were also her own. And the two got along remarkably well, compared to the helpless friction she always saw in humans. Neither she nor her master cared enough about the other to find friction worth fighting over. They had no desire to grow closer together. They had no invisible bond that demanded they find some fulfilment in the other's indulgences. They simply did not care. And they certainly did not care about each other.

One night, as the wind swayed the forest trees around her, she descended into the city to find what may be found. The master had risen with her, and without a word had left toward the southeast.

She kept a small villa within the city now, and it was here that she came first. The gate was locked and undisturbed. The walls were too high to climb, and the weeds around the place showed no signs of being disturbed. Good. That was good. Though no one would be able to find her treasure buried deep within the floor, she preferred the place was left alone. This was her domain, her own refuge. And as far as she could tell, not even the master knew about it. Though it would matter little in the long run if a mortal were to stumble into here, she still liked to have that one piece of reliable routine that never changed: that one constant in her life. Her villa was that constant. The bones of many of her victims littered the floor, long since rotten and picked clean by the buzzing flies and rats that overran the place.

She went into the main house, not bothering to close the door. The temperatures from the outside could not disturb her, and she only wanted to relax in solitude for a moment before she began her hunt for the evening. The night was quiet and she could hear the wind off the hills in the distance. People were sleeping, yet others were awake, many others were awake. These people, these night crawlers, were out and about every night, wandering through the streets as grapes to be plucked from the vine. Most of them were busy getting drunk, but still others just wandered, too restless to be able to sleep. She hunted them all.

But right now, she just listened to the wind, and felt the presence of the night as one eternal, never ending abyss that she was swallowed up in, like being on the bottom of the Mediterranean for all those countless years, separated from the passage of time by the death of Kerisa so many years ago.

Her contemplations were disturbed by a crash at her gate, followed by another one that rendered the gate useless and burst it open. Curious, she walked to the front door to see eight men stumble into her villa. They were angry looking, and definitely not from these parts. They were soldiers, of a sort, but lacking in discipline and order. They were dirty fellows, with blood and dirt on their clothes and searching, hungry eyes. They carried their luggage with them, and weapons, and large sacks of leather she could only guess carried their plunder.

She leaned against the doorpost to the threshold of her house and crossed her arms. They stared back at her, taken back by the fearlessness in her posture. A few of them noticed the skeletons of the dead lying around the place, thrown where they now rested when Aphrodite had tossed them aside. None of them seemed afraid.

"Welcome to my home," Aphrodite said sarcastically. She made no move toward them, content for the moment to look at them from across the courtyard separating them.

A few of the men made a move toward her, but were held back by their companions. "We need this place for shelter," one of them said, apparently the leader. It was not a request. He spoke with a rich accent.

Aphrodite laughed. "If the price is right," she said. "You may keep it."

Again, one of the men made to walk toward her, but he was restrained.

The leader only looked at her as if she were mad. "We will not pay," he snorted. "It is you who will pay."

At that, the man that was so interested in dying was finally allowed to cross the distance between them. The others watched as he came toward her, and they remained where they were in frozen terror as she sucked the life from him and cast him aside. She made the death quick, pulling the blood from his neck as fast as she could. It had only taken a few moments, yet all the while; she had kept her eyes locked on the leader of these raiders while his man died in her arms.

Satisfied for the time being, she stretched her arms and inhaled, relishing in her kill. The night was still young and full of promise with so many men trapped within her villa. "Who's next?" she asked casually.

No one moved toward her.

"Who are you?" the leader finally asked.

"I am known as death's mistress in Venice," she answered truthfully. "My name is Aphrodite."

"Aphrodite," he repeated. He would never forget that name.

"What's in the bags?" she asked, nodding to the leather sacks over the shoulders of a few of the men.

The leader motioned for them to dispose of the bags, and the men carrying them stepped forward. Taking turns, with much bravado, they spilled the contents into a heap in front of her. She was right. It was plunder; gold, silver, jewels, all intricately crafted into beautiful displays of craftsmanship in everything from plates to necklaces. In all, the plunder could hardly compare to the wealth Aphrodite had hidden within the villa, but it was interesting to see what mortals considered wealth. As the last of the men took his turn and upended his sack onto the growing pile, Aphrodite's interest changed. Last to spill from the sack was a golden cross, identical to the one that had helped drive Aphrodite screaming from the hamlet along the banks of the River Rhine.

"Where did you get that?" she asked, wide eyed and in awe.

"Deep in the wilderness," the leader said suspiciously. "In a hamlet on the bank of—"

"—the Rhine," she finished for him, never taking her eyes from the cross. "I will buy it from you," she said breathily, looking up at the leader of these raiders.

"If the price is right," he mimicked. "You may keep it."

Without another word, she left them and went back into her house. She had to have that cross. She had no illusions as to what these men had done to that building and its amulets that could burn her so painfully. But this cross, taken from that place, was just a gold statue, and lacked its power, had been stripped of its power. What a trophy! She had to have it. She was obsessed with having it.

Using her supernatural speed and strength, she tore at the floor of her house and dug up the earth with her hands. In a few moments, she pulled a large, oaken chest from the pit she had made and hauled it into the courtyard. The raider's eyes went wide as she upended the chest, much larger than the combined weight the leather sacks had been, into a pile of her own. Gold, silver, copper coins, diamond necklaces, opal statues, jade and ivory, rare and priceless trinkets of immeasurable beauty spilled out into a small mountain in front of them. A deep silence of awe spilled out over the men with it. They had never seen so much wealth in one spot.

"All this for the cross," she said. "And I won't kill you."

The night, so young, was promising more and more to her. The leader, without arguing, reached into the pile and handed her the amulet, robbed of its power as it had been robbed from the building it was taken from.

"The church it was found in lies in ashes," he said proudly.

She looked deep into his eyes as he said this, and then smiled, allowing her fangs to show under the moonlight. "I know," she said happily as she hugged the cross tight to her chest.

And now it was hers!

* * * * *

He waited until they had settled in to another endless predictable existence in Orleans. There was no sign of this ever ending, and no hope of finding respite. Aphrodite did what Aphrodite did, and he did what he did. He noticed Venice had put the fear of fire into her, and he was amused as she grew in wisdom and experience that would forever be second to her power. Aphrodite seemed like a young Anubis pup to him, always stretching the full length of her leash, and he wondered what he had ever found about the female vampire that was worthy of interest.

Silently, they awoke together and arose together, the lids to their coffins crashing to the stone floor of the cold root cellar simultaneously. They sat up and glanced at each other, and then, without a word, they went their separate ways.

He brought nothing with him but the ring and the clothes he wore. Luggage and slaves would only slow him down on his journey. He would take what he needed when he needed it. He had no fear of going without. So, he turned toward the southeast and struck out across the uncharted wilderness, moving through dark and uninhabited forests with the supernatural speed of the undead. He could not be moving faster if he had been on horseback, galloping down a road that led straight to his destination, veering neither left nor right from its desired course. Iminuetep was pleased.

Even taking shelter from the sun under the rotting moss and leaves of the great sentinels around him brought him some comfort. He sought no protection for himself during the day. His dark presence alone was enough to drive any predators away from his temporary grave. Animals were so much smarter than humans in that regard and he respected them for that.

One night, ravaged by the vampirism that owned him, he stumbled into a clearing, shaking with the need to feed. Moonlight filtered through the darkness, and though he had sensed the human long before his arrival, an old man gasped with fright when he saw Iminuetep appear from the shadows. Iminuetep pitied the old man his fright, though respected him for his wisdom. Something in the human knew instinctively what Iminuetep was. Iminuetep nodded as he accepted the fact, and looked at the old man, who looked back with astonishing acceptance.

"I prayed you would come," the man said.

Iminuetep strode a few paces into the clearing, closer to the man.

He was in pain, severe and crippling pain that brought the tears to Iminuetep's eyes when he sensed it. "Who do you think I am?" Iminuetep asked compassionately.

The fear in the man was subsiding with each step Iminuetep took toward him. "You are death," he said.

"And this is not a bad thing?" Iminuetep asked.

There were tears in his eyes as he shook his head. "No," he said. "The pain must stop. I came out here to find you, to get away from the pain I was causing my family. It is my time, and I did not want them to be tormented by disease."

Iminuetep nodded again. This man was wise. "You have cancer," he confided quietly, gently. He sat down across from the old man, careful not to draw too close and frighten him. "You are in a lot of pain."

"I have never heard of this 'cancer' you speak of," he admitted. "But I believe your words."

"You will die," Iminuetep admitted. "I am glad I found you."

"Will there be pain?"

Iminuetep shook his head. "No. Not any more. You will only go to sleep. You will know rest."

The man sighed with relief.

"Do you want me to bury your body?" Iminuetep asked.

He shook his head. "Let the dead bury the dead," he said. "And I sense you have a long way to go this night."

Iminuetep nodded and the old man reached out to him.

"Do it now," he said. "I am ready. I have made peace with God."

Iminuetep looked at him and wondered about his words. Yet he kept his questions to himself and complied, doing it quickly and compassionately.

There was no pain, as Iminuetep promised, and as the memories and emotions swept through Iminuetep, he knew the man's life as though it was his own, appreciating the full and wondrous experiences, his sorrows and laughter, the death of his wife, watching his two children, one son and one daughter, grow to maturity and have children of their own. He remembered the human's pain as the sickness began to take him, and the constant care of his daughter, the worry of his neighbours, the pain. There had been so much pain. And now, as the last of the flickering light of his life was slowly fading away, there was only peace, peace and acceptance and a great appreciation for Iminuetep and what he had done.

Iminuetep held the lifeless corpse in his arms for a while. Then he gently placed the body on the forest floor. He would not bury the body, as the man had asked. But he would do something more for him. He bent his head and concentrated a moment longer. Then a wave of intense emotion, a copy of the peace Iminuetep had felt from the human, washed out from him as though a rock had been tossed into the centre of a pond. The air about him rippled, the leaves in the trees fluttered, and Iminuetep knew that those who loved this old man would feel that emotion and know the torment had ended. If they responded to that inner feeling, they would find his body.

Satisfied he had done all he could, and appreciating the newfound strength of the blood that flowed through him, he rose to his feet and looked down at the sleeping body one last time. He truly had found peace, and Iminuetep envied the man for that, vowing in his heart to do the same, if he could.

Then he struck out again, not knowing where he was going, or even why. But his thirst was sated and he could not be angry at himself for what he had done.

He did not know exactly where he was going, only that the seeds of a place called Romania were beginning to germinate. And he wanted to see what was taking place within this mysterious land. He did not want to waste time, nor energy, conserving his new found strength and vowing to make it last as much as he could. The perpetual shadows of the forests blurred past him with his supernatural abilities to exist as one with the darkness. The nights wore on until he lost count of the days that passed.

Then, eventually, his timeless flight came to an end. He had been following an inner hunch, an instinct similar to those animals use to migrate. Something, a feeling, a desire, told him he was near his destination, and though he knew nothing of what he would find, he knew what he sought was close at hand nonetheless.

Early one night, as he traversed across a treeless expanse over a barren mountain range, he came across the ruins of an ancient stone temple. The crumbling structure had been built to withstand time's cruel and heavy hand, yet the ageless temple was still crumbling under the weight of countless years passing. The roof of the building had long since vanished. The walls were nothing more than low heaps of rubble that came to his knees in a large, octagon shape that centred a raised dais of stone. There was a stone stairway that led to the top of this dais and hundreds of stone statues surrounded him, scattered around and throughout the rubble in silent, eternal solitude. Many of them had survived the test of time better than the temple itself, and Iminuetep, drawn fascinated to one of the carvings, shivered as he looked into its lifelike eyes.

The statue was alive. It was an immense creature that did not comprehend him, strong inhuman hands and arms that dug into the stone at its feet and a bald head with pointed ears and a slanted, inhuman face. It wore clothes, though only a stone portrayal of a pair of leggings. It was hunched over and looked off into the horizon with such a rapt expression of awe and devotion, that despite its ugly nature and the obvious destruction for which it was made, Iminuetep glanced off at the direction this monster was gazing at, desiring for himself whatever end this creature had found.

Iminuetep saw nothing but the night. Still, conscious that he might be blocking the gargoyle's view; he stepped out of its way and walked over to another one. This statue was just a statue. There was nothing lifelike about it, yet it caught the artist's rendition of anger as only a masterpiece could. Iminuetep wondered if he himself could rise to the challenge of carving something as masterful as he looked up at the human figure that raged in silent, everlasting fury. Probably, though it might take him a while. He walked around the statue and saw another gargoyle had taken up a chisel and mallet and was frozen in a pose to drive the chisel through the statue's back. The artisan that had created the angry statue stood frozen in time, himself immobilized as granite stone. He had created an image of himself, and now, for whatever reason, had become a part of that image, caught forever in a pose of killing his own darkened intent. His face lacked any of the anger Iminuetep had seen in his self portrait, though the work had been exact in detailing a replica of the man. The only expression the artisan had was one of fierce determination. Nodding his respect at the work of art the mysterious artisan had made himself part of, Iminuetep moved on.

Another gargoyle sat chained to a wall. He had been dressed in rags when he was turned to stone, and a pile of refuse and dirty straw had turned with him. He had been captive for how long Iminuetep could only guess, but the vampire thought perhaps he had been that way his entire life. Though still in rags, and still chained, the creature now wore such a look of fierce and royal freedom that Iminuetep envied the man and his royal state despite the chains. If only Iminuetep could find what this one had found, he would no longer care about such temporal things as rags or chains.

Compelled by forces beyond his experience, Iminuetep turned and glided toward the dais in the centre of the temple. He had to weave between gargoyles packed inside the temple, so many of them there were. It took Iminuetep some time to reach the dais as he stopped to study each one. When he moved on, he longed to find what they had found. When he did reach the bottom step of the dais, he was shy to move forward. He looked up at the top, seeing that a few other gargoyles were kneeling on the steps or standing with hands and heads raised to the sky.

One gargoyle had her back turned toward him. She was kneeling just about at his feet, with her elbows resting on the stairs in front of her. Her head was tilted toward the top of the dais. She wore a robe that covered her completely, though what colour it had been before she was turned to stone had been replaced by the granite it had turned to. Her hair, also now colourless, was full and long, and tumbled down her back in rivulets. Captivated by her, Iminuetep moved forward to see her face and was struck dumb when he saw her. Her eyes shone, though they were still made of stone. She was the embodiment of all that was good and right, he could see that by the inner life that still held tightly to her through her eyes. Yet her mouth was opened to reveal a strong and powerful set of fangs that would have dripped with the blood of her victims in another time and another place. She had once been a vampire; yet now, she was free of her bloodlust, even though she had been petrified in the midst of the terrible thirst that drove all vampires to take their victims.

That was the last straw. Turning from her, he strode up the steps of the ancient platform and came to a stop at the top of the stairs. He looked up at the stars and raised his hands above his head. "What has taken these!" he cried out to the wilderness. "Let also take me!"

Instantly, a bright white light washed over him. He closed his eyes and felt all his endless days and the burden of his existence wash away from him. Finally, Iminuetep knew peace. It felt as though a great fire had ignited inside his chest, and though the vampire should have been terrified, he embraced the warmth and entered into an existence outside of eternity, far removed from his daily sufferings, where no tear was ever shed, nor any addiction ever ruled.

Iminuetep's body had turned to stone. The gargoyle still had his hands raised, his head back, and his eyes closed. His face said he had found a peace that would outlast the wars that raged inside of time.

* * * * *

These raiders called themselves Vikings. They were Normans, originally, and yet they worshiped a violent pantheon of war gods that demanded blood sacrifices. To appease their gods, they had to travel far from their homes every year in search of new places to raid and plunder. She liked them immensely, and had them go out into the city and bring her back a living sacrifice just to prove to them that she was at least equal to one of their gods. They did this, and found the entire experience entertaining as they stood in a circle and watched her suck the life out of a young woman they had ravaged along the way. She killed the woman on top of the pile of wealth she and the men had collected, and it was an experience, the first of many, that would not be forgotten by any of them.

During the night, she told them of her special needs, how she had to seek shelter from the sun during the day, how she had to have blood, and how she had other dark passions that consumed her every given moment. The men swore, after sharing in some of these baser passions with her, to not reveal her to anybody, to keep her existence a secret. When they did, she just shrugged and said, "I'd hunt you down and kill you if you told anyone anyway." The men laughed and cheered her as they got merrily drunk that night amongst the dead bodies of Aphrodite's victims and the stolen treasure they had massed together.

Near dawn, she took her cross, and not trusting her new companions enough to sleep in her villa, bid them a good night. She did not return to her master's estate, but instead went deep into the forests surrounding Orleans. She covered herself with the decay of the earth and the trees and fell asleep with a smile on her lips as she hugged her trophy.

They were waiting for her when she arrived back at her villa just after sundown. "Mistress!" one of the Vikings called to her when she jumped down from the wall surrounding her villa. "We leave Orleans!" he cried happily.

"Then I go with you!" she cried just as happily as she shook some of the dirt and foliage from her hair.

Her announcement was met by cheers all around, and they set out immediately into the night.

Their pace was slow, but she was in the company of mortals, so she kept her complaints to herself. Yet, in the never ending face of the night, time meant nothing to her, and whatever pace these fellows kept would ultimately matter very little to her. Wherever they were going, they would get there eventually. That was all that mattered.

Conversation was kept to a minimum, yet she could feel the admiration of the men around her. About halfway into the night, she saw a young couple, arm in arm, oblivious to all else around them but each other. She made her leave from amongst the Norman invaders, to their quiet encouragement, and slipped into the shadows around them to become the huntress once more. She had vanished from their sight, and her efficiency to do so startled them. But that was all behind her and her kill was before her.

She took them both and made the woman watch as the man died in her arms. Then she relished the woman's terror as she made it her own. Too soon it was over, and Aphrodite quickly looted the corpses of anything that might interest the Normans. She found a pair of matching gold rings, and scarcely little else except for a purse of a few copper pennies. Silently, she left them to their death and glided back to the Normans. Without a word, she slipped the rings into the purse and tossed it to the leader. He upended the purse into his hand and laughed when he recognized the wedding rings for what they were.

That was her last kill in Orleans. By the end of the night, they had left Orleans behind them and were heading deeper into the Carolingian Empire, always migrating closer to the Atlantic Ocean.

* * * * *

Blood rained from the sky. Men screamed and died all around her in a mass of confusion as horrors unspeakable occurred in an endless sea of rage and madness. It was her first real battle and the mistress of death laughed at the shear chaos her soul enveloped as the seven others of her band of Vikings fought in a tight circle around her. They fought not to protect her, for the barbarians believed her to be immortal, but to win favour in her eyes, and they fought only to kill, and to shed the blood that she gloried in. Sensations unlike anything she'd ever imagined cascaded around her, to collide with her and wash her away in the glorious life that was ending. Aphrodite laughed again and flew at her opponents recklessly, breaking out of the knot of men that surrounded her and wading into the wall of shields and spears that sought in vain to keep her at bay.

She was naked, and her face was painted blue, yet in the watery moonlight and the blood that she bathed in, she looked like a demon risen from Hell to inflict vengeance upon those that stood to oppose her.

The Atlantic Ocean stood between her and the far off horizon, and as she fought along the beach, empty handed and with her fangs revealed to the horror of every soldier that saw them, she felt as though she had truly come home.

These that opposed her marched under a flag with a cross on it. She had seen them kneel before the blacked robed priest at the beginning of the battle, and the light that had emanated from his blessing filled her with fear and loathing. But as the battle wore on, the light faded, and as these soldiers brought forth the violence deep within them, the light of peace that could so readily drive her screaming into the night had faded until all that remained was the angry testosterone of a mass of killers. She waded into their midst fearlessly. And the blood continued to fall.

She was giddy with the passion of it, able to taste the blood from any and all of them at any time she wished. And caught up with the anger that flooded through them, she added to those sensations a new level of fear and terror. She would not let them escape. These men were hers, this blood was hers. This death that they so readily sought to inflict was hers. She was death's mistress, and it was time they paid their taxes to her. It was time she collected. And collect she did.

There was over two-hundred men that came to oppose their small band of marauders. Rumour of their passage through the Charlemagne Empire had spread before them, and when they had long last made their way to the Atlantic, these soldiers were here to greet them, just after sundown.

The fools.

Chapter Thirteen

After the victory for the Viking invaders upon the shore of the Charlemagne Empire, the opposing forces retreated, leaving Aphrodite with a secure location on the coastline to mass her force of invaders. Her own small band had come into the empire from the east, sailing along the coast until they had struck inland and had eventually discovered who they called the Mistress. Their longboat had been lost and yet their riches had grown immense with Aphrodite's help. Now they were back and they took good care of the Mistress in style she was finally growing accustomed to.

In a plantation that overlooked the ocean, they watched their forces grow, watched a fleet of Viking longboats collect along the exposed waterfront of her nest. This was her land now, and as one Viking after another was brought before her and placed their weapons and their lives at her feet, Aphrodite's ambitions grew with it.

"We stay here," she declared to her general, the same Viking who had given her that first cross back in Orleans. Now, they sat across from each other at a large wooden table. Under the light of a myriad of tall candles, the collection of jewel encrusted crosses and crucifixes glittered with an inner life that had nothing to do with the power that could so easily defeat her. She sipped warm human blood from a crystal wine goblet while he feasted on a table full of the choicest foods taken from the surrounding hamlets.

General Theilbold only nodded with a mouth full of food. In one hand he held a matching goblet full of red wine. In the other, the leg of roasted duck dripped grease over and across his chin.

They were alone except for a slave standing mute and afraid against one wall. She was ready to jump to do any bidding commanded. She had been taken from the household of the estate. Aphrodite had chosen her for her beauty, yet she was off limits to her men, and they did not push the issue. Her intelligence, however, was without measure. Aphrodite had felt it appropriate to rip out the woman's tongue and help insure her silence. She had also eaten the delicacy before the scholar's eyes and had secured her loyalty in doing it. Every other original member of this household had long since died.

"For how long?" the Theilbold asked.

"I know you are not challenging what I say," Aphrodite admitted.

The general, fearless, shrugged and then continued eating. "Your will is my command, mistress," he admitted without looking up. That was no big surprise.

"Until we have taken all we can," Aphrodite declared. "All we want before it gets too expensive to stay."

"Then what?"

"Across the channel to Britannia," she declared.

"How much blood do you want?" he asked, in awe. Blood for her meant wealth for him, and yet she had never taken from him, never bitten him. It had become customary at the beginning of their meetings for him to bleed, to cut himself and fill a goblet with his blood so that she may know of his experiences, his battles. It was his blood she sipped on now, relishing in his life just as he did. She dwelt within his memories now, seeing every murder, hearing every scream, smelling the smoke from every fire as it clogged out the light from the noonday sun. And she tasted the lust in every rape as she felt the sensations that went with it. She could see the violation on the faces of his victims as their life spilled from them and feel their will crumble under his ability to extract information from his captives.

Yet she had not touched the blood that flowed only the width of a sheet of paper away from her. She wanted her men strong, immortal even, if she could make them. And she had spent much of her inexhaustible energy to make them such. She trained them personally, pushing them with sword and shield, with bow and spear, running them into the ground in practice that they may not tire in battle.

And her officers had been taught everything she could teach them about trade.

Theilbold was running through calculations in his head as he chewed. "Eight months to a year," he said thoughtfully. "We can move anytime within those four months and it won't matter," he said. "At your pleasure, mistress."

She took another sip of his blood. "Do you know how to read, general?" She knew the answer better than he, had taught him herself and had known what it was for him to learn.

He stopped chewing as he returned her gaze. "Not one word," he said. "Teach me, mistress. I am yours to command."

She laughed at his response and drained the rest of his blood. Then she placed the empty goblet on the table and rose to her feet. She walked around the table until she was standing behind him as he ate.

Aphrodite bent over him and kissed his neck through his beard.

"Thank you for the gift of blood," she said breathily into his ear. Then she motioned to her slave. "Janelle," she said, not unkindly before continuing to kiss Theilbold, mouthing his neck as she gently toyed with the hairs on his neck with her fangs.

The slave stepped forward, acutely aware of all her mistress's whims. Her stone expression remained as such as she stepped to the table and took Aphrodite's empty wine goblet. Her emotion never changed as she rolled up the sleeve of her arm. Deep gashes and ragged scars crisscrossed the woman's entire hand and arm. Her expression did not change; she showed not one whit of pain as she found a spot that would serve her purpose and drew a knife she kept tucked in the sleeve of her robe. Expertly, she traced a deep enough cut down her arm, weaving it between the scars in an attempt to add aesthetic value. She was pleased with what she had done to herself. But by then the goblet was full, and her mistress was served. She returned to her station against the wall and the knife vanished into one of the folds of her robe.

Aphrodite took the goblet without looking up from what she was doing. A moment later she turned and walked into the adjoining bed chamber.

Her general took another bite from his roasted duck before throwing it onto the table. He pushed his chair away from the feast, and keeping his wine, followed after her.

The men knew their jobs. The two of them had time to spare this night before Aphrodite would make an appearance before the men before dawn. She would stand before them naked, as was her custom, and upon a mountain of plundered wealth drink the blood of a sacrifice brought before her.

Janelle, her mute slave, stood at the ready as Aphrodite and her general coupled in front of her. And still the Viking longboats grounded upon the beach in greater and greater numbers, each filled with a crew of capable sailors, killers eager to swear allegiance to the Mistress of Death.

* * * * *

The boats were ground to shore on the soft beach before the plantation. Twenty-eight of them in total, each able to hold twenty men, they sat as silent sentinels, they had carried a wild, ungodly celebration to the coast of the Charlemagne Empire. The wealth was moved onto the beach and placed in a pile upon the shores of the Atlantic. It glittered next to a bomb fire that gave off enough heat to keep the Vikings away from it.

Her men danced and celebrated in wild, frantic fashions. Fresh women had been brought in from the hamlets surrounding them, and yet the favourite ones were present as well. Loyalty was something that Aphrodite demanded, and the price for breaking her law was unthinkably high. She kept her side of the deal; traitors were given over to the men, that they may prove who had the most loyalty to their mistress of death. The flayed bodies of a few fresh corpses hung skinned on crisscrossed wracks at appropriate distances from the fire while tanners watched over the skins with masterful eyes for detail. Some of the heads had remained intact, and these were looked after more carefully than anything else while the blood was scraped from the skins and then burned in the flames. Barrels of salt were close by what was left of each of the corpses. These skins were being preserved while many of the bones still glistened wetly as they served as candle holders, part of a silent army of the dead that held everlasting tribute to their victor by holding a candle high in her memory. The candles stretched the breadth and the width of the sand, covering the entire length of the waterfront within sight of Aphrodite's nest. She had no need to illuminate anything else with fire. This was enough.

Aphrodite appeared at the doorway to her villa. At her side, her mute slave stood with her. Aphrodite was naked. The slave wore only a shawl that covered her arms to her fingernails. The outfit supplied her with a deep black hood, should the lady wish to use it. The shawl was down, exposing her untouched, beautiful face. The rest of her body, save her shoulders, was traced with intricate blue tattoos. When she had run out of room on her arms, the slave had turned to decorating the rest of her body. The cuts were shallow, yet longer, and flowing in repeated contours that brought out the beauty of her flesh. The tattoos had been placed to bring out the cuts. No man within the camp touched her, and she wanted none of it. They did not look at her, simply ignored her presence, and many of them had since forgotten she was there.

She wore gold ankle bands, and if she turned her neck, one could catch the glimpse of golden chain mail laced with diamonds that surrounded her neck like a sea of stars cast upon the ocean waves and then frozen in timelessness. She wore gold-plated bracers under her sleeves and kept two knives hidden away, one up each sleeve. One knife was an ornamented, slim weapon that ended at her elbow. But the other was simpler, smaller, though no less lethal. Janelle kept it tucked away in her right hand. This was her knife and she would carry it with her always, though she could chose any blade she wished. The Vikings kept their swords only at her whim. Her mistress would not have to concern herself with her own protection.

Slightly behind Aphrodite's left shoulder, she remained ever silent and watchful as they walked toward the army. Halfway to the fire, the general greeted her with a kiss and took his place at her right hand. The Vikings cheered her on as they approached the bonfire, and when it became too unbearable, Aphrodite walked on alone while Janelle and the general stood in silence.

The silence spread as Aphrodite gazed out at her army. "Tonight!" she called out. "We move from this place. Tonight, we go in search of greater treasure than this!" Her men roared their approval as she took her sacrifice and forced him to the mountain of treasure beside the fire. And under the light of the fire, with their worldly treasures mounted nearly as high as their heads behind them, Aphrodite drank the man's life away. She tried not to show her disappointment from the experience. He had been a farmer, a free man, a relatively educated man who had learned to make extra money for his family as a mercenary to the local lords. But once he had learned of Aphrodite, his resolve had failed him. He still worked just as hard as ever, but he came before her fearlessly, dead inside. Terror had already burned out his soul, and this was only the welcomed end he had been waiting for. Now his nightmare would end and he would know peace. Aphrodite imagined that drinking his blood was as tasteless as water.

She looked at her slave Janelle when the deed was done. Janelle nodded reassuringly. She would give her mistress another sacrifice from her own flesh once they were alone, something that would be able to nourish her properly. Aphrodite was able to give a bold and victorious front to her men. The cheering renewed and she let it swell to a maddening pitch as the men chanted, "Death's Mistress!" over and over again.

She suddenly shot her arm into the air and the chanting stopped immediately. Only the crackle of the fire was heard along the beach.

Aphrodite held the silence for a little while, letting the anticipation build in her men. Finally, she knew they couldn't take the suspense any longer. "Weapons and armour before Janelle!" she commanded. She waited until her men had their weapons safely out of their hands, then cried, "Divide the plunder! We go to Britannia!"

The men roared their delight and dived to the task of salvaging as much of the gold as they could as it melted into itself. Aphrodite and her general, with Janelle ever at her heels, strode from the fire and the madness behind them. Someone had figured out a new use for candleholders and had dipped the end of a leg bone into the melting gold to use as a club against his brothers in arms. The pile was being torn away and the mock battle that ensured brought laughter and curses to everyone's lips. Yet Aphrodite's mind was elsewhere. Her original crew of Normans, the seven of them, now her officers, and Janelle, the ever present assassin, followed from close behind, empty handed but for the weapons on their backs. Their gear was already stowed on board.

They commandeered the fastest ship for this voyage, and Aphrodite helped push it into the ocean. The boat surged into the froth as the Vikings struggled aboard, and still the Mistress of Death added her strength and her will to the speed of the boat as the unlimited confines of the Atlantic Ocean opened up before her.

* * * * *

Aphrodite pulled herself from the ocean once the men had found the rhythm of the oars to keep to the speed she had set. Janelle stood with a tankard of blood in her hand and handed it to her. She eagerly reached for the blood. For the most part, the sailors ignored her now. They had a job to do, and while the general stood at the rudder, she looked to the night skies and commanded the sails to be unfurled. Then she found an empty spot at the oars and lent her strength to their journey while the men took shifts beating out the cadence of their movement on a war drum that echoed over the still Atlantic night. The coastline receded into the darkness behind them.

When dawn began to approach, she left her men to their work and bid them cut the pace, that they may save their strength for the night. The general respectfully declined to follow the suggestion, and she did not order them to stop. She smiled instead. "I guess you will keep the sails up as well?" she asked. Black as night, the sails were a telltale sign to all who saw it what they were and what they would do to any who approached them. It was also a challenge, and they were entering into uncharted waters, with unchallenged natives.

"To take it down would be an insult to your greatness, mistress," General Theilbold said, not taking his eyes from the stars overhead.

She laughed quietly to herself.

"Have a good sleep, Aphrodite," he added into the silence.

Aphrodite nodded her thanks and flipped open the lid to a coffin that sat in the center of the ship. It was simple, made of dried balsam wood, yet polished to a glistening sheen. All thought had been given to the speed of their journey, and this simple coffin was lighter than the gold-plated ones she had settled into with her old master. Lighter meant for a faster voyage across the channel.

"Good night gentlemen," she said as she closed the lid over her. Janelle guarded over her while she slept. The general guarded over the ship, and the men gave it their full strength until they feared to risk the wrath of their mistress the previous night. Sundown was only a few hours away and they would not be caught exhausted when she rose from her coffin once again.

* * * * *

Aphrodite awakened to mist and darkness all around them. Before she opened her eyes from her sleep she could sense the shallow depths of the waters below and feel the earth of Britannia before them. She smiled and pushed the lid to her coffin open as quietly as she could. She slipped out of it and glided wordlessly to her general, who crouched against the gunwale.

She tapped his shoulder and he did not jump at the sudden impact with what was not there before. Instead, he turned slowly and regarded her through the darkness. She motioned with her hands, and they bent their heads close so that he might better see what she said. Her lips did not move, but as her hands talked for them, he nodded or shook his head, depending on his answers to her questions. "Yes, the mist came on us about an hour before sundown. No, we have not seen any sign they know of our approach. Yes, we've seen several fires already. No, I'm not sure for certain what they are, but my guess is campfires. Yes, they are keeping watch. No, we wait your command. Yes, I thought you might want to be the first overboard." The meanings to her questions were clear, as were the meanings to her answers.

Then his hands began moving, though briefly in the silence. "Drink well tonight, mistress," he said silently with his hands.

She smiled and slipped from the boat, eager to feed on a nation that knew nothing of her coming.

* * * * *

The tired citizens of the port city Pevensey groaned as sunrise slowly drove them from their unrestful slumbers. Aching with bedsores and chilled with slight fevers, not one of them had managed a good night sleep. Yet the reason for their nightly turmoil escaped them. Restlessness was not unheard of, and they had yet to discover that this strange plague haunted them all.

General Thielbold looked on in silent satisfaction as he watched the still mostly sleeping residents drag themselves from their huts and force their hands to the plough once again. The marketplace was opened, though more behind the sunrise than usual, and common life in the city resumed a tired lethargic pace.

A few simple monks walked amongst the city, noticing with quiet eyes the difference that had so come across the people of this land. Anderita was commonly a harsh, ambitious place, yet now a quiet hung over the morning air as all that the monks looked upon seemed too exhausted to rise to the challenge of the day with the energy and aggressiveness they usually had.

General Thielbold did not notice the few plain monks as they faded into the wilderness to return to their monastery with their strange report.

Instead, he was too caught up in the size of the victory that awaited them. Anderita could be theirs in a few more days. In one deft move, Theilbold and his mistress could take the city with little more than the handful of men they had taken with them, before the rest of the fleet managed to catch up to them from across the Channel.

"Let's take it," one of the officers said, seizing the opportunity to invade the city while its citizens laboured under the early sun in exhaustion. He moved to leave the shelter of the trees they hid in, but Theilbold was quick to grab him from behind and force him to a stop.

"No," he commanded quietly, with infinite patience and the firm authority that his men would do as they commanded. No one would challenge his command and fear the mistress' wrath. "We wait," he said. "Let the mistress do her work."

"But—" the argument faded into silence as he looked into his general's eyes. "We wait," he said, agreeing with the general.

"And then we take it all," Theilbold announced. "In one night."

That night Aphrodite rose from her coffin and politely refused the draught of blood that awaited her. "Thank you, Janelle, but I want to be hungry when I attack Anderita once more." She had drunk so much pure and innocent blood the night before that she had puked on her way back to the ship. It had been glorious, and she wanted to save her hunger for what was to take place again this night. The citizens of Anderita were unknowing victims in her quest to take it all. The few churches in the place had been left alone; the huts that huddled close to them had been passed over. The more wretched places near the waterfront and the wealthy areas next to the forests or in the centre of the city had suffered her thirst.

The ship had been well hidden in a cove not far from the city. It had been ground to shore, the sails and the mast had been taken down, and the ship had been overturned to form a kind of shelter for Aphrodite's coffin. The officers and Janelle had set up a well organized and quite hidden camp, and clothing had been found for the women. Now the deadly nature of Janelle and the inhuman death incarnate that radiated off of Aphrodite had been partly hidden by simple, unadorned peasant's clothing. Still, Janelle was loath to give up her wool smock with its blades ever sheathed at her ready. But Aphrodite needed no such weapons, and to all, the pair of them looked like simple peasant women from afar, though nothing could hide their unmarred beauty that would surely give them away as easily as a war banner. They kept their hoods pulled over their heads and their gazes at the ground. The men kept their weapons concealed. Years of raiding and ravaging had taught them well, and they knew the merits in stealth when it suited them. Even without Aphrodite's wishes made known, they would have still followed a similar course of action, though the scope of her ambitions could not fully be grasped by the men. Still, they trusted her, and if she felt like she could take this city before the rest of the army crossed the channel, then they would conform to her battle plans.

She emerged from under the hull of the overturned long boat and crouched before the fire the men had made.

They sat looking up at her from their places, anxious to just look on to her face.

"The people were tired this morning, mistress," General Theilbold stated gleefully.

"Give me two more days," Aphrodite declared. "And they will be exhausted and sick in their beds. You can take the whole city unchallenged, the seven of you alone."

The Vikings grinned. They had no displeasure at the thought.

Aphrodite smiled back at them and rose to her feet. Without another word, she faded into the darkness surrounding the fire and disappeared into the night.

Chapter Fourteen

Though the sounds of the ocean surf may have bounced off of the mighty Roman Port of Anderita, the timid monastery sat amidst a cushion of wooden pillars. The slight noises that blew on the hazy morning wind were comforting, soothing. The disease called Vampirism cringed under the weight of a granite shell while Jason slept quietly in peace and oblivion. The gargoyle stood with his arms crossed, waiting patiently. An immense grey and black wolf sat on its hunches. It was passive and content; its joyous panting was in rhythm with its heartbeat and the forest around them.

In time, a pair of monks emerged from the clearing. They were jogging, sweating with perspiration. Yet their strides did not waver or grow weak, and the determination in theirs eyes burned as fiercely as the wolf's. He sprinted down to greet them when he saw them. They jabbed at him with their feet, kicking playfully where they knew he'd not be. He dodged their kicks happily, going through motions the monks had thought up for him during their training sessions together. He was having fun, yet they could not afford too much time for the play and he soon understood to follow from behind.

The gargoyle came out of his sleep before the two travellers could notice him standing there. He smiled when the monks came to a stop in front of him. "Gregor, Kelly," he said with a nod. Shaking off her disguise, the woman smiled as she pulled her hood off and shook out her long blonde hair. She nodded to Father Jason and to Gregor. "If that'll be all," she said. "I'll be preparing for mass."

"Mother Superior," Gregor nodded back and she flashed a smile to Father Jason on her way out.

Some time ago, rumour had reached the monastery that the wolf god Fernir was in the area. They had sent the dog out for a look, but he had been wounded during the night. Jason tried not to think too hard on the scandal that must have taken place once daylight struck the walls of the sheltered convent. But Christopher had insisted until he was blue in the face and threatened by castration by one of the wolf's keepers that all was well. Still, it had not been a complete disaster. His quick wits had the screams silenced and into quiet concern in moments, and Jason gave the boy respect for how fast he had made it home after that, with two other experienced riders close on his heels. The Mother Superior and her dear daughter, the one who had found the dog originally, had come to prepare for the worst. Even now, their training was continuing to advance.

It had been agreed upon that as few as a dozen sisters knew of the battle Christopher and his kind were raging. But they had become eternally grateful he was there.

Now, on this sunny morning, he had discreetly disappeared into the forest before his transformation had taken place.

"Good dog," Jason mumbled to himself.

"What was that?" Father Gregor asked. Jason looked down at the broad smile Gregor wore.

"Nothing. How was your early jog?"

"Not good. We had to ride two of the horses back to cover the terrain faster."

Jason grew serious. "And?"

"The people are plagued with sickness."

"What?" Jason asked. He fought the urge to detract his fangs and kept the other priest from seeing the tips of their jagged edges.

The priest only nodded and kept at his story. "Anderita is exhausted. They had little or no sleep last night. And they look like they are all catching the flu."

Jason grew pale. She was here. "Send runners out to prepare for tonight," he said. "War has come to Britain."

Gregor's eyes grew wide and afraid. "War cannot reach us here," he said stubbornly. He was thinking of the werewolf and their earlier days together.

"It's not from Fernir," Jason said finally. "It's from something else." He paused to look at Gregor, wishing he had time to explain it all to him in ways that would not harm him. But there was no time, and though what he was about to show his brother may cause the dear man permanent harm, Jason realized he had no choice. "It's from this." He let his fangs slide free and his eyes shine with the hunger of the undead.

Gregor stumbled back in fear, fell, and then continued his mad fright as Jason hid the vampirism once again.

Just then, Christopher emerged from the woods. His brown wool robe kept his strides to a shuffle, yet he did not seem to be in a hurry. "And do not let the boy know," Jason finished. "This is not his war."

Gregor hurried to his feet and glanced at Christopher as he approached. "Of course," he said. "I'll send those who are not his keeper."

Jason nodded. "That would be wise."

Then Gregor was off at a run.

Christopher caught up with Jason in the kitchen. "Hungry?" Christopher asked.

Jason shook his head. "No," he said happily. "You?"

"Starving!" He went for the cupboard and pulled out a raw roast.

"Figures," Jason said as he watched his son push the haunch of meat onto a wooden pole and thrust it into the kitchen fire.

Christopher grinned until he pulled the roast, charred black, out of the open flame and push it onto a plate on the counter.

"Christopher," Jason said, choosing to his next words carefully.

"Father," he answered with his first mouthful of food.

"We're going to the waterfall."

"When?"

"The day after tomorrow."

"Why?" Christopher asked with his second mouthful.

"Training day."

Christopher only smiled and continued eating in silence. He needed his strength. It was legend that the ancient Spartans would push their warriors until every one of them dropped of exhaustion. It often took a few days. What Christopher was about to go through was different. He did not drop of exhaustion. He only dropped dead until the creature from within awoke at sunset.

Unfortunately, not enough time would have passed for that to happen, but still he was sure he and the wolf would have a good time anyway.

Chapter Fifteen

The shadows embraced her as she pulled the plain wool cloak over her head. She had no need for flamboyance or greatness this night. Tonight she was in her element, and as a gentle breeze ruffled the curls of her hair that stuck out from beneath her peasant's garb, she was comfortable with what had to be done, revelling in her new home and the promise of conquest that lay under her feet. She walked, relishing in the quiet of the night, listening to the sounds around her as though listening to a conversation with an old and familiar friend.

Through the darkness, on the path before her, two simply dressed men walked toward her with the same disposition as her, no doubt mistaking her for a simple peasant girl. She saw them long before they could have seen her, and the smile grew as Aphrodite began planning her first seduction of the night. She would take the blood from these two and throw their bodies in the ocean, despite what she had told her men. Two simple peasants would not make a difference to the Normans anyway. They were here for greatness, for glory, for wealth. They were here to carve their places in history. They would not discredit their mistress her own wiles.

As they neared each other, she could not help but noticing that neither man showed the slightest interest in her, though they seemed content enough with their surroundings and her approaching them. They felt as safe as she. They were not going to threaten her, but were to let her pass by politely and safely. She smiled as the fangs slid from her gums with the same familiar agony that had been with her through the millennia.

This would be too easy.

She kept her head down, and the bloodlust began to flow through her veins, taking hold of her and bringing her nearly breathless with longing. Yet she did not change her pace and kept ambling toward them like a mortal would.

When they were close enough to not raise an alarm, she drew her head back and let her face be seen in the moonlight. They did not stop their own pace, nor show anything but calm and gentle resolve, though they must be able to see her fangs. Perhaps, she reasoned with herself, these two peasants were simple minded; or perhaps their mistake was not that they were without fear, but that they pitied the poor peasant woman her terrible deformity. She smiled all the more as they came within easy reach.

She grabbed one of them, and her hand exploded into flames.

She screamed in pain and pulled the flames away from the man, shocked at what was still incinerating her. She looked from her closed fist, inflamed before her widened eyes, to the men who had stopped before her. Their own eyes were icy with determination, though there was no hatred there. "Be gone from us, Mistress of Death," one of them said smoothly.

She did not move, not able to understand what was happening, too shocked at the flame that still burned her hand. *How could they know who she was?*

"Now!" the other commanded angrily, suddenly.

Both men seemed suddenly released with fury, as though a spring had been coiled deep within them and was suddenly released upon her. Too late, she realized the trap that had been set for her. "In the name of the Christ!" the other shouted as he ripped a wooden crucifix from around his neck. "Depart from these shores!" The night around her exploded into a brilliant, searing ball of fire.

That said, she screamed in terror as the familiar horror of this treacherous light engulfed her. Shrieking, she burst into flames and fled from these two, back to the ocean, back to its familiar depths and its darkness and its icy oblivion in a desperate attempt to block out the horror and the shame of her easy dismissal.

She gave no thought to her victory as she plunged into the ocean once again, seeking only the quiet oblivion and the healing affects of her own death under the dark waves.

Chapter Sixteen

War.

Studying amongst the vaults of the monastery of Signa Aquainnus, Christopher listened carefully to the echoes of the rumours that filtered down to him and his quiet, removed life of self discipline. There would be no way for war to penetrate so deeply from the surface of the world to the dusty bottom of the ancient libraries he kept.

Yet knowing that records of the beast and his workings in the not so distant past had been removed painstakingly from the records, Christopher could not help but still be worried that greater men than he would find a legend or a folk lore and trace them back here to him. He worried that the powers he had so diligently kept locked down inside the deeper recesses of his belligerent soul would be discovered, and he would have to let them resurface in the name of politics and greed.

Christopher shook himself out of his dark thoughts and went back to copying the work placed before him.

They would not find him. They could not find him. And even if they could, they would not be able to call upon the darker powers of his soul to help in the name of right. Such a thought, such a theology, could not be reasoned through, could not be justified, and yet Christopher could not help but wonder what greater good still lay in store.

His work progressed through the timelessness of the place, and yet he could not find the comfort in its unmarked passage. Page after painstaking page was copied by the lowly hands of a simple scribe, and when the words of the greater books seeped into his mind, they found fertile ground in humility, soil rich and waiting with the fertility of genius.

At last, the bell sounded for mass, and Christopher cleaned his quill carefully before replacing it next to the ink well on his desk. The pages before him were still wet with ink, but he did not dare touch them with the sand. *Better to let them rest where they were,* he thought. No one would be coming down here anyway, except for the aging Father Jason, perhaps. And he would know better than to touch what needed not to be touched.

Christopher climbed the stairs quickly, taking two at a time, yet not breaking sweat. He did not know how much of his night gifts affected his body, or how much of a remarkable miracle rested in his hands. He did know, however, that the world was a dark place, and he kept the potential of what that world represented locked tightly within his chest. Not even Saint Peter himself would dare unlock what was within, and he was at peace with such knowledge.

What a ritualistic routine that affair always seemed. When the residing father was finished reciting the homily from a book, Christopher couldn't help notice he'd read from a copy Christopher had made. The words seemed fresher in the scribe's mind than they'd been in the father's voice. A few chants were poorly sung, a few prayers were said, a few candles were lit. Then everyone seemed to hustle out of the building as quickly as they could, leaving Christopher and a few others on their knees and scattered throughout the sanctuary, contemplating the mysteries of the Eucharist and of more subtle puzzles placed before them.

Father Jason approached the lowly scribe. His gait of late seemed to be stumbling into that of a stooped old man while the cough in his lungs seemed to be thickening. The dampness of this place could not be good for the old man. Christopher mused that perhaps it was time to find a healthier environment for the godly man limping through the corridors.

He watched silently as the old man sat down beside him.

"I'm fine," Father Jason said stubbornly. "I just need a little fresh blood, that's all."

Christopher smiled. "There is war coming, Father," he said. "I have heard of it."

"Set your mind at ease, son," Father Jason said. "It has naught to do with either of us."

"And yet can the greatness of God or the mysteries of the ways of his Spirit be fully understood?"

Now it was Father Jason's turn to stare.

"I cannot shake my mind from the creature that I guard."

"It is your duty to be its guardian, your calling. You are doing well."

"I cannot think that perhaps it could be brought to bear in the war that threatens this place."

"No war threatens this place," Father Jason said defiantly, stubbornly.

Christopher tried another route. "Father?" He scratched his nose to buy time. "Do you not have a pet dog?"

The priest smiled. "As a matter of fact," he laughed. "I have a pet wolf. I thought you were unconcerned with such things."

"Yes," Christopher said thoughtfully. "Usually I am. And does this wolf, is this wolf mean in any way, a menace, even?"

The old man smiled. "No," he said, recollecting his companion. "The wolf is good to me."

"What is its name?" Christopher asked.

Father Jason looked at Christopher and tried to keep the hurt out of his eyes.

"I will not be offended," Christopher prodded gently. "Please."

"His name is Beast," the father said simply.

Christopher snorted. "Fitting," he said. There was very little pain in his chest as he said it.

"Why do you ask?" the good father asked.

"Would not Beast," he said the word with only a tinge of sarcasm. "Would not Beast serve as a protector as well?"

"The time has not come for such a thing," the priest stated flatly.

"And even if it was?"

"I would collar the wolf with a leash," Father Jason said angrily as he stared deeply into Christopher's eyes.

"Father," Christopher said, "No collar can hold that creature. There is no leash he cannot snap. You know this. There is only one bond that holds him at bay and that is the bond of love. There is only one cage that can keep him subdued, one debt he cannot repay and seeks continuously to do so. That is the debt of love; that is the cage of love. And that is his den. The beast does not sleep. The beast never sleeps."

"I did not know that," Father Jason said quietly.

"No. It is only I that need rest. It is only I that must sleep."

"You mean there is no part of yourself that is not in that creature, my companion these long years?"

"Every part of me is in your precious wolf, Father," Christopher said. "Otherwise…" He shook his head to dispel the image. "Only, I sleep. That is when the beast has control."

Both were silent after a time.

"What does that change between how you feel about your companion?" Christopher asked.

"Nothing," Father Jason said at last. He was silent for a moment, while he contemplated what Christopher had said. Then he stirred himself from his musing and looked at his son. "Ready?" he asked. "We're leaving for the waterfall soon?"

Christopher nodded. "Just let me get my pack," he said as he rose and left the sanctuary, going to one knee and crossing himself on his way out.

Chapter Seventeen

The eyes of the sunken corpse opened. The fangs of the demon retracted, and Aphrodite pulled herself from the murky bottom of the Atlantic Ocean. Restored, she was famished; defeated, she was furious. Only one thought penetrated her mind as she surfaced from the ocean before Janelle and the anxious men under her command.

Revenge.

She came from the waters furious, striding forth with a set determination to abandon all of the fear and the horror of the night before and make the people of this island pay for rejecting her so quickly.

"With me!" she cried furiously, striding forth, ignoring the waiting cup Janelle offered her.

They all went with her, anxious to please, and Alexis set out at once for the churches of Anderita.

"Burn them!" she commanded hatefully. "Burn them all to the ground!"

Her men jumped to fulfill her command, as did Janelle, yet Aphrodite was quick enough to hold the assassin back. "Stay by my side this night," she confided to her mute servant. "I have need of more than your blood."

As the flames began to lick at the sides of the first church, the alarm was sounded, yet Aphrodite killed the first of the peasants to wander into the night, relishing not in their blood, but in the efficiency and the fury she disposed of them.

"Back to your homes!" her general roared angrily with a torch raised high above his head as more peasants fearfully stepped from their mud and wattle huts. "Or face a similar fate!" The peasants, shocked at the blasphemy they witnessed, took note of the Norman's angry determination and scurried away from the rising flames, taking shelter in their quiet lives.

The church behind them was quickly engulfed and they moved to the next building, striding through the streets of Anderita unopposed by the still lethargic and shocked defenders. No one resisted them.

The second sanctuary went up in similar flames, and this time a priest, enraged at what was taking place, stormed from a nearby shelter, his fist shaking with fury. "In the name of God!" he cried, and Aphrodite flinched with pain.

"Kill him," she said to her silent slave. "Do it quickly."

Janelle jumped to do her mistress's bidding, and thrust a knife through his abdomen. Angrily, she pulled the blade from his gut and let the man, sputtering in horror and pain, drop to her feet. Only then did she turn to her mistress, who stood back at a safe distance.

"To the next one!" Aphrodite cried.

They did not bother to sack the churches before they were engulfed. Time was on their side, and both the general and Aphrodite knew a fast and effective strike would cripple these people of their potent faith, with their fire that could drive her into hell.

When dawn finally began to creep up on the horizon, Aphrodite returned to the ocean bottom, knowing that no search would be able to find her there. "Fare well," she said to her men and Janelle. "They will be hunting us, now."

"I will find you tonight." Then she was gone, below the surface to the sleep that would waken her once again to a dance with this cursed city, and she would let these people court her, for she was the mistress of death, and she had come to claim her place amongst their ranks. Her fury had not nearly begun to be sated.

Chapter Eighteen

Gregor stumbled into the small cabin, exhausted and grief stricken. The place was a checkpoint between Anderita and Signa Aquainus, a place where monks and travellers could stop to refresh themselves before continuing on their pilgrimage to the holy monastery. Yet there was none of the pious quiet devotion in him as the monk threw the door open to let it crash against the wall.

The other monks, three of them sitting around a wooden table in the centre of the room, jumped when they saw him enter.

"Dead!" he cried. "They are all dead!" He looked around the room; his eyes were wide with shock. To the other monks watching, it looked like Gregor had gone insane.

"What is it, brother?" one of the monks asked, rising from his seat to help Gregor. "What can we do to help?"

"Send runners!" he cried. "The churches. They've been attacked! Burned! The priests, dead! Send help!"

The monk slowly sank back into his seat as the gravity of the news washed over them all.

"What's wrong with you!" Gregor cried. "Father Jason needs to know!" Then he realized that none of the monks present were Christopher's keepers. They were just simple monks, not nearly up to the challenge of running the distance between Signa Aquainus and Anderita. And, it was already dark out.

He realized he would have to go himself, and wait until morning. Defeated, he too sank into a nearby chair and stared into the silence as he listened to the weather turn bad outside. He began to wait for the rest of the night to pass.

Chapter Nineteen

The rain poured down through the darkness while Beast gazed silently out into the night. Little did the weather concern him, but it masked the scents in the air, and helped to dampen the sounds of the forest night. Still, his dark eyes pierced through the shadows, and he was content to remain where he was, as motionless as the night itself while Christopher slept silently deep down in the centre of Beast's being. His tongue lolled as a sign of contentment.

The good father was resting fitfully out of the shelter of the rain in a small cabin that did little to keep the damp cold air out of his lungs. The wolf watched over him silently while he coughed through the night, and as the dawn began to approach, the rain began to fizzle itself out. In the darkness before dawn, there was but a mere drizzle to mark its passage, yet the priest's coughing continued undisturbed.

The wolf, sensing the stirring of the soul within, instinctively sought a warm, dry place to rest and had to content itself with the floor of the cabin. It managed to find a way in through an open window, and Christopher would later wonder if it was left open on purpose, despite the father's cough. Silently, he glided into the darkness outside the cabin and lay down, resting his maw on his outstretched forepaws.

Christopher awoke.

The wolf glided effortlessly back into the suppressed shadows of the mind.

Though in the time between times, when sleep and awake are one, Christopher met the wolf briefly, was able to pat the creature's thick mange of black fur that hung about its neck, and bid it a fond rest. The wolf brushed up against his leg and receded into shadows, stoically ignoring Christopher. Beast was always aware of Christopher and had no reason to even acknowledge him now.

Christopher smiled as he watched the wolf disappear into the obscurity of his mind and then opened his eyes to find himself face down on the cabin floor. He was cold, and wet, and quite naked. Yet the darkness afforded him privacy enough, and his clothes were within reach on a chair nearby.

He dressed quickly and silently so he could listen into the forest in an effort to find out where he was. Yet Father Jason's coughs continued, and Christopher was disturbed by what he heard. He dared not light a candle to dry the air out. The priest needed as much rest as he could. Instead, he sat down in the now empty chair and watched thoughtfully until sunlight began to creep in through the closed window.

With a start, Jason awoke and sat up in bed. He was dressed in his robes, no doubt for the added warmth.

"How did you sleep?" he asked, when he noticed Christopher watching him.

"Like always," Christopher commented. "Like the dead." His gaze remained fixed on the priest. He did not need to ask the father how he had slept.

The priest remained silent.

"We're leaving," Christopher said at last.

There was silence.

"Where are we going?"

"Anywhere but here," Christopher said more harshly than he intended. "Away from the coast," he corrected himself, trying to soften his words. "Away from the rains."

Father Jason nodded. He knew it would do no good to argue, it would only waste time.

They left that night, just as the sun was going down. Father Jason spent the day resting, while Christopher packed their few meagre belongings together and made their intentions known to Beast's keepers. The other monks stoically agreed, seeing that decision would be for the best, and they began to break camp. They would make a game out of trying to catch Christopher and Father Jason and wanted to give them as much a head start as they could once they agreed Christopher was to head west, deeper into Britain and Fernir's territory. Whoever this other werewolf, the monks were secure in knowing that Fernir would not be able to stop resist all of them. Perhaps it could be agreed upon whether they would take the creature's pelt.

No better diversion could be thought up for Christopher. It got him away from the coast, and the war that raged there.

Chapter Twenty

Anderita waited for her with a fury that matched her own when she stepped at last upon its shores one more time. Scattered and hiding, her men and her assassin waited for her to collect them and bring them to force once again. Their camp had been found, their longboat had been burned, along with the coffin her men had so painstakingly crafted for her.

She looked over the remains of their home and couldn't ignore the lump that rose to her throat. "To Hell with them all!" she muttered darkly as the angry mob of militia and soldiers waved torches through the wilderness in an angry, determined search for the invaders.

She shook her head at how easy they had made this for her, and soon men were falling as they screamed to their deaths, one at a time, scattered throughout the wilds, cut off from each other and unable to collect quickly enough to gather against the supernatural strengths of the darkest of nights.

Her men, hearing the screams, shouted their own war cries as they rose from their hiding places. Janelle was a silent shadow of death with her two knives in each hand and her naked body reflecting the strength and horror of what she had become. Anderita was completely unprepared and fell before the dawn had once again come upon them.

"Victory," Aphrodite panted, "will be ours." Her men and Janelle stood surrounding her, equally exhausted and suffering only a few minor scratches that would heal soon enough.

"An army is coming, mistress," General Theilbold reminded her.

She rose to her full height as she caught her breathe and stared at her men, measuring their strength against what she had found in Britain. "Let them come," she said at last. "And let them die."

Chapter Twenty-One

Gregor stumbled into the monastery, breathless and shouting as loud as he could. "Where is everyone?" he cried out it despair. No one answered. Two steps away from falling, he reeled about the empty hallway, determined to continue on until he found one of the Keepers. Miraculously, he prayed it would be Christopher, but he didn't keep his hopes up. Anyone at this point would be better than no one. And someone had to organize their defences. He didn't know for how long he could continue.

Knowing he could not quit, he set his feet toward the front door and stumbled toward the waterfall. It took him not as long as he thought to reach the bottom of the valley. The downhill slope gave him rest, and he was able to finish his trek despite the vomit that rose to his throat with every step. Joshua was there, packing up the remains of their camp and carefully stowing away Anubis' pelt into its chest.

"Where is everyone?" Gregor asked, breathless.

"They went after Fernir," Joshua said. His face went pale when he saw Gregor stumbling toward him.

Gregor only looked at the questions in his eye and nodded. "Vampire!" he gasped as he collapsed to the forest floor. Joshua returned his nod and dropped the chest, going after the Keepers at a run, leaving Gregor and the pelt in the valley behind him.

* * * * *

It was night, deep inside the forests. A statue stood passive in the centre of a clearing while moonlight filtered down through a thin dusting of clouds that flipped the light around the clearing in a gradual blur of movement.

Nearby a cave had been carved from a massive rock. An iron grate had been built into the cave's entrance, and immense oaken bolts placed across the front of it. Scars on the gargoyle, huge gashes frozen in place by the flash of immortality that had transformed the creature to granite told Christopher and his men whatever had attacked the creature was a werewolf.

Two warriors dressed in black cloaks with hoods up stood transfixed on the door in front of them. Swords were partially drawn as they stood ready to strike.

The gargoyle was a werewolf. Seeing the creature brought an angry wrath boiling out of Christopher's skin and he flung himself at the statue as he sought to pour forth the anguish of his own soul.

His men, seeing what had happened, jumped after him while the warriors dived in to intersect. The battle was fierce, though there were more Keepers than there were of the mysterious clan. No killing strike found its mark while Christopher was free to avenge himself on the gargoyle, instinctively seeing the wrath that was frozen in place, finding a safe place to vent his own unending frustrations at last.

Oblivious to the mortals and their deadly dance, he heard the first time a crash sounded against the iron grate.

More men, more darkly cloaked assassins, were pouring into the clearing. His keepers were now hard pressed, ringed around Christopher and the statue in an arc that let no one through. Yet the assassins were drawing the Keepers off, trying to spread their defences away from Christopher. It was an interesting battle, as no one continued to strike a killing blow.

Then, the door exploded outward and another werewolf roared as he ripped through the jagged hole he had made in the cave. Beast jumped at the new threat, tearing a path through the men, who dived and scattered to get out of the way in time.

The werewolves clashed with a battalion of barred teeth and outstretched claws. The noise was deafening as they engaged each other madly, ripping and tearing before they broke apart and went galloping into the woods in a maddened war with no reason.

The men remained motionless, considering the dead and wounded that were left behind. Finally, one of the assassins pulled back his cloak. By the look of him, he was a Norman invader. He glared at the Keepers hatefully, realizing full well the damage that had been released this night. "This is your mess," he spat in a rich accent that spoke of truth. The Keepers avoided his eyes as he glared at them. "You clean it up."

Then, he and his men set out after Fernir, and Christopher's Keepers did no less.

* * * * *

Exhausted, Joshua found the abandoned gargoyle at first light. He stumbled into the clearing, saw the ruined holding cell and the carnage of the dead and wounded men around him. Then he fell amidst them, too weary to do anything else, and cried out in despair. His voice was only one amongst the anguished survivors.

"Where is Father Jason?" he cried.

"The priest is still at camp," another monk answered miserably. "What brings you to our disaster, brother?"

"Anderita is under attack!" he wailed.

More than one of the Vikings grinned wickedly. "What you have delivered to us now consumes you," one of them said cryptically.

Joshua glanced at the Norman angrily. "A vampire leads them," he said. Then he collapsed, too spent to bother with more words.

* * * * *

All through the night and into the next day the Vikings and the monks chased after Christopher and the other werewolf, Fernir. Their trail was not hard to follow, but as they jogged through the endless miles, both parties knew they would not come upon the werewolves as mortal, not this day. The two would stick close together while mortals. Yet when the sun had set, they would return to their maddened battle. Only time would tell if their guards would be able to catch them after that. But their pursuers had no choice but to try, becoming grateful for the animosity between them that fed their determination as the day wore on.

Just after midday, the Keepers realized Beast was trying to get back to the statue of Father Jason. Without saying a word to the Vikings, they simply broke from the trail and scattered into the wilderness, cutting through the underbrush in a path they forged in front of them as they went. The Vikings, knowing the determination needed to keep a werewolf amongst them, followed, realizing they would find their pets sooner if they cut away from the trail.

* * * * *

Christopher stumbled into the clearing at dawn. He had left the confused and maddened soul behind him, doing what he could to outdistance the man. But desperation and determination drove the madman on, and he needed Christopher's reassuring presence, knowing that the monk had the same nightmare demon lurking behind his skin. He would not lose the security he had found in numbers. And he dogged Christopher's steps tirelessly as the monk fled toward his father.

The gargoyle dissolved when Christopher returned to him, and Jason stood before him. As fast as the transformation had taken place, Jason's expression had dissolved from heavenly to terrified. "What has happened?" he asked.

"Fernir," Christopher said quickly. "He is not alone." He grabbed at a set of clothing and began to dress. "It's time to go," he said as he pushed Father Jason out of the clearing. "He's chasing us."

Chapter Twenty-Two

Two wet and weary travellers clung to each other. The one coughed labouriously and full. His wracking sobs clutched him uncontrollably, bending him in half. The other slaved over the old man, afraid and destitute, flinching at shadows. The road was uncommonly used, and the going was much easier than Christopher had expected. But he was thankful as well. These trails were making it easier for the old man.

Several hours later they stumbled onto a road.

Refugees struggled through the weather one weary step at a time. They were weighted down by hundreds of pounds of luggage. They wore ragged, thread-bare clothing worn in tattered layers about their shoulders. They counted in the thousands of starved and sleep-deprived men, women, and children who had seen the horrors of unimaginable terror brought to life before their eyes. All of them kept their faces away from the coast, struggling to free themselves from the mountains of their home.

"What do we do now?" Christopher asked into his father's ear. Terror was raging through him and he struggled with his lack of faith until his eyes became downcast and repentant. He crossed himself, yet the old man seemed too weary to lift his arms.

A strand of men dressed in leather and carrying swords walked through the crowd, who struggled to give the rough soldiers a wide enough birth to pass by without drawing attention: though there was little effort left within them.

Christopher and Jason watched them come, too intent on their flight to care. The danger was behind them, not before them. Yet when their eyes met those of the men, they knew fear once again.

The last of the men, a wiry, thin man with a touch of insanity in his eyes, gazed deeply into Christopher's eyes, and something in them froze Christopher in his tracks. The wolf within him raged against his cage, coming fully awake and shaking the bars of his den so hard that Christopher's heart skipped a beat and he swooned with the effort of holding the creature at bay. Father Jason's hand under his elbow supported him until he could regain his balance, and in a moment, his strength had regained as well. By then, the warrior had passed and continued on his way with the rest of his band.

"We are getting off the roads," Christopher whispered urgently. Travel through the woods would be slow and perilous, but both knew they could be comfortable in conditions where others would perish. He was plagued by the fear of Fernir now, and needed to see his father safely away.

Father Jason nodded at the wisdom of his words and holding each other from falling, they weaved their way through the crowds until they were clear of them on the other side, and hurried as fast as they could for the shelter of the trees some distance away.

Soon after, Fernir's host stumbled out of the bushes and onto the road. He was still naked, yet oblivious in his determined madness. He pushed through the Viking raiders, spewing a few curses at them in Norse for being in his way.

One of the Vikings watched him for a moment and then said, "We go this way."

The others nodded and relayed the message up the line. They turned and followed their companion's suggestion wordlessly, hungry for what their man had in mind.

The forest was dim in the sunless drizzle, yet Christopher found their way through it easily enough. There was nothing to do about the wet that soon had them drenched to the skin in heavy robes that weighed them down and had Father Jason shivering with what was becoming a fever.

But there was that deep, primordial instinct pounding in Christopher's chest that told him to run, to run and to run, and he pushed them onwards despite the old man's labours and failing health. At one point during the day, his concern for the old priest forced them to stop for a brief rest.

Father Jason dropped from exhaustion, too weak to cough, yet barely able to draw breathe and not daring to speak.

"It is He who gives us strength, Father," Christopher reminded him.

Jason nodded as he reached into a fold of his robes.

"You brought some of it with you?" Christopher asked.

With shaking hands, the old man pulled out a few pieces of broken bread and held them reverently between them. The two regarded the bread for a moment in thoughtful reverence. Christopher bowed his head and made the sign of the cross as they worshipped. Father Jason took a piece and placed it in his mouth as he closed his eyes. Immediately, strength began to return to him. He breathed in and then out, forcing the air through his congested airways. Then he looked at his companion. As he chewed the bread, he held out a piece for Christopher, who took it solemnly.

"His body," Christopher mumbled. Then he took the bread and ate it.

"His blood," Jason added as he carefully replaced the remaining pieces into his robe.

Wordlessly, he pushed weakly to his feet.

Christopher shook his head at the stubborn persistence of the man and followed, quickly taking his elbow and lending him his strength.

The wolf's beating heart forced Christopher onward again, and for the rest of the day, his attention was given completely over to finding the easiest paths through the forest.

The raiders followed far behind, taking their time to avoid the thicker tangles of wet foliage. Yet there was assurance in their stride, an arrogant swagger in their steps as they silently fanned out through the forest. They were in no hurry. They could easily follow the trail of the two weak and frightened monks. But these monks had come from somewhere, and no such place was supposed to exist in these parts. Most of these communes proved to be of value, many of them being rich in plunder. Taking their time to track these two was worth the effort.

Near sunset, Christopher and Jason stumbled into a clearing and Christopher's eyes flitted over the place, searchingly. Though what he was looking for, he could not say. *Stay here*, his instincts told him with a calm sense of wordless authority.

He looked about the clearing, and then at the sky overhead. The rain was stopping and it would be better for them to make camp in the clearing than under the dripping eaves of the trees surrounding them. And soon, it would be too dark to travel. Christopher would need to sleep through the darker parts of the night. He was not worried about the safety of his companion once that happened. And a fire would help keep the other creatures of the night away from them. He nodded as he decided about the place, then he halted

Father Jason in the middle of the clearing.

"Here is where we stay," he said at last.

The priest did not argue, but only sank to the ground in weary resignation.

Christopher had a flint stone and dry shavings in one of the folds of his robe, and quickly began to build a fire next to the old man. Yet when it was time to strike the spark, the priest placed his hand on his arm and drew his attention away from the fire.

"It will not start in the damp," Father Jason said. "Not like that." He pulled out a piece of parchment and held it out for Christopher.

The younger man's eyes grew round at the magnitude of the sacrifice the priest was making. "Father," he stammered. "That is paper."

"I know what it is," Jason said almost angrily. He paused until his voice was under control. "Burn it."

Recognizing the command for what it was, Christopher took the page in his hands, fearful of looking at it and seeing what writings it may contain. As the spark caught and flame ignited, a tear streamed down the side of his face over the magnitude of their loss even as the warming flames grew in strength and insured their survival.

Chapter Twenty-Three

The following night a more organized mob of soldiers waited for them outside the gates of Anderita. These Aphrodite quietly ignored as she told her men to wait while she scouted the city. Monks roamed the streets with armed guards to protect them. Using torches to light their way, they made no secrets about being there, often shouting encouragements to the city that huddled in fear, now shouting challenges for the demon to come out and show herself. Aphrodite did not like the boisterous resolve she saw in those streets, and wondered if vampires could burn to death. This was not good.

She quietly returned to her men and told them of what she had seen.

"What are we to do?" Theilbold asked fearlessly. "We are outnumbered."

"You draw the soldiers from the gates off," she announced. "They'll see you and they'll give chase, leaving the monks behind. Then we strike them all down."

Theilbold grinned. The tactic, though called cowardly, worked in other places and at other times. It would work here as well.

Without the command, General Theilbold rose from his hiding place and the rest of his men followed. Janelle sat silently by Aphrodite's side, awaiting her mistress's command.

"Soon," Aphrodite whispered to her companion. "I will have need of you again before long."

Janelle looked at Aphrodite questioningly.

"The monks," she admitted. "They have something that can destroy me." Janelle showed shock on her face.

"It is true," Aphrodite said. "But they are vulnerable to other mortals, weak in comparison. I do not dare approach them now. But you," Aphrodite looked at where the assassin kept her knives sheathed under her long sleeves and shook her head. "If you were like me, you would feed this night," was all she said.

Janelle seemed pleased with the prospect, and Aphrodite was happy for her.

The Vikings closed with the Britons in a reckless assault that caught the defenders off guard. Though there were only a few of them, the Normans threw themselves into the attack, and with surprise on their side, managed to drag a good number of them to death before the Britons repelled them and gave chase. There were about twenty of them close on the heels of the Normans, and three more monks that laboured to keep up behind them. But the Vikings were lightly armoured, the Britons were not. And there were no horses amongst them. The monks, unaccustomed to running, were already showing signs of slowing as they trudged along in their long wool robes.

Aphrodite pulled Janelle to her feet and pointed to the monks. "Kill them," she whispered heatedly. The bloodlust was already beginning to take control. "Let them think you are me."

Janelle nodded and ran to intersect the monks while Aphrodite turned her attention to the heels of the Britons disappearing down the road in front of her. She ignored the monks' screams and gave chase, confident Janelle could dispatch of the deadly threat behind her.

The first of the Britons fell, then the second and third, until Aphrodite found her predictable pattern of death and the defenders began dying all around her. Her men, realizing she had caught up, checked their flight and charged fearlessly into the fray, confusing the already terrified Britons and cutting through them in a swathe of blood.

It was over quickly enough, and Janelle was trotting down the road to meet them.

"Good," Aphrodite said. "This is good."

With that, she turned and led them back up the road to the undefended gates of Anderita.

By some signal, the other defenders roaming the streets had been called to the gates, and Aphrodite did not like what she saw once Anderita came into view once more.

Monks lined the streets, bathing in supernatural light that only she could see. The soldiers with them took notice of the Normans and their mistress with Janelle. But they did not move, nor did they leave the silent, prayerful monks locked in concentration before them. Some of those monks were on their knees, clutching crosses or crucifixes before them that blazed with flames Aphrodite had to wince away from if she stared at them for too long.

"This time," Aphrodite called to her men in a voice that carried to the awaiting Britons, "We take the city." She was angry and determined to end this war over Anderita before reinforcements from either side came. And she knew any day the armies of either Britons or Normans would show up to change the tide and break this deadlock between them. She would have that deadlock broken before hand, thus giving her Vikings a safe landing on a foreign land of plunder.

"We are ready to fight by your side," General Theilbold announced. "We are ready to die by your side."

She looked at him and was filled with a fierce love for the man. On impulse, she grabbed him by the neck and held out her wrist to him. "Drink," she said heatedly. "Drink and never die." Then she bit into his neck, and he into her wrist, and the blood flowed between them in a heated bloodlust. When enough had been shared, Aphrodite pulled away and forced the general away from her. He stumbled to the ground, as if too drunk on wine, holding his head and moaning in pain. Aphrodite herself could not stop the spinning in her own head and forced herself to remain motionless until the world slowly stopped spinning.

Still, the defenders of Anderita watched, waiting for the moment of the attack and not daring to be drawn off by the spectacle before them.

Janelle was beside her, holding a cup out to her, and Aphrodite drank gratefully. Immediately, some of her strength returned, yet it would take the restorative sleep of the dead to replace what she had given this night. General Theilbold crawled to his knees, still holding his head between his hands. Then, he slowly rose to his feet and filled the air with a wicked, thick laughter. He pulled his hands away from his face and turned to face the Britons before them. His fangs were already showing in the moonlight and he laughed again as he watched the ripples of horror rush through the waiting ranks.

"Kill them," he muttered quietly. "Kill them all."

"General," she said quietly.

He turned and looked at her. He was pale from the need for blood and waited for her command.

She motioned for him to spread out with four of their men, while she would take Janelle and the other two and attack the other side of the Britons. He nodded, reading her battle plans in the deft motions of her hands, which now moved faster than he'd ever seen them. Yet he could follow their meaning, and his eyes shone with the torches from the Britons. They would be victorious this night. He never stopped smiling and when her commands had been relayed, he nodded and left her side, taking his men with him.

The Britons were growing more and more afraid as they witnessed the efficiency of command from Aphrodite, and she stared at them for a moment before she and the remaining half of her force walked toward the British flank.

The Britons eyed them fearfully as they split apart, and then, when they were far enough apart to divide the British defences in half, they attacked. Theilbold and Aphrodite controlled their movements to match the strength and speed of their men, and the defenders opened up a path through the middle of them, unaware of the supernatural strength before them. Once engaged, Aphrodite released her speed, as did the general, and the two of them seemed to reappear in the midst of the soldiers, behind them, while they fought the handful of men and the woman assassin on either side. The vampires cut them apart as fast as they could, ignoring the blaring light and fire that engulfed them. Searing pain was weakening them, yet they fought on, until, at last, most of the soldiers were dead and what was left standing would not carry any threat. Now it was the monks, and only the monks that posed a threat.

"Retreat!" Aphrodite commanded through gritted teeth. General Theilbold was fighting with a rage that deterred the flames, though they ate at his clothes and his back. "Retreat!" she shouted again, trying to get his attention from the hunger he sought to quench.

Still he fought on, locked in his new passions. His men followed her as she pulled back, and Aphrodite was grateful once the fire was out of range and could not harm her any more. Theilbold was surrounded by a tight knot of fierce soldiers, the last of them, while surrounding them, the monks closed in a tight circle. Fire exploded from the centre of the circle, and Theilbold cried in horror. All at once, he tried to escape, yet though he quickly, recklessly, dispatched the soldiers, he could not break the concentrated determination from the praying monks as they linked their hands together and lifted their voices to the skies. They were offering up a liturgy of prayers to some god Aphrodite did not know of, and the intensity of those words grew as the light and the flames from the general grew as well. He screamed again, and she cringed in knowing pain. Then, suddenly, she too exploded in flames, and crying with his loss, she fled to the safety of the ocean.

She forced herself onto the shores as fast as she could, and managed to regroup within a few hours. A few of her men were gone. Theilbold, somehow, was still alive. *Perhaps vampires could not die,* she thought to herself. There was precious little left of him. He had been burned to cinders, yet he lay too weak to moan, in agony beyond what any mortal could bare.

She looked on at him in horror, and he slowly moved his eyes to peer into hers. She cringed at what she saw there, and without hesitation, she vowed that vampires could die. Straight away, she ignored her men, who had rescued Theilbold from the gruesome vengeance of the now dead monks, and grabbed up a broken spear shaft. Angrily, she strode over to Theilbold's body and without hesitating, she thrust the shaft through his heart. The spear slid through his burnt and broken body, and he shuddered as he looked up at her. Then the light of their life extinguished from his eyes and he lay dead at her feet. She sighed with relief that his pain had been extinguished at last, and turned to look at the remaining force of her men. Only three of them and Janelle remained. Her men looked shocked, surprised. And Janelle had been crying.

"What happened here?" was all Aphrodite asked.

"The monks, mistress," one of her men stammered.

"What about them?" Aphrodite asked. She could see her men were shocked by what they had witnessed, so she gave them time to answer when they could.

"They forgave us," one of them said simply.

Aphrodite shook her head and blinked her eyes in disbelief. "What?"

Another Viking nodded in agreement with the first. "It's true, mistress. They forgave us and said they hoped we would be freed from our turmoil?"

"What turmoil?" Aphrodite cried.

The Vikings shrugged. Yet Janelle was looking off at the distant wilderness with longing in her eyes. She was not listening to what they were saying. "Some of the others," the Vikings continued. "They began to cry with shame. They did not dare to dishonour you, so they helped kill the monks. But when they were done, they relinquished their swords. There they are before you." The Viking gestured to the small pile of abandoned weapons. "They left. They knew you would find them, and perhaps kill them. But they said they could not do this anymore."

"Do what?" Aphrodite asked, horror stricken.

"Destroy," the Viking answered. "They could not destroy anymore."

Aphrodite sighed and thought for a moment. "Let them go," she said at last. "They deserve that, at least." She looked over the body of her general, at the awaiting city.

"There are no more defenders," she said at last. "Anyone who wants to pillage what they can, I suggest you do it now. There will be more tomorrow night."

Without another word, she picked up the body of her general and carried the corpse to the beach. Janelle and the Vikings followed her without a word.

She placed the body on the beach and sat with it through the remainder of the night. The sun began to lighten the horizon, and still she remained where she was. Janelle grew fearful for her, but Aphrodite waved her off, staring at the corpse as she had done all night long. She deserved to feel the flames that would claim his body to eternity. She would give him that much. And the sun, with its claustrophobic terror, was not such a big threat in comparison with the horror the two of them had suffered this night.

She had never sat through a sunrise before. And the horror of the engulfing light was dispelled only by the comforting proximity of the ocean. The sun did not hurt her yet, but it did terrify her, and some detached part of her mind was fascinated with the experience she was suffering through. Her men and Janelle stood in a semicircle around her and the general, grieving in silence for the two vampires. Then, when the sun finally did crest the horizon, flame ignited on their bodies and slowly spread over them both. At last, Aphrodite pulled away from her general, and engulfed in fire, dived into the ocean and its depths.

As the darkness swallowed her up, the flames died. The pain of her tormented body would subside in her sleep, but the aching in her heart would be with her for ever, she was sure of it. She fought off the sleep as long as she could as she tangled her body into the weeds at the bottom of the ocean, to stop it from floating to the surface and crisping again.

Finally, the darkness swallowed her, and she fell asleep.

Chapter Twenty-Four

Night grew on around them. The clouds tapered away, and the crest of a full moon offered them its shining light as the clouds blew across it. The raiders saw the fire in the distance and approached it with new determination as they smiled to each other with dark, humourless grins. This night they would make a sacrifice to their war god, and he would be pleased. He would be very pleased. The cursed one with the madness in his eyes, the one they'd followed into the wilderness, walked onward purposefully, giving himself over to his hunger and ignoring his companions with his inner searching. They nodded to each other as they cast knowing glances at their companion, and the smiles never left their faces.

They stepped into the clearing and spread out, staying just outside the ring of light at its centre. Christopher and Jason saw them, but gave no sign of it as their eyes communicated the fearful reality of their predicament. Father Jason coughed weakly and Christopher finally tensed as the warrior that had caused him so much fear finally stepped into the light across from him. Christopher stared at him through the flames and waited for him to speak.

"Mind if we share your fire?" the warrior said with a rich accent that told Christopher he was not from these shores.

"Do what you came to do," Christopher said flatly. The beast within him raged to be released, and Christopher feared the leash was about to snap.

"As you wish," the other said as he smiled. He roared out into the night, given over to his lusts and his cravings. The other warriors cheered him on with upraised weapons, and met his battle cry with their own. He shouted a second wordless scream into the night and suddenly, the unthinkable began to occur. Christopher struggled to his feet in horror as the hackles rose on his neck. The warrior's voice deepened into a growl before it rose to an inhuman howl. The man shook his head and fangs began to grow in his mouth as his nose and lips pushed out away from his face. His clothing ripped and fell from his body as it grew in size and changed in shape. Hair appeared on his arms and chest and face, covering him with a shaggy mane of fur.

In horror, Christopher looked on at his kindred, shocked that the man would give himself over to the beast within himself like this. The man seemed to be goading the beast on, whipping it out of its cage, forcing it to surface and go to war. The beast seemed tired and worn out, and as their eyes met, Christopher could see the dead look of one who had been the cause of uncountable death and misery. Yet the moon was full this night, and the beast came out with all of its strength. Half man, half wolf, it stood savouring the reaction it saw in Christopher. Then it turned its gaze upon Father Jason.

With a roar, Christopher wrenched the bars free from his own inner companion, who sprang from its cage snarling at the hunger it saw in its primordial enemy. No one, nothing, no force on this earth, would be able to stop the beast from protecting the father, and Christopher would not stand in its way any longer. Instead, he gave himself over to the wolf, lending it his intelligence, his faculties of the mind.

Werewolf once again, Christopher ripped from his robes as though they too were paper. The simple wooden cross around his neck was the only ordainment that still fit and was the only thing that truly identified the one beast from the other. Christopher did not hesitate, did not stop to question.

Instead, he lunged for the other creature's throat, his claws stretched out before him to tear and render the monster in front of him useless and lifeless if he could. The other wolf, caught off guard, managed to save himself in time. He reached back, away from Christopher's snapping jaws, and instead, Christopher sunk his teeth into the creature's shoulder.

Howling his fury, the raider embraced Christopher by the neck, and the two went down in a heap, snarling and biting each other as they continued to morph into the wolves that they were.

The warriors looked at each other fearfully, silently, as the two combatants tore and thrashed amongst the clearing. Father Jason remained motionless and stared at the flames of their fire, saddened by what this night was brining on.

The father began to cry as his heart broke by the sacrifice Christopher was making.

As for Christopher, rage consumed. It was simpler than that. Rage held him. He was one with his desires in his righteous war, and he had no compunction about killing the monster before him, none at all. The other wolf felt the same, and the two continued to snap and lunge at each other, blood flowing fresh with each contact they made.

The night wore on, and still the fight raged, though now both wolves were slick with blood and wounded beyond recovery. But gradually, it was Christopher, whose fierce and pent up will had been exploded from within, who began to get the upper hand. The other wolf, weary from his never ending war, felt each tear upon his back as hopeful release, as perhaps the end of his ongoing nightmare, and the resolve of the man quickly fled, until Christopher was fighting only a wolf, a stupid creature that made mistakes.

Christopher quickly took more control of his mind, enough to grasp a branch from the fire. This he took up as a hefty club, and swung the one burning end into the face of the wolf. The creature snarled and checked its flight as the flame came up between them. Their eyes met. Covered in blood from head to toe, both knew there was only one course of action, and that was to finish this. Yet in that moment, they both knew who the victor would be.

"Come to me," Christopher snarled in a tongue that was just barely human. The other warriors cringed to hear the quiet command, yet their god knew no such emotion that would allow him to cringe away in defeat. This was the full moon. Sacrifice would be made.

He sprang into the air, and Christopher roared as he swung the branch full into the wolf's face. The fire caught as the branch broke upon the jaws of the wolf's snout. The creature whimpered in pain as Christopher turned back into Beast and sprang at the other wolf's neck. Blinded by fire and pain, the other was caught off guard and still in the air while Beast's jaws sunk into to his jugular and tore it from his neck.

They landed in a heap, motionless. But then Beast struggled to his feet and looked at the other warriors, who stared dumbstruck at the body of their dead god.

Beast dropped the flesh from his mouth and then retreated back into his cage.

Christopher, wounded and exhausted and dying, stood on unsteady feet, naked before his enemies except for the cross that still hung around his neck. He was silent for a long while as he regarded them, and they him. No one moved. The warriors had the good sense to know trying to escape from the werewolf would be useless. Finally, it was Christopher who spoke. "Take it and go," he said as he motioned them toward the carcass of the wolf.

He stood where he was as he waited for them to go, and then turned back to Father Jason. Exhaustion finally overtook him, and he collapsed into the bloody grass. Quickly, he fell asleep, and Beast manifested through the broken body once again. Whining, the wolf crawled over to the father and collapsed against him, offering the priest the warmth of his fur coat, slick with blood though it may be.

The scent of blood, of wolf blood, filled Father Jason's nostrils and worked through his senses until he seemed coated in the stuff himself. He closed his eyes. "His body; his blood," he mumbled as he retrieved another piece of the small, unleavened bread from his robe. He crossed himself and then ate of the bread, trusting in its nourishing presence to see them through the dark remains of this night.

Eventually, Beast stopped whining. His breathing slowed, and his eyes closed. The wolf died. Under the pale moonlight, the carcass's coat of black fur began to slowly change colour. As if washed in the liquid light, the blackness of the pelt began to dew with dripping light, like weightless mercury. The drops of light clung to the coat like the dew of the morning upon the forest floor. And gradually, the drops soaked into the fur, bleaching it to silver and white. Jason continued to cry as he ran his fingers through the coat of fur, grieving over the loss of his friends, both the animal and the man.

Yet when the sun crested over the horizon, even as the moon still hung in the air, the dead body of the wolf began to change slowly back into the body of the man. Unlike the times when Beast and Christopher were alive, this time the change was gradual, peaceful. As the sun rose, the body changed, and as the body changed, the wounds healed and were gone. When the first rays of the sun touched the body, it suddenly, violently, drew breathe and came alive once again. Christopher awoke with a start and sat up.

He was in full health, and fully rested. His body wore no traces of the fight of the night before. He looked at the priest and sighed in relief. "That was interesting," he said at last.

Jason nodded wordlessly. His health, too, had seemed restored, if only a little bit. But it was enough, and he knew he would survive another day.

The Keepers found them soon after that, surrounded by their Viking counterparts.

"The other has gone on," Christopher said to them, recognizing them instantly for what they were. They nodded, and without bothering to exchange words with the monks, they chased after their charge, disappearing into the wilderness once again.

The Keepers collapsed into the clearing and Christopher started to salvage the fire. They would camp here this night before returning to Anderita the following day. Father Jason hoped that had given the others time to dispel the vampire attack before Christopher knew of it and released Beast upon the unsuspecting citizens. He was confident the threat would be ended soon enough. Yet as dusk began to settle about them, Joshua, left behind in the mad chase through the wilderness, stumbled into the clearing.

"Anderita," he gasped. "She killed them. I don't know how, but they are dead. Everyone is dead. Anderita is vulnerable."

Jason rose to his feet next the fire, his men rising with him. He glanced at the sun and after understanding the sacrifices made for him, could do no less in return. He looked at the edge of the clearing and allowed the strength of vampirism to flow into his veins. Usually suppressing the maddening thirst, he now let it flow forth. His fangs grew and his eyes darkened as he flinched painfully at the setting sun. The monks and Christopher stumbled away from him in fear. Yet Christopher, understanding what was happening, dared to approach the morphing body in front of him.

"Let me come with you?" he asked.

The vampire turned and looked at him with alien eyes. "You will only slow me down," he said in a voice Christopher did not recognize. He did not try to hide his surprise. "I am not your father this night," he said. "My name is Iminuetep." Then he was off, disappearing in front of Christopher's eyes even before the sun had set.

As he ran he summoned the child vampire to his side with a strength and determination he knew she had never before encountered. With the Keepers so far away from the monastery, and the others dead, it would be the only place safe enough to meet her, to try to contain her and get her away from the town of Anderita.

He made sure he stopped at the waterfall to retrieve the pelt of Anubis.

Chapter Twenty-Five

"Janelle!" she roared angrily before she was even out of the water. "Have reinforcements arrived from the mainland yet?"

"No, mistress," one of the Vikings reported coldly. "They have not."

Janelle looked apologetic as she held out a goblet of blood for her.

Aphrodite started to refuse the drought offered to her, but then changed her mind. She would not feed on the weak to indulge her senses this night. She took the cup and drank the entire thing down while her men and Janelle stood patiently by for her commands. When she was done, she gave the cup back to her slave and said, "With me." The men knew what she meant and jumped to follow her into the night.

She was at a loss. Until her forces came, she had no army. All she could do was continue to weaken the city through plague, and this she did, vengefully, draining the blood from her sleeping victims while the Vikings and Janelle awaited close by, should another monk venture to try to stop them. No one did, though she had no doubt the vicious creatures were searching for them. But the few of them were easy to hide, and Aphrodite feasted and feasted until she vomited again and again. When her army arrived, they would lay waste to this city and claim it as their own.

Yet it seemed like an empty victory, and Anderita would have no doubt summoned help from the surrounding cities. But none had come yet, and none would be able to stand against her anyway. It was only the monks she had to contend with, and she had already proven she could defeat them, though at a terrible cost.

Midway through the night, a powerful premonition took hold of her, and she turned to the wilderness surrounding Anderita. Her master was close and was summoning her. He knew what had taken place within this city, and he was calling her. She crept from the hut she was in and looked at her handful of loyal servants.

"I must go," she said to them. "I don't know how long I will be gone, but the city is ready to fall. Once the Vikings arrive, tell them what has happened here, and take the city. I will be back as soon as I can."

Janelle reached out to her mistress imploringly. But Aphrodite restrained her.

"No," she said to her servant. "You cannot come. You would only slow me down. No worry, I am in no danger." She leaned close to Janelle. "My master summons me," she whispered into the slave's ear. "I must go to this summons."

She pulled away from Janelle and held her at arms' length peering into her eyes to see the understanding there.

Janelle and Aphrodite both nodded and then the women embraced. Janelle kissed her mistress on the cheek and held her at arms' length once again. "Come back to us," her eyes said. And Aphrodite nodded her promise that she would.

Then Janelle knelt before Aphrodite and the Vikings followed her example and gave their Mistress of Death the homage that she deserved.

"I will return," she said at last. Then she was gone, following her premonition deep into the uncharted wilderness of Britania.

Chapter Twenty-Six

The sun set as the spirit of a vampire, dressed in the carcass of a dead werewolf settled onto the balcony. The ghost passed through walls and windows alike, as like smoke. But he appeared as solid as any apparition, and could move as cunningly as he wished. Fully awake and alert, the spirit passed from room to room, silently diminishing the light that had been gathering in the corners of the monastery. Darkness filled each hall as he went, moonlight extinguished candle flames. Mist covered light and trees stopped swaying as they shook off their autumn leaves. The whole place from within and without was sheathed in gentle fire, its presence too subtle for mortals to see; but enough to drive the child into a mad flight if she even caught a hint of its being here.

With each phantom breathe from the vampire more of the monastery fell asleep under the darkness. Yet the gargoyle standing in the courtyard of the house marked the barrier he would set, should the trap work. He knew Aphrodite had to be stopped, but he would not suffer the loss of seeing her destroyed. Signa Aquainnus was a good home, and many good memories were built into these walls. It would take a long time for the child to resent her prison. It had been he who had told her vampires never died. He needed to put her somewhere. His first concern was of drawing her away from Anderita. His second concern was for her.

The gargoyle boiled within, each hidden fireball reaching new degrees with every breath of darkness the ghost took.

He sought her out and realized she was on her way; she would meet him at the balcony of the dining room.

As she glided into the room on rays of silver moonlight, the drapes billowed out on a silent wind. He chuckled as he sat waiting for her before a glass of red wine. She was always one for flare.

"You," she said huskily, aching with desire. She pushed through the air in her effort to stand against the table between them, exhaling a hiss of desire as her back arced and her fangs glinted in the darkness.

He looked at her thoughtfully. He had one night to show her the way, one chance to conform the vampire to a higher level of existence, of life.

"What is it you want from me?" Aphrodite asked huskily as she walked around the table and threw herself into his arms. She began kissing his neck, not realizing that what she kissed was but a reflection of the true spirit within the gargoyle.

Iminuetep picked her up into his arms and walked into the moonlight on the balcony. He looked down to see his body, burning from within yet oblivious and at peace from without, in perfect harmony, in perfect balance. He transported them there and held her up so that she could see its face. Sensing his wishes, she looked up away from him and was instantly amazed, transfixed by the expression that was sculpted into his features. She reached out her hand and ran it over his granite skin, feeling each nuance of peace and contentment that shaped itself across the indestructible surface.

He put her down on her feet gently, careful not to jolt her out of her experience. She seemed to look into the creature's soul and mirrored the expressions across her distorted and evil face. The glowing hatred of her eyes was replaced by the restful passage of the moon. The fangs of the Mistress of Death slowly retracted into her gums and her expression was passive as it slid back into the sleeping human form it took during the day, when death kept the soul locked deep within eternal slumber.

Then, not needing the aid of a ghost image, the phantom stepped back and faded into a mist that only helped distinguish the fires of life even more. Within, the gargoyle burned with an explosive power of infinite degrees of heat while the inner layers of rock were seething with the intensity.

She looked at the statue and remained motionless, captivated, as the sun began to rise. Then, all at once she exploded into flames. The first touch of morning had found her out. Knowing her time was up, she pulled her eyes from what she thought was a statue, and walked into the house. The fire extinguished as she entered the shadows and sought out the deepest cells within the roots of this castle.

The gargoyle smiled. For all Aphrodite's lofty pride, and amongst the vast wealth the creature would lavish in, she was choosing to make her residence within the kennel.

He kept watch over her through the day, and she approached the gargoyle when she arose, once again. Wondering where Iminuetep the master had gone, she nonetheless placed a hand on the gargoyle's face appreciatively, then set out to find the master sculptor who had fashioned his own perfect image as a memorial to his greatness. Anderita not only groaned under its heavy burden of wealth, but the statue, as decoration, wore the pelt of Anubis immortalized into stone and draped about his shoulders. Magnificent, she thought. Then she was off, searching across the desolate wilderness.

The phantom of Iminuetep appeared next to the statue, and he set off once again to bring her back to the house.

When she saw him she was relieved and followed him back, unthinking, knowing that her men and Janelle would seek her out if she did not come to them. Her victory was complete.

He took her to the stone statue once again and allowed her to slip from his arms. She knew its features well, yet she was still pulled into the look in its eyes. The ghost shook his head and walked away from her, fading into nothingness once again.

Sometime later the night shifted and a twig broke the silence over the monastery.

Startled, Aphrodite came to herself with a start and looked around the courtyard, wondering where Iminuetep was. Instantly, she sensed the other vampire's presence, as if summoned to her by her desire. She looked back at the statue, and was mesmerized once again. Only this time the statue became animated, awakening from an inner sleep.

Deep inside the impenetrable skin of granite, the gargoyle's interior core of light and flame pushed out against the darkness with a righteous anger that seethed with the need for release. The gargoyle's face slid from peace to expressing that need, though the change was gradual and took them deep into the hours within the night. Yet that whole time Aphrodite remained just as still and mirrored his emotions on her own face. She went from sharing his peace in equal measures to experiencing a terror unlike any she had encountered. She still did not comprehend the power of life building from within the gargoyle, yet she grew aware of the power to keep her transfixed throughout the night. She was caught in an awakening level of terror, beginning to realize the power this statue possessed was as equally out of her reach as the ability to stop the sun from rising.

And still the heat boiled from within until the eyes of the statue came to life with a blinding light that engulfed the perimeter of the monastery in a solid wall of flame. Aphrodite screamed in terror and ripped her gaze away from the statue's eyes, and instantly everything returned to the way she had found it the previous night. Shadows reigned and there was no trace of that holy fire. Yet Iminuetep was still nowhere to be found.

She glanced over at the statue. And for a third time she was transfixed in place. The gargoyle's eyes were now mere molten portals. Though they seethed with liquid fire, the statue remained as indomitable as always. Realization dawned on her that this statue was the master, that it was alive and becoming animated. She ran her fingers tenderly across its face, marvelling at the power the master possessed. Then she stepped back away from the statue, not understanding the dangers that could consume her so readily.

Lines of light began to appear across the surface of the gargoyle as the stone began to crack under the pressure boiling from within. The cracks grew as the magna pushed above the rock layers, and gradually, all that remained of the once dead statue was a living tongue of fire pressed into Iminuetep's body. The pelt of Anubis turned into a real werewolf skin as he glided toward her.

Still in awe, and relieved the fire within him did not burn through the surrounding night, she stepped aside and returned his stare as he glided past her and then up onto the balcony of the dining room. She followed, watching him as he entered the house. As the shadows embraced him, he was sheathed in an illusion of a man dressed as a monk, or a priest, the perfect illusion to accompany the dead trophy of this monastery he languished in.

He walked to the head seat at the table and pulled the chair away. Then he sat down and motioned for her to do the same to the chair across from him.

"How did you defeat the hell flame?" he asked quickly.

"Is that what you call it?" she asked back. "Is that what it is?"

Jason nodded. "I will share my knowledge with you, child. I have grown powerful in your absence."

"I see that, Master. What hidden knowledge drives you to this awakening?"

Jason smiled. "The hell flame is a source of perfect light. Vampirism is a source of perfect dark. While we are slaves to our passions, we live empty, ceaseless lives that endlessly torment us with eternity."

Aphrodite knew what that felt like, though her men had given her enough distraction in the last few years to forget about the mundane. "I just began my reign of conquest, and wasn't about to weep for my loss until I mimicked Alexander the Great and mourned because there was no other empire to conquer. But until then, I will grow and think up things to do to pass the time until I rule the world in a fist of death. Despite your power, I pity you for even acknowledging that disgrace."

Iminuetep looked at her and sighed. "I remembered the immeasurable wealth of Egypt I once massed, and wonder what you could possibly do that was as great as the monuments of stone left behind as their legacy. And you think you will be able grasp all of it." He sipped from his wine glass, savouring the taste upon his lips and soul. "History has been written by the hands of mortals who passed to dust. The records of the past and the present and the predictions of the future are nothing more than the desperate scribbles of men and women who need to feel as though they themselves have contributed to the passage of time. Yet history, past present and future, is something that only the immortal mind can express, can contemplate. Vampires are but shadows and dust, but unlike the mortals who desperately seek to find an excuse for crawling around on a planet, given breath for only a handful of moments, vampires know of the empty endlessness of it all. And it is the vampire mind that waits patiently for the judgement to come and fall in merciful finality.

"We are the damned. We are the lost. We are those who walk the halls of darkness night after night with nothing but the minds of our victims to pass the time.

"Humans, in their meagre existences, have it far better than the rest of us. Yet all are destined to fall under our path. All are destined to either walk this path with us, or crumble to dust at the beginning of this eternal tread.

"It is a mercy either way. Yet all of us seek light, seek a way out, seek something beyond ourselves. And religion, usually a front for our night time workings, none the less is based in a truth that many of us have found and embraced. Mortal and immortal alike, we are all now free, seeing uorselves all as equals, no matter our stage in life. We are waiting for the final judgement to set us all free of our earthly, deprived cravings while this truth gives us the strength to resist even the power of the terrible vampire thirst."

He looked at her closely. "What makes you think you can obtain anything close to what I have already done?"

"Because I can," she answered defiantly.

"And will that bring you the fulfillment I have shown you in the last few nights?"

She was silent as she considered his words. Finally, she was forced to admit the truth to his words by the evidence before her. "No."

"Then relinquish control," he said calmly.

"No!" she shouted as she rushed to her feet and threw the chair she sat on against a wall in rage. "I will not!" she cried as she turned back Father Jason. "You may be the master! But I am the mistress! The very fires of the cross could not stop me from Anderita! I am indestructible!"

He rose to his feet. "And blood?" he asked. "Will you ever grow tired of your thirst and seek to put it to rest? Will shedding the blood of innocents ever amount to enough killing to quench your desire for plague and death?"

"No," she admitted. "But it will be enough!" she vowed as she held her hand in a fist she held before her.

"If it is blood you seek," he said. "Take mine."

She expressed her surprise and delight by letting her lower lip quiver with excitement.

He was offering her the spoils of war.

Quivering, she sided over to him and breathed onto his neck, savouring the moment. Then she plunged her fangs into his jugular.

Fire exploded from the wound. The amulets flared to life like mirrors pointed at a sun. Darkness ceased to exist as liquid gold seeped through Jason's wound and healed it.

In terror, she stumbled back. "Hellfire," she muttered, trembling on the floor.

Jason looked down at her. "I didn't win, Aphrodite. I lost." Then he strode past her and returned to the courtyard.

In time, she could climb to her feet and stumble from the house. The fire had dissipated when he left the room, and the dizzying pain slowly lifted from her. She walked onto the balcony and looked down to see the gargoyle statue frozen into its place once again. It was at peace, it was at rest. And Aphrodite shivered as she realized the spirit within that statue was hellfire itself.

She approached the gargoyle, already mesmerized by what she saw there. Then, with a terrible effort, she tore herself away from the expression on its face and walked into the darkness surrounding his house. Instantly a wall of fire shot into the sky, sending her reeling in terror as she stumbled back into the courtyard.

The fire winked out and the night returned to its sleeping death. She looked at the gargoyle suspiciously, and realized she was his prisoner.

Chapter Twenty-Seven

Christopher was the first to reach Signa Aquainnus. Leaving his keepers behind in the night, Beast had sensed something was wrong and was driven with a determination as Christopher slept. The night glided past them in a continual blur of shadows and patches of moonlight, but Christopher slept soundly while Beast pursued his instinct through trails that drove them straight as an arrow and just about as swift to the front doors of their home.

Once there, Beast calmed and went dormant. Still asleep, Christopher pitched to the ground, where he awoke with a start, wondering how long he'd lain there, but not questioning how he'd gotten there. He knew where he was, and he approached the silent, sleeping monastery cautiously, not knowing what awaited him within.

No other monks were about. Christopher surmised they'd gone to Anderita to help protect the city from the same vampire Father Jason had been confident enough to face alone. He wondered how the other monks fared, but pushed his fears and doubts aside as he summoned Beast forward to help search the empty halls with their shared night vision.

Eventually, they came upon the dining room, gliding silently into the room to find a female vampire staring out into the courtyard below. She sensed his presence and turned to face him. Then she attacked.

She flew through the room in a blur, but the moon was still growing, only a few days from being full, and Beast was not tired, nor weak. He saw her coming and before she had bridged the distance between them, he was snarling and baring his teeth in warning.

Shocked, Aphrodite stopped. She was confused by this strange animal's speed and ability to see in the dark. Mere paces from him, she asked, "What are you?"

Still snarling, half human, half wolf, Christopher and Beast snapped at her. Not bothering to answer, Christopher released his control on Beast and allowed him to attack instead.

The wolf plunged and grabbed the vampire's shoulder in its powerful jaws. Instantly, she exploded into flames and screamed in terror and pain. Startled, he tossed his head and threw her into the far wall. Still screaming, she came to her feet and fled the monastery. He followed and caught up with her moments later, cowering at the foot of a granite statue. The flames were tapering out in the night, and the vampire was too terrified to look up at the werewolf standing over her.

The wolf looked up from her to the statue and the werewolf melted back under his skin as Christopher gazed upon the pained expression of his father.

The priest ached with a longing to protect Aphrodite, even as he held a fierce determination to deliver the sentence that she so readily deserved. Christopher was sure his father had been powerful enough to kill the creature while he had the chance, and just as assuredly, Christopher could finish this at any moment he wished. Yet his father pleaded, his love for Christopher was just as obvious in his silent, still expression. They were like two of his children, Aphrodite and Christopher, and now they were locked in a struggle of good versus evil that rendered Father Jason's heart with each blow that was exchanged.

Still cowering, the flames now totally extinguished, Aphrodite clutched at the base of the statue. "Master," she cried weakly. "Please, have mercy on me." She was pathetic, spent, and trapped between the gargoyle and the werewolf. Both could burn her in an eternal flame she had no power over, and she was at their mercy, defeated even as victory lay within her reach.

Christopher saw the compassion on his father's face and stepped back, confused and angered by the mercy Father Jason showed her. Still, the werewolf was determined to end this war and knew little of the power Jason held over her. Then, sensing the unspoken question, the gargoyle's head slowly tilted toward the sky and a silent prayer was sent to the Heavens as the statue's expression changed from compassion to pleading.

In response, the gargoyle began to grow wings. Quickly, they appeared from behind him, stretching outward and around him as they embraced Aphrodite in a protective alcove of rock. Not touching her, they extended all the way from his shoulders to the ground, and left an opening wide enough for her to slip through should she ever want to leave his embrace. Yet the determined set of his jaw told Christopher Jason held her on a tight leash. Whatever power he held over her would not let her roam very far. He was her captor now, as well as her protector, and she would not be allowed to harm anyone for a long, long time. The determined set of the statue's gaze told Christopher that much.

Bitterly, knowing he had lost his father, Christopher looked down at the vampire. "You are defeated," he said. "Father has given you this place, but I swear, if you so much as set foot outside this place again, if he releases you for whatever reason," he pointed up at his father and then back down at her. His hand was shaking, he was so angry. Then, he relinquished his anger to Beast and went to sleep. He morphed completely into the wolf, letting her see the power the white wolf possessed. She shuddered all the more as she looked on at a creature of the night more powerful than her. Beast snarled and snapped at her, showing her his teeth and the never-ending determination in his eyes.

Christopher's meaning was clear. Leaving her to her fate, Beast slunk into the forest to look for the rest of the invaders. The priest had dealt with one; let him deal with the rest.

* * * * *

The thick wavering crest of the partial moon hung low over the horizon, hiding Christopher's grief and disappointment as he stood before Aphrodite's men and her silent assassin. Beast had found them quickly enough, and then had awakened Christopher, letting them see him for what he was. They were shocked into silent pacifism and did not attack him on sight. Instead, they listened carefully to every word he had to say, even though they knew him to be an enemy. "Tonight the power has been granted," he growled through gritted teeth, caught between rage and grief. "Tonight your mistress has won you the right to walk forward into the halls of greatness and invade the strength of this land itself."

Her men and Janelle were too tired and stunned from the previous night to rejoice in the haunting victory. Yet Christopher took no gratifications in their limited grieving and strode past them, signalling her flagging handful of servants to follow him into the hollow depths of the forested mountains. They followed, given strength to their bodies by the powerful will to serve Aphrodite's every command. She was the great one, and they would not allow their exhausted, staggering losses to dampen the size of the conquest at her disposal.

Christopher morphed back into Beast and led them deep into the hills. The night continued to deepen around them until they had to stop and light torches. They were in foreign country, and though the werewolf slowed not one step as he padded silently away from the ocean, the men and even her trusted assassin stopped to give themselves light to see by. They had a labourious night ahead of them, and all knew it would be difficult to keep up with this creature.

They jogged through the night, hungry for vengeance and power, though still numbed by the monks that had left them feeling haunted and helpless. By the light of the nearly full moon, Beast finally led them into a clearing and waited for the Normans to catch up. The men were hushed, awed by the spectacle of Signa Aquainnus, laughing as they recognized the tell-tale signs of a monastery filled with riches, ripe for the taking. A few of them looked over at Beast in utter shock. He was ignoring them and staring at the monastery silently. The others tore their eyes away only after their companions were sprinting across the lawn with hoots and shouts of happiness on their lips.

They crashed through the front doors before even checking to see if they were unlocked and smashed everything they could see, whether it be planked boards or mirrors of immeasurable value. Their torches led the way and they knew the only resistance they'd face would be something to appreciate. There was no need to mask their invasion with soft steps.

Janelle remained outside with Beast, eager and concerned for her mistress. She looked at the werewolf and in answer, Christopher morphed back to his human self. "She is in the courtyard in the back," Christopher said bitterly, answering the mute's unspoken question. Janelle nodded and began to run after the men, yet following them across the lawn on a different course than the one they had taken. She disappeared around the side of the building and was gone from sight.

Christopher watched the halls of his home for a while longer, silently saying his goodbyes to his father and his home. Then he went to collect what remained of the monks of Signa Aquainnus, his Keepers. He set his mind resolutely on driving Fernir from the coasts of Britain all together, preparing for the day when his father would release the vampire he kept imprisoned. When that day came, Christopher did not want to fight a war on two fronts, though the vampire had easily been beaten the first time.

He could do nothing for Anderita or Signa Aquainnus. His home had become her prison. His genius mind calculated how far ahead she had gotten from the rest of her fleet, estimating how long it would take for the flagging army to gain the shores of Britain. He shook his head at what he guessed and bitterly realized that Anderita was lost.

At dawn, the shouts of the invading war fleet echoed across the waters as the peasants of Anderita cowered in their beds. The Vikings walked into the village and took control of the port without so much as having to unsheathe a sword. The Britons were more than compliant with all of the Vikings' commands, down to their smallest dark wish. And they recognized within hours the tell-tale sign of a select few of them, men, women, and children, with stunned eyes paralysed with fear. They were the smartest, the strongest, best looking. They were men and women of potential, and the Vikings took special care to offer them all the courtesies they would to Janelle. For these people carried the signature that they belonged to the dark one and were not to be touched. Each one of them had their tongues cut out soon before the Vikings had arrived. Yet the wounds were healing remarkably well, as if they'd been removed by a surgeon whose skills were far ahead of any others of that time.

Soon enough, the first wave of the army of her grateful men brought forth the shaking victims as they came to stand at the head of a long oaken table, polished to gleaming a glossy black that reflected the candlelight that filled the great hall. Aphrodite studied the fire as it danced off of the surface of the blood in her hands. The goblet she drank from was made of pure gold. She smiled and finally allowed herself to look up at the offerings brought before her and savoured every drop of her victory, even as the statue of her master paralysed her with a fear she could not hide from her men.

Chapter Twenty-Eight

In January of 1066, when the wind and the snow howled about the walls of Aphrodite's Manor, now a fully fortified castle, one of her men came with news that brightened the ambitious glint in his eyes.

"Mistress!" he declared happily, first embracing her and then dropping to his knees before her in reverence. Before he pulled his eyes from the ground, he drew a knife across his hand and squeezed the blood into a small crystal glass. He held the blood up to her and only after she took it from his hands did he smile and look up. "I have news!" he declared happily.

Aphrodite smiled mischievously as she rolled the goblet back and forth through her hands. One sip of this and she would know all he knew, experience all he had experienced. "Pray tell," she declared with mock excitement. "And what is this news?"

"The English King is dead," he said breathily as he rose to his feet before her. "Duke William of Normandy will succeed him."

Aphrodite smiled and drank the blood in one gulp. Then the smile left her face.

The English King Edward the Confessor, had died. Yet rather than the crown passing to his Norman kinsman, the earl of Wessex had been crowned in his stead. Though it was still winter, a campaign had to be launched from across the channel within the next season. Otherwise the upstart earl would have firmly entrenched himself upon the throne of England and the true

Norman King would be want of a kingdom.

She said as much to her man standing before her, adding that he had no fleet, and no way to transport the horses across the channel. It would take an expert fleet of navigators to ferry him and his horses across to Brittan, as well as a safe place for them to disembark. The Viking looked saddened by what she said. But he brightened immediately when she added, "And where could he find such help as this?"

"Where indeed?" the man answered back, took two steps away from her and spun on his heel. "Before the end of the year," he called over his shoulder, "You will taste the blood of kings!" And then he was gone, leaving her alone with his promise.

Aphrodite only smiled to herself and delicately drew her finger along the inside of the small glass. She brought the last remaining drop of blood to her mouth and savoured its taste as she contemplated what her warrior had shown her.

By spring, the message had come to her. The Duke was on his way. The Duke was grateful for her assistance. The Duke would not forget her help when he assumed his throne. The Duke would continue to add promises and declarations, one after another, until Aphrodite got bored of reading the message.

Good for him, she thought to herself. After countless centuries, she was slowly losing interest with the ambitions of the human race.

Yet when word came that between two to three thousand horses were landing in her port, Aphrodite felt interest reawaken and was lured onto her balcony overlooking the waters. She tried to ignore the statue of her captor, but even as she witnessed the magnitude of the incoming fleet, his presence still haunted her. Janelle came to stand at her side and offer the silent support of her comforting presence. Although she kept her gaze fixed on the ocean, Aphrodite was still grateful for her maiden's presence.

The ambitious duke had not only recruited the Norman help of her fleet, but by the looks of it, he had salvaged Viking longboats from all over the known world. Suddenly, it occurred to her that he would win, that the Norman invasion would be successful. She had to smile at that. Vikings would rule the world once again, and their lust for glory would feed her lust for blood.

Yet, as the ships docked and the troops began to systematically unload, one handful of a growing army at a time, the cross of the Christ hung off the banners of the ships in the bay. Aphrodite shuddered, grew very cold, and backed into her castle once again, closing the doors behind her so that she did not have to see that cross again.

"Janelle!" Aphrodite said shakily. Her face was pale. "Send this message to the harbour. Duke William of Normandy, I rejoice with your success in overthrowing the English tyrant from this land of tyrants. Yet I fear I have taken ill and cannot see you off to defeat Edward.

"Sign it any way you think is befitting one who would fight under a Christian banner," Aphrodite snapped angrily as she strode from the halls, leaving Janelle and her perfect memory patiently writing her words in a perfectly fluid hand.

The following night, the duke himself came to her and knelt at her feet. "Mistress," he said excitedly.

She offered him no reaction as she looked down at the top of his head.

Nervously, he looked to her men for support, who motioned for him to continue. He drew a knife across his arm and blood welled up.

Aphrodite rolled her eyes impatiently as he awkwardly collected as much of the blood as he could into a crystal wine glass and held it before her.

"Tell me, William," she said to the still kneeling form before her. "Has this blood ever been inside a church? Has it ever watched the candles burn through the night, or has it ever seen the sun come up through the stain glass treasures that so plague these buildings like I do the night?"

The duke thought for a moment. "Yes, mistress," he answered. "I guess it has." Still, the blood was held out before her.

"Than what makes you think I would drink such an offering?" she asked flatly, though not angrily. She strode past him and he lowered his hands as he rose to his feet.

"I can still give you this," he replied.

"What, William?" she asked, spinning back to face him. "What can you possibly give me that I don't already have?"

"Title.

"Death's Mistress of the old world," he declared in a formal voice accustomed to shouting commands. "You are now the Duchess of Pevensey, sole and uncontested owner of these lands. Your children and their children's children after them shall hold this land as part of their royal lineage throughout time."

Aphrodite laughed bitterly. "I can't have children, William. And I would outlive them anyway."

"Then you," he emphasized the words as he spoke them. "Will forever rule these hills. And I can promise you that as long as I shall live, no Christian cross will ever again be found within these lands."

Aphrodite rolled her eyes again and shook her head. She did not bother to tell him what her treasure room contained.

"You make me a prisoner in my own lands, William," she said.

"And yet, mistress," he said innocently. "Isn't this all you want?"

Now it was her turn to take pause. "Yes," she said thoughtfully. "I guess it is."

The duke only grinned and offered her the glass of blood once again. This time she took it and drank, at last savouring the flavour of kings.

Chapter Twenty-Nine

The years passed in comfort and prosperity as the Normans grew accustomed to the wealth and the slaves at their disposal. Thoughts of the bleak Norman way of life were hard to find in this quiet pagan village along the Eastern shores of Britain. Though the words were spoken on Sundays, and the respected shrines were bowed to as the villagers passed, the power of these icons remained lost on the Mistress of Death in her castle atop the hill that overlooked Anderita. A view had been cleared for the mistress, exposing the fort's military advantage once again. But it also gave the village a view of their mistress's tomb.

With mortals, it was the little things that Aphrodite found kept them loyal in the long run.

Occasionally, she would venture out from her fort and walk amongst her people, who gave her reverence and mortal fear in equal quantities. Her men, her aging, fattening, dear sweet Vikings that had stormed the Charlemagne Empire and the British Coastline, still burned bones on the beach for her, honouring her at banquets and celebrations with glasses of wine made from their own wine presses. But more and more she watched her warriors become more concerned with tomorrow's weather, the harvest season, or a long dry spell without any rain. They brought before her less and less gold as the years passed and more and more wine or wheat or cattle from the harvest. She smiled at their docile natures, glorying in their new lives through the living blood they brought before her. Yet, even as the years passed, her men dwindled from her cult of followers and from the village, losing their interest in her in their newfound freedom from violence.

She had little doubt where they went, or who they served now. And although she knew her men loved her still, the light she feared so terribly was stealing those she loved, those closest to her. And a shadow seemed to pass over the castle that was quickly becoming an empty and desolate place. Weeds grew over the lawn, trees began to hide her from the memories of her people, and one by one the tired and old loyal companions of the Mistress Of Death lay down their heads and died, leaving her behind with their bones and their memories, to live eternally alone with what she had left, haunting the graveyards to be close to the people who's lives had created the memories that she now carried as her own.

One night in late Autumn, Janelle, the last of her slaves, came before her in silence. Once proud and regal with her scars and her assassin's skill, with a mind of a genius and a scholar's knowledge to shame that of any man of her time, with a naked body exposed proudly for all to see as she went to battle, Janelle was now clothed from the chill of the weather, stooped with age, and aching from a thousand wounds across her scarred and creased body. She limped on a cane as she came forward, slowly.

Aphrodite, still as young as the day they had met, folded her arms and leaned against the doorpost that led out into the cold of Autumn. She waited patiently as the best of her best came forward labouriously, considering what it could be that Janelle wanted of her now.

The tired assassin finally made it over to Aphrodite and stared at her mistress in the eye. Aphrodite stared back, watching with keen interest the play of emotions that worked their way behind Janelle's eyes, though her face showed no hint of expression.

Finally, the assassin unsheathed her knife from where she kept it in her sleeve and went to cut herself for her mistress.

"Don't," Aphrodite said as she gripped the bare blade in her own hand. The blood flowed, swelling up through her closed fist, yet Aphrodite paid it little heed.

Janelle froze when she saw Aphrodite's grip, and only her eyes moved as she stared at the blood swelling up from under Aphrodite's hand. The vampire removed her hand from the precious weapon, and still Janelle followed the wound with eyes wide with horror.

Aphrodite ignored the cut as though it was nothing and looked at the knife in her friend's hand. "There is my blood," she said. She crossed her arms once again and watched Janelle carefully. "The choice I leave to you," she added.

The assassin stared at the weapon for a moment, for a long moment, contemplating the offer that had been given to her. Finally, her mind resolved to the choice she was making, she carefully, reverently, retrieved a fine linen cloth from the table and wiped the blood from her knife. Once clean of the dark substance, Janelle limped over to the closest candle and set the linen on fire, forever destroying the one chance she had to share immortality with her mistress of death.

Once the cloth had been burned to ash, Janelle looked at her mistress with tears in her eyes and Aphrodite had to swallow the lump that rose in her own throat.

Janelle returned to her place next to the wall, and remained as attentive to her mistress's desires as she could, though now age seemed to have dulled the wits with which she served the great dark one.

Aphrodite imagined the human's funeral.

She would kneel over the coffin of Janelle's body and whisper a few final words over the wooden box. Young and immortal still, she would keep back the bitter tears that stung her soul more than they would her eyes. The villagers would be there, still, kept in the grip of fear by long practices of tradition and ritualism that ever ensured her people would remain loyal to her. Yet ignoring the faceless, nameless humans, she would thank her servant for her years of service and devotion, and then watch the coffin be lowered solemnly into the hole in the ground at her feet. She would wish she could throw herself into the grave as well, but she knew she would become restless eventually, and would climb from the earth as she always did, night after weary night.

It was better to let the body of her maid rest in peace, though it would mean nothing in the long run. Aphrodite would laugh bitterly, surprising some of the peasants with her outbreak. Then she would turn her back on her people, on humanity, and lose herself in the shadows of her great mansion. There were catacombs in there, with ancient bodies of the dead long since rotted to dust. She would be there, rather than out here, sealed up within walls that were not so easy to break through as the loose soil at her feet.

And she would not be so easily disturbed by the human mortals that tried so desperately to forget her, though they remained enslaved to her still.

She laughed bitterly again, this time coming out of her morbid day dream, and looked at her hand maiden, old and withered. "I don't think so," she said.

"You will not defy me in this." Then she had Janelle by the throat and was pressing her wrist against the human's mouth. Wide eyed and afraid, Janelle stared at her with pleading eyes, swearing she would not be forced to drink Aphrodite's blood.

Aphrodite only laughed again and bit into her servant's neck.

She did drink. It was a reflexive instinct to remain alive that all humans had. She drank for a long time before Aphrodite pushed them apart.

Janelle coughed and sputtered, trying to spit out the blood she'd already swallowed. She sank to one knee under the weight of her years and the vampirism quickly took hold of her. Aphrodite watched patiently as she cried, weeping for her lost humanity. Yet when she finally looked up, the eyes and the fangs of a vampire met Aphrodite's inhuman gaze with an all too familiar lust for blood. All signs of her old age were gone. Where one powerful vampire had been imprisoned under Iminuetep's eternal vigilance, now two young immortals would watch the endless years slide by together.

Book Three
Thorns of a Rose

Chapter One

Aphrodite waited amongst the dying ruins of her cavernous fortress. She was an old woman now, shrivelled to near her death by the bitter wind around her. Janelle came forward on slow, weak steps and sank into the chair at her mistress's feet. "All will be well once again, mistress," she said silently as she looked up at Aphrodite from knees that would not give out, nor would her arms stop animating by the will of vampirism. She was dying, and yet her spirit refused to fade away from the corpse that rotted around her.

Aphrodite shook her head in amazement and painfully lifted her sister from the side of their bed. The chill of the winter wind rustled against pains of shattered window glass and shutters that moaned when the attic creaked. Yet Iminuetep's cherished pelt of Anubis had managed to keep them warm if they huddled under it through the endless nights while they were awake. Many, many years ago the statue had relinquished the pelt as Janelle had stood transfixed in front of it one night. Tears had sprung to her eyes as she'd taken the fur coat and embraced it to herself. But even with the supernatural insight of a vampire, Aphrodite could not get her to relinquish what the gargoyle had told her. Still, she was grateful for the pelt, the kindness Iminuetep had showed them.

There was no longer a view of the ocean from their vantage point atop the mountain peaks deep within the rugged terrain. Cliff faces and frozen swamps crested the hill of an overgrown graveyard instead.

Neither of them would die this night, and they both knew it. Vampires did not die. There would not come a time when the nights of eternal, agonizing torment would stop. The winter winds would warm, eventually, lessening the ache in their bones, but without fresh blood to sustain them, their bodies would continue to decay, letting them grow older and older, tormenting them in ways no mortal had ever suffered. Together, they helped each other stand before the rotting doors of their once proud fortress.

The fortress they rested in was invincible.

The presence of the gargoyle glared down at them eternally from its painless stance against the rising full moon. They gazed upon the final death of one of the great ones and shuddered at the hideous monstrosity. It stood unwavering, unflinching, the corpse of an immortal high god, now nothing more than a slave to something even greater again. It posed, motionless, in a place outside of time, where its soul changed expressions with the coming of the seasons. Yet its body, though now nothing but a captured memory, was weighed down with wings that looked like they'd once been melted, though now they were impenetrable granite stone. He had been hypnotized by the hand of the god that controlled him, and now even the demon blood of vampirism bent its knees in subjugation to this eternal horror.

Anubis stalked the streets, or rather Fernir now. Popularity for the werewolf spread like lemmings through the minds of the mortals in the city before them. Many nights the werewolves found their way into Aphrodite and Janelle's prison. The ancient creatures seemed to find refuge in the dead and decaying relics of Aphrodite's haunted house. They would wander dazed and confused through the halls of the vacant and rundown monastery. It was believed that vampires had canine guardians that watched over them as they slept, yet Anubis looked on at the shrivelled vampires as weak and detestable creatures worthy of his disdain. Not once did he crave their blood. Anubis could dine on the young and the ripe in the fields outside their prison.

The wolves were insane creatures, nothing like the passionate Christopher Aquainnus. Yet, they searched for something, and when they came across the gargoyle of Iminuetep, whatever they looked for, they seemed to find. They would leave at peace, and Janelle and Aphrodite would never again see them.

Time had brought on a terror. Periodically, an immense set of piercing white eyes roamed over their graveyards, filling them both with dread. Aphrodite would rage at the gargoyle with no affect, while Janelle stared out at the human race, wondering if she was still able to enter her place amongst the living.

Yet, though Aphrodite and Janelle could not hide behind the exposing glare of the headlights, they both heard the violence in the abandoned alleyways that bordered their land, the nightly rape and murder of young women crying out for mercy. Yet Janelle and Aphrodite stood firm against the onslaught of torment. Death had given the mortals a way out. The gargoyle reminded the imprisoned vampires of that and saw that they would never forget.

Janelle would look on at the gargoyle with envy. She believed her life would be brief, but she believed she would find the eternal rest she sought. There would be two gargoyles standing amongst the living, moving too slowly to distract the attentions of the humans as they continued to salute their killer, their god.

Aphrodite stood staring out at the old stone in horror while Janelle gazed out in rapt attention. She was immortal, a vampire, yet only an aging old woman within these halls. Aphrodite flinched under the excruciating gaze of another set of headlights while Janelle stepped quickly into the engulfing darkness of the closest shadow. At once, the car lights came jostling toward them, careening dangerously up the road that led to their front door.

The wealthy remembered their dead in this small country town against the waters of the Atlantic Ocean. The funeral pyres were kept burning as a reminder, though over the years the ceremonies had been reduced to one mere candle placed on a stone altar before the gargoyle. Aphrodite would shudder every time she tried to think who would drop that candle off during the day.

The signs that hung on the rotting fences around their silk prison still bore the legible words, "Enter at own risk." But still the onslaught of the reckless flight up the boulevard continued until the car smashed headlong against a memoriam. Immediately, Janelle set out to retrieve the soul crying out for death. But Aphrodite restrained her, placing a hand gently on her shaking arms.

Both women stared in rapt attention as the young woman struggled toward them. Her hair gleamed in the terrible watching eyes of the passing traffic with a youthful vitality. Yet she dressed in what Janelle and Aphrodite perceived as rags, blue leggings torn at the knees and clinging to her hips and thighs. In her hand was a bottle that sloshed excess in wild abandonment with each step. She was bleeding from her neck, as though she had teased a lover's kiss beyond what he could endure.

Aphrodite and Janelle watched together, holding each other's hands in the excitement of fresh blood as she stumbled into the stone courtyard and saw the gargoyle. Mere paces away, through an abandoned doorway, stood the model of youth in all of its unabashed splendour. But for the moment she was transfixed with the statue before her, and Aphrodite and Janelle had to give respect where respect was due. They waited impatiently for eternity to stretch out before them as they watched the young woman. Nothing happened.

Then, with a resolute, fixed stare, she looked up at the moon still rising above the gargoyle's shoulder.

"I will not suffer the wrath of the parents upon their children any longer," the spirit within the gargoyle rebuked Janelle and Aphrodite, making them cower in the darkness all the more.

"Save my child!' the woman cried finally as she collapsed into a foetal position at the gargoyle's feet. She began to change, morphing into a werewolf as she clutched her unborn child protectively. Janelle and Aphrodite glanced at each other as they watched this new development, realizing for the first time that the hosts of Anubis did not all know they were werewolves.

Instantly, the woman began to change to stone. Caught somewhere within hidden passions of a bruised soul and the maddening cravings of the demonic, the woman's face froze. Dripping fangs dried up with startling speed, leaving gleaming ivory canine tusks embedded indestructibly into granite skin. Her body was that of a woman, yet she bore the head of a dog. She did not show her pregnancy yet, but that meant nothing.

Iminuetep's wings began to move. They stretched to the sky, melting out of the ground as they did, then enveloping the woman in an eternal embrace, hiding her completely from view.

No one else approached Aphrodite and Janelle throughout the endless, eternal winter. Yet the two stood motionless before their useless windows with the moonlight and the aching cold. They hoped they might find fresh blood once again, but darkness settled over the haunted manor, offering no respite from their eternal thirst.

But then the snows began to melt. Still, Janelle and Aphrodite yearned toward the statues in the courtyard. Iminuetep had left enough of a gap in his wings to let Aphrodite and Janelle see her cuddled in peaceful sleep. Her youth had been preserved despite the terrible transformation, and in the spring, the sounds of angry wolf puppies could be heard as they ripped free from their stone womb.

Janelle's eyes widened when she realized what had made that sound. All at once, she made her choice. "Puppies!" she cried suddenly. Her tongue had grown back in the instant she'd chosen to follow Iminuetep's fate. Even as Aphrodite watched, her withered form melted away and was replaced by youthful vitality.

"Janelle!" Aphrodite cried, realizing she had lost her hold over the only friend she had left.

Yet the young lady discarded her memories and abandoned the vampire to what she was. She sprinted toward the wolves as they yipped and whined into the warming spring air. One of them, toothless and blind, struggled as pitifully as the rest, yet Janelle knew something was wrong with him. The puppy fought to open his eyes, and although he struggled, Janelle knew he would not survive long.

With all respect, she knelt over the tiny creature and scooped him up into her hands. Then, she carried the hairless, mewling creature to her mistress's skeleton form and looked deeply into the vampire's eyes. If it was up to her, eternity would continue with them remaining together.

Bitterly, Aphrodite could not resist her own blood lust and bit into the creature, ignoring its confused and merciless cries while Janelle stood in perfect glory before her, in restored health and new life Aphrodite knew would transcend death itself. Janelle had become human, had managed to remerge into life. She had given herself over to the vampire death and had embraced the source of hellfire that destroyed darkness forever. Life shone in her eyes and Aphrodite did not have to look inside the slave's mouth to know a stone tongue had grown back to replace the one Aphrodite had devoured so long ago.

Youth was restored. Aphrodite laughed when she realized what headlights were and she ached at the need to experience the roaring combustion of flames and noise and speed all at the same time. She looked over the corpse of the puppy at Janelle with renewed respect and strode to the bed they had huddled under throughout the agelessness of the passing of time. She threw off the pelt of Anubis and approached the high priest for the first time since he had taken his eternal vigilance over her. His wings spread to accompany her, stretching out to the sky in welcome. His hands, once hidden, were now revealed holding a female child cupped safely away and looking up at him with rapt awe. She was perfectly human and beautiful, and slept in the most comfortable cushions of love Aphrodite had ever seen. The monstrosity of the female werewolf was nowhere to be seen. Aphrodite would not soon forget this image, she who had just eaten the first born puppy from a litter of Anubises.

She cast the fur coat at Iminuetep's feet and the puppies began their slow and steady crawl into the midst of the soft fur down. "Puppies!" Janelle cried again with a tongue she never had before. "Mistress!" she cried for a third time, scooping up two of the wolves, one held in the crook of each arm.

"Yes," Aphrodite said, more to herself than to Janelle. "We have a litter of puppies." She was already looking out at the vast unknown outside their eternal prison.

"No, mistress," Janelle corrected respectfully.

Aphrodite looked at her sharply, demanding why the slave dared to contradict what Aphrodite had said.

Janelle stared back at her fearlessly, capturing Aphrodite in a timeless spell that lasted until the morning, when exhausted, Aphrodite crawled away from the stone statue Janelle had become. Aphrodite took refuge in the cellars of decay around them.

At sundown, she crept back to the motionless statue still staring into the space Aphrodite had inhabited when the transformation had taken place. The wolves, the pair of them, had both been crystallized into granite that awoke when Janelle chose to animate herself from her eternal freedom in death. "The master has a litter of wolves," she finally got around to explaining to Aphrodite.

"The little demons are hungry," Aphrodite said bitterly, abandoning the only friend she ever dared to have.

Iminuetep's statue shifted ever so slightly as it looked at her with disappointment. His stone hand stretched away from the manor house, casting her away from his home and into the world once more, freeing her from her prison.

Aphrodite walked away from her stone halls and reentered the world of mortals. She clothed herself in the fashions of secularism and was lost to the timelessness of another game. Janelle and her litter of werewolves could rot in their decaying hole, for all she cared.

Anderita had proven indestructible, yet not defendable, and Aphrodite needed something she could control.

* * * * *

The years passed. The Manor House of Anderita grew in wealth and respectability as the young lady known as Janelle established her network of trade throughout the known world. Janelle's furs were the perfect quilt, turning to stone or the softest down, or both, depending on the need. And they stretched from the most pliable limits of any trampoline to the impenetrable indestructibility of legendary vampire armour. But another power was rising as well, a monolithic corporation that specialized in the production of pornographic material. The corporation was constantly under suspect and investigation, though nothing was ever found that could jeopardize the business's continual success, a business simply called, "Aphrodite." Aphrodite took the name of Alexis to better blend into the modern world, and her network of illegal operations and movie productions took control of it, squeezing the wealth of the world with corruption too tantalizing to turn down.

The ancient enemies looked warily at each other through the windows surrounding their estates, and power came with an extreme measure of wealth. Lady Janelle, in all her finery, was going to crush her enemy in bloody jaws and devour her living heart if she had to stop Aphrodite.

"Let it come!" Alexis would scream defiantly, humiliated beyond reconciliation as memories of sunlight tormented her with phantom flames. She had been forced to drink the blood of a dog!

Janelle would only smile back at her through the satellites and television network systems while images of Iminuetep and hellfire flooded through Alexis's dreams throughout the day.

"Vampires do not feel," she would tell herself each and every day. Usually emerging from a limousine to glance fearfully at the moon, Alexis would then disappear under a conglomerate of international intrigue and resurface upon the heights of the building tops around her. Sipping the warm red blood of her last victim from a priceless heirloom, usually once belonging to a taken mother or grandmother, she would call forth her tired human slaves from their beds and set the day's events into motion. The ocean stretched its endless cold embrace away from her; and she tried to tell herself that it meant nothing that Anubis' children were becoming sane.

The wolves still roamed the streets fearlessly, and though Anubis was proving too powerful for any vampire, the mad and homeless werewolves that Janelle could not recruit and rehabilitate created enough of a smoke screen of madness for Alexis to hide behind. Timelessness continued with one war after another, raging through the streets continuously as thousands of her own still worked as temple prostitutes. Anubis, Fernir, the rebel child of Anubis, Osiris' pet dog; whatever they called themselves, it mattered not; werewolves bathed the streets in violence, whether they were locked in stone holding cells deep inside the agencies of counter terrorists, or locked inside the twisted and lost minds of mad men.

Janelle would never find her, not behind this wall of destruction.

Chapter Two

Years passed and Janelle's puppies grew to adolescence. Young and troubled, the unruly teenagers were almost impossible to control. Yet with the years Janelle grew in understanding. Her wisdom deepened with her love for the light that burned so fiercely within her.

Iminuetep remained immobile as a stone statue. But she soon realized that if she stared at him long enough, she could communicate with him on a deep, emotional level. Many a night passed while she stood transfixed before him, herself turned to stone without her realizing it.

They talked of many things in their way, and it was in this manner the younger gargoyle began to think of her elder as her father. Through him she learned many things. He emptied the storehouse of his experiences to her, giving her access to all of his memories, from his time in Egypt to the timelessness in Romania where he'd first discovered their kind.

Yet he chose to remain a statue, impervious to the passage of time, to the rain and the snow or the never ending cycle of the sun as it set and rose over their manor. Janelle did not resent him his rest. As a gargoyle, the perpetual thirst of vampirism was put to rest, and he could know peace, at last.

Through Iminuetep Janelle learned everything there was to know about werewolves. And with the advantages of the modern world, she learned more still. Her manor became known by those sane enough as a haven of rest; yet to those controlled by Anubis' passions Aquainus Manor was nothing more than a nameless source of fear, of agitation: one more excuse to drive Anubis to commit atrocities unspeakable.

Yet perpetually troubled, Anubis continued to seek out Iminuetep's statue. Wordlessly, he gave the troubled souls rest and healing as Janelle stood by and watched from the shadows. She no longer feared the wolves as she had as a vampire, but her new appreciation for the light gave her a deep sense of righteousness, a deep desire to do what was right. She gave the wolves their privacy with their master, knowing first hand of his healing affects.

Many wolves chose to stay and join Janelle's growing army of immortals. Yet many chose to leave, howling and cursing into the night with their demonic madness. Though few ever spoke of what went on in front of the statue, it seemed to Janelle Iminuetep had given them a choice; continue to live as slaves to their passions, or be rehabilitated to freedom. Iminuetep promised to show them the way.

The battle was long and hard. Yet Janelle channelled all her resources to aiding the werewolves in their inner struggle. And though many decided to fight for their sanity, a few even made it far enough to embrace the same God Janelle and Iminuetep had, unexplainably changing their own coats of fur to a pure snow white colour.

Still, there were casualties, and many beasts grew too unruly even after they'd chosen to stay. With the incredible potential for destruction, they weren't permitted to live.

Ruthlessly, they purged the evil from their ranks, suffering losses from those they'd sought to save. Wolves died from both sides until Janelle's people began to refer to themselves as the Rebel Children of Anubis.

One night, as Janelle sat gazing out across the courtyard to Iminuetep's statue, a werewolf with the white coat of one of the redeemed glided out into the moonlight and came to stand at the base of the statue.

Janelle held her breathe. She didn't recognize him as one of her own. He appeared confused and half mad despite the colour of his coat. Still, he approached the statue of her father uncertainly, as if he wasn't sure what awaited him.

With his back turned to her, she couldn't be sure of the reaction the statue had on the wolf, but his shoulders shook, as if he was sobbing. Silently, Janelle crept forward, her interest perked.

The wolf let her approach, keeping his attention on the statue until she was nearly beside him. Then he turned to face her. His eyes held intelligence, but buried within great wells of grief.

She gasped as she recognized him and watched as Anubis melted away from his face. Christopher looked back at her, the grief not at all lessened by his human features.

"It's been so long," he began, glancing up at the figure of their father, then back at Janelle.

Speechless, she didn't know what to say. "Christopher. I—" her voice trailed off into silence. She wondered if he remembered her as the evil assassin that accompanied Aphrodite so many years before.

He reached out and felt the collar of her coat. "Werewolves are stronger than vampires." Apparently, he did. "How did you take this?"

She looked down to see the white pelt of Anubis, or rather, of one of his children. "The war. One of ours was killed. The human soul past repair. The wolf was killed as a kindness. I wear the pelt to remind myself of the loss of a friend. The others don't mind."

Christopher glanced over at the house. Werewolves hid in the shadows, watching them with curious, shining eyes.

"And the pelt father wore?"

"We sold it… with others."

He turned back to the statue.

Both were silent as they gazed at the peaceful form. Finally, it was Christopher who broke the silence.

"It's been so long," he admitted softly. "I've been lost. I finally drove Fenir to America, but it's been an empty victory. And now there are so many others, I feel I've lost anyway."

"You don't have to fight alone, now."

Christopher turned to her. "I came back to kill you. You and the other one."

Janelle smiled. "I've already died." She gestured toward the statue. "Father showed me the way."

"Father?"

"Iminuetep. Jason. We are the same now, he and I."

Christopher was shot through with a pang of envy. He looked back at the statue.

"He's spoken often of you." Her words were unsteady, knowing she had no right to stand beside him like this.

"Does he ever animate? Turn from stone back to flesh?"

"Never. He's grown tired of the pain, of the thirst."

Christopher nodded, remembering what his father had said so many years

233

ago when he first revealed what he was. "I won't take that away from him.

"And you can talk to him when he's like this?"

"When I rest, yes. I make it a daily practice to turn to stone. It helps keep the thirst down when I'm awake."

Christopher was silent as he contemplated what Janelle had told him. "Does he ever mention me?"

Janelle smiled. "Often. He's dreamed of your return."

Christopher looked at her again.

"Your place is here." She held out her hand. "Brother."

Hesitating, he took her hand, and then with a rush of emotion, embraced his new sister thankfully.

There were tears on both their cheeks when they pulled apart.

"Welcome home," she said wiping her tears away with the sleeve of her coat.

Chapter Three

An army stretched out before a wooden platform set low into the pools of a waterfall that ran down the centre of a natural amphitheatre. They were shadowed deep inside the overwhelming presence of old growth trees that dwarfed their significance to the utmost secrecy while the rest of the world outside this forest knew nothing of their presence. The walls of the cave glistened as if alive with fire where the water had splashed high and then caught the light of two immense bonfires built to either side of the stand. The army was spread out in lines, the soldiers perfectly distanced from those all around them, though the trees had given them difficulties on their own: and obstacles gladly overcome. The walls of tall cliffs rose up sheer against the sounds of the thundering presence of the waterfall. Yet the trees kept their frightening silence just as forceful as they reached half as high out of the sink hole hidden away in the rugged terrain. Nearby, a monastery sat perched precariously upon the edge of the falling rocks, boulders the size of trees themselves, only just as round. The scenery seemed frozen in the grip of immortality's merciless grasp, a continual morbid reminder of the nature of those that drilled mercilessly beneath the canvas of leaves overhead. Only one amongst their kind would chose to break out of this terrible curse this night, and though there might be two pelts cut, wars would be prevented, wars that would otherwise stretch across mankind's powerless hopes of control. And one of those two pelts would be white.

Janelle, herself sheathed in a white fur cloak that hid her completely from collarbone to toe, would gladly rejoice with her ranks. Her army of werewolves respected her. She was untouchable and they rejoiced in the presence of their sister as she fought alongside the best of them. Today, however, she remained calmed and passive as she paced back and forth before her soldiers, studying their every move and continually finding new weaknesses to exploit.

As the day's sweltering heat continued throughout the hours in unending predictability, drill after drill pressed the sweat from their brow. Christopher Aquainnus, in the forefront of the ranks, though off to the side and away from the centre stage, managed to see her face now and again. Whenever she passed she managed to lock eyes with him, even though the wooden practice staff shook in his calloused hands from the effort to keep it under his control.

She had practiced already during the early hours before dawn began to filter through to the still sleeping soldiers. He had been awake, dressed in black, stalking her endlessly, silently, through the still bodies of their brothers and sisters. He had not been alone, yet though there had been a few others to balance the odds, still she had pounced and pounced again. Her one dagger glistened now and again as it glided by the dying embers of a camp fire; but that was her only weakness. Christopher smiled as he recounted how she had killed him time and time again, thankfully all in mock battle that left him with only the finest of scratches that had faded before sunrise had fully come to an end. He might have stabbed her once, though for all the good it did to slow her down.

She was caught by his smile and walked by to return it; neither one hid their devotion to the other, for all were brothers and sisters here. The hosts of Anubis thought with one mind, were driven by one turmoil that pushed aside all others. They would conquer the beast within. Janelle would see that happen.

Endlessly, the hours continued to wear on. Yet though the sweat pushed from Christopher's skin and his muscles were on fire from within, though his breathes came in jagged, rhythmic gasps and his long staff shook, Christopher did not grasp the passage of time, so absorbed was he in the patterns he and the others danced into the forest's floor. And in this ignorance he found bliss. The beast that raged seemed to calm, his hunger seemed to dampen, and as Christopher grew tired and worn, the force of the wolf's presence gave him strength, even with the sun arching overhead. It filtered through the trees on dust clouds like the eyes of a leviathan searching out its next prey.

Eventually, the drills were over. None collapsed into exhaustion when the command to rest was given. Rather, many soldiers angrily tossed their staffs onto the ground or struck them against the trunk of a tree as they tried to break the wretched things; few did. Everyone kept their complaints to themselves, however. And most of the weapons were returned to the armourers and their awaiting transport vehicles

Campfires had been made in preparation for the hungry wolves and their human twins. Both were fully awake and dangerous. The balancing act between sanity and confusion had been left behind. As the sun set, more and more of the dangerous Anubis made their presence known. Yet not only was Anubis' children here, but Fernir's bloodline also glided through the trees to sit silently and obediently in line as food was passed out in dishes. Ancient wars between brothers were being put to rest under the common banner of good; any werewolf that turned away from its evil past was welcome amongst these ranks.

Those that still wore the bodies of humans, or at least human enough to hold a bowl of food, would help those that chose to remain in the skin of a wolf as they headed out amongst the trees. Many couples discreetly slipped into the trees. Man and wife, the soldiers took their dinner and left, seeking solitude within the endless bounds of the forest around them. Many, many more remained to feed the intellect of the genius minds that had found peace within the confines of a wolf's body. Discussions were loud and heated as shouts and laughter pealed against the amphitheatre's walls, though once out of sight, the waterfall quickly blanketed any other sounds to hide their presence.

Christopher did not bother to seek the attentions of his sister right now. The vampire was busy. Suffering from her own hunger pains, she was wreathing with the need to kill and eat. Yet though she walked under sunlight and spoke with the tongue of an angel, she was still a vampire, and refusing to release her hold on time altogether, gargoyle skin was crawling, branding into her from within. She stayed close to the waterfall. She was meditating on the battle against her bloodlust and her body swung from contorting against the hellfire from within to eerie silence as the death of granite took her away when the pain grew to be too unbearable. Her torture drew flinches and angry curses from the werewolves that tried desperately to ignore her, yet she remained with them for as long as she could, until finally she passed into a few hours of silence. When her death came, it came suddenly, cutting off a scream at the pinnacle of pain. Christopher smiled when he heard the echoes end. When he glanced over at the gargoyle, he saw her standing tall and proud on her feet. The werewolf pelt, though never touched with the poisonous blood of vampirism, had turned to stone around her.

She was carefully avoided until the fur melted back into soft down and life returned to her fair skin once again. Christopher had seen the scars God had not removed, scars that covered her from neck to toe. He knew her passing into her gargoyle sleep had been an easy weight for her to bare.

Campfires had been set up in her absence. Containment units were brought forth, vans lined with concrete walls, equipped with mesh cages and tranquillizers, their doors left open in preparation for any who had to seek refuge against themselves. Any who had slunk off into the woods now returned and joined the festivities. They ringed the bonfires, not concerned with gathering too closely around the flames, but careful to complete a rough circle around each one.

When Janelle awoke, she stepped from her frozen place with gradual abruptness and headed toward the fires with determination in her step. She found Christopher quickly enough and glided quietly up behind him as he laughed with the merriment going on around him. The others, seeing her come, kept their smiles behind their hands or looked away as their eyes danced with merriment. A knife slipped free of its sheathe in her sleeve and glistened in the campfire as she brought it up and close to his neck. Christopher caught the glint in the corner of his eye, wondering if she had given herself away on purpose, or she no longer cared, thinking she had not given him enough time to react before he lost this match.

He was moving as the knife came up behind his ear. Not wanting to sacrifice the beer in his hand, he caught her wrist in his other hand and then pinned her knife hand to the side of his neck. He sank to his knees as her other hand swung at his exposed right side. She grabbed a handful of his hair as he put his beer down. Then he sprang to his feet and threw her high over his shoulder and into the air. She kept her grasp, though his scalp ripped away from his head, and she landed on her back in front of the campfires. A cheer erupted from the crowd around them, saluting both combatants with mugs raised high.

Christopher smiled as he felt his scalp. The blood of Anubis glistened on his fingertips as his hair grew back.

Janelle had not moved from the ground. She was looking up at him and smiling. *This one would be hard to take*, she thought to herself. *Let Alexis do her worst.*

Christopher laughed as he reached down with his clean hand and helped her to her feet. They embraced and when they broke apart, he offered her a taste of the blood on his fingers. She refused. She had come from the gargoyle's timeless presence with all her needs satisfied. Heaven had been good to her, and she had no needs. They laughed and then she was off, pouncing determinately at someone else.

This time, the woman caught her at arms' reach and snarled at her as she held Janelle at arms' reach. Janelle hissed back with her fangs baring and her inhuman predator eyes of a vampire caught in the grasp of her bloodlust. In a moment, the wolf threw her away, back into the circle toward the fire. Once Janelle was out of her reach, the werewolf's womanly features returned as she laughed with the rest of them. Janelle's eyes now held nothing but human amusement as she used the wolf's momentum to clash against another wolf. She had taken the opportunity to unsheathe her other dagger and both were extended in a poise to kill when the soldier grabbed at her and tossed her over his head as if she was weightless. He laughed when the encounter was over, though a little uncertain and shaken by the determination with which she had struck.

And then Janelle was gone. Christopher doubted he would see her again for a good long while through all the amusement, not until the coat had been taken.

Finally, the sun began to set in truth, and a young man was brought forward under guard. The soldiers quieted when they saw him. Many looked into his eyes and looked upon the madness that Anubis gripped his human hosts with. No angry snarl erupted from the silencing crowd, though a few sorrowful whines filtered around the fires. The man had been found huddled deep within the streets of a sprawling metropolis in North America and had been transported here. He had been treated well, compassionately. He had been fed and bathed, clothed in comfort and every need had been met with merciful smiles. But though he was tended to with caring hands, those same hands guarded him well, tirelessly as he was shipped here on one of Janelle's private jets. The journey had been quick as the moon grew in size daily. But he had been found only days after the full moon; and his life had been longer and fuller than most. Janelle and the children of Anubis saw that his life had been a good one as they suppressed the beast he had not known was there.

Still, he had refused to give up control. He had allowed Anubis to take his mind and his will, and now he could not imagine living without the demon's powerful dread hanging over his life. He stood before a crowd of werewolves, knowing that Anubis could not possibly be triumphant in the battle that was about to take place. Yet though very few rational thoughts echoed through his confused mind, enough of the man was there to smile darkly as he looked around them. "Sacrifice will be made!" he shouted gloriously as he threw his hands into the air. Christopher looked away sadly as the force of Anubis' growling voice took over.

Sane wolves manifested fully, rising to the challenge of containing the evil beast for as long as they could. It was going to prove to be a long night; for no one sought death but the evil mad man before them. Still, death would come, and though it did not matter to the wolves how much, for death was death and it would be grieved over, they were all willing to pay the ultimate price.

This was a war between the wolves. Only one wolf would come forward this night from amongst the ranks. Though many would howl angrily at the alpha, none would contest her right. Christopher had no way of knowing if she would walk away with her life, but he hoped she would. He glanced over at Janelle, to see her holding herself fast in a helpless embrace. Her wolf's pelt of pure white fur, softer than any down, did little to comfort her. She felt his gaze and their eyes caught, and he motioned for her to come join him by her side. Sadly, she shook her head and moved one of her hands. Firelight glistened off of a point hidden amongst the fur and he nodded respectfully. The vampire had work to do.

The alpha was in the back of the crowd. Knowing her time had come, she kissed her husband with human lips and stepped away from her human life. Gradually, painlessly, her own coat, as white and soft as the wool of a lamb, grew over her shoulders and back as her clothes ripped away from the morphing shoulders of the awakening creature sleeping under her skin. "No sacrifice will be made tonight except that which you have brought upon yourself," she said to the raging demon before her.

The monstrous head of a werewolf roared back at her hungrily, and by then she had gone to four legs and was galloping toward the monster in front of her. She snarled and barked as she lunged into the air and they went down in an onslaught of roaring determination as they snapped at each other. Go for the heart, Christopher hoped silently. Go for the heart. Yet he knew she would not remember any such reasoning. The human woman had gone to sleep. Now, she dreamed blissfully of being in her maker's caring arms. She was being shielded from the nightmare that raged without, and she would simply not awaken from her bliss if the battle was to be lost.

The wolf tore herself away from the demon and blood flew from a wound on his arm. Yet she exposed her flank and the werewolf managed to sink his teeth into her before she could turn and find a hold on his throat. He did not let go, though she had him. The battle was to the death, and neither cared little how big the sacrifice was. The alpha realized she had no choice and tore out a piece of the creature's neck even as the werewolf finished his own transformation into a wolf and ripped apart her hind leg.

Now, both mortally wounded, the wolves turned back to each other and lunged once again, before their strength had time to falter. Janelle looked away sadly and walked away from the crowd. Christopher saw her leave and followed quickly, even as Beast took over and he went to sleep. He wanted to leave the nightmare of the war behind him, even as he knew she had no choice but to witness it all. The last thing he remembered was Janelle's hand sinking into the fur behind his neck. He knew the vampire was sensing his peace, his oblivion, even as she remained awake and alert.

When it was possible, death would come quick for both wolves, she would make sure of it. It was either that or allow the humans underneath to suffer never ending. Neither would be free of the terrible pain until they were killed. As mortals, the children of Anubis should quickly die by their wounds, yet as the immortal force of Anubis, only two things could kill a werewolf, and both had to happen at the same time.

They had to be skinned alive, and they had to have their hearts destroyed.

Janelle knew of the surgical procedures that could take the pain from the victim and hide the nightmare from the surgeons. But there was nothing that could kill faster than a vampire.

The madness of the human soul trapped within the evil werewolf would in itself become an anaesthetic, helping to ease the dim senses of the groggy human that would instantly become awake, though still tired and struggling to grasp why it was caught inside the body of a wolf. Awake and conscious were two different things, and the human would not comprehend the sufferings around him. For Patricia, the alpha that had sacrificed her own life, she would simply stay asleep, oblivious to the death that had secured her within its grasp.

It mattered not how fast the heart was taken after that. Destroying the heart would kill the human, while the spirit of Anubis would be locked into the body of its dead host. Allowed to bleed, it would flow into the pelt and disperse to whatever business it had within the afterlife.

Beast shook as if warding off an invisible chill and Janelle crossed herself as she looked up at the sleeping fortress above them. With her penetrating eyes, shining orbs of light, though casting no light of their own, she looked up through the terrible darkness around them.

Though the evil nature of the vampire within her was dead, the gargoyle steeled itself as it stared up at the castle. Pain cascaded through her body as the fire reserved for the spirit of vampirism rose up and exploded around her. Her body turned to liquid magma under the immeasurable heat, though it did not release Janelle's mind from the torment it was under. Still, she smiled at the greater healing life that flowed through her spirit, embracing a force of life and immortality that gripped her just as fiercely. In her mind, the pain was only a dying meteor that crashed into the cool waves of a never ending ocean. The pain would not even make a ripple amongst the rhythmic pulsing amongst the waves of love.

Janelle and Beast turned toward the campfire once more. The night was not over. The silent crowd of mourning soldiers parted to let them pass while two weak and angry wolves glared at each other, oblivious to the life that flowed out of them. The pain was last in the madness of the minds of the dying mortals, yet the werewolves, one with a mortal host soaring free in Heaven and another with the lost soul in purgatory, stared out across the bridges of death and looked at their eternal fates.

Pamela's spirit danced before the throne of freedom already; a staff of gold and a banner of truth already in her hand; yet the gold was weightless and the banner's white and shining linen never touched a drop of blood to stain its surface. The nameless man was going through something else entirely, even though the werewolf's anger kept him strong and awake.

Stone fangs lunged at the white animal first. It was Janelle's choice, and it was right for her to make it as she wished. Blood gushed over the gargoyle's stone surface while Janelle's knives flashed. Beast held the alpha's body in his powerful jaws and the pelt was removed in one swift jerk. Moments later the gargoyle had her heart in its hand and destroyed it just as quickly. When it was finished, she and Beast turned to the glaring werewolf that had just seen its own end.

"I will not go peacefully," it snarled. The stone statue shook its head sadly and Beast came forward silently. He broke the werewolf's neck, paralysing the creature, and then the gargoyle swept in with the supernatural speed of a vampire.

In the morning, two wolf furs, each priceless fortunes, were carefully drying by the fire under the watchful eyes of master tanners. Though they'd done this enough times to finish the tanning with their eyes closed, they saw through a blur of tears while an endless routine of drilling prepared the children of Anubis for their next fight. Spirits were high, knowing they had a full month to prepare. The suicidal madmen locked inside the bodies of Anubis still roamed endlessly through the streets of mankind. There might be more than one next month, or none at all.

However it went, they'd be prepared.

* * * * *

The small convenience store nestled tightly between two taller buildings that stretched into the sky like two hostile trees in the wilderness of a great and deadly jungle. An overpass stretched across the view from the front door, casting the little store into a world of perpetual gloom that changed only when it rained, and then only dampening and darkening the world it belonged to. Bars were on the windows and door. A dead bolt of the heaviest kind insured no one would be coming through that door when the store was closed. There was no back door. Whoever designed the store in the distant past knew that this place would become the centre of a world abandoned and forgotten, and back doors would sooner or later only lead to misadventure. Yet the store had stayed open faithfully for years and years, becoming an icon to be ignored and taken for granted by those that adventured down here as they passed by in the routine of their daily lives. There was a sign on the door that said, "Closed on July 31 for holidays," and those that saw it marked the day with disinterest, keeping in mind they would have to go somewhere else for that one day.

Just after dawn, someone screamed outside, a high-pitched female scream that soon brought the roar of sirens and the eerie light of their flashing lights over the brim of the overpass above. There was a crowd gathering on the overpass, and the police were diligently pushing people back, angrily shoving cameramen and reporters off the bridge and stretching a wall of yellow tape between them and the audiences gathering on each side.

No one noticed a skinny, homeless man stagger away from underneath the overpass, wearing only rags he'd managed to find himself wearing when he awoke from the noise. Dazed and panicked by the confusion above, he fled the crowds and the horror of what was being veiled from the eyes of society. He stumbled toward the little convenience store and forced the door open, collapsing on the inside of the thresh hold. The door closed behind him and for a moment he was at peace, knowing he was alone. But then, slowly, he realized he was being watched.

In horror, he looked up to see the store clerk looking down at him with calm, protective diligence from his mighty place behind the counter. His arms rested on the counter at each side of him as he leaned over to look at this new matter of interest.

Eyes wide with fright, the vagabond looked up and shuffled against the door to get that much farther away from him. Something had shocked the man, and the clerk did not need to imagine what it had been. The lights nearby still cast their unearthly glow over the store, though the cars and the commotion were far removed from this little world of outcasts.

The man looked around the store quickly, as if just realizing where he was. The confining space panicked him even further, and he pushed to his feet and fled. His steps echoed on the pavement until the door banged shut.

"Closed on July 31 for holidays," the sign taped onto the door said. The clerk smiled when he saw it. Less than a month away, and he would be able to take the day off.

That easily, the panicked man was forgotten.

* * * * *

The sun was coming up over the mysteriously silent overpass. It was though the events of the day before had sent out silent, horrifying ripples through the city. Though it was covered up and spoken only as whispers, people still avoided the place where the gristly evidence had been found. It was though instinct was telling people to stay away and hide in fear, while intellect and the demands of routine kept people from acknowledging their fears. But they did stay away. And so the sun rose in silence: just beginning to touch the convenience store with its light.

The little chime above the door rang out as a poorly dressed man stuck his head uncertainly into the store. He looked at the sign beside him, then looked around at the rest of the store. As if seeing everything for the first time, and as if everything he saw frightened him, he nonetheless kept his composure. The fear only showed in his eyes, which were as wide as they could go and shifted endlessly around the place.

The clerk smiled at him as he approached the counter. The man looked past the clerk to the rack of cigarettes behind him and pointed to a pack.

Following his outstretched hand, the clerk retrieved the smokes and placed them on the counter between them. "That'll be nine ninety five," he said as he punched a few keys on his worn out cash register.

The man fished out a handful of wrinkled dollars and imitated the clerk by placing them on the counter between them.

The clerk sorted through the pile and took a ten dollar bill. Then he pushed another button and the register slid open. His customer jumped at the sound but remained where he was, caught between an uncertainty of how to react and a need to run. The clerk handed him a nickel and smiled, trying to disarm his fears. He looked at the coin as if he'd never seen one before and then up at the clerk with a vacant expression on his face.

"Have a nice day," the clerk said, realizing how lame that sounded in his own ears. The customer remained motionless for a moment, then grabbed his fistful of dollar bills and his pack of smokes. He fled the store.

The door with the sign that said, "Closed on July 31 for holidays," banged shut behind him.

* * * * *

Crowds pushed by the store as they headed home for the night. They kept their heads down and their collars tucked up against the bitter chill that hung in the air. The mists were damp and cold against their skin. The weather made bones ache and people stay in steaming hot showers rather than invade their precious routines. Alexis watched those below her shiver with her passing as though she herself was the cold.

A thin, frightened looking man pushed through them self consciously as he headed for the store, and Alexis was amazed at the emptiness of his life she learned during their brief contact. He had very little experiences, virtually no memories, and only a vague sense of restless fear that goaded him on toward the convenience store as though it could somehow save him from the nameless terror that plagued his steps.

She watched as he disappeared into the store, squinting at artificial light that flooded through the door and into the street below. But such light did not hurt her, though she knew to respect the simple reminder of what real light could do to her. But quickly enough, the light was shut out from her world once again, and she was shaded in peaceful oblivion in the minds of her potential, tasteless victims.

Soon enough, the hapless soul reappeared, slipping back into the night. The door closed behind him as he fished through the pockets of a black overcoat. He looked out at the world around him from under the dark brim of a black pull over held up by a baseball cap. He was too preoccupied with his search to take notice of, let alone be concerned with the weather.

He found what he was looking for and pulled a lighter from his pockets.

There was a cigarette in his other hand, and he lit the thing as he drew a relieved breathe off of the end of it. He exhaled with a sigh of relief and then pulled the stick from his mouth so that he could look at it in admiration. He chuckled to himself and shook his head. Then, relieved, he placed the smoke back in his mouth and his hands in his pockets.

He plunged back into the flowing traffic of human flesh, quite content and at ease with the weather and his smoke.

Alexis rolled her eyes and disappeared into the night, looking for more adventurous blood than this.

* * * * *

"Given over to hallucinations," the doctor had said to the officer in charge. For some reason the patient seemed to hear those words and they echoed through his mind with the voice of cohesion. There was something here, something that he must find before he could slip back into the reality of his mind. He blinked and tried to shake what felt like sand out of his eyes. Nothing worked. He tried to wipe the sand from his eyes. Again, nothing. It was turning out to be a miserable night.

These people were not his friends. He did not wipe his eyes again and kept them frozen open. Tears wept and coursed down his dust stained face. He had been sprayed with fine silver, and the shards of what was still there cut into his eyes.

Both the police officer and the superintendent of the hospital froze when they noticed him come to.

"Thank you, ma'am," Christopher said politely. "That will be all."

Without another word, she blew him a kiss and left.

Yet his eyes never left their patient.

"Who is this doctor?" the man in the trench coat asked through a mouthful of broken teeth. He hadn't realized he was wearing a tight leather coat under his trench coat, or that it would be so sore to move. His skin-tight leather clothing creaked slowly, revealing to them both how truly weak he was. The vagabond held his ribs tenderly. Both sides ached from a beating. With horror, he looked up at the man standing before him; his conceit faded. "Who are you?"

Christopher stared at his patient until the man flinched and looked away. "It's been a long time," he said as he circled to stand in front of him. They were in a prison cell, an encased questioning room. There were old-fashioned tools on an old wooden bench with chains that supposedly never broke hanging on the walls. Christopher looked at the chains fondly. He'd tested them well, but he was sure they still had a weakness in them. He was determined to find it by the end of the full moon.

In horror, the man looked up at him, as if seeing him for the first time, but with an understanding that brought him nearly full cohesion. "The other god," he said, understanding the dream that plagued him. He was a werewolf. The man standing in front of him was the white beast with the silver cross. "Who am I?" His eyes bled as he looked up at him.

Christopher crossed his arms and took his time to study Anubis' host once again.

The vagabond pulled his two last cigarettes out of his pocket and held one up to the monk, who took it and lit it up. The vagabond did the same. Silence passed between them.

The smoke was thickening and Christopher just shook his head as he blew out another puff of the stuff, adding to the cloud around him. "I want to kill you," he said politely. "I've done it before, and I'll do it again. But you taught me how to be me, and how to stop people like you." He looked down at his old enemy, who cowered in his seat as if he could hide behind it.

"And you don't even know who you are."

The werewolf shrank into his seat as he remembered a distant past. "It has been awhile," he nodded. "They wanted to keep us in vaults back then, locked up during the night in concrete slabs," his eyes passed over the strange room. "Just like this one. I remember."

Christopher slapped the stone behind him affectionately and then sat down at the table in a spare chair next to his patient. A bottle of bourbon and two shot glasses sat between them.

"It was you I was running from," he said fearlessly.

"Not really," Christopher replied. "Try not to make any sudden moves," he added. "I had to break a few of your ribs." He held out a glass brimming with the fine beverage. "I've managed to acquire a fine taste for this," he said. "Try it. You'll see."

The werewolf stared at the man and then at the drink in his hands. It was amazing how potent some drinks could become over the years. He smiled and slammed the drink back, holding the smile as he felt the burning sensation drop straight into his stomach and stay there before the poison shot lightning quick through his veins to filter away at the tips of his fingers and toes. Once the spasm passed, one quick jerk, enough to kill a train load of innocents, faded away he returned the glass to the table.

"Thank you my friend," he said respectfully. "That came remarkably close to killing me."

Christopher looked at the glass in his hand and then poured another drink into the spare one. This one he downed himself. "Care for round two?" he asked when he was finished his own convulsion. He took the glass and poured it. "You first."

The werewolf took it and looked at it for a moment, remembering that he was a prisoner here. "We'll drink this one together," he said to Christopher.

Christopher nodded and filled the second shot glass to brimming. He watched the wood from the table steam when the bourbon splashed upon it and the other wolf stared at the liquid just as fondly. Together, they both reached out and grabbed the shots. Not spilling a drop from either, they slammed the drinks back and the world went black in relaxing peace. Both came to, too dazed to shake their heads, and too dull headed to remember how. Gradually, they regained movement, swaying as they held their heads in their hands. They remained motionless for the whole time, too weak to break from behind the barrier of a paralysis.

"I've got to get another pack of smokes," the vagabond in the trench coat said as he stretched to his feet.

"I can't stop you," Christopher announced, savouring the taste of the cigarette.

As if the whole conversation had been recorded, a slight electronic buzzer sounded from somewhere overhead.

"Thank you," the vagabond announced as the door slid open. He turned back to Christopher as he stepped over the thresh hold. "I'll see you soon."

"There's a full moon coming," Christopher announced as he stared through the smoke at the wall across from him.

"I don't think I could ever have enough fun in here," the vagabond said as he looked around him. "Sorry, officer."

"Day after tomorrow's a full moon," Christopher warned for a second time.

"I don't know what that means," the vagabond admitted. Then he turned and walked away.

Down the hall directly in front of him was the door. He was calm as he walked away. The door to the inquisition room remained open and yet all eyes and ears were turned to him as he passed. In the room behind him, the white wolf ripped through Christopher's skin and clothes with an euphoria of death that brought Beast clean out of his skin with hardly any pain brought to his human counterpart. They howled, first in pain, then for the other wolf to hear their plea, then a third time in an emotion far more complex than those a human could grasp.

The wanderer pulled his coat tightly around him before he pushed the front door of the building open. Before he could let the door close, he admitted to the wolf, "I need a smoke."

The wolf behind him looked up from inside the concrete and brick room. It was a room inside a room, one that might hold the weight of two unleashed werewolves. Yet it was surrounded by a forest of desks, of coffee makers and the noise of human involvement. The wolf began howling again, and the door to his pen slammed shut. It was nearly thick enough to block the sound, but the wolf rose to the challenge and reached a higher pitch still.

The door behind the vagabond slammed closed, shutting away the monster in its cage with its organization locked up with their bright white lights and their hypocrisy. All about his head, the mists hung thick, closing him in to a cocoon of oblivion. He needed a smoke. The warning his friend had given him put the fear back into his bones. These mists were not enough, not nearly enough to hide the terror that was falling upon him once again.

But soon he was there. The smoke was bought. The lighter was found. And all was well as amnesia closed around him once more.

* * * * *

Once he began to wake up, he knew that last smoke of the day waited for him. Throughout the day, he had a pack near at hand, but as the sunset approached, one cigarette after another was lit up and drained away, until he knew he could not put it off any longer.

He was out there. He was watching. He would punish him.

The vagabond knew what he had to do and had practiced it for an entire month. If he could get to that smoke before the beast exploded from within him, he would pacify it and all would be well.

So as the nearly full moon began to rise, he plunged into the darkness of the streets and fled to the convenience store.

The clerk was waiting for him with a smile on his face.

"Good to see you, my friend," he said quickly.

"And you," the vagabond answered.

The man handed him a pack of cigarettes, his pack of cigarettes. He pocketed the smokes and then handed the clerk a twenty dollar bill.

"Keep the change, Toni," he said. He held up his smokes. "They await," he declared happily.

The clerk laughed and saluted his friend with the fist that held the money. As the door banged shut, he shook his head and punched a few buttons on his cash register. The clerk would see him again after the store reopened for holidays.

* * * * *

Excited and sure in himself, the wanderer approached the convenience store under the shadow of an overpass. There was a lightness in his steps, and even though he was alone, he did not feel ill at ease with the night. He was confident, and in a few minutes he would have his smoke. He always had his smoke. And everything was always all right after that.

Amnesia plagued him and had thrown him into a treacherous world perpetually against him, but one thing was always certain, and that one constant always brought him a remnant of peace. His smoke waited for him.

He stepped up to the door and tried the lock. The door would not give and everything was dark inside. "What? No," he said to himself, too shocked to be able to cope with his disappointment.

It refused to register. "No," he repeated as he tried the door again. He had to have that smoke. Still, the door would not give.

"No!" he shouted as he punched the door. He stepped away from the store, enraged, and shouted, "No!" one final time before the wolf ripped agonizingly through his skin, bursting the leather bandage that had been holding the human's ribs together. But the beast within knew of no pain, and the ribs mended together during the transformation.

Half human, half wolf, the monster roared in frustration and attacked the door, putting its open hand through the window and then tearing the door off of its hinges. It roared again as it stepped into the building and began destroying everything in sight.

* * * * *

Christopher picked through the carnage carefully, though with every step his feet crunched broken glass. He was amazed the building was still standing, and everything was torn to pieces by the onslaught the wolf had done to it. Now, Christopher was standing on the second floor, in what once was a small

250

apartment overlooking the street and an overpass. Blood had soaked into the carpets and upholstery. It was splattered on the dry wall and plaster torn from the walls. Human remains, torn and half devoured, lay scattered as macabre surprises throughout the ruined apartment. Christopher did not need to look at the carnage. He only sighed as he stepped carefully, coming to stand at the front of a broken window. He looked out at the drab scenery and kept his focus outside, away from the horror he was standing in.

Other police officers followed into the apartment behind him. One gasped as he stepped into the room. Another vomited and fled the scene. Christopher could not blame him; but he kept his gaze outside and refused to look at what remained of the body or what had once been its home.

Surprisingly, the other police officer found the man's wallet. He slipped on a pair of gloves and carefully picked it up. "His name was Toni Harison," the officer said. "He owned the convenience store underneath us."

Christopher nodded. "Just needed a smoke," he mumbled to himself.

Dawn was approaching. The wolf would have gone to ground by now, yet Christopher knew who the creature's host was. The law now permitted him to take custody.

He turned and faced the police officer. "Have all the evidence collected," he said sternly. "I'll be by the precinct in the evening to pick it up."

The police officer nodded and grew pale at the look on Christopher's face. "Yes sir," he said.

Then the monk, sworn to a life of servitude, left the apartment and the crime scene, stoically ignoring the other police and slipping discreetly past the press. They did not know he existed, and it was easy for him to keep it that way. Safely away, he pulled a cell phone from his pocket and pushed a button. Then he held the phone to his ear while he opened the door to his car. He looked around quickly to make sure he had not been followed, and then slipped into his vehicle and closed the door behind him.

"Yes," Janelle answered groggily.

"Janelle," Christopher said, swallowing the lump in his throat. His free hand began moving across the keyboard of his onboard computer. The casual resolve he was masking himself behind melted away as the computer screen flashed under his command. Everything fell into place inside that space behind his eyes. His detective's mind led him to where he'd wanted it to go for months, yet he was still unhappy with what he found.

"It's four in the morning," she said miserably.

"Sorry," Christopher lied flatly.

"No you're not."

"No I'm not."

Both Christopher and his commanding officer sighed at the same time.

"What have you got?"

"Turn your computer on."

"It's on."

"Then turn the monitor on."

There was another tired sigh coming through the receiver cradled between his shoulder and his ear. He could hear her moving, and then a, "Good God!" More silence.

Christopher waited quietly: too wary to reach for his coffee cup. The coffee would be cold anyway.

"How long have you been obsessing over this?"

"Too long," Christopher admitted. He left no satisfaction at cracking the case at last. "How soon can we have the warrant?"

"Half an hour," Janelle said quickly.

More silence. "It's the only real perk of this job," she admitted over the phone line.

"What's that?"

"Waking our superiors up in the middle of the night."

Finally, Christopher smiled. More silence as they shared the joke.

"Good work, Christopher."

"It's still going to take me awhile to find him," he said.

"You have a month."

Christopher ground his teeth in determination. "It won't take that long," he vowed.

"Then take the damn compliment," Janelle commanded.

Christopher was silent for a moment. "Thank you, Jan."

Then the line went dead in his hand.

Chapter Four

He was born a monster, with the bloodlust and the violence, the strength and the speed of a creature of the night. Yet he remembered very little of it. Creatures such as this beast often think more animalistic than animals as they roam the fields and forests in the dark. Yet in these days he was a vagabond, a homeless refugee running, always running, with the paranormal terror of his unknown victims flowing through his veins. If he had known enough of what was happening, he would remember he was lost in oblivion and terror. His body was always racked with sickness. His bones ached as though they were rotting from the inside out. Not only was he constantly fleeing from phantom fears, he flinched continuously as if hunted by an unknown stalker –the embodiment of terror. He would have very short life times. Then he would die and be reborn during the night of the full moon, to live another life of terror, reborn from the blood of a tragic massacre, the sole survivor of a hideous bloodbath psychologists say he had no awareness of. They hypothesized it was due to the fact that the memories caused such emotional trauma that he suppressed the incident by entering into an alter reality he created. They said he suffered from paranoia, schizophrenia, Multiple Personality Disorder, and amnesia. They couldn't even fathom the half of it.

At night was something different. Creatures of the night prey on each other. They prey on humans. They prey on animals. They prey on themselves. On the night of the full moon he would drink his fill at the apex of life and death, strength and weakness, at the apex of chaos and lust, anger and pain. Oh the glorious pain. Oh the glorious pain indeed. He basked in it. He drank his fill of it then craved for more, leaving him empty of life even as it filled him with the immortality and the eternity of death.

It was the night after the full moon, and he was as cowardly weak as a newborn pup, timidly learning his senses and honing his skills for the hunt with teeth that had not yet grown from his gums. Alexis remained where she was when she first took notice him. He was loping down the sidewalk, confused and dazed as werewolves generally are, and she was in no danger.

Her heart was breaking with the tired endlessness of her eternal cycle of life. She was bored with the drab and inferior human intellect crawling around on the planet. Walking sacks of water and vitamins, essential nutrients that she needed to survive, yet spiced with the finest wines of the world the blood of her victims remained forever the flavour of the mundane. It was watered down with overplayed radios and reruns of prime time soap operas and reality TV shows; with shopping malls designed to make people wander without purpose yet with an illusion of importance. Their schedules repeated themselves every seven days, and the humans walked around in the same sleep Alexis embraced every day. Even the rocks pulsed with more interesting noises than a society raised to mimic whatever Hollywood could think up.

She was thirsty all the time. She had had to feed and feed and feed with the unquenchable thirst that stereotypically marked her kind in the tomes of legend and myth. Once repulsed by the thought of dog meat, and still furious at Janelle for her betrayal, Alexis watched the werewolf, half beast, half man, lope into view, still far, far off as he walked somewhere between the sleeping and the dead.

She was propped up on the top of a building, yawning with the sleepy euphoria of a fresh though unremarkable kill. Hidden deep within the shadows, she sat watching the traffic in the streets below. It was a warm night, with not a cloud in the sky, though weather did not matter to her. The roses were out in bloom, and on the gentle breeze her supernatural senses were filled with their aroma from the park across the street. Alexis watched the beast cower from the flow of human traffic and was surprised at how well he hid from them, crouched low or huddled in the deep shadows amongst the branches of park trees. But she soon bored of this as well and drifted to sleep while she contemplated about the werewolves.

Suddenly, she snapped awake to an utterly abandoned city street. Without humans around, the wolf was secure enough to roam openly.

This was something new, something outside of the eternal reality TV.

Vampires are more superior intellectuals than humans. They're smarter, faster, usually a lot more resourceful, and have the years of time on their side to fill their indulgences and grow bored. Werewolves, however, are superior animals, filled with emotions and irrationalism that fuel passions and exploits into the night, night after night, in an ongoing quest of adventures and experiences. Alexis would be jealous except that they lived for the moon and died by it, only to be reborn and suffer through another month of the same repetitive life, again and again, and again. And again.

Who wanted it? Certainly not Alexis.

This particular werewolf froze suddenly and sniffed at the air. She melded quickly back into the shadows, thinking of the sudden danger she was in. Had this been two nights earlier, that beast would surely be half way to her throat by now. Had it been the night before, he'd be enthralled in an orgy of blood and death that Alexis would wish she couldn't survive through.

As it was, the full moon had passed, and all werewolves everywhere were at their weakest. Mister Wolf had only just noticed the roses, and was enraptured by the experience. She shook her head at the stupidity of the beast and was emboldened enough to abandon the shadows altogether. She perched on the very edge of the roof she was on. All of this was simply too good to be true. With his snout continuing to sniff the air, the wolf involuntarily followed his overactive nose down the street a ways, struggling to maintain his balance and keep up with his outstretched and disproportionate neck at the same time. He finally stopped in front of the largest patch of flowers, and Alexis had to get a better view. There was a gazebo nearby, and completely without his knowing it, she passed over him and took refuge in its shadows.

With his back no longer to her, she could clearly see the tears forming in his eyes. Waves of emotion were emanating off of his enraptured being and she leaned closer, drawn by the sheer will of his presence like a moth to the flame. He was in wonder; he was in awe, in love.

Lost in some kind of overwhelmed trance, he reached out a hesitant, shaky paw and caressed the delicate petals of one rose as if he'd never seen anything so beautiful, so perfect. He reached out his other hand and cupped the rose in his palms. His whole body began to shudder, and Alexis suddenly realized he was sobbing, weeping with the beauty and perfection, the completion of the rose in full bloom.

This was too much for Alexis.

Torn between scorn and curiosity, she advanced down the steps of her poor shelter. Now fully in the open, fully exposed and vulnerable, she was confident he was too absorbed to see her. Had she walked right up to him and brushed his furry back with the fingernails of her hand, he wouldn't have noticed, so long as she was enhancing his mesmerizing emotions and not distracting him from that flower.

He withdrew his hands tenderly and stepped back from the rose. His eyes remained fixed on it, and in a moment, he wrapped his paw around the stem. He would have this rose. He would pluck it from amongst the other roses in bloom and possess it, just as he, in all his ignorant passion, believed it had possessed him. When he tightened his fist, he recoiled as if struck by a physical blow.

The betrayal. The violation. The disappointment. He'd caught a thorn and it had cut into his flesh, cut deeply, leaving a fresh drop of blood glistening on its stem.

He howled in agony, in frustration, in pain. His heart had been broken and the grief of his howl was enough to make Alexis' head swim. Then he howled again and she fled from the park to watch the rest of this show from the safety of distance. He was now enraged, enraged at the rose, at the pain in his hand, at the night and the illusion he had been drawn into.

Alexis cried out. She didn't mean to, and she wasn't heard over the animalistic din he was making. But she found herself stricken by the grief he was in, as if she was the rose and truly returned his feelings.

Still roaring, he swiped at the rose with his animalistic strength, sending petals scattering. Then he was wading into the thicket of thorns and petals, thrashing this way and that, seeking retribution for the betrayal and ripping deep gashes into his body even as he thrashed at the roses around him. His pain was continuing to mount. His lust to destroy deepened at the beauty denied to him. He made quick work of the park, and then raised his bulging arms to the sky, his fingers outstretched like claws, and howled his frustration at the moon. In a final burst of speed, he fled from the park and down the street from whence he came.

This was too much. Alexis found herself amidst the ruined roses before she even realized what she was doing and, more importantly, why. She needed this. She had to have it. After countless nights of the same deadness, the chance to experience something new—no matter what it was—was simply too much. Besides, there was only enough for a taste, a sample: surely not enough to do any damage, if there was damage that could be done. But enough blood had been shed to experience what he felt, what he had lived.

She sampled the blood from a ruined stem gingerly, experimentally, lapping at it for just the smallest taste, the smallest sample. Suddenly, she was seized by an emotional ecstasy so overwhelming, she felt her loins quiver as they grew moist with the longing, the blood lust, and the need for something real, for this.

She too made quick work of the roses, moving not with animal speed, but with superhuman precision and total abandon until her mouth remained full of blood, torn from the thorns of a rose. Whether the blood was hers or his, it no longer mattered. Their blood was now mixed. And it was oh so sweet, oh so real and altogether different than the hazy, sleeping bipeds she'd been feasting off of before. She staggered with the weight of her discovery, with the wealth of it. Her head swam and the last she remembered of that night was the ground reaching up to meet her in a soft embrace. The grass had never looked so green. The moon had never looked so vivid, and Alexis had never felt so alive.

* * * * *

Confused, the beast's host woke shivering with a damp cold that had found its way into his very bones. A light mist was in the air and his breathe frosted when he finally opened his eyes. He was lying on a fire escape in the foetal position, quite naked and with a slight fever. A window behind him was open, and without knowing how he knew, the apartment within that window belonged to him.

He went to get up and groaned with pain. His entire body, every muscle in it, screamed at him in agony. A second attempt found him swaying on his feet, though the effort of it caused him to faint for a moment as he sank to his knees and his head sank to his chest.

It was then that he noticed he was covered from head to toe in lacerations, shallow, jagged cuts that had left long red welts across his skinny, malnourished frame. Shaking with the fever, he stumbled through the window and pitched head long onto the kitchen floor. He moaned, lay prone and motionless where he fell, then moaned some more. Water from his hair and body pooled under him on the floor, tainted ever so slightly with red.

From what he could see, the apartment was absolutely barren of any furniture. The floors were covered with a pale white tile; the ceiling was painted with the same pale white. The place was sterile and empty, though the kitchen countertops were stained a darker shade of wood-brown to match a ceiling fan. He could see it idly making its rounds down the hall in an endless cycle.

For the first time he became aware of the noise of traffic sloshing through the lightly falling rain outside. He struggled to his feet and shut the window and the noise outside. He suddenly felt very helpless, as though the walls were closing in on him. It was like being in a bear trap that he had stepped in, and he knew beyond doubt that if he remained here for very long the hunter would be along to check his trap lines.

Stumbling now in as much panic as pain, he made it down the hall to the bedroom. There was a bed there, with a mountain of blankets and rags piled on top of it. Clothing lay strewn across the floor, clothing that looking to belong to him.

He reasoned that it must be his, because it fit, and soon he was dressed in blue jeans and a grey pullover with a merciful hood. He found a pair of boots that he jammed his bare and bleeding feet into then threw on a black overcoat. There was a set of apartment keys in one of the coat's pockets.

He fled the apartment without checking to see if the keys would work on the door.

Shuddering, he went anywhere. He just had to keep moving, he told himself, and he would be able to stay ahead of his mysterious pursuer who caused such terrible anguish. He didn't know how long he wandered, or how far. He only knew that when he came across the ruined flower bed and saw the woman sleeping there, he was immediately afraid for her safety as much as he was for his own.

He suspected it was human nature that had left her to lie upon the wet earth. That part of the race of man that looks away or pretends not to see calamity when it pushes itself on other people had discreetly left her there to her fate. Perhaps people are so afraid to face their own mortality that they deny mortality when they see it in others. Perhaps it is the fear of the unknown that terrifies them so, that they have no room in their precious routines to extend the same courtesy to another that falls to their unfortunate, secret dread.

Whatever the case, Anubis' host was suffering under no illusions and had no luxuries to lose. He hesitated for only a moment before wading into the scattered thorn bushes and lifted her labouriously into his arms.

She said something unintelligible and draped an arm across his shoulders before passing back into a death-like sleep.

How he carried her home, he never knew. Where he found the strength to keep putting one foot heavily in front of the other forever remained a mystery to him. But he did it, though the world seemed to descend into silence and empty haze. The noise of the traffic faded from his mind, as did the buildings and the people on the street. The only things he was aware of was the sound of his own footfall on the damp pavement; his laboured and wracked breathing, and the deep, immortal beauty of the peace he could see on this woman's sleeping features. She was beautiful, truly. With long brown hair with a hint of red in it, and strong cheek bones under smooth and pale skin, he took her for a business woman by the way she was dressed, one of the sophisticated career types who lost her briefcase when she fainted, lost it or had it stolen.

But by then he had her in the lobby of his building and was hurrying her into an empty and open elevator. He automatically pushed a button, hoping it was the right one then slid to the floor in utter exhaustion, the dead weight of his new and mysterious friend still in his arms.

When the door reopened, he jammed it with his foot then struggled into the hallway, draping the woman by her arms, with her heels scraping along behind them. In this manner he got her to his apartment, then through the door and into his bed.

He buried her as much as he could under the blankets he heaped on top of her, leaving her head uncovered so she might breathe. Then taking a worn blanket for himself, he collapsed onto the floor and passed into a troubled sleep full of nightmarish terrible images. He was still feverish.

* * * * *

Alexis woke with an immediate return to consciousness. Her eyes flew open in alarm. She knew exactly where she was and how she had gotten there. This wasn't what had caused such alarm, however. It was the fact that she had been out in the daylight and was still alive to remark about it. Even now, there was the last remains of a fading light filtering through the window onto the back of her head.

A part of her had remained aware of what was happening around her after she had passed out drunk on werewolf blood the night before, as if she had watched the day's events through a television screen. Yet what struck Alexis was not the sense of danger that radiated over him. It was the sense of awe or wonder that radiated through her at his presence.

She had been reduced to a glowing teenage girl at the sight of her chivalrous knight in shining armour. She had been turned from a creature of fierce independent nature, a huntress of the night, to a helpless and grateful woman in love with an abandonment that was alarming. She was her lover's and his desire was for her.

Now, though, as she looked at the wretched man on the floor, she could only chastise herself for her behaviour from earlier that day. The huntress had reawakened and calmly pushed the girl deep down inside where this pathetic counterpart's emotions were of no concern. There was a werewolf about to awaken in the room with her. And that was never a good place to be.

Still, as she sat up in bed, she was struck by how weak and vulnerable he looked. It must have been a huge sacrifice to bring her here, to the place where the roaming demon would return, night after night, and where this poor, confused man would wake in terror and oblivion each morning after. But he did bring her to his lair, and she suspected it was not entirely out of compassion, as he thought. He must have sensed the kindred between the two of them, not so much the fact that they were both anomalies of terror. Had he known she was a creature of the night, he would have fled from her. It must have been the blood in her, his blood, calling out to him in the same synchronized rhythm of emotion as his own. Alexis guessed she must have been feeling very frightened and exposed out there in the daylight. Yet she had never felt any such emotions for herself since she drew her first draught of human blood from her first terrified victim.

So, the werewolf blood did have a downside to it. It may have given her experiences and strength far beyond what vampires usually get to revel in. But it also made her feel vulnerable, weak, and in love. It was creating in her a second identity, a second personality that would awaken for brief interludes during the day. This new identity was a complete stranger to her, alien in her humanness as his human host was alien to Anubis. But she was grateful she was at least aware of this human, whereas the wolf would know nothing of the man, and the man nothing of the wolf.

Mister Wolf was awakening by then. It appeared to be a slow and painful process, one which he fought valiantly in his feverish state. Deep down inside, the man was being overcome by the fear that stalked him throughout the day. From the deepest recesses of his mind, the creature would come from his hiding places to consume his human alter ego. The human was whimpering pathetically. His body twitched spastically upon the floor.

Acting out of a sense of obligation she did not quite understand, Alexis rushed to his side and bit into his wrist.

The night before she had drawn blood from the wolf. Now, she drew blood from the man and took all of his terrors and incompetence into herself. Blood was blood, though. And this blood, this remarkable blood, was still the same as it had been the night before. It still had the same effect. It was glorious.

But it was not for her that Alexis had done this, and so she pulled away from the physical effects it was having on her body. Instead she concentrated on him. In her mind's eye she was greeted by the terrified man and his inner beast as it fought for dominance over his mind and body.

The man was weak and yet he idolized the very sight of her, very much the way Alexis' new day walking counterpart had looked up to him. The wolf, however, was enraged at the vampire's presence. Yet there was an unspoken truth between their kind, a fact both of them had known about for countless years; here, she was the stronger. Here, she was the master. Here, she held all the authority.

She remained calm and passive as she stared the wolf down. He tested that authority only as far as to take a few hesitant steps toward her before turning and retreating back into the darkness of subconscious.

Another time, vampire, a thought floated out of the caverns of this bruised mind.

"We'll see," she muttered as she turned to the awestruck little man at her side. Now, his eyes shone with as much fear and respect as they did with adoration.

Trusting in Alexis, he let her lift him into her arms. She must have stopped drawing on his blood then, because they both found themselves back in his little apartment at dusk. He was still in her arms, looking up at her with such a sense of relief and relaxation written on his face. His body was putty in her arms.

Carefully, almost fearful of hurting him, she placed him on his bed, where he had earlier placed her. "Sleep now," she muttered kindly as she reached out and closed his eyes for him. Enwrapped in the bewitchment of the vampire, he passed into sleep immediately. "And know peace, for a time," she added: not knowing if he would or not, but hoping nonetheless.

Before she could stop herself, and not understanding why she did it, she bent over him and brushed a kiss against his forehead. Then she fled from the apartment to vent the aggression beginning to surge through her veins. The strength of the werewolf was now hers, for all of its good and bad.

And she had to hunt.

She was careful to leave the kitchen window open. The wolf would eventually awaken. But she would need a way back in when she returned.

Chapter Five

That morning, two confused and very dazed people woke up side by side amongst a pile of rags. Both were so inflicted with mental illnesses that neither had the faculty to speak. The man, conscious that he was naked, covered himself quickly as he realized he was not alone. The woman looked at him strangely as she pushed her way out from underneath the pile of dirty clothes and worn blankets. She was dressed in a wrinkled, conservative suit of clothing, and so felt none of the shame the man was suffering through. Experimentally, she stood on shaky feet. Though her balance was uncertain, she found that she knew how to walk, though she had no conscious memory of ever having done so before. She was hungry, though she loathed leaving him for even a moment. She found the kitchen and realized there was no food in the apartment, so she slowly made her way back to the bedroom. By the time she got back, he had already dressed and was standing at the side of the bed, confused.

"Where am I?" he asked.

The daywalker, still lacking the faculty to talk, could not comprehend what he said. Grieving, she silently pleaded to him with her eyes.

"I am hungry," he said after a moment. He looked at her carefully and steeled himself against the terror of having to go find food. "You need to eat."

His mind made up, he walked past her and she grabbed his arm. He turned back to her and looked deep into her eyes. There was only love there, and her desperation faded. "I'll be back in a little while," he said with a smile. "You're safe now." Then he left her in their apartment and ignored his terror as he stepped out into the unknown world.

The woman, confused but controlled by instinct, knew all would be well. She looked around at the messy bedroom as if seeing it for the first time. Then she began sorting through the laundry with practised movements she did not know she possessed until after she had begun the chore. She found a washing machine and drier in a closet in the hallway and was surprised to find a half empty bottle of detergent as well. Her hazy confusion was fading the more she moved through the apartment, though she retained no memories. Her mind was blank, yet she was waking up, ever so slowly. She lost track of time as she gave herself over to the chore, and before she was aware of it, the first load of laundry was finished and drying, while the second one was already in the washing machine. She smiled to award herself for her accomplishment and then looked up as she heard the door open.

He had returned and smiled at her as he came through the door. In his hand were two paper bags. He had managed to find a fast food restaurant nearby, had managed to conquer his fear enough to approach the building and then the counter. He had spoken to the person behind that counter and money had been exchanged, though he scarcely knew how it had happened. Unsure of himself, he had waited at the counter and was rewarded for his vigilance when the server handed him his food.

Now, he was back. And wanting to share his prize with her, held out one of the bags to her. "Food," he said as she took the bag.

She smiled her gratitude and went into the barren living room. He followed her in and sat down next to her on the floor. Then, together, they opened the bags and pulled out whatever breakfast he'd managed to find. She smiled as, famished, the aroma of the fast food filtered up and filled her sense of smell with the sheer goodness of it. Then, as he bit into his own meal with the ferocious determination of a dog, she bit into a breakfast bagel and sighed as she tasted the glorious food upon her tongue.

Then, hideously, her stomach turned and she dry heaved the food out of her mouth. Her hunger forgotten for the moment, she dropped the bagel onto the bag in front of her and rushed to the kitchen sink. Her stomach convulsed and she dry heaved painfully into the sink, though nothing came out of her stomach. She moaned at the pain of the spasm, yet in a moment, it passed and she righted herself, holding steady to the kitchen counter. She composed herself and returned to the living room, where her kind and mysterious lover looked up at her with terror shining in his wide eyes. His mouth was full, yet he dared not chew his food as he stared up at her.

Trying to reassure him, but lacking the words to do so, she came over to him and sat down, leaning against his arm. She put her head on his shoulder and sighed, feeling comforted just knowing he was there, next to her.

In a moment, he relaxed and returned to his meal, tearing into it just as savagely as before.

She closed her eyes with relief, glad that at least one of them was eating.

When he was finished, he looked at her own meal longingly, left abandoned in front of her. Though she could relate to how hungry he was, she pushed the bag toward him. The food had become an alien thing to her, detestable and uneatable. She would not attempt to eat again, and chose to live with her hunger as it gnawed ceaselessly at her mind. At least she had him, and that helped ease the torment a little.

A moment later, he started in on her breakfast as well. And when he was finished eating, his own hunger had subsided.

* * * * *

Plagued by lack of memory and paranoia that could not be reasoned with, the ragged and confused couple found comfort only in the arms of each other. They gripped each other fearfully, silently reassuring and lending as much strength as they could as they walked down the sidewalk, wide eyed at everything around them. He was too afraid to say anything; she had forgotten how to talk. Other people walked past them as they made their way slowly along, yet no one bothered to acknowledge them, instinctively sensing that something was wrong with them.

That was just as well; neither was really sure if they could handle attention being drawn to them, and both were thankful for the oblivion.

Shopping malls and sky rises surrounded them, blocking out the noonday sun and casting them into shadow. They smiled hesitantly at each other and conquered more of their fear as she pulled him to a stop before a department store window. It showcased a mannequin dressed in clean, new clothes, not the worn and ripped jeans, or the faded and stained tee shirt the man wore. He looked at the display in the window without interest for a moment before he looked back at the woman he was with.

She was smiling and staring up at him. Unable to speak, her intention was lost to him. But after a moment of thought, she patted his arm and pointed at the set of clothing in the display. He shook his head and shrugged his shoulders to tell her he did not understand what she was saying. So she patted his arm for a second time and pointed at the mannequin again. Again, he shook his head.

Pursing her lips together, she searched her groggy mind for a way to explain what she was trying to say. She looked at the sign over the front doors and pointed at it.

He looked at the words, spelling them out in his head. When he was sure he could pronounce them properly, he looked at her and said, "Tommy Hilfiger." Then he shrugged again and asked, "What of it?"

She patted his arm a third time and pointed at the sign this time.

"What are you trying to say?" he asked.

She grew very still and then said, "Tommy Hilfiger."

Amazed that she spoke, he burst into laughter and embraced her.

But determined to get her message across, the lady pulled out of his hug and patted his chest as she searched his eyes for understanding. "Tommy Hilfiger," she said as she held her hand against his beating heart. With her other hand, she pointed at the mannequin, and then back at him. "Tommy."

Finally, understanding dawned on him, and he kissed her passionately, not only because she had spoken, but also for the compliment that left him at a loss for words. Tears were in his eyes as he finally pulled away, though she hungered for the kiss to continue. "Thank you," he said through his onslaught of emotion.

Then they kissed again, forgetting about their fears for the moment.

The following day, Tommy gathered the nerve to go back to that store and buy the clothes they had seen on the mannequin. He also bought a new set of clothes for her, somehow keenly aware of what would fit her and what wouldn't.

* * * * *

Lying on their bed between freshly washed sheets, she smiled as she looked deep into her lover's eyes. Breathless and tired, he forced himself to stay awake as he watched the slight nuances of emotions that filtered across her face.

Not able to bear the silence any longer, he asked, "Who are you?" The compassion in his face and the open desire to know her was so obvious that she reached beyond her own limitations and pulled from her mind an image lost to the ages. Unsure of what she would say, she nonetheless forced her mouth to work and betray the silence and oblivion she had always known.

"My name," she said, forcing herself to continue despite the surprise at her own success so far, "is Jemma."

Tom sighed contentedly as his eyes dropped shut. "Jemma," he said, more to himself than to her. Then he drifted off into sleep.

She watched him lovingly as sunset began, and then as it darkened outside.

Then, suddenly, she blinked. And that quickly, Alexis awoke and the day walker, Jemma, was asleep.

Thirst.

Alexis shook her head and rolled her eyes at the day walker's crazy emotions. "Jemma," she mumbled. "Why that name?" she asked herself out loud. All she could think of in way of an answer was the gnawing worry that Janelle would find her and set her dogs onto her. "Let her try," she said again. "I have my own dog now."

Tom was beginning to twitch as the wolf began to manifest.

It was time to sate her thirst.

When she was done, the werewolf had already awoken and stared up at her weakly, powerless. The blood was drained from his body. Enough blood had been taken to kill a mortal, yet Anubis clung to life, too stupid to die.

She shook her head at the entire pathetic situation and laughed as the werewolf's heightened emotional blood made her feel alive once more. The day walker and her lover were far beyond her when she left the paralysed body in the bed and dressed herself quickly. She had an empire to run, and with his added strength coursing through her veins her other slaves would be easy enough to control.

* * * * *

Laughing together, Tom and Jemma ignored the press of the crowds around them as he pulled her onto his back and galloped through the crowded mall. He jostled her purposely to make the ride harder for her, yet this only brought more peels of laughter from his passenger as she clung to his back for dear life. Every reaction from smiles to outright laughter met them from the crowds, who parted as they watched the two lovers, oblivious to the attraction they drew to themselves. They flirted inside their own private world of paradise and no one else mattered except the two of them.

Tom saw a water fountain in the centre of the mall's food court, and headed there with determined steps as he bounced Jemma around on his back. She saw where he was headed, yet powerless to prevent his course, only laughed all the harder as she tried to gather her breathe. "Don't you dare!" she finally managed to laugh. "Don't even think about it!"

Tom ignored her and raced toward the water, laughing at the prospect. She squealed and laughed with him, already planning her revenge should he go through with the drenching. But at the last second, at the very brink of the fountain, he stopped and swung her into his arms. He dipped her over the fountain and she screamed and laughed all the harder as she clung desperately to his coat. Yet, instead of dropping her, he kissed her, holding her secure in his embrace. Eventually, trust returned to her and she relaxed her grip on his clothes. She brought her hands up behind his back and lost herself to their kiss. Breathless, he pulled her to her feet and set her down next to the fountain. They stared into each other's eyes for a moment longer before she grabbed at the nearby spray and deflected it enough to splash his face with cold water.

Laughing, they both collapsed at an empty table and looked at each other across the space between them. Eventually, their laughter faded away and they caught their breath.

"Are you hungry?" he asked.

She looked at him sorrowfully. "Always," she admitted.

"I am too," he said. "Want anything?"

Jemma held her hand to her mouth and tried not to vomit at the thought of food. She paled and shook her head.

Regrettably, he nodded. "We should get that checked soon," he suggested.

"I know," she admitted. "But I'm not unhealthy, not yet."

"It's been nearly a month, though," he said, worried.

"I know," she repeated, echoing his worry in her own voice.

They were silent for a moment as they contemplated her eating disorder.

"We should do it today," he suggested.

"You can't. You have to work today," she reminded him.

He looked at his watch quickly.

"What time is it?" she asked.

"Time to eat," he said as he slapped his hand against the table and stood to his feet. "I'll be right back." Then he kissed her on the top of her head and blended in to the crowds of streaming people. She watched him go, smiling, and then sat patiently for his return.

* * * * *

Tom recklessly stumbled into their apartment and slammed the door behind him. Jemma sat on their couch, looking up at him oddly.

"Why aren't you at work?" she asked as he rushed past her to their bathroom. He flung open the toilet seat and vomited painfully. "I guess that's why?" she said from behind him. Then her face paled and she grew angry. "What happened to your back?"

Spotted with blood, it was as if he had been stabbed. In truth, he had been, several times. But unknown to either of them, the wounds had closed in his drunken flight from the pub. He didn't want her to know what had happened, so he lied. "I got in a fight and was thrown to the pavement," he said once the spasms had passed and he could talk again. The room swayed dangerously.

"What!" she asked. "Who did this to you!" she roared. "Who are they!"

"No one," he said quickly, afraid she would discover what he had done. The bar was in ruins. People were dead. He was the only one that escaped alive, and even then, he did not know exactly what had happened, only that there was a monster involved. And he did not want her to be taken by that terrifying creature.

"You were at The Blind Duck again!" she roared angrily.

He moaned and pulled himself to his feet. "I'm fine," he growled as he stumbled past her into the hallway, putting himself between her and the only way out.

"I'm going down there!" she swore. "I'm going to find out who did this to you, and I'm going to press charges against the animals!" Her voice had risen to an angry shout.

Tom swallowed the fear in his throat, fear he had for them both. Steeling his resolve, his determination, he pushed his emotions to the side and looked into her eyes. "No, you're not," he said calmly. And he placed a hand gently on her solar plexus.

Outside, the sun was setting. The full moon was cresting above the horizon.

"Yes, I am!" she screamed angrily as she grabbed his hand.

Tom roared and the beast of the werewolf ripped out if his skin as he blanked out.

He came to moments later. Jemma's body lay in a heap on the floor, broken and bleeding, and very much dead. He screamed as he realized what he had done and fled in panic from their apartment.

He did not stop running when he reached the street, nor did he risk glancing over his shoulder as he ran. He needed to get as far away from what happened as he could. The sun was still up, and in the filtering light, he ran.

The wheels of a car screeched past him as he ran. He ignored it in his mad flight and did not have the mental functions left to realize he should change directions when the same car came to a halt at the intersection in front of him. A man jumped from the driver's side door and vaulted over the hood of the car. He did not hesitate, but flew at Tom with a determination Tom could no longer ignore. Seconds later, Tom was sprawled out on the pavement, looking up at the sky as the awakening stars spun wildly out of control.

Christopher plunged a needle into his neck and emptied the syringe. Once the tranquillizer was in Tom, Christopher tossed the syringe onto the street and hauled the now morphing werewolf to his feet. Tom was only aware of the passenger car door opening before he was thrown headlong into a wire mesh cage and the door was slammed shut behind him. Then darkness took over and he lost consciousness.

* * * * *

The sun set completely and Alexis came awake. Suffering from bruises and broken bones, she pulled herself slowly to her feet amongst the pooling blood. She needed to feed before the regenerating effects of vampirism could heal her body from what the wolf had done to it. The ongoing saga between the day walker and the werewolf could wait until morning. She was starving and could not care what Jemma would do when Alexis went to sleep again. All that mattered to her now was her blood lust. Her only remorse was that she had not drunken a drop of Tom's blood before he had tried to kill her and then ran screaming from the apartment.

Chapter Six

The rain was coming down in torrents, making Christopher's vision blur as his Buick Regal slid sideways along the treacherous roads. Thankfully, the night was still young, but time was never on his side. Anubis, locked in the meagre cage behind him, fought the tranquillizer with confused anger, staring out at Christopher through blurred vision. He looked back, just as heartless, just as cold, and Anubis looked away. Christopher readjusted his rear view mirror and kept his attention on the road ahead of him.

Anubis was always the same. Angry, passionate, stupid, and completely irrational, the only thing that stopped Christopher and Beast from ripping this werewolf's skin off right here and now was the confused and frightened sleeping soul locked deep down inside this creature's body: Tommy Hilfiger.

They pulled onto a winding street that hugged a cliff face to their right. A sheer drop was on the left, and mercilessly, the rain did not slow down, forcing Christopher to adjust his own speed instead. He looked at the clock on his dash board and then chose to pointedly ignore it from then on. "We'll make it," he told himself. "We'll make it." Silence answered him, and he preferred it that way, steadily climbing up the mountain and away from the city Tom had been taken in.

Eventually, the rain did begin to slow down a bit. They were still climbing a mountain, and the rain was being left below. All at once, the cliff levelled out and the car pulled onto a wide, broad plateau stripped clear of any vegetation. An air strip ringed with a chain link fence and barbed wire kept back civilians that might wander this far up. A guard station with a barricade marked the end of the road.

When Christopher saw it, he punched a button on his cell phone and speed dial took over for him. He readjusted his grip on the steering wheel and accelerated to still higher speeds. When the phone came alive in his ear, he said, "Open the gates." Someone tried to question him, but Christopher shouted over the protests. "Open the gates now!" Then he slammed the phone shut and threw it into the passenger seat next to him.

In the distance, the gates began to open and the barricade moved aside.

He waved at the reluctant guard as he flew by, then kept his attention focused on where he was going. Moments later, the car slid to a sideways stop next to a jet whose engines were flaring to life even as Christopher cut the power to his own vehicle. He jumped from the car and pulled a pistol from its holster under his jacket. A van was pulling up beside him as he threw the passenger door open and fired a round into Anubis' chest.

The creature, still dazed and weakened by the tranquillizer, was cooperative enough as Christopher threw him to the concrete between them and the van.

A containment crew took over after that, shackling the beast and tazering it with electric rods as they forced it into the back of the van. Christopher had seen hundreds of containment cells before, even tested a few of them out himself. They never held for very long. Still, he watched Anubis being unloaded from the van, now locked inside the steel enforced cage. He frowned at the locks on the doors then looked reflexively at the sky.

Though the rain came down in torrents, hiding the full moon from sight, he still guessed where it would be in the sky, gauging the time he and the other werewolf had left. Not much.

He looked around at the crews of Janelle's secret army of mortals and then put two more rounds into the werewolf through an open grate on the side of the steel cage. His weapon illuminated the night like falling lightning, yet Christopher still heard the werewolf fall dead from inside his cage.

Relieved, he put his weapon away. "Load it onto the plane," he commanded as he strode toward the walkway leading into the plane. "I don't want to look at it again until we get back to Anderita."

The crew leapt to his command, using a forklift to load the cage into the cargo bay. Christopher decided to board as a passenger this night. There was no need to upset the humans any more than they already were, and secrecy amongst the ranks was always a good thing in his line of work.

He was handed a towel by an awaiting stewardess who smiled invitingly when she saw him. He took the towel from her and asked, "I'm told there was an intensive care unit on board?"

"Yes sir," she answered. He never gave his name, and she was smart enough not to ask, though he could tell she wanted to.

"Where is it?"

The stewardess swallowed her disappointment, though she could not hide the hurt in her eyes. "This way." Frowning, he nodded and followed her deeper into the plane.

A section of the room had been set up like an intensive care hospital room. A bed rested empty, with a life support system ready for whoever might need it. Christopher needed it tonight.

"There's a nurse on board," he stated. "Who is it?"

"That would be me, sir," she answered, looking up at him.

Sadly, he looked down into her eyes. "What's your name?"

"Synthia."

"Well, Synthia," he said. "I guess you've been briefed."

"Not really," she said. "The lady said you'd explain it to me once you got here."

Christopher shook his head, frustrated. "Was she wearing a white fur coat?"

"Yes sir," Synthia said.

Christopher was silent as he tried to guess what Janelle had in mind. "Well, Synthia," he said. He shook her hand and then said, "I'm sorry you had to see this."

"Why? What is going to happen?"

"I'm going to die."

Then the plane began its descent down the tarmac.

The stewardess smiled sadly, unsurprised. "Christopher," she said quietly. "That is all right." She placed a hand on his shoulder and led him to the bed, pushing him onto it. Too shocked that she even knew her name, he put up little resistance. She looked down at him and dared a smile through the tears that were blurring her vision. "You've heard of the Sister Mary Margarette," she said.

Christopher nodded. "She was a nun in the middle ages."

Synthia knelt before him. Her hand was still on his shoulder. "She didn't stay a nun," she answered. "I am her granddaughter."

"Her what?"

Synthia nodded. "You were the priest that married her off."

"Why don't I remember this?" he asked.

"After Iminuetep turned to stone," she said. "You lost your memory for a time. It was Janelle that helped you bring it back."

Realizing he had nothing to fear for her, he all at once broke into a sob and allowed himself to relax. The wells of emotion, of years of beatings and violence, of loss and pain, came pouring out of him and he wept uncontrollably as he fell into her arms. She held him while he broke, not trying to stop the flood of pain that rushed from him. "You are safe now," she said gently, not understanding, but knowing how to stop him from hurting more. "You are not in the field anymore."

He remained in her arms until he cried himself fell asleep. And in peaceful silence his heart gradually came to a stop. The plane crested above the cloud covers and flew by the light of the full moon. Those that were on the plane kept to themselves in silence, not wanting to disturb his rest, and lost in their own contemplation about the war he fought for them.

Not once did Beast manifest through his body. The creature slept as well.

* * * * *

In the morning Christopher awoke to a sun filled cabin inside the plane's gradual descent to Anderita. Refreshed, he pulled himself from the bed and disconnected the monitor systems that were still flaring to life. He still wore his wet field clothes, noticing that they had dried during the night. He wondered if Synthia had set the room temperature to do that on purpose. He got up and set out to find her.

He did not have far to go. She was in the hallway with two cups of coffee, looking at her watch as he came through the door.

She smiled. "Morning. How did you sleep?"

He chuckled and reached for one of the coffee cups.

"No, not that one," she said quickly. "This one's yours." She handed him the other coffee."

He took it suspiciously and sniffed at it. "Why? What did you do to it?" he asked.

She looked at him fearlessly. "I made it the way you like it," she answered. "My stomach can't handle that. Especially this early in the morning."

He laughed. "Janelle!" he said thankfully. "She gave you my file!"

"Yes, she did," Synthia said. Then she placed her free hand on his shoulder. "Welcome home." They embraced in a fierce hug.

"Thank you," he said gratefully, overcome with gratitude. "Thank you so much."

"You're welcome," was all she said.

Then she led him to the cockpit so he could finish the rest of the flight with his pilots. Knowing they had important business to attend to, she discreetly left them to it and closed the door behind him.

One of the pilots had a travel chess board waiting. Pieces were already set up; the game was unfinished.

"Morning gentlemen," Christopher said, smiling.

"It's been a long time," the pilot with the chess set said angrily.

"He's been stalling," the other pilot joked.

"It's been two days!" Christopher cried.

"Give it a break," the pilot with the board mumbled. "You're still stalling."

Christopher only shook his head. "Fine. Pass it here."

The pilot beamed from ear to ear as he passed the board up.

They arrived at Anderita at midday. Christopher was the first off of the plane. He didn't bother to wait for the stairs to be rolled up, instead jumping from the plane before the latch had been fully up.

Janelle stepped from a limousine and laughed as he watched him gallop toward him. She took a few steps to clear herself from the limousine and kept laughing as he careened into her at full hilt. They both went sailing into the air, laughing and wrestling with each other as they impacted the concrete beneath them.

"I don't know who's worse," Synthia said as she and the rest of the crew walked down the stairs. "Vampires or werewolves."

"I'll let you know," the pilot carrying the chess board said.

"Have you won yet?" Synthia asked, referring to the ever present board.

"Not yet," the other pilot answered for him.

"Not once," the first admitted honestly. "Not once."

Tommy Hilfiger was unloaded from his containment cage and chained and shackled. Dazed, but respected, he was guided toward where Christopher and Janelle were still trying to playfully kill each other. Seeing him coming, they detangled themselves and rose to their feet, trying to salvage some of their dignity in his presence.

"Mister Hilfiger," Janelle said as she greeted him and shook his hand. "I trust you did not have an unpleasant trip."

"I don't remember it," he answered truthfully.

She smiled tensely and held the car door open for him. "That's good," she answered. "Please don't mind the restraints," she said. "They are for your own protection."

Then the three of them climbed into the limousine and she closed the door behind them. Christopher looked at Tommy for a moment, considering. Finally, he leaned into Tom's face. Instinctively, he flinched back, afraid of the sudden proximity and the authority Christopher wore. "Do I have any lipstick on me?" he asked, turning his head first one way and then the other.

"No," Tom said.

"Are you sure? None on my collar, or behind my ear?"

"None," Tom answered.

Christopher sat back triumphantly, gloating over his victory with Janelle while she feinted an exaggerated sulk. "How is Jemma?" he asked.

"Oh, Jemma is fine!" Tom answered with exaggerated pleasure.

"Who!" Janelle asked. Then her eyes widened as she realized what Christopher was hinting at. "Alexis," she muttered darkly.

"Tommy Hilfiger," Christopher said, pointing at Janelle. "I'd like to introduce to you the Countess of Anderita Manor, Janelle Aquainnus, my sister."

Tommy looked at her, perplexed. "I don't understand," he answered.

Janelle, in her fur coat and limousine, only stared at Tommy, as surprised as he was, yet waiting for his slow mind to at least grasp a part of what was going on.

"It seems Tommy is no longer Fernir," Christopher began to explain, feeding her another piece of the puzzle. "He is Anubis."

"So. He has help." She looked at Christopher. "And you think whoever Tommy's in love with is a day walker? Why would that happen?"

"True love," Christopher answered. "It happened to Father. It can happen to anyone."

Janelle nodded. "It happened to me. Yet this thing inspired it?" she asked as she motioned toward Tommy and the werewolf that lurked underneath.

Christopher nodded. "It seems that way."

"What does Beast think about it?"

He shook his head. "I haven't let the creature near him. They're old friends anyway. We and Fernir here used to be neighbours just before you and Alexis stormed the Manor."

Janelle nodded. "This is the one you chased to the Americas."

"Kicked his hide from one side of Europe to clear across the Atlantic," Christopher remembered fondly. "He never did get the message."

"But you weren't permitted to kill him, then?" she asked.

Christopher looked at her realistically. "Didn't know how."

"And now?"

"Now there's a day walker involved. Besides, I have a whole month this time. And he remembers most of last month."

"It might not be Alexis at all, just some leech the dear sister toyed with at one time. And it might not even be a vampire." Janelle leaned in to look straight into Tommy's eyes. "Whoever this Jemma is, she's a rose with a thorn."

Christopher swallowed. "That's a little harsh, isn't it?"

I'm a realist, brother," she said as she leaned into him and kissed him on the cheek. "Do what you can with him and then go after the vampire. You have a month."

"I won't need a month," Christopher answered as he wiped the lipstick off of his cheek.

"Then good work."

"Thank you."

They passed the rest of the ride in silence, considering the mountain that rose up before them and considering the paths best to take.

The limousine pulled up to the front of Aquainnus Manor and two bodyguards stepped forward to open the doors. Janelle took Tom's arm while she pulled him out of the car and Christopher stepped from the other side.

"How was it?" the body guard asked. Both Christopher and he watched as Janelle led Tom away.

"Painful," he said.

"We have a holding cell waiting, if you need it," the guard reminded him.

Still watching their captive, Christopher smiled. "Concrete walls? Wall shackles? All the rest?"

"Even a neck chain for Anubis to throw himself against."

Christopher nodded appreciatively. "Is it big enough for two of us?"

"It is." Janelle and Tom disappeared into the house and Christopher faced the guard.

"Does it have two leashes?"

The guard shook his head. "The cell is to small."

"Then get a bigger cell," Christopher responded, deathly serious. "And do it quick. I want to start tonight."

The guard nodded and tapped his ear. He glanced at Christopher and nodded goodbye. Dismissed, Christopher nodded and jogged after Janelle as the guard started issuing commands into his sleeve.

Christopher caught up with them in the courtyard with his father's statue. He sank to his knees in reverent devotion and crossed himself quickly. He stood just as quickly, wiping a tear from his eye. Tom and Janelle stood before the statue, he in awe, she transfixed in quiet conversation with her kind.

Then, very quickly, the wings of the gargoyle opened to receive her and she stepped forth into his embrace. Quietly, the wings folded back, not touching her but shielding her protectively from the threats that surrounded her. She turned very quickly to stone, the soft fur coat turning just as hard, just as quickly.

Chapter Seven

Set deep into the cliffs of the forested mountains, a cave, one of many, had been carefully carved out of the rock face. Its entrance overlooked a picturesque view of a waterfall and a canopy of mammoth trees with leaves the colour of golden sunlight. Some thought had been given to the construction of this holding cell. Love had been placed behind every blow of the hammer upon the chisel, the walls were smooth and carefully carved. Yet though the attention to detail remained obvious to any who saw it, none could ignore the bloodstains on the walls, or the chains sunk deep into the living stone of the mountain. Not even an immortal could break out of those chains, nor could any amount of scrubbing remove the macabre evidence of past failures, despite Janelle's best efforts to prevent those tragic incidents.

There were only two chains in this cave, leashes with shackles that fit around the necks of immense steel collars. They were at opposite ends of the rectangular room, with the entrance between them, allowing the setting sun to filter through the autumn leaves and illuminate a patch of light against the far wall. And both chains were occupied. Christopher Aquainnus and Tommy Hilfiger sat calmly against the walls of their temporary prison, staring at each other as they tried to ignore the pain the metal shackles were causing. They were shirtless, and wore baggy sweat pants. Their bare feet were a little cold against the cool stone, yet Christopher knew the discomforts would soon pass and his assurance to Tom kept them both waiting patiently for the sun to set.

"I still don't understand why we're down here," Tom said, perhaps for the tenth time.

"We are dangerous creatures," Christopher explained again.

"No, we're not," Tom said quickly.

"Yes, Tom," Christopher said, deadly serious. "We are."

Tom swallowed as the look in Christopher's eyes demanded he admit the truth to his words. "Then how come I don't know it?"

"How long does your memory go back?" Christopher asked.

"To Jemma," he answered quickly, smiling at her memory.

"No farther?"

Tom thought for a moment, then shook his head. "No," he admitted. "But why would it need to? She is everything."

Christopher nodded. "In truth," he said, "You are much older than that. Hundreds of years old, perhaps thousands." Tom chuckled at the ridiculousness of that statement, but Christopher raised his hand and silenced Tom's ridicule. "I know how it sounds," he said. "But you don't remember anything. The memories you do have are hazy and short term, at best. You have within you a creature that is so much more than you could ever be. And right now, it owns you completely. It is what you fear, it is what drives you restless day after day. It is your secret terror that you've been hiding from."

"How did you know about that?" Tom asked.

"Because Tom," Christopher said. "I am just like you.

"But unlike you, I've got reason to remember, reason to tame the beast and conquer the fear." Christopher looked at the patch of sunlight sinking steadily down the wall between them. They were running out of time. Any minute now, he would be able to show Tom what he was talking about. And after that, it would have to be up to Tom to chose. He dreaded the thought of another pelt being taken, but ultimately it would be Tom who chose.

Tom just shook his head. "I don't believe you," he said. "How could I?"

"Even after Janelle turned to stone?" Christopher asked. "Is it so unbelievable after everything you've seen, with the jet and the limo, and your transportation here, all the resources that have been spent, the people involved, that there is at least a grain of truth to what I say? Maybe the world isn't what you've been raised to believe it is. Maybe the world is bigger, more frightening, and so much more dangerous." He could already feel Beast stirring beneath his skin.

Tom could feel Anubis as well, but his instincts were fighting the transformation, denying his unrealistic passions behind a flimsy wall of reason, a wall that always collapsed once the fierce determination of Anubis was ready to break from its shell. "I need a smoke," Tom said as he shook his head.

Christopher laughed. "Then I'll show you," he said. And Beast came snarling to the surface, yipping happily to be free once again.

Tom screamed in terror, subconsciously recognizing the demon he'd been running from throughout the millennia. And Christopher, out of compassion for his new friend, let Beast subside back under the surface. The werewolf morphed painlessly back into a completely human form and Christopher looked at Tom with the infinite patience of one who'd seen a similar reaction from thousands of other people before him.

"What the hell was that!" Tom screamed, rising shakily to his feet, despite the heavy weight of the chain that dragged at his neck. The anger of Anubis was already surfacing, and Christopher had little time left with someone sane.

"That," Christopher continued, still sitting and watching his patient from the floor of their holding cell, "was what I've been trying to tell you. You're a werewolf, Tom. And the reality of that fact is so terrible, so unacceptable to you that you'd do anything to suppress that fact. But here's another terrible fact to burden your already terribly troubled mind. If you don't come to grips with what you are, if you don't find a way to defeat your fears and learn to control the darker side of your nature, then you remain a slave to your passions. And countless more people will die because of you."

"I've killed?" Tom asked, heart broken, yet believing what Christopher was saying.

"Thousands of people," Christopher answered. "And we," he motioned to Signa Aquainnus and the organization around them, "can't let that happen any longer."

"What do I have to do?" Tom asked quickly.

"Find a reason worth remembering. Find something, anything, worth fighting this battle for. Then fight. Fight with everything you've got. I won't lie to you, Tom. The battle is terrible, and the victories are small and gradual. It will take time, but all you have to do is chose to overcome, and chose to never give up. And eventually, if you can hold on to this conviction, you will win."

"It's that easy?"

Christopher shook his head slowly. "Not at all," he said.

Tom was silent for a moment. "Jemma," he said quietly, under his breath. Then he nodded and looked at Christopher. "I will fight," he answered. "And

I will win. I won't be afraid anymore. Not anymore."

"Yes, you will," Christopher corrected him. "But sooner or later, that too will end. I promise you."

Tom stood waiting, willing the transformation to take place. Nothing happened. "What now?" he asked.

"Just let go," Christopher answered in a low, inhuman growl. He rose to his feet. "Some part of you embraces this destructive nature, while the other part of you is repulsed by it, ashamed of it. What you have to realize is that it's not bad to play rough. It's just bad when you hurt someone. You can't hurt anyone here. So, let go. Eventually, you realize you enjoy it, and come to rely on the release. In fact, you need the release. That's what makes you dangerous in the first place." His voice was slowly growing harder and harder to understand, and Tom was staring at him in shock. "But, enough words," Christopher said. "I doubt you could understand anymore anyway."

Beast came lunging to the surface, happy to play with this new wolf amongst their pack.

Tom, lunged back against the wall behind him, terrified.

"Let go!" Christopher snarled. "We can't hurt each other! The chains will hold, and keep us apart." Then he growled and lunged again, trying with all his strength to break the chain behind him.

Tom, still terrified, grew angry at the horror in front of him, at the challenge rising from Christopher. "How dare you!" he shouted. Then he too let his inner irrational beast surface, and he lunged with claws outstretched, doing what he could to grasp the werewolf in front of him by the throat.

Yet, just as Christopher declared, the chains held them apart, one angry, snarling werewolf with death in his eyes and one playful creature in a white pelt, ignoring the anger it sensed from its brother. They snapped at each other and pulled against their chains, retreating to the walls of their confines and then lunging at each other again and again, trying with inhuman strength to break their bonds. But thanks to the miracle of modern technology, these steel chains refused to budge, refused to even come close to breaking, and held them securely throughout the night.

Then, late in the early morning, Christopher finally grew tired of watching Beast and the other werewolf. His aggression was spent and he happily retired to sleep. Beast morphed fully into a white wolf, and continued his play for a while longer. Yet Tom, still holding to his unreasonable anger, refused to go to sleep, refused to relinquish his control. The battle raged within him as much as it ever had before, and the night dragged by for the tormented soul much like every other full moon before that.

Soon, Beast grew tired of antagonizing this angry creature and returned to his wall and lay down. He watched the irrational werewolf as it raged through the night, then grew tired of even that. Finally, he closed his eyes and went to sleep.

Eventually, Anubis, still raging, grew so angry, that he began to claw at his own chest. As each gaping wound was rent from his flesh, he only became more infuriated, more impassioned by the pain he was putting himself through. Lacking anything else to take his aggression out on, he quickly ripped his chest apart, and then collapsed onto the floor of the cave. As Beast's heart gradually stopped, as it had every other full moon before this, Tom's tormented Anubis died from his wounds.

Silence settled over the valley and the moon eventually set.

Sometime in the morning, Christopher awoke from a peaceful sleep, though he found himself on the floor of one of the holding cells, with an uncomfortable steel collar around his neck. He remembered where he was, and much of what had happened the night before. Without sitting up, he called out, "Tom?"

On the other side of the cell, Tom lay in a pool of dried blood. There were bags under his eyes and every muscle in his body ached. There were scratches over the front of his chest, scratches that felt like they were on fire. He felt ashamed and exposed, and pretended to be asleep. His head throbbed, as though he had the worst hangover he'd ever had.

"Tom?"

He groaned, realizing Christopher had no intention of leaving him alone. "You alright?"

"No," Tom said as he forced his eyes open and stared at the wall in front of him. Dried blood was everywhere. His blood.

"But you'll live?"

"I guess so," Tom admitted.

"Do you remember anything?"

"Not very much."

Christopher was silent for a time. Then he asked the question that had to be asked. "Do you remember what you are?"

It was Tom's turn to be silent. "A werewolf," he answered.

Christopher sighed with relief. Tom had chosen to live, and the battle had been engaged in earnest. "I hope she's worth it," Christopher said.

"She is," Tom answered, still staring at the wall in front of him.

* * * * *

"How does this work?" Tom asked. "How can you justify killing werewolves to fund your quest to rehabilitate them?"

Janelle sat across from him at a table brought out and placed before the statue of her father, Iminuetep. She looked at him for a moment beneath the soft fur of her own pelt of Anubis, trying best to find the words to explain to him all that she had to explain.

Finally, she looked at the statue of her father. "That is a real person, beneath that granite," she said. "He is very much alive, though not entirely here with us."

"I gathered," Tom said as he glanced at the statue nervously. "But I still don't understand it."

"We," she said, motioning toward her and the statue, "were once vampires. We're not anymore."

"Vampires," Tom said sarcastically. "Two days ago I would have laughed in your face. Today, after what Christopher showed me last night, I believe you. Though it's difficult."

"Do you want proof?" Janelle asked.

Tom shook his head quickly. "No!" he nearly shouted, holding his hand up in front of him. "I'll take your word!"

Janelle nodded, though it made little difference to her. "Vampires can't die," she said. "And eventually, this fact becomes a curse too unbearable to live with.

Tom nodded as he considered this.

"But, Father Jason here, along with a few others of our kind, have found the way out."

"What, pray tell, is this way out?" Tom asked.

Janelle smiled. "You just said it," she answered. "Prayer. Simple prayer, and faith in a greater being than us, a creator, a god of gods, the Christian God, the Christ. He sets us free of our desires for a time. And while we're encased in stone, we know peace."

Tom sat back, shocked at what she just told him. "That's it?"

"That's it."

"A Sunday school service?"

Janelle shrugged. "I'm glad you've heard it all before."

He was silent for a moment. "Than where does that leave me? Am I going to have to accept this ridiculous notion of a god?"

Janelle only smiled. "The seeds have already been planted. They have but to break the surface."

"What makes you say that?"

"You chose to live," she answered. "You chose to fight for your life, for your sanity."

"Only because of Jemma," he answered.

"No. Only because of your love for Jemma," Janelle corrected him. "And God is love. Some part of your love for her has been put there from God, and as long as you hold onto that, God will see you through these next nights of hell."

Tom nodded, refusing to argue against something that was as good and pure as that, yet still not quite believing what he heard. "You've given me a lot to think about," he said instead. "Thank you."

She nodded and held up an empty tea cup. He lifted a full cup and toasted her, then drank as she watched him.

"I've never seen Jemma drink anything either," Tom admitted.

Janelle only smiled mysteriously and looked off into the forests around them. Whatever she had to say, she was keeping it to herself, and Tom knew not to press the issue. "Without this love sustaining us, both vampires and werewolves alike, we kill," she said. "We are given over to our dark passions and we kill, feasting on mankind, tormenting them. It is our way, our nature.

"Signa Aquainnus does not execute werewolves because they refuse to accept a religion," she admitted. "Far from it. You haven't accepted what I say, and still, you remain alive. And Christopher and I are very confident that you'll remain that way.

"We execute animals, the monsters that hide inside of you. If you and your kind do not take responsibility for these demons, this Anubis creature, than someone else has to. And we cannot let werewolves run loose, terrorizing and murdering at every full moon."

Tom nodded. "And once I'm totally rehabilitated?"

"You'll be free to leave, or stay as you wish."

Tom nodded. "That makes sense," he admitted. "But Christopher told me that the last time someone refused to tame Anubis, one of your own died as well."

Janelle looked at him painfully, not trying to hide the hurt in her eyes. "Wolves only attack one on one, when they first engage each other. It's not until after one falls that the rest of the two packs collide. Sometimes, the wounds are too mortal to heal, even with the werewolves' supernatural ability to heal themselves."

Tom rubbed his aching chest. The proof of that was serving all too well as a reminder of last night.

"It's a mercy that they are killed when they are," she admitted. "You have to understand that you are not mortal. You are not human. The rules are not the same for you and I as they are for humans. Though your soul is every bit as mortal as anyone else on this planet, your body cannot die. You would suffer the very pains of Hell and still be trapped in your body."

"So what happens when this takes place?" he asked.

"The few times we've seen it," Janelle admitted, "your body goes into shock. You become a vegetable. Then you starve, and all that remains is Anubis, awakening from a vegetable, a brain dead container, past redemption, past rehabilitation, to feed on mankind night after night, until he too is destroyed.

"Our own sign legal documents, ensuring that should any wounds ever occur, they are to be put to sleep before their own wolves grow mad without the sane half of their minds to keep them in check."

Tom nodded. He would do the same, if given the choice.

Chapter Eight

Morning crept up on the sleeping city and found Alexis' body falling deeper and deeper into the death sleep of her kind. She had spent the night following Tommy's abductor to the airstrip, but had lost them when the plane taxied into the storm. Since then, she had settled for human blood to satisfy her cravings, but compared to the feasts from the werewolf, the human experiences seemed mundane, tasteless. She went to bed bitterly disappointed, wondering when she would taste dog flesh once again.

Jemma rose the moment the sun struck her face through the window. She awoke with a start, jolting out of a painful, terrifying nightmare that was lost to her the second she opened her eyes. She sat up in bed with a start, and still shaken by her nameless night terror, went to the window to watch the rising sun. In a moment, she shuddered and closed the drapes to block out the view.

Tom was not in bed. Her head seemed groggy this morning, slow. Yet she chastised herself for not remembering where Tom was. But try as she might, she could not remember anything that happened the night before. She thought about him for a moment, and then set out to find him. He wouldn't be far.

* * * * *

Alexis rose from slumber as if awakening from a bad dream, only to find that the creature, the being she had watched throughout the dream was herself. She shuddered, thinking how despicable and weak the creature in her dream had acted, how incredibly pathetic her emotions had been, her wallowing, her whining throughout the day as she used every piece of tissue paper in the apartment, and then had moved on to the linen as she sobbed and cried with agonizing human humiliation. The day had crept by and the tired, exhausted day walker had finally drifted into a troubled sleep while Alexis had risen in her place.

Furious, she made her tear stained appearance look presentable and then grabbed Jemma's purse on the way out. "Thank God for late night drug stores," she fumed, punching the elevator buttons. Then, too angry to wait, she abandoned the elevator and stormed back into her apartment.

The fire escape opened onto the roof, and Alexis was there in seconds, then in the air, as the substance of vampirism dissipated into a cloud of mist.

She passed into the sky and began travelling over the buildings. Then something made her infinitely grateful she had chosen to travel like a vampire and not like a human this night. Anubis was out in full force. He seemed everywhere, watching from the quiet corners of the city where darkness fell the thickest. It was unlike the werewolves to remain so passive, yet there were also too many of them to dismiss as well. This many wolves in one place would have, by necessity, caused some kind of a fight, yet these creatures of madness remained quiet and hidden, watching—just watching—from their places.

She suspected the dogs were beginning to pack; and this made her think of Jemma's precious Tommy, Alexis' own font of the passionate experiences. Perhaps he had betrayed Jemma, drawn away from her by these other creatures and somehow turned against her.

Alexis laughed at the thought. She knew Tommy's motives, his experiences, as thoroughly as he: more so because of her superior intelligence. No way would Tommy allow himself to be taken away from Jemma, and she doubted there was a prison cell on this earth that could keep him from her for long.

It would only be a matter of time before he returned to her. Somewhere deep down inside her, a sleeping day walker was reassured in her grief. Her lover had not abandoned her: he would return, and she would not be alone for long.

But then Alexis was settling to earth in front of a drug store. Still angry at her human counterpart, she straightened her skirt and stormed into the store.

* * * * *

That morning a confused and terribly grief stricken young lady awoke from her nightmare plagued sleep. The night had been full of dark images and impressions of dreams she only half remembered. Driven through the night on wings of evil itself, she was haunted by memories of lust and murder, and of a hunger that reached beyond any she'd remembered before, driving her on through the night on wings of evil itself.

She stumbled from bed, confused and tired, vaguely aware that the morning was well spent. She'd slept through her alarm and was probably missing work. For some reason, that didn't seem to bother her, though she couldn't remember why it should. She made it to the bathroom and pushed open the door. The first thing that caught her attention was the mirror, and shocked, she stood looking at her reflection. Her hair was now blonde where before it was red. Yet that wasn't the only change. She had fallen asleep with her makeup on, makeup she'd never worn before, colours she'd never liked, applications she always thought she'd hate. Yet looking at herself in the mirror, she had to appreciate what she'd done to herself and wondered how hard it would be to do it again.

The bathroom was full of cosmetic boxes. Bleaches and makeup cases were strewn carelessly throughout the little room. Yet the garbage can was empty. She opened the medicine cabinet to see that it was full of the new makeup, the new look. She must have already thrown out her old supplies.

"There's no going back to it now," she shrugged to her strange reflection. Then she set her mind to getting ready to go out. There was also no reason to sit around and wait for Tommy to come home. Something bad had happened to him, and she would find out what it was.

* * * * *

As the church bells sounded high in the tower overhead, Christopher was reminded of his home in Anderita. Nostalgically, he continued to think of Signa Aquainnus as he filed into the church with the rest of the crowds, conscious to pay attention to anything suspicious. Always on the lookout, he could not afford to take the time off to appreciate mass, yet as a monk and then later as a priest, Christopher knew he had heard the homily the priest would speak, even copied out the scriptures the priest would speak on. Christopher would not miss much, yet he did wish it could be different.

As the service went on, he noticed a young lady, apparently grief stricken and looking as if she had insomnia. She kept her composure throughout the service, yet there was something strikingly familiar about her. Perhaps it was just attraction, he reasoned with himself. It was a shame he had no time to pursue a relationship, and even a bigger shame that it would not be fair to introduce a young lady such as this to the darker world he belonged to. Besides, he was a priest.

Best to let it be, he thought to himself as he returned to studying the church and the parishioners therein. He categorized even the smallest details, filing them away in his memory for later use, should the need arise. Tom had been taken from the area and it would serve Christopher well to remember the faces of the people he saw here today. By the very fact that these people were at mass under the sunlight told him they were not on his suspect list. Being sane told him they were not werewolves; for he, like the rest of Anubis' rebel children, could recognize each other on sight, and there were no others like him in this place.

As mass let out, he filed past the young lady he had noticed earlier and had the opportunity to look into her eyes. She was tired and worn out. She was sad, so sad. His heart yearned to comfort her somehow, but he knew he did more for her by remaining unknown in his battle with the darkness of the night, and so he let her go without saying a word to her.

Night was still a few hours away, and he had work to do before Beast could be unleashed.

* * * * *

Night was setting in. Confused and alone, Jemma stumbled out of mass, her third one that day, wondering when she would find respite for the grief that was killing her. Yet as the cold, uncaring eyes of the people around her moved past, not seeing, not concerned, she wondered if she would be noticed if she simply lay down right here on the steps of this great building and died. She was so tired, so very tired. She could barely put one foot in front of the other as she trudged past the priest, not seeing him, and he not seeing her.

Then, under the moonlight on the steps, she stopped walking and lost consciousness.

Alexis blinked and shook her head, bringing herself fully awake. She looked around at the people around her with an instinctive fear. But there was no hellfire here, only dead mediocrity and watered down hypocrisy. She laughed as she filled her senses with the blood of these people and then laughed some more as her fangs slid painfully from her gums.

The people, so uncaring, so unconcerned with Jemma a moment ago, now looked at Alexis oddly, giving her an ever widening berth as they filed past her.

Still laughing, she teased her senses with the ease of the kill at hand and spun around slowly, facing the church once again.

The priest, noticing the disturbance, was coming out to see what was the matter.

She did nothing to hide her fangs, or the inhuman glow in her predator eyes.

"Daughter?" He was unnerved by her deformities and not understanding what he saw. "May I help you with something?"

Alexis laughed again and looked at the priest, seeing only the blood that was about to be spilled. "Forgive me, Father," she said as she outstretched her hands to mimic the figure on the crucifix above the church doors. "For I am sin itself."

Then she attacked, and there was nothing present that could even come close to challenging her.

* * * * *

The outside lawn was covered in loose rubble. The parking lot was a glittering arena of glass shards and broken hearts. Blood flowed amongst the glass while a crowd of spectators stood around a perimeter of yellow tape, holding tear stained faces in shaking hands and staring on in disbelief and outrage. The building had been attacked from within. The victims had been at mass, and were caught unaware. The church crucifixes and relics were smashed and defaced, lying scattered amongst the rubble like so much cast aside waste.

"Detective!" someone cried, and Christopher looked up from the ruins. "Over here!"

He picked his way across the ruins, taking his time to chose where he stepped. Officers were gathered around the awaiting evidence when he reached them and pushed his way through. "What's so important?" he asked, "that an entire team of investigators has to stop an active investigation at the crime scene!"

Hesitantly, the crowd dispersed and the officer who had called him over pointed at a golden box cast aside amongst the ruins. Christopher smiled to himself and knelt next to the box.

"You can rule out theft," the other officer said.

"Not necessarily," Christopher said thoughtfully. He tore his gaze away from the box and pointed over to a section of the wreckage. "Check over there," he said. "Look for gold plates and chalices. They shouldn't be hard to find if they're there."

The other officer stepped back and called the search to the place where Christopher had suggested.

Alone, he turned back to the box and carefully pulled a pen from his pocket. Ever so careful, he unfastened the latch and opened the box. Inside was a golden cross and a small plate of white bread. He sighed his relief and crossed himself as he pulled a carry pouch from the inside pocket of his coat. Not worried about fingerprints, he took the bread, still just as careful, and secured it, placing it into his carry case and then the case back into his pocket. The cross he was equally careful with, until he saw there was no more of that precious bread inside.

Satisfied, he placed the cross and the plate back into the box and closed the lid, mindful of fingerprints once again.

"There isn't any gold over here," the officer shouted.

"Thank you, officer," Christopher said back.

"Animals were involved?" she suggested.

"Not necessarily," he answered, rising from the rubble. "The killers you're talking about don't care about the Eucharist," he explained. "And they're too dumb to take anything."

"This was an act of passion," the other officer argued. "It fits all the criteria for the serial killers who'd do this."

"You think I don't know that!" Christopher shouted suddenly. The other flinched and Christopher looked around at the crowds of people. Then he forced himself to calm down once again and he muttered, "It wasn't wolves," quiet enough so no one else could hear what they were talking about.

"Than what could have done this?"

Christopher looked around the scene, taking in the amount of people picking through the rubble. "I'd rather not say," he said. "Not until I'm absolutely sure." *A vampire did this*, Christopher thought bitterly.

"I bet it'll make an interesting report," the officer said, challenging Christopher.

"You'll never know," he answered. Then he turned away and took the quickest path out of the rubble.

"Should I have anything tagged for you?" the officer shouted after him.

"Nope!" he shouted back without breaking stride. "There's nothing here!" He was already punching buttons on his cell phone.

"Christopher," the voice on the other end answered immediately. It was Janelle.

"Hold on," he muttered as he opened his car door. Once the door was closed behind him and the crowds of human casualties were behind him he told her what he had found. "It was a vampire," he started.

"A vampire!" Janelle responded, unbelieving.

"Guaranteed," he responded. "Everything fits like a wolf did this, but the Eucharist hasn't been touched, neither has any of the other sacraments."

"What do you mean, none of the other sacraments? How can you be sure?"

"The rectory was left alone," Christopher explained. "And though the priest died on the front steps, he wasn't the only priest in attendance. The others had already left and weren't touched. Also, ironically, the confessional was left standing.

Janelle snorted. "Whoever did this fears hellfire," she noticed.

"Exactly. Worse, he didn't know where it could come from." They were both silent while they thought about what this could mean.

"It wasn't a gargoyle then?"

Christopher snorted. "Not even close. It was made to look like a wolf attack, and no blood was taken from the victims. It was almost like the creature was repulsed by the thought."

"A day walker," Janelle answered assuredly.

"Someone likes the taste of dog meat," he added. "And is going without. Any other cases like this?"

"Not yet," she answered. "I'll let you know." Then the phone went dead.

Soon after, the phone rang again. "Yours was the first," she was shouting. In the background it sounded like the end times had been released into her offices. "Churches all over the coast have been hit!" Janelle shouted. "Same profile, same results! There's signs of hellfire in some of the places, but no burnt vampires. Nothing! The whole Florida coast looks like an old Norman invasion!" She had to shout to be heard over the pandemonium being unleashed in the background. This was the first time Christopher wished less wolves worked at this level, and more level headed humans instead. Yet even as he did, the emotions began welling up inside him and he was thankful for the tinted windows to his car as the tears and the grief began swallowing him whole. "Find this creature!" Janelle cried. "Find it and kill it fast!"

"Vampires don't die, Janelle," Christopher reminded her bitterly.

"Than show us the closest thing to it!"

Then the line went dead.

If this was a vampire, it'd have to be brought in. Christopher had no idea how that was going to happen, or how Janelle planned to contain it, but he had a sick feeling it had something to do with his father's statue in Anderita.

* * * * *

He returned that night, bitter and disappointed, and out of options. The chances that the creature would ever return were next to none, yet knowing every second counted, Christopher had no better options left to him.

The moon was well hidden by an overcast sky, and as Christopher cut the engine to his car, he wondered vaguely if the weather would hold out. He hoped so, the rain would be a hamper against his scent of smell. Yet it mirrored his inner turmoil, his feelings of helplessness. People were dead, a lot of people. And for the first time since taming Beast, he felt like he could do nothing about it.

How was he supposed to catch a vampire? No such thing had ever happened, that he knew of. And he had no idea how to track one, at that. They could virtually disappear into smoke. They could fade into the night in ways that not even Beast could follow. And they could kill. They could kill and kill with an unquenchable thirst that had nothing to do with werewolves and their madness. Vampires killed because they had to, werewolves killed because it was their nature. Nature could be suppressed. Vampires could only choose to turn to stone.

The spectators had tired of the ruined church and had long ago gone home. The police, satisfied that nothing more could be learned, had left the crime scene. The people who ran the church had taken what valuables could be salvaged from the wreckage and had left the rest to the clean up crew. But as he ducked under the yellow tape, he surveyed the carnage once more and realized that much more had been lost than what appeared. The feeling left him hollow inside, as though he had already lost the war and there was nothing left for it but to lie down and die.

He sighed and looked up at the cloudy night sky. It was a full moon tonight, Beast would have to be let out to roam before their heart stopped beating again.

At least Tommy had chosen to be reformed. That was something, anyway. One less wolf pelt was always a good thing, because it meant one less needless death. Yet whoever had done this was somehow connected to Tommy and knew that Janelle and Christopher's secret order within the church had taken him away. But other than Tommy's lover, he had no clues. Still, the day walker would just about be asleep by now, regressing back into the subconscious mind of the vampire she emerged from. Even if Christopher could find her, she'd be of no use by now, too confused to offer any help. The vampire, whoever she was, probably kept the day walker locked up somewhere and out of danger while the vampire slept. No, Christopher knew he would not be able to find her.

"Where are you?" he shouted into the sky.

A soft, feminine laugh answered from the shadows. He spun around, trying to find out where the voice had come from. But then he was struck by a blurred shadow that knocked him sprawling onto his hands and knees. When he looked up again Beast's muzzle of fangs was already protruding out of his face; a menacing growl rumbled from deep within his throat. He roared, and lunged to his feet, letting Beast rip through his clothes as the werewolf was fully unleashed.

"Where are you?" he shouted again, this time barely human.

No answer was coming.

Beast and Christopher stood amongst the ruins, feeling cheated, realizing they would not get a second chance this night. No vampire was stupid enough to challenge a son of Anubis during the full moon. Christopher had lost his one opportunity.

Then he felt the gash on his neck and reached a hand to it experimentally. His hand came away wet with blood: his blood.

Beast melted back into the recesses of Christopher's mind as they stared at the blood in defeat. He'd been bitten. That meant the vampire who had done this now knew what Christopher knew, and now had the same passion that Beast had. The day walker would reawaken for a few days and there was no chance he would find her now.

He sank to his knees, still staring at the blood in his hand. "No!" he cried to the moon hidden behind the clouds of darkness. Beast came ripping out of his skin for good, and Christopher let him come, giving the wolf full control until he was asleep and only a wolf stood in Christopher's place. Beast howled their grief and was answered by dogs all over the neighbourhood. Shocked, he shook himself free of Christopher's clothes and began to run. He would return to this place before he had to rest. He was well trained. But until then, he needed to run off some of the frustration Christopher had been gathering for the last few days.

Alexis watched the wolf disappear into the night. She savoured the blood on her lips, contemplating what she'd learned.

"So," she said once she was sure the wolf was too far away to hear her. "The wolves are beginning to pack."

Her thoughts turned to Tommy. "Bad dog," she muttered.

Then she began to prepare for her trip to Anderita.

Chapter Nine

Days crept by, each one crucial as a potential turning point in the war Christopher and Tom fought, one battling desperately from within, another roaming the streets without, both hunting an allusive enemy. Tom was having more luck than Christopher: his inner beast was being subdued with a steady patience and the unlimited resources at Signa Aquainnus. Yet though Christopher raged against his own lack of success, no other churches were attacked, and no other vampire attacks were reported that mimicked the werewolf passions his organization hunted. He soon returned to Signa Aquainnus and waited for the day this mysterious vampire would make a mistake.

The day came when the full moon crested above the horizon, and while the sun still lingered in the sky, very human eyes watched with apprehension for the time when the shadows would be cast deep enough upon the earth for the passions of Anubis to be released.

Christopher, with Beast always at the ready and near the surface, had planned the night off, taking the opportunity to allow the wolf to hunt within a game persevere Janelle kept for this very reason. Tom, still on the premises of Signa Aquainnus, was packing his few meagre belongings in preparation to return to his beloved Jemma. After tonight, and the manifestation of the wolf within, he would be free to leave and enter the world once again. Signa Aquainnus would always be open to him, day or night, with the support he would need to help regulate the destructive forces that raged within his being.

He was eternally grateful for what Janelle and her people had done. He had never felt as sane, as strong, as sure of himself. But the most remarkable thing about his newfound confidence was the utter and total lack of fear that had plagued him throughout the millennium. He could not wait to find Jemma again, and share with her his new self.

As he continued packing, he felt the werewolf presence rippling across his skin. He smiled as he realized he was even now manifesting, even as he finished packing and put his bags by the door. Then, as a werewolf, he left, and went into the courtyard to join Janelle and the ever present statue of her father, Jason Aquainnus, otherwise known as Iminuetep, priest of Osiris and keeper of Anubis.

Janelle, herself a granite statue, melted into her human form and turned to face Anubis and Tom as they approached her. Unconcerned with his presence, she recognized him immediately and smiled. "The night is yours, Tom. I suggest you head that way," she pointed toward the wilderness behind Signa Aquainnus, toward the waterfall and the tracts of forest she'd left undeveloped for her army of wolves to prowl through. "You'll need to sleep sometime tonight. And we'll talk more before you leave."

The werewolf nodded at her gratefully. Then he began to run, and the sheer joy of the experience took away all else.

The night was his.

Moonlight filtered through the treetops like liquid silver that cast its surreal shadows over the forest floor. An invisible wind swayed the trees and made those shadows seem alive in a world where no human would belong to. Surrounded in a cocoon of light and noise, no human being would be this far into the wilderness, not in this modern day and age, not unless flashlights or at least a campfire could be used to dispel the fear that would come with such a place.

Yet the human soul, once afraid even in the daylight, relaxed luxuriously in comfort and security, half asleep, half awake. His body, as if it belonged to someone else, pushed through the underbrush, seeing paths through the darkness and trails through the forests. As if watching a movie, or being in the passenger seat of a vehicle he was only a witness as the wolf stalked the night tirelessly, content and at peace with all that was around them.

The werewolf, both man and wolf, had never felt such freedom, such liberation from the fears that had always stalked it. Always had Tom been played by a host of emotions that ranged from terror to rage, but never peace, never like this.

The wolf was on the prowl, looking patiently for prey, some wild foul or rabbit startled from its nocturnal rest. Yet it was content with not finding anything, with just simply roaming the forests, away from humanity, away from civilization, and the terror, the rejection it knew would come in such places. Even now, it caught the scent of several smaller animals sleeping or cowering in their dens nearby, yet the wolf passed silently by them, leaving them alone. Should one of them decide to give him a chase: that would be different, something different entirely. But small, defenceless creatures were just that, and the wolf knew they would give him no sport.

The last month had been the hardest thing Tom had ever gone through in all the countless years of his never ending life. Yet Janelle and her people were there, offering the full support of Signa Aquainnus. Yet though they had to wait until he asked, they knew better than he what was happening to him. At first, he would approach with a question, and Janelle or one of her people would wait patiently for him to try painfully to explain what it was he was suffering from. Then, after the words were scarcely out of his mouth, the remedy was there, ranging from medication to holding facilities, from photos of him and Jemma taken during Christopher's investigation to assurances that she would still be there when he was finished. It did not take him long to realize that she ran a well thought out operation, and that they knew better than he what needed to be done in order for his rehabilitation to become a success. Yet they still waited until he asked, and he did ask, not ashamed of relying entirely on Signa Aquainnus, even as his requests became a simple, "Help!"

And now, it was done. She and her people were on the far side of this vast track of wilderness, near a waterfall where they were venting their own full moon hormones and celebrating his success as they trained for the next month and the next Anubis they'd manage to pull off the streets. Tom hoped with everything in him they would manage to find another one, no matter the outcome. But for the moment, he was barely awake, allowing the wolf to roam freely, while he dosed in freedom.

The wolf caught the scent of something new, yet familiar. Its snout quivered with the familiarity of the scent, and its instincts twitched as though encountering the threat of an ancient and hated enemy. Tom groggily noted his counterpart's reaction, then he went back to his light sleep, letting the wolf deal with this new interest however the beast felt best. One thing Tom had learned through his training was that the wolf knew how to take care of itself—and Tom, if he had the courage to let it.

The creature shifted directions, gliding through the underbrush and the shadows just as silently as before. Only this time, its entire body was focused on one point far off in the distance, on one destination. Still aware of everything around them, it would not be distracted from this new protrusion into its senses. The creature wasn't angry, not yet. But it wouldn't be hard for it to become so, especially if something dared threaten this place it had come to think of as home. This was its territory now, its domain, and no one, nothing, would threaten it, or Tom, or any of the other wolves that were far, far away on another corner of their shared reserve.

Standing in the centre of a pool of moonlight, far out from the enshrouding confines of the trees, Alexis stood waiting, fearfully, apprehensively, chastising herself for being insane to dare to face a werewolf during the full moon. Yet she sensed the presence of the dumb creature, and more importantly of Tom, barely conscious under the surface, as they glided through the forests toward this clearing. Her body shook with the need for blood, for his blood. And though apprehensive, she was confident she could control Tom as he controlled the wolf, something utterly unthinkable for her to try alone.

The werewolf stopped at the edge of the clearing and looked at her warily, cautiously. Something of the beast told her it remembered her all too well, remembered the times she had drained his blood, gorging on the creature as it would have done to her, if given the chance. The creature knew caution now, and was not quick to attack.

Yet Tom recognized her on sight, and his love for Jemma leapt into his throat, bringing him instantly awake, if not still groggy. In this place, with the Anubis bloodline fully manifesting, it would always be confusing for him, caught between a place between awake and asleep, where dreams and reality were one. But he knew one thing for certain; this beautiful woman before him loved him and he loved her. There was nothing to fear; she was what had given him the strength to see him through his ordeal of the last month.

He subdued the wolf's caution and they approached her with a mix of excitement and dread, mindful of each other's feelings and compromising by not running to her, but loping to her slowly, stopping every few paces to test the air for changes. She waited calmly, forcing her heart to a steady pace. She needed this; Jemma needed this. And she would not fail. The threat of hellfire loomed all over this animal reserve, and even being this close to Signa Aquainnus was reason to be nervous. Her feelings matched his mixed emotions perfectly.

She remained totally still until the werewolf was close enough to touch. Then, the creature knelt down before her and looked up at her with searching eyes. She was taken back by what she saw there, the absolute lack of intelligence, yet the fierce and unyielding loyalty. She suppressed a relieved laugh and placed a hand on the werewolf's head. The wolf did not move, a soft whine escaping from its throat. Then, just as tenderly, she leaned into him and began whispering into its ear, telling Tom of Jemma's feelings for her, and the wolf grew even more passive, though it remained just as alert, wound like a spring waiting to explode at any moment. She kissed his mane gently, muttering softly between each kiss.

Then her other hand came up to the other side of his neck in an embrace, and the wolf closed its eyes, terrified of her, yet trusting in the control that Tom exercised over it.

She bit down. The wolf tensed and tried to pull out of her embrace, but she held him fast with practised technique, struggling against his terrible, superior strength. She pulled the blood from his wound so fast that he swooned and fainted within moments, growing weak enough in her embrace that she could drink her fill without endangering herself further. Quickly, he became a dead weight in her hands, and they both fell to the ground, passing into a dreamless sleep as their minds were wheeling with an overload of mixed emotions.

In the morning, as dawn crept up over the sleeping forests, Jemma and Tom awoke, even as Alexis and the wolf still clung to consciousness, eager to see how this night would end. They were still entangled on the forest floor, early morning dew had soaked them both. The vampire fangs and the glistening inhuman eyes had been replaced by Jemma's smile and her innocence, while the werewolf manifestations were quietly and rapidly fading back into Tom's skin.

They stared at each other wordlessly, searching each other's eyes for understanding. Jemma did not understand what she saw as the wolf went dormant, yet Alexis, so engorged on the werewolf blood after her fast, was still awake, hiding within Jemma's own consciousness. She was an invisible, wordless force, reassuring and confident. Jemma had never felt so alive, so mentally aware. And she was not hungry. Tom was unaware of his hideous deformities, those that were quickly fading under the approaching sunlight. The wolf felt weak, like lead in his bones, but Jemma was in his arms.

Then, suddenly, he pulled away from her and felt his face, the inhuman distortions that rippled across it. He was horrified that she should see him like this, and he covered his face with his hands to try to block her vision.

"What is it?" she asked, still thinking she was dreaming.

Convinced he was dreaming as well, he pulled to his feet and turned his back to her. "I will come to you soon," he said.

She lay in the grass, looking up at his naked form. "I will be waiting," she said dreamily.

Then he ran, fled from her presence, using the tired strength of the werewolf to carry him as close to Signa Aquainnus as he could get before the wolf went totally dormant.

Eventually, Jemma found her own feet, and headed off into the opposite direction. Though she did not know where she was going, she knew it wouldn't be far. And led by a certainty in her instincts, she came across an airport, found her way into the crowds of humanity, and managed to board onto the next flight back to the Americas.

She slept like the dead on the plane.

Arriving in America at sundown, the exhausted yet very sane young lady exited the plane and stumbled from her terminal in a daze. Her mind was racing with in a thousand different directions, and yet very little of it made any sense to her. She pushed through the crowds of people as memories rushed in on her. Then, all at once, Jemma slipped into sleep.

Her steps faltered, as though she lost her balance. But before her body could pitch to the floor, Alexis recovered and continued to make plans for Tom's re-entry into her and Jemma's life. She bought a cell phone at a nearby kiosk and ordered a limo to pick her up from the airport. With her photographic memory already razor sharp, she went to work, punching numbers into her new phone and issuing commands without bothering to greet her minions.

As far as she knew, Tom was already in America, and there was no need for her or Jemma to live the life of squalor they belonged to before. The vampire and the werewolf were now as much a powerful team and integrated into each other's lives as Tom and Jemma were. Life in America was about to change.

* * * * *

Everything inside him screamed to be released. The wolf, yet still on the horizon, ate at the ground in great, powerful strides that left rend marks upon the earth as he pulled himself along with over proportioned claws and the intelligence that far outweighed that of a mere man like Tom. Its jet black fur glistened, slicked back in the onrushing air. Its destination was unknown as it gave itself over to the sheer pleasure of the chase. The full presence of the sun was over its head as it ran in new found freedom.

Tom sat up with a start, finding himself in a bed made of fine silk sheets. The chandelier in the ceiling cast a fine bright glow in tall white candles. The servants had replaced them that evening before sunset. It was still early on in the evening.

Beside him slept the translucent form of a golden ivory body, usually pale, now awash with the soft brilliance of the light of the night. Her back was turned to him as she slept partly on her side, leaving a slight curve of her breast tucked into her arm. Her hands were folded under her face as though she were at prayer rather than asleep. Tom sighed as he brushed a strand of her hair out of her face and watched her peaceful expression under the candles' brilliant glow.

Not wanting to disturb her, he slipped out of bed and pulled the blankets up over her shoulder. She responded in some sleeping mumble of love and he smiled. Not daring to kiss her and disturb her even more than he had to, he turned to the desk at the side of the bed and pulled on a robe he kept over the back of a chair. The mirror greeted him with the same stoic loyalty it always did as it reflected back the image of a man Tom had never been able to get to know.

The wolf was passive for the moment, and Jemma was asleep, safe in her own arms. There was an ivory wash basin in front of him, and grateful, he splashed some of the water over his face to distil some of the shock of the dream. It didn't help. Yet, this was Jemma's place, these were her servants. They were blindly loyal to her and to her alone. The amnesiac millionaire was in her villa with her lover who had mysteriously rescued her from the streets of the city.

Tom shook his head at the incredible magnitude of the story, imagining it as though it had happened to two other people. He couldn't. And he smiled as he realized how much help she had gotten him, how much better they had both gotten, how much recovery had gone on. Now, the terror of his inner demon had receded to a powerful nightmare that still made it difficult to sleep. And Jemma was safe from harm.

* * * * *

"Going to sleep so soon," Alexis asked. She did not try to hide the evil from her voice. Tom, still unaware of Alexis' façade, was caught off guard by the dark intent in her tone. But he smiled as he yawned.

"If that's okay with you?" he asked, putting his fist to his mouth in an attempt to stifle the yawn. It didn't work.

"Of course," Alexis said reassuringly as she sidled up against him. "Just let me have one good night kiss." Then, ever so tenderly, she pushed his chin away from her face and drew closer to his neck. She exhaled with passion as she felt her fangs sliding out from her teeth, breaking the skin and her gums with an age-old pain that was more relaxing now than it ever could bring terror. Her breath blew softly against the nearly invisible hairs on his neck.

Then she bit down.

He swooned, and fainted in her arms. Instantly, he stood beside her in one of their shared dreams.

"Tommy," she said nicely. "I need you to step aside for a moment." Aware that he still thought her as his lover, Alexis brought as much passion to her voice as she could, but she knew how young the night was, and how much Mister Wolf must want out of his cage. She craved with him, desiring the essence of his experiences that would make her feel alive.

He nodded and stepped back, though she could read his desire to embrace her. That would help; Mister Wolf would be drawn to her as he was, would share in his reaction to her. "Come to me," she said throatily, desiring the chase once more.

The wolf glared out hungrily at her from the shadows. Its beady black eyes shining as its muzzle was cast partway in shadow and partway in a lesser gloom allowing him to be only a bit visible. He still hung back, though she could sense the hunger coming from him. Perhaps one or two of his beatings had been too severe for him in the past, and now he craved no more, learning shrewdness and caution to size up his victim. All he had to do was find a way to get past her, into the world of the seven senses and out of this small mind, and not even his mistress, his guardian, would be able to hold him back, not even her.

"Come to me," she insisted once more, nodding her head ever so slightly in silent, insistent encouragement. Every fibre in her strained toward him as her body silently screamed her desires out to him. Then she fled the dark recesses of Tom's mind, and the beast exploded past him, knocking him to the side.

He remembered falling to the floor, but wasn't sure if he was only dreaming, or if he had too much wine and had swooned in her embrace. She would have placed him on the ground as his strength had given out.

But Alexis was nowhere near his falling body. Like a gust of wind, doors blew open and windows smashed as she dived through them with the superhuman precision of her kind, the living dead. The wolf morphed through Tom's body, catching it before it fell limp to the floor. It landed on all fours and sprinted after her, tearing through their apartments with the animal strength of a caged animal finally set free.

* * * * *

Darkness. Madness reached out to embrace the entrapped soul. Tommy Hilfiger screamed in pain as the corruption reached out for him, touching him. He recoiled in fear and loathing; he roared into the night. He shrank away from the ferocity of the noise and the body of the beast shrank with him, whimpering in the shadows as he huddled against the corner of a stone building, cowed by its own ferocity.

Alexis looked down on the poor creature and tried with all her might to give Jemma a memory she would cherish.

Instead, she kept occupied by passing overhead, close enough to keep Tom from passing out. The very sight of his lover and her assuring confidence as she blended fearlessly with their surroundings coaxed the whimpering wolf from its hiding place. The beast sniffed at the waning fullness of the moon overhead, testing the air for her scent. Alexis alighted beside him and scratched his head. Comforted, a quiet growl of pleasure escaped from his lips. "Remember to hold onto you," she had said earlier, now the memory of those words echoed through Tom's mind and he looked up at her with big trusting eyes.

"Come," she said, motioning with her other hand.

Then she was off, keeping low to the ground that Tom and his beast might follow. She raced through the night with the werewolf close on her heels. She raced down a darkened alleyway and vaulted into the air as she soared to the top of the building at the end of the alley. The wolf, with Tom at its centre, went on all fours and vaulted off of a stack of crates to one side of the alley, sprang onto the edge of a window sill, then up over the ledge where Alexis had vanished. Its tongue lolled in its mouth as it painted after its mistress happily.

She giggled as she lunged across another alley. She felt the beast close on her heels and did not turn around; she knew he could follow at any speed this night, traverse anything with her. Tonight, the night was theirs.

Buildings and street lamps slid by as shadows and lights that they traversed effortlessly, as though all was made from mist.

As the night wore on Alexis focussed more on where they were going rather than the sheer joy of the chase. Their flight slowed and he kept pace accordingly, not overcoming her, nor lagging behind. She led him to the top of a tall building and slowed to a soundless glide. Creeping along behind her, his nose twitched as he sorted out one new scent from another. There were many to choose from, but his mistress was unconcerned.

This is what she had come to show him.

Down below, in the streets, flashes of bright white light momentarily pierced the dark while moving red shadows cast a continuous hue between the buildings.

The beast, puzzled, made to approach the moving lights.

"No!" Alexis hissed.

The beast froze and looked at its mistress.

She smiled and went to him and scratched the top of his head again. This time, he would not be distracted from the unspoken question in his eyes. She motioned with her hands for him to follow and crept to the edge of the building—looked down into the streets below.

Police cars and city detectives flooded over a scene of gruesome macabre. Flash bulbs from cameras still occasionally punctured the night. Tommy ducked lower to the ground to help hide from the flashing lights, but Alexis remained motionless, trusting the shadows would hide her.

In the midst of the carnage Christopher carefully picked his way through the gristly evidence, left alone to find what he needed his way.

As much as he wanted it to be, this was not the attack from a wolf like him. The gruesome, random act of violence had the same passion to it, but by the way the bodies lay, whatever had done this had managed to creep up unsuspecting amongst the crowd before attacking.

No wolf could have done that.

"What do you think, Lieutenant?"

Christopher looked up from his work and shook his head. There were many things he could not talk about, and this was one of them. Stepping over the carcasses, he walked over to his companion's side. He was silent as he looked up at the rooftops thoughtfully. He would come back later once the lights weren't against him and take another look the way he knew worked best. Right now, he couldn't see anything. "I think," he said finally, "there are some sick people in this world."

Back in the shadows, Alexis and Tom watched silently. At last, Alexis bent close to the beast's face and pointed to the streets. "Bad," she said to the beast, which looked up at her questioningly. "Bad men," she repeated. "Stay away from them."

Understanding dawned on him as his head nodded ever so slightly.

* * * * *

Lat one night, Tom sat in a shadow as he watched the moon, only days from becoming full, cresting over the horizon. The wolf was growing in strength daily. And unlike last month, in the forests of Signa Aquainnus, the beast was angry, restless, vengeful. As far as Tom knew, it had yet to manifest through their body. But the moon was continuing to rise and fall, with the same steady regularity as an hour glass. Destruction and death were the only outcome. Tom glanced around the room, at the expensive finery that surrounded him, noting the graceful influence of his lover in everything around him. Then he began to cry, weeping silently as his gaze returned to the moon once again.

He'd been keeping a journal, something he'd been taught at Signa Aquainnus. Although the wolf in him lacked the intelligence to speak, it was passionate, emotional, and while at Signa Aquainnus, Tom had discovered poetry as a way to try to give his darker side a way to express itself. Though his journaling this night had been an attempt to settle the beast, instead, his thoughts and his feelings had returned again and again to Jemma, to his own grieving heart.

Alexis found him like that, staring at the moon with his journal in hand, and caught her breathe when she entered the darkened chambers. He stirred and looked at her, pretending not to see her through the darkness. She was staring right at him, as if he'd become something alien to her, something dangerous and uncontrollable. There was no love in her eyes.

He only kept up his weeping and looked away from her.

"Tom!" she asked, calling into the darkness as if she wasn't sure she could see him.

The beast within silently roared with pent up rage. There could only be one outcome from the next full moon.

"Tom!" she asked again, feeling her way into the room as though the darkness refused to give up its secrets to her.

Tom only shook his head. Whoever this mysterious girl was, she was changing, daily. There were still moments during the day when Jemma, his Jemma, loved him with a passionate devotion that outshone the sunlight. But more and more he was seeing something alien lurking in the shadows; the fearful distance their servants kept from them, the way she stared at him hungrily, the way she hovered near him when he was drifting off to sleep, the nightmares, the strange terrible nightmares of violence and death that was becoming more and more vivid as the nights continued their dreaded countdown toward the full moon. And there was the wolf's smouldering hatred, its feelings of helplessness when she was around. Its fear.

If nothing else, the wolf could not be ignored.

His mind made up, he called out to the creature he did not know. "I'm here," he said.

She responded and glided toward him through the darkness as though she was a cloud of darkness herself. "Aren't you tired?" she asked as she touched his ear, his hair. Something in her voice was edging on panic, on desperation.

"No," he lied. He turned and looked at her through his mask of tears. He looked straight into her eyes, and neither of them could deny they saw each other. "I'm not tired," he said. Tonight he was going to take the beast out for a run, and he wanted to be conscious, to feel its concerns.

She nodded as she looked back at him. "Something is happening to you," she said.

"Me!" he shouted, suddenly furious.

Jemma took a quick step backwards. Her entire body was instantly tense, prepared. In less than a second, she'd become a deadly creature of the night, prepared for anything. Her eyes gleamed in the darkness with frightening, inhuman intensity. She kept her mouth closed so that he wouldn't see her fangs.

He looked at her, shocked at the abrupt change. "You can see in the dark," he said, forcing himself to calm down once again.

"So can you," she pointed out.

Tom shook his head. "You couldn't before, now you can."

"Neither could you," she said feebly.

He smiled sadly and shook his head again. "Yes, I could," he announced. "I could always see in the dark. I'm changing you, and it's not for the better." He rose to his feet, dropped his journal on the windowsill and walked past her. As he neared, she quickly glided to the side, still tense, still an alien killer, though very much afraid of him, of his strength, of the werewolf strength.

"Where are you going?" she asked to his back.

He did not turn around as Anubis manifested over his face. "I need to leave for a few days," he said. "It's important."

307

He could feel her growing terribly sad.

"Jemma," he said as he forced Anubis below the surface and turned around.

She looked up at him through the darkness.

"I'm coming back." He paused to look at her, to memorize the way she looked. "I love you."

Alexis stared back at him. Her eyes and her fangs were poorly concealed by the darkness and the searching eyes of the werewolf in front of her. He would catch the lie, so she reached deep into herself and broke through barriers of darkness that had always defined who she was, first as Aphrodite, then as Alexis. "I love you too," she admitted, for the first time in her life.

The wolf inside Tom responded to the truth of those words. He felt like a giddy school boy, in love for the very first time. He smiled and then left for Anderita.

Alexis watched him leave, stood where she was for a mere heartbeat, and then walked over to the abandoned journal. He'd dog eared a corner of the book and she opened it, discovering his hidden talent for poetry and what he'd just finished writing.

How many roses
Hove withered and died?
How many tears
Were shed in the night?

How many people have
Cried out in vain;
Broken and tormented,
Dying in pain?

These are questions
I'm afraid I can't ask;
Lest I invoke an
Invisible God's wrath.

But I will adhere
To the promise I made
Forever and always. Even as
Her love fades.

She sobbed as her hand flew to her mouth and she dropped the book. Another sob later and she sank to the floor and wept. She was in love, the Mistress of Death was in love. Jemma's feelings were now her own, and she was painfully aware of how much she truly wished Tom could know who she really was.

And yet, she needed to feed, perhaps not tonight, but soon, before his return. She would follow him to Signa Aquainnus, feed, and be back before his return.

They'd figure it out then.

* * * * *

Alexis thirsted as she crept closer to her lover's body.

Tom hung from shackles in an ancient room deep within the catacombs of Alexis' ancient home. He hung there, motionless, as though he were asleep. But he still carried his weight on his legs, so she couldn't imagine he was too asleep. Still, the beast was manifesting to the point where the transformation was nearly complete. She couldn't imagine Tom would be awake for such an event, or even that he would be present. Tom would be sleeping deep within that monster's chest, and no amount of pain or horror would bring him forth this night. Jemma's lover was safe.

But for the blood of the beast Alexis would sacrifice almost anything. She was shaking with the anticipation of it as she came face to face with the sleeping monster. His head hung limp on his shoulders while his hair hung in long ringlets over his face. She would not disturb him this night, nor do anything to threaten the safety of this beautiful man. But she had to have it, it had been so long, that now her legs quivered with longing.

Hesitating, she shyly placed a hand on his muscular chest. He breathed deeply at her touch, as though some part of him knew she was there. Then, tenderly, she brushed a kiss against his shoulder before she bit into his chest. He stiffened with the pain and then relaxed again as she drank his glorious blood. The sensations ran through her, washing her in experiences and emotions that she had not experienced since the last time she had tasted of him.

She lost all track of time, but when she pulled away from him, just as shyly as she had approached, Tom was staring at her.

He was fully awake, fully conscious. He looked at her as if seeing her for the first time, as though he did not recognize who she was. Then, recognition slowly dawned on him as the swooning effect from her drinking wore off. His eyes teemed with shock at first, then sorrow, then betrayal as he recognized Jemma's form standing next to him. Finally, they blazed with anger as she, still caught in the weakening effects of what she had done, wiped the blood from the corners of her mouth.

"Christopher," he growled angrily. He took hold of the chains binding his wrists and with an inhuman growl, tore them from the wall and was gone.

"Christopher," she repeated slowly. Tom was going to get answers.

Christopher, the other wolf had those answers. Then she too was gone. Christopher was going to die this night, before he could convince Tom to betray her.

Chapter Ten

As a warrior priest, Christopher stood at the front of the sanctuary. He was dressed all in black leather amour that creaked above the noise of the rainfall from without. Today he had stood vigilance, tonight he knelt in prayer. In the morning he would finally receive the knightship, a promise given to him in a bath of blood.

He knelt, resting his hand on the pommel of his sword, an antique he cherished as an heirloom from the old wars. There was speed in his movements, a quickness of agility that despite his best efforts told of a warrior's crouch he was only able to hide from the other parishioners by the leather cape he kept close to his body as he would the robe of a monk.

The priest overseeing the ceremony was well accustomed to warriors and their ways, being a Chaplin for Janelle's army. Yet, he was only human, and was continually reminded of the longer life spans of the wolves around him. Their devotion to their faith was deeper than his, given countless years to develop into something beyond what he could even begin to grasp. Yet he was up for the challenge as he made the sign of the cross above Christopher's head.

Sensing his thoughts, Christopher raised his head from deep prayer and met the old man's gaze unflinchingly. He too, was up for a challenge this night.

Lightning cracked with the clap of thunder that shook the candles in their sconces. Movement. The priest saw it, Christopher sensed it. Both froze and focussed their concentration on the intrusion.

The shadow, knowing its disguise had been penetrated, abandoned its hiding place and began to run down the side of the immense cathedral.

"It seems God has granted your wish, Father," Christopher said, watching the demon run toward them. He kept the smile from his lips, though his face quivered with the effort. "Your faith will indeed be challenged this night."

"At least it won't be a dull night," the priest said with calm, patient eyes. Quietly, he whispered, "With the blessings of the Church, my son. May your sins be absolved in the holy war before you."

Christopher did not wait until the end of the ritual before he was smiling and turning to face the creature of the night. "Everybody out!" he bellowed in a deep resonating tone that filled the mighty halls with a musical voice trained in the melody of Gregorian chant.

The priest, just finishing all his appropriate "In-the-name-ofs," had reached the few others kneeling in prayer and was herding them into the side passage leading to the Rectory. "Just stay away from the statues this time!" he added.

"The Lord moves in mysterious ways, Father!" Christopher bellowed as he laughed and strode down the central isle, his sword still sheathed. This wasn't the first time the sanctity of this place had been challenged.

"Just try, then!" the priest answered, aggression finally creeping at the edges of his voice.

Christopher laughed again and pulled his sword free. The fist sized ruby in the hilt glinted in the candlelight in a reflected flash, as though an eye had opened. His sword had awakened for battle, and Christopher held her free in his hand once again.

Suddenly, the doors to the cathedral crashed open and his mood changed. "Get everyone out!" he shouted just as powerful as before, though now anger touched the tone of his voice.

The door slammed shut just as every light in the entire cathedral went dark.

"A dull night, indeed," the priest mumbled quietly as he herded the worshippers before him.

Close to the ground, where Christopher had stood, a low, menacing growl was the only response.

Sensing the peril the situation was quickly becoming, the priest was quiet from then on.

"Where is your God now, Father?" a female voice accused from the darkness, after the priest had left. With canine perception, Christopher listened out into the blackness, separating one falling raindrop from the next. Yet the voice that spoke came from all places at once and nowhere at all.

The human side of Christopher searched the darkness frantically. The rest of him stayed perfectly still and silently tested the air for scent. Nothing.

"Oh, you'll see once you taste the fires of hell," he said in a very human, very commanding voice. He smiled through canine teeth as he caught the scent of fear. "What could possibly possess you to come here? To make such a stupid mistake?"

Grasping his sword in a hand half changed to the forepaw of a wolf, the leather amour creased as he hunched over. He dived to the side then swung at the darkness as he rolled to his feet. He knew the creature was a vampire, and had practiced long and hard to hunt vampires. Janelle would have been proud as he felt metal strike flesh.

The shadow he had first seen let out a high pitched squeal of pain. It was a female voice, high and painful. Something about it seemed familiar, though it escaped him as a dream would in the recollection of it. Gradually, the shriek gave way to a menacing, mocking voice.

"Alexis?" Christopher shuddered as he called out into the darkness. "What are you doing here?"

Now would be the night. Too soon, perhaps, but he had the sinking suspicion that both Tom and the vampire were in this room with him, that the war he was fighting would at last come to an end in this final battle. Either he managed to defeat the vampire and Tom chose to help, or he would defeat the vampire and Tom chose not to. He did not like the choices ahead, but that was the fate God had decided, and he adhered to the decision, clearing his mind for the task at hand. Such things as death and his own desires would only serve as distractions in times like these.

"Jemma sleeps," the vampires explained as she materialized from the darkness before Christopher. He was startled by her appearance. It seemed Christopher's sword did little to slow the creature down, to even wound it, for that matter.

"It seems you have some explaining to do, Father." The voice in the darkness coalesced behind and to the side of Alexis. Tom the wolf stepped closer, into the dim light from the storm lit sky.

Alexis purred through fanged teeth as she stepped closer to the werewolf and seductively ran her hand over his shoulder, feeling the coarse muscle through the coat of fur.

Repulsed, Christopher never took his eyes off her: His sword stayed unwavering in his hand.

He could only guess how Alexis had found them at last. He could only imagine how painful to her it must be to be so close to the light of true faith. Yet here she was, and with the other werewolf. Tom looked none too pleased, either. Alexis would be a master of lies, and Tom, still young in his walk of rehabilitation would be easy prey.

Christopher was right. Tom roared and lunged. Christopher sidestepped and spun around to face Tom as he passed. The sword swung a deadly arc between them. The swing was cast wide in the hopes of glancing Alexis in the side even as it kept Tom from ripping out his exposed spine.

"Why!" Tom roared in the dark. The sound of wood ripping in the dark followed his angry accompaniment.

Christopher had no idea what he was talking about. "Alexis drinks your blood," he told him. He rolled to the side as a bench crashed into the place where he stood, clipping his shoulder and spinning him onto his back.

Alexis pounced, aching with the need for blood.

Fearlessly, Christopher brought the sword up between them and sheathed the blade to the hilt in Alexis's stomach as he regained his feet.

"No!" Tom roared as he lunged toward them.

"Get back!" Christopher warned him, and he stopped in mid step. He was looking at Alexis, amazed that she was still very much alive. "Or I'll decapitate her right here and right now!" Christopher cried angrily.

Tom nodded and faded back into the night.

This was to be a night of revelations all the way around.

Christopher smiled as he turned back to her.

Alexis tried to speak as the air rushed from her diaphragm. Shyly, her fingers brushed against Christopher's leather clothes.

Still gripping the sword, Christopher wordlessly held the vampire in place and looked deeply into her eyes. She had no mesmerizing power over him, and he wanted her to realize that. He may be a wolf, but he was no creature of the night. He was a man, and such things as this demon had only the power over him that he gave her, which would be little enough. The light of the cross burned within his chest. The presence of the Holy Spirit pumped through his veins, and this vampire had reason enough to fear both. Now, realizing who he was, her demeanour changed. She would be as meek as a lamb now, lest he command her to burn to death.

Tom staggered back a step when he felt the authority Christopher had over the vampire. The beast in him grew instantly terrified and cowered like a new born puppy, but the rational side of him told himself that this was his friend, his ally, the man that had helped him save himself.

Tom suddenly realized what he was doing and dropped the attack. He couldn't hurt Christopher, and if the throbbing in his shoulder was any indication, he couldn't even if he wanted too.

Alexis stood rock still, impaled to the hilt of Christopher's powerful heirloom. She stared at Christopher hungrily while her hands brushed his clothing and her lips mumbled a silent incantation of some kind. For his part, Christopher only looked at her angrily, but the life did not flee from her body. Her eyes, though full of pain and an indefinable hunger, did not dim in death. Angrily, Christopher jerked the sword from her spinal column, and unsheathed it from her abdomen. Alexis miraculously kept to her feet, though she was in too much pain to move.

She turned her head slowly and looked at Tom through the darkness. She could see the shock and betrayal, the horror and relief all mixed into one painful expression that rent her insides more painfully than the sword had.

"What is going on here?" Tom whispered.

Alexis only blinked, but Tom knew she had heard the question loud enough. "This can't be," Tom mumbled quietly.

"Think Tom!" Christopher roared. "She's a vampire!" he cried as he pointed at her. "This one is called Mistress Of Death. Jemma is a product of your blood and this creature's thirst!"

"No!" Tom shouted. He spun on his heel and crashed through the nearest window, fleeing into the night

Satisfied with the realization he saw register in Tom, Christopher stepped back and raised the point of his sword into her face.

The vampire winced, but kept her feet. She looked up at Christopher and nodded. She knew she was defeated. She was too weak to even move, for fear of pitching onto the floor.

"For what it's worth," she said quietly, "I do love him."

Christopher's sword arm shook with the desire to end this.

"Chris!"

It was Janelle, dear sweet Janelle. She'd appeared in the hole in the wall Tom had made, and was climbing through it even as she shouted his name.

He did not dare look away from the vampire, or lower his weapon.

No light was needed to guide her path as she came to his side. Her eyes were gleaming with the vampire blood. She looked at Alexis, tenderly holding her wound. "Good work," she said as she continued to stare at her ancient enemy.

Alexis stared back, in too much pain to answer right away. "I guess it's too late to turn myself in," she said.

Angered, Janelle only clenched her teeth and shook her head. "Bring her with us," she said as she spun on her heel and walked back toward the ruined hole Tom had made in the sanctuary wall. "You don't need to be gentle."

Christopher finally sheathed his sword and tossed Alexis over his shoulder. She cried out in pain, but he ignored her. "Be content I don't cauterize the wound with fire," he said as he made his way to follow after Janelle.

Alexis bared her teeth, but remained quiet as she was carried before the statue of Iminuetep. Janelle was waiting in the rain on the other side of the clearing, across from him. Christopher set her down between them and retreated out of the courtyard to stand at the side and watch.

"You will not leave this courtyard," Janelle announced. "Father and I are in agreement with this."

"How would you know!" Alexis tried to shout. She pointed at him. "He's a statue!"

Instantly, a wall of flame shot into the sky, surrounding the three of them in an impenetrable circle. Alexis cringed from the heat and faced Janelle angrily.

Yet it was Iminuetep who spoke. "You have nothing left, Aphrodite. You are through with second chances."

Alexis spun to face him. He was very much alive. And in his arms was a sleeping girl child, the spirit of the Anubis who had been dying at his feet, so long ago.

"You cannot hold me like this forever," she rebuked him.

"She's right," came Christopher's voice through the flames. She looked for him, but could not see him through the flames.

"Tom will be back," Janelle announced.

Alexis smiled. "He will. And then there will be hell to pay."

"I can deal with Tom," Christopher's voice again.

"No, you can't," Alexis said honestly, her eyes never looking away from Iminuetep. "Not during the day, not when Jemma will be standing here instead of me."

Chapter Eleven

Shaking with fury, Tom ran through the night. Rivulets of water washed over his skin as the storm seemed to match his rage with an equal measure of its own. Fueled with the monstrous strength of the werewolf blood, and hurt beyond reconciliation, he clung to consciousness as he allowed the wolf free and unbridled control over their body.

He gloried in the instincts that fueled the beast, the anger that drove him, the knowledge that nothing, no force in the universe, was powerful enough to stop him.

They were fast approaching a city. The lights from the street lamps were blurred with each step he took, as they cast a haze onto the low-lying clouds. Humans were about, stupid enough to be out in this weather. And right now, Anubis hated them all.

The first victim didn't have time to scream. He was standing on the outskirts of a crowd of people with his back toward Anubis when Tom and the wolf came upon him. Anubis grabbed him by the shoulders then pulled. He tossed the broken body aside like a rag doll.

The man had been talking to a woman, whose eyes widened in shock when she saw the werewolf standing where her friend had been less than a moment before. Anubis reached out and grabbed her by the face, even as she was opening her mouth to scream. His grip cut the air off from her cry, covering her nose and mouth in its broad, misshapen hands. He pulled her close to his own face, imagined she was the vampire Alexis and then roared. The force of his voice was enough to blow the wet hair out of her eyes, eyes gone insane with fright.

He tossed the woman into the crowd behind her as people began to scream in terror and scatter before him like chickens before a fox.

Then he waded into them, his superhuman strength making them sluggishly slow before him. He tore with his claws, bit with his teeth and killed again and again until he was covered in the blood of his victims.

When he was done, there were still a handful of survivors left, scattering in every direction. And it was not enough, not nearly enough. Most of the humans, four of them, had remained together and were running down the street in front of him. He would hunt every one of them down this night, but he decided to go after the group first.

If only his lover could see him now. What was it Christopher had called her, Mistress Of Death? He laughed bitterly as he ripped into the humans, not caring that the sound that issued from his throat was more frightening than anything he had ever heard before.

Only one person out of the three remained alive now. Tom stood watching her through the rain as she ran, looking over her shoulder as she screamed something over and over again into the night.

She was crying out in English, yet Anubis' ears twisted the words and he could not understand what she said. They were in a courtyard, a vast ancient thing with cobbled streets and a water fountain in the middle of it. Most of the original buildings had been torn down, but one, a heritage site, was opening its doors for the woman. A foolish thing to do, considering no door, no wall, no force on this earth would be able to hold Anubis back, and this only gave him a target.

He walked across the courtyard as she sprinted ahead of him and pushed past a terrified man in black who stared out into the rain unbelieving as the werewolf stalked toward them. The woman was looking over his shoulder, rather than trying to hide inside the building, as though something inside her knew if he crossed this thresh hold, nothing could stop him.

Tom didn't care; it was not the chase he relished in tonight. It was the kill.

She had taken refuge in a church; the man standing in front of her was a priest and if the house of God would not protect her, nothing would. Slowly, Tom came to realize these facts, began to recognize the ancient building for what it was, to see the priest for what he represented, to begin to understand the words spoken to him in a human tongue.

"—a house of God!" the priest was shouting. Yet he grew suddenly silent when he realized Tom understood him.

He looked at the priest and saw ignorance behind his eyes and fear, a whole lot of fear. Yet though he did not understand what stood before him, perhaps did not fully understand the meaning behind the words he used to try to drive the werewolf off, Tom wondered if anyone could, if anyone could fully grasp what it was to be evil, or understand the magnitude of love it would take to set one free of that evil.

It was obvious the priest did not understand, and his thoughts turned to Christopher, to Janelle. They made no secrets about not understanding as well; but they were free, unarguably free, as they basked in the love handed down to them through their ridiculously simple faith.

Tom looked at the woman standing behind the priest. She looked as though she possessed the same faith as they. Though she was terrified beyond reason, she nonetheless stood her ground with a certainty in this mysterious love that left Tom shaking his head in wonder.

He could no longer bring himself to crush these people. They reminded him all too painfully that this love, given to something as powerful as Jemma the vampire had brought him to murder, while the same love given to an invisible god had left these mortals the courage to stand and face the worst terror of the dark.

Suddenly ashamed, he turned and, sobbing, stumbled into the night.

* * * * *

Eventually he stumbled across a stone statue left in the centre of a street. This too was some sort of an ancient monument of some kind, with a plaque embedded into the base of the statue.

It was a cross, a stone cross, the kind found in cemeteries. He looked at it, and unbeknown to him, came to stand before the very same cross Christopher had found, centuries before.

"Please!" he mumbled. "The weakest of mortals have something I do not have, something better than this," he motioned toward the invincible body of a demon, the body he wore. "If I could change," he said bitterly. "I would. But I can't. Take this evil from me," he said, utterly defeated. "And give me what they have instead." He pointed at the mortals cowering inside that stone building. He did not dare count himself worthy to be compared to Christopher and Janelle. "I give my life to this end." He meant every word.

319

Suddenly, red hot flames erupted over everything in sight. The cross, the street, the buildings, even the rain as it fell from the sky, contributed to the hissing inferno. Tom erupted into flames, felt the heat from within and without. But though he should have burned, he did not. Instead, he stood before the cross in wonder, staring at it and then at his burning hands in turn. He could not grasp how he could still be standing there, when he understood what he deserved was to die in the flames.

Yet as the werewolf stood under the burning sky, he knew something of himself was burning away. The pain, the anguish, the grief, the guilt; all of it with his fears and hatred dissipated into the flames around him. And as he stood motionless before the cross, the fur of his Anubis coat became ignited, lighting up like a human torch. Yet Tom bore it all, determined to see the destructive nature within die to this terrible living force of unconditional love.

He stood there for a long time, and eventually died, as was his destiny on this day of the full moon. Yet though the flames were roaring about him when he lost consciousness, when he awoke well before light, all was peaceful and quiet. The rain had stopped and the mortals were still asleep or cowering from the nightmare incarnate that had stalked them during the night.

Tom looked down at his body and was moved to tears when he saw his pelt had changed from black to white, to a pure and clean white pelt with not a blemish or a scar on it.

With a supernatural resolve to face Signa Aquainnus and Alexis again, he rose to his feet and glided into the morning, using his new werewolf form to distance himself from the human city behind him.

At dawn, he reached Signa Aquainnus.

* * * * *

Jemma stood with her arms crossed against the cool morning. She stared at the statue of Iminuetep, fascinated, not understanding that it was more than what it appeared. She was caught by the life like qualities of it, the realism behind every smallest detail, including the wolf pelt that hung about its shoulders. The statue of the lady was as just as real, her own fur coat just as detailed, but Jemma could not take it all in at once, and so she took her time appreciating the craftsmanship surrounding her.

She did wonder how she came to be here, but that was part of her condition, this cursed amnesia. And one thing was always certain, Tom was nearby.

He came toward her silently, wearing nothing but a pair of sweat pants. Though the morning was cool, he seemed not to notice, nor care. There was a confidence in his step, a security that hadn't been there before. She couldn't put her finger on it, but she recognized the change immediately. He did not look happy to see her. No, he seemed to dread what he was doing, but his jaw was clenched in determination, so she watched him come, appreciating the new muscles across his chest.

He said nothing as he came to stand beside her, turning to face the gargoyle before them. She rocked onto her toes and kissed his cheek, and he flinched from her touch.

Slowly, she pulled away, sinking back onto her heels as she grew afraid. "What's wrong?" she asked.

He looked at her. There were tears in the corners of his eyes. He was searching her for something, and seemed to find it, though the thought brought him no happiness. Jemma yearned to be able to take his pain away.

"Do you believe in dreams?" he asked. "Even if the dream could never be real?"

"Sometimes I think it is easier to believe in a dream," she said.

"Than to face reality?" he asked.

She nodded.

He reached out to the stone statue before them, to the stone fur, and pricked his finger on the jagged surface. A tiny droplet of blood swelled from the pin prick.

"What are you doing?" she asked.

He held the finger out to her. "Taste it," was all that he said.

"What? Why?"

"Wait." Then he leaned in and kissed her. To Jemma, it felt like a good bye kiss. Then he held the wounded finger out before her again. "Now taste it."

She looked him in the eyes as she took his hand in her own. Then she leaned in and put the tip of his finger into her mouth.

She blinked, and memory returned to her.

She closed her eyes and pushed Tom's hand away from her. Then she turned and faced the other statue, the one of Janelle. She was quiet as she walked away from Tom. "She'd give up the rest of her life to keep me here," Jemma said sadly.

"Not you," Tom corrected her. "The other one."

Jemma laughed bitterly, and her laughter quickly became a sob.

Tom rushed her side, but before he could embrace her, she held a hand out before him and collected herself with an independence Tom had never seen her possess.

He suspected the other one was this independent, though.

"What have I done?" he asked.

Jemma crossed her arms again and then looked at him. "What was right," she answered.

Tom began to cry, thinking the worst. But before the tears could seep from his eyes, Jemma placed a hand on his chest and pointed at rising sun. "Alexis could not survive under that," she reminded him. "I am the one who loves you."

Tom nodded. "I'll be right back." Then he disappeared into the house, only to return a moment later with a table in his arms. She looked at him questionably, but he only smiled as he placed it in front of her. "It's going to be a long day," he said. Then he was off again, returning with two chairs and two jackets that would take the chill away from the early morning.

As he put the chairs down, she took the clothes from him and shook one jacket out to look at it. It was grey, with an insignia of a wolf with its jaws open in a silent roar. She looked at Tom questioning.

"The colours and the coat of arms of House Aquainnus," he admitted as he pulled the other jacket on. It was identical to hers. She did the same, then sat down at the table across from him.

"So what happens now?" she asked.

"How much do you remember?" Tom asked her.

"Everything," she admitted. "Every single moment of every single day I've ever been alive. From the time of my first love, James. To the time of my second love," she pointed at him. "You."

He seemed jealous. "I didn't't know you had another love before me."

She laughed, though she was dangerously close to crying again. "That was a long, long time ago," she admitted. "But I think I remember biting you once while I was in the Mediterranean. You came from Egypt, not Scandinavia."

Tom snorted. "What does that have to do with anything?" There was no way for him to prove or disprove her claim. The past was buried to him. Signa Aquainnus had not been able to help him remember it. Nor did he really care to remember.

"You come from the Anubis blood line," she said with a shrug. "Not Fernir, like they thought."

"So?"

She only shrugged. "It's good to know who your family is," she admitted, trying to keep the conversation light.

He looked at her, appreciating her beauty, but not forgetting the monster that had created her. "We've done some terrible things, you and I," he admitted.

She nodded. "I know."

"So what happens now?"

"Alexis thought you'd free me in the morning," she said.

Tom shook his head sadly. "I can't do that. Alexis is too dangerous."

Jemma began to cry. "I know," she admitted. "I know."

They spent the rest of the morning enjoying the presence of each other and the fragile dawn that was spreading across the lawns of Signa Aquainnus. Then, as the sunlight took away the chill from the morning, Christopher appeared at the doorway to the manor house. He held an immense thermos and two mugs in one hand, and a silver platter covered against the cold by a silver cover in the other. He smiled at them when he saw them, and strode toward them with a confidence and a fearlessness that took Jemma's breath away. Even Tom cringed away from him, knowing that the deliverer of their sentence walked so fearlessly toward the two greatest enemies he'd ever known.

He placed the platter and the thermos down on the table between them. "Sorry to break up the party," he admitted. "But werewolves must eat." He pointed at Jemma. "You can't have any."

She laughed at the light-hearted comment, the lack of hatred she so expected to be there. "Hello, Christopher," she said.

"Alexis," he answered as he poured coffee from the thermos into both mugs he carried. She noticed he could not look into her eyes when he spoke. He handed one cup to Tom. "It's strong," he said.

Jemma looked down at her hands, ashamed. As Christopher sat down beside her, he finally did look at her.

"What?" he asked.

Tom pointed at the sun. "This isn't Alexis," he reminded Christopher. "It's Jemma."

Christopher nodded sadly. "The dream."

Finally, Jemma looked up at him. "Alexis' dream, if that means anything."

"Even if she would never admit it," he agreed with her.

"Oh," Jemma turned to look at Tom. "I think she would."

Christopher lifted the cover to reveal a steaming mound of pancakes, some syrup, and a block of butter. There were no forks, knives, nor even plates.

"You've got to be kidding," Jemma cried.

Christopher smiled at her, even as Tom was already reaching for a pancake.

She laughed and shook her head, then turned away from the two of them. "And I thought Tom was the only one," she said, averting her eyes from the way they were attacking their breakfast.

Tom grinned at her through a mouthful of food.

"You were wrong!" Christopher announced happily.

She didn't dare look at him. Her stomach lurched at the thought of food, at the best of times. Instead, she left the table and walked over to Janelle's sleeping form, the stone gargoyle standing guard over her wayward sister.

"There was a werewolf attack in a nearby city last night," Tom admitted to Christopher.

"I know," Christopher said. "The description we received was of a black and grey beast."

"What are you going to do?" Tom asked.

Christopher shrugged. "It all depends on tonight. Everything depends on tonight."

Jemma knew they were talking about Alexis. "This is a nice fur coat!" she announced, still studying Janelle's motionless form.

"You can't tell when it's stone," Christopher said. "But it's white, perfectly white, like mine."

"I've got one," Tom admitted.

Christopher looked at him, surprised. "When?"

"Last night, after the holocaust."

Christopher nodded, smiling with new found respect. "It was like that for me too." He reached around his neck and pulled a silver cross and a chain over his head. He held the cross out to Tom.

"I couldn't," Tom admitted, shocked by his friend's gift.

"Take it," Christopher demanded, thrusting the chain even closer to Tom. "I can get another one. But I'd like you to have this one."

Tom smiled and nodded as he reached out and took the cross. "Thank you, Christopher," he said. There was a tear in the corner of his eye.

Christopher wiped his own eyes as they both looked at Jemma. She was watching them, remaining silent as Tom slipped the necklace over his head, not bothering to tuck it into his jacket. "It's going to be an interesting night," she admitted as she watched the two werewolves, now armed with a weapon far deadlier than the immortal bodies they wore at night. "At least Alexis won't steal any more of your blood," she admitted to him.

He looked at her sadly. "Then you'll grow tired and fall asleep."

She shrugged and turned away again. "Finish your breakfast Tom. So I can hug you."

He and Christopher did what she told them. They enjoyed their food, though they were saddened to see it gone. Tom lifted the thermos and gestured toward Christopher's empty mug.

"That's okay," Christopher said. "You keep it. Something to drink later on."

Tom nodded his thanks as his friend cleared the table. Once everything was loaded back onto the tray, Christopher turned to Jemma. "I hope I see you again," he said quietly.

She nodded, not knowing what to say.

"If it's any consolation," he admitted. "I know you better than you know yourself right now. It won't be as bad as you think."

Doubting his words, she nonetheless nodded her thanks.

Saddened, he returned her nod, then nodded at Tom, and left.

At sundown, Jemma placed her head on Tom's shoulder. She stared up into his eyes as the sun set and it grew dark around them. They'd already said their goodbyes, kissed their last kiss. Now, they waited for the worst, for one or both of them to fall asleep and have the war begin once again.

Eventually, all light faded except for the lights that came from the house. It was growing late, and still they sat, motionless, staring at each other with mounting dread. When Tom grew tired, he did not bother to suppress the werewolf manifestations. They rippled over his skin, indeed showing off his new white coat. "Aren't you tired?" he asked.

She sat up straight, watching his face change into the wonderful creature she'd come to love. The jacket he wore stretched with his changing shape, as though it'd been made for werewolves. "I love you Tom," she admitted.

Then she blinked.

Tom looked at her. There was no change. But he knew. Jemma had fallen asleep. Yet there was no change. "How is this possible?" he asked.

"Maybe you just can't see the difference," Alexis answered.

"No," he said, shaking his head. "I would."

Sadly, Alexis folded her hands in front of her and lowered her head. "Maybe I'm not tired," she said. "Maybe I'm still Jemma."

Tom knew she was lying.

"I'm sorry I'm not the person you love," she admitted. Then she closed her eyes.

325

The night burst into flame around them, encircling the courtyard with a wall of fire that shot into the sky. Janelle and Iminuetep stood on either side of them, all semblance of granite lifelessness gone from their stance. Janelle was crying.

"Are you ready?" Iminuetep asked.

"Does it hurt?" Alexis asked.

Iminuetep smiled, though he nodded his head. "Oh yes. It hurts a lot."

Alexis nodded. "I'm ready." Then she kissed Tom one last time. He was too stunned by what was happening to stop her. "I'm sorry," she said.

She closed her eyes and looked into the very vortex that was her centre. For years there was nothing here, nothing at all but darkness. Yet she knew nothing of that, for to have darkness one must have light; to break the law, one must have a law to break. She had simply existed as a collection of passions playing upon the mind of the body that had died when she had been bitten so many, many years before. But now, something was birthed within her, and though it was on the verge of dying itself, it still struggled for breathe within her. In her mind's eye it shone with a bright white light and was curled in a foetal position as it slept in the crux of a black endless vortex Alexis knew represented herself. Jemma seemed to radiate with love –the love Alexis was beginning to experience.

There was no good in Alexis. She knew that. The realization brought her no joy, but neither did it bring her any grief. It was a simple truth, and like the many empty eons that passed without Jemma, the truth was empty. Jemma was all that mattered. Jemma was all that remained.

Humans had a soul that contained passions both good and bad. They had intellect that controlled these passions, and some of them had a spirit that fuelled their souls with an eternal light Alexis was afraid to approach. Jemma had such light. And it was now burning away at the inside of Alexis' mind.

Werewolves were all soul and all intellect, with their bodies as mere manifestations of what went on inside them. But Alexis was different. She was a vampire. She was darkness. She was passion. Yes, she existed as a separate entity, a unique entity for the time being. She was cut off from the rest of evil by the sheer mindlessness of it.

"Evil can be thought of as a wind," Christopher's voice filtered through her meditations. She looked up at him to see him standing amidst the fire, though it did nothing to burn him. He wore a white coat of a werewolf, yet his face was completely human still. "It is simply a force, with no thought, no reason, until it possesses the mind of a person, where it can take shape, take form. Where it can assume a will through the reasoning of the individual soul it possesses, like air inside a balloon takes the shape of the balloon, but gives the balloon a new shape as well, in its expanded form."

"And now you want to pop the balloon and release the air back into nothingness," Alexis declared bitterly. Tom choked back a sob and looked away. Such a thing could—would—kill Jemma. And they both knew it.

"The Holy Spirit can be thought of as the same thing" Christopher said patiently. 'Accept Jesus Christ. Seek a personal relationship with him, and let the Spirit of love mix with the evil of your kind. When this happens the spirit in Jemma, the light you are so afraid of, will continue to banish the darkness from your mind."

"Just one question," Alexis asked. "How is it that I can even contemplate this if I am darkness incarnate?"

"Jemma is even now fighting against you," Christopher admitted. "She is already beginning to annex you, your attitude, your will."

"Then why must I succumb to this willingly, at all? There is now life in me, in my body. It is killing me, but I can't tell, so it is killing me in theory only."

Christopher reached into his robe and pulled out a silver cross. It erupted into flames in his hand. "If you let it burn from within, Jemma lives. Otherwise...

"The only difference is that your mind will embrace the light of God as Jemma is doing right now. You will always dance this dance of rebellion, or Alexis will. But Alexis will grow faint and Jemma will grow strong."

She nodded, made up her mind, and looked into her soul once again. The pain numbed her. Yet it held no fear. It only comforted her, and as it did she realized that it comforted not her, but Jemma. She was becoming Jemma, leaving Alexis behind.

She saw within her mind's eye the light wash across her entire vision, "Take me," she said. "I have nothing left anyway."

The light of love engulfed her.

With a shriek of pain, Alexis turned to stone. The granite statue looked in pain, with such a tremendous burden of grief and guilt on her face. But she also had a look of wonder in her eyes, a look of awe, of surprise. When Tom saw her, he knew that one moment later, all that pain, all that grief, all that guilt would cease to exist, whenever she chose that moment to be.

But for this moment, the spirit of the woman he loved so much was free.

Epilogue

Darkness and rain. Tom stood amidst them both, dressed like a man in a gray uniform. Yet underneath his clothes, the body of a monster was tense and prepared, like a sheathed and sharpened sword waiting to be used in the line of duty.

Jemma's body, the gargoyle statue, was in a posture of prayer. Water ran down her fair skin, yet she did not notice it was there. How long she'd remain like this Tom could only guess, and he knew he could not disturb her sleeping form. He'd tried in the past.

Hesitating only a moment, he came forward and placed a fur coat around her stone shoulders. "Something to keep you warm," he admitted to her, though he knew she could not hear him. The fur melted to stone as he arranged it over her. Then he leaned in and kissed her on the cheek.

"Oh give me a break!" Christopher cried.

Tom stood up and looked at his friend. He was wearing the same uniform, imperious to the rain, as he was. His body was disproportionate as well, as though he was a world class body builder that could not hide his physique under the clothes he wore, no matter how baggy they were. "You'll see her in the morning," Christopher announced. "We have work to do!"

Tom nodded and stepped away from the stone statue. He made to leave, but a voice caught his attention and he froze in mid-step. "Tom," she called to him.

He turned around to see Jemma, soaked to the bone with a werewolf coat about her shoulders. She was smiling. "Hurry back," she said.

Tom smiled back at her. "As soon as I can," he promised.

"Come on, will you!" Christopher barked. He grabbed Tom's shoulder and began to drag him away. "Later Alexis," he said with a nod.

She nodded back at him, her smile still on his face. "Bring him back alive!" she called.

"So what if I don't!" he called back.

Then, just like that, the two werewolves had faded into the night, back into their secret war.

Alexis sighed. "I guess it's time," she muttered to no one in particular. Then she reached for her own cell phone and went to work.

Printed in the United States
61335LVS00003B/7-57